"*The Altarpiece* is literally and figuratively a hidden gem."
—*The Marblehead Reporter*

"Fogle Boyd's passion for history and art comes alive in the book's pages to create a riveting period piece that will appeal to art lovers and fans of World War II literature alike."
—*Merrimack Valley News*

"*The Altarpiece* is impressively written in both the gritty realism it portrays and the impassioned story from both sides of the front." —*North Shore Art Throb*

VISIT THE PICTURE
GALLERY AT
WWW.LAURENFOGLEBOYD.COM

THE
ALTARPIECE

LAUREN FOGLE BOYD

Lucky Bat Books

For Pippa, our little artist.

EUROPE

Prologue

✝

Berlin. November, 1933

FASSBINDER WATCHED HITLER from the darkened shallows of the alcove off the main corridor. There were many such alcoves in this museum, where small pieces were hung or delicate objects were displayed in glass cases. Fassbinder was sweating despite the time of year and the draftiness of the old building, so he removed his wool coat and draped it over his right arm as he craned his neck to see what Hitler was gazing at. A Kandinsky—a large one. A riot of color, shapes, and angles. Geometric faces stared out from the corners of the canvas.

Hitler inspected the painting with the same intensity with which he did everything. His hangers-on hovered close to him, but not too close. The Führer must be allowed his time to reflect, after all, he too was a painter. Hitler shook his head several times while staring at the Kandinsky, then turned to an associate and said something that Fassbinder couldn't quite hear, but that clearly impressed the surrounding crowd. Murmurs of approval rippled across the rows of invited admirers, even reaching Fassbinder in the alcove.

Then something strange happened: two museum officials produced two ladders, mounted them, and took the Kandinsky down from the wall. Hitler looked at it for another few seconds as it stood upright in their hands, then walked away followed by his handlers and the majority of the crowd. The museum officials began carrying the Kandinsky down the corridor toward the freight elevators, followed slowly by the director of the museum. As they neared the alcove, Fassbinder stepped out.

"Did our Führer object to the placement?" Fassbinder asked casually. He addressed this to the director, Hans Steiglitz, who was Fassbinder's longtime acquaintance.

"I'd get out of here if I were you, Friedrich," Steiglitz responded coldly.

"Why?" Fassbinder asked, shocked. "I was invited."

"Don't be obtuse," Steiglitz said, facing him eye-to-eye. "You know the Führer's tastes. This isn't it. It's being removed. Since everyone in Germany knows you specialize in collecting and selling Kandinsky, Beckmann, Klimt, and Junger…," he trailed off, the color rising in his cheeks.

"Are you being serious?"

"Perfectly. Listen, I'm on your side."

"We're taking sides? About art?"

"The Führer is. Keep your head down. Tell your friend Junger to do the same. I admire him and I'd hate for anything to happen…," he trailed off again and began walking after the painting.

Fassbinder watched his balding head recede down the darkened corridor. The museum wasn't open to the public today, just invited guests. He had originally felt elated at receiving an invitation. He had taken it as evidence that his success in Bavaria was now noticed in Berlin. But now, and forever afterward, he saw this day as the moment his eyes were opened. The day Germany decided to end its own phenomenal dominance in modern and expressionist art. Nothing was ever the same again.

As he waited on the train platform an hour later, Fassbinder felt the optimism he was known for draining away from him. He had always promised his friends and colleagues that Hitler wouldn't interfere with art. He had assured them that the Nazis couldn't dictate taste. He clenched his fists in frustration. He must speak to Junger immediately. Junger needed to be careful. He had Anke to think of.

When he was settled in his first-class seat on his way back to Munich, Fassbinder closed his eyes and recalled one of the happiest moments of his life…six years ago, at the Brosslers.

Munich. September, 1927

MRS. BROSSLER TOLD HER SON that if he asked about Anke Junger one more time he would be spending the party in his room. Her eyes were kind, but her tone was verging on anger. Erik knew better than to pester his mother when she was preparing for one of her parties. His father certainly did and had spent the day sequestered in his study, respectfully avoiding his wife.

To be fair, Lotte Brossler was known as one of *the* party planners in Munich. She had grown up amongst celebratory people; her father had owned a silversmithing empire that provided the flatware for all the best tables in Bavaria. Her maiden name, Klein, was delicately engraved on the back of each piece, even the smallest sugar spoon. Lotte felt it was her duty to keep up the family tradition of hosting soirees, even after she married the relatively poor art historian, David Brossler. Lotte's inheritance, including the house, kept them in style and David's circle of artists, art dealers, writers, and other intellectuals kept a steady stream of interesting people, some even famous, flowing through her door. This more than made up for her husband's dismissiveness of many of her former society friends. All considering, Lotte was content.

She glanced at her son who stood sulking on the stairs.

"I'm sure she's coming," she said, gently. "Dietrich always brings Anke. Why should tonight be any different?"

That seemed to do the trick and Erik skipped off toward his father's study. Lotte returned to her task—arranging a massive display of flowers, including the hard-to-find birds of paradise, on the hall table. This wasn't just any party. Tonight they would celebrate the fortieth birthday of Friedrich Fassbinder, art dealer to the rich and powerful of Munich. The turnout would be large, perhaps the largest ever for a Brossler event. A handful of well-known artists were planning to attend, as well as many patrons of the arts including several from as far away as Vienna. To be safe, 100 bottles of champagne had been ordered and a similar amount of Riesling and Bordeaux.

In his father's study, the twelve-year-old Erik surveyed the scene from the worn leather divan. He peered out the windows that faced the back garden and watched the servants covering long tables with white tablecloths and setting them with the china and Klein silver from his mother's considerable collection. The garden featured a wide, sloping lawn that spilled into a massive fishpond stocked with eels. Grandfather Klein once told Erik that the Romans used to build eel ponds behind their villas. "So, why shouldn't we Germans have the same?" he asked. Their quiet neighborhood was fashionable and filled with stately homes with manicured gardens, but Erik's grandfather boasted that his was the only residential fishpond of any size in north Munich.

Watching the servants, who were hired specially for the occasion, Erik only briefly forgot about the issue at hand. Was Anke coming? His mother had said she was, but this was most likely said to appease him and put an end to his questioning. He decided to ask his father.

"One never knows if Junger will come or not," his father said not looking up from his book. "But if he does, he will surely bring Anke."

Anke was the only child of Dietrich Junger, the painter. Junger was just now achieving fame in Germany and France and had recently sold two paintings to a New York dealer who planned to sell them to a new museum called the Museum of Modern Art, which was opening in a few years time. Fassbinder had brokered the deal. Erik's father was a professor of art history at Ludwig Maximillian University and a longtime friend and supporter of Junger. For years, when Anke was very young, Junger frequented the Brossler's art parties, or "salons" as Erik's mother called them, and brought his little girl with him. Her mother had died when she was just two, so she was usually cared for by the Brossler's housekeeper, Trudie, who took her to play with Erik's old toys and put her to bed in one of the guest rooms until Junger came to take her home. He often left in the early hours of the morning and bundled the sleeping girl to an awaiting taxi.

Sometimes Erik would stay up late listening to his parents and their guests from the back staircase. Junger was one of the most interesting because he was usually very quiet, which made the guests seek his opinion all the more. He rarely rejected other artists work or made negative comments, but he did occasionally dole out praise for the likes of Emil Nolde, Marc Chagall, and especially Ernst Ludwig Kirchner, who Junger very much admired. But what especially intrigued Erik was Junger's attachment to his daughter. There were nights when he couldn't bear to be parted from her and she slept on his lap as he sat on the red divan in the main parlor. Erik had even followed Junger on one of his trips to check on the sleeping Anke in one of the guest rooms and watched him gently kiss the little girl's forehead, first brushing away her blond curls.

As Anke grew older, she and Erik began to interact and he showed her his toys and art supplies in his room. She loved to draw, so they drew together while their parents were downstairs until Trudie came to take Anke off to bed. The last time Erik had seen her, some months ago, Anke looked quite different. She had just turned nine and her hair had pretty ribbons in it, a gift from her father. She was moved to the same school Erik went to and was only two classes behind him despite being three years younger. He had heard his father and Junger discuss Anke many times and her "talent" for art history. Brossler had promised Junger he would tutor Anke and help prepare her for an eventual entrance to Ludwig Maximillian University. Erik was also planning to go there, so he and Anke would be together. Erik felt that was only right, that they would be together.

As THE GUESTS BEGAN TO FILE IN for Fassbinder's party, Erik stood watch on the main staircase hoping to see Anke and her father emerge from one of the many black cabs lined up in front of the house. The servants raced up and down the stairs, carrying the capes, cloaks, and light jackets the guests had worn on this September night. They glared at Erik for being in their way. Finally, after what seemed like a hundred arrivals, he saw her. She was taller than the last time, and thinner. Her hair ringlets stuck out from underneath her black cap and her cheeks were pink from the fresh air. Her blue eyes were warm as she greeted him at the stairs and handed her jacket and hat to the awaiting maid. Erik said nothing so she spoke first.

"My father says I can stay downstairs for the entire evening if I want."

This was indeed a major shift in policy and Erik needed a minute to digest. He had assumed she would accompany him to his room to draw and play with his telescope as usual. He was desperate to be alone with her.

"If that's what you want," he stammered, unsure. He followed Junger and Anke into the main parlor but lost his nerve and retreated briefly to the stairs. Finally he joined her on the divan, bringing her a cup of punch. After a long silence, she saved him.

"I am happy to go look through your telescope again, Erik. If you want to, that is."

The look they exchanged was not unnoticed by the Brosslers, or Junger, and several smiles were suppressed as the youngsters bounded toward the stairs, hand in hand. Lotte fantasized for a moment about Erik and Anke being married and how wonderful it would be to be related to an artist like Junger, even by marriage. She soon forgot all about it when Max Beckmann and Paul Klee arrived and she hurried to greet them at the door.

Upstairs, Erik and Anke held hands for a long time. Eventually she broke away to look through his telescope, though the sun was only just setting and she couldn't see very much. Outside, the torches were lit and the guests mingled in the warm September dusk. A delicate bell told them dinner was being served.

Anke and Erik ate sitting on opposite sides of the table, which had grown to forty people by the dinner hour. Junger watched his daughter watch Erik and felt himself relax slightly. It was too early to tell, yet he couldn't help but feel that an association with the Brosslers would be a good thing for Anke. David was an art historian, one of the most prominent in Germany, and Erik had already shown an interest in medieval art, which was Anke's budding passion as well. They were perfectly matched. Anke's mother was dead and Junger had never dared think about Anke's life after his death. They had few relations, but as he looked around the table, many friends.

When dinner was done, Lotte carried out an enormous birthday cake and set it down in front of Fassbinder, who immediately stood up. He toasted his friends with tears in his eyes.

"Who has ever known such wonderful people?" he asked, truly moved. His wife, Jutta, stood next to him giggling and clapping. He kissed her tenderly and everyone applauded.

"Come help me cut this thing, Anke darling," he said, wiping his eyes. She started toward him, but Lotte intervened, insisting that the cake would be cut in the kitchen and then served by the servants. Fassbinder laughed and deferred to the hostess, but wanted Anke to visit him anyway. Her father switched seats with her and she sat next to Fassbinder who was dabbing at his eyes with his handkerchief.

"Anke, darling. Are you enjoying the party?" he asked her, grinning.

"Yes, it's wonderful."

"Thank you for coming, it means so much to me. Your father and you…mean so much to me."

"I know."

"You do?" Fassbinder looked surprised.

"You never had any children," Anke said softly, as if it was a secret.

Fassbinder smiled and embraced her. "No," he said. "But you are like my child and I will always be there for you. Do you understand?"

"Yes," she said smiling back. She glanced at Erik and he was watching her. The flush came back to her cheeks. They felt hot to the touch.

1

The Degenerate

✝

Anyone who sees and paints a sky green and fields blue ought to be sterilized.
—Adolf Hitler

Cambridge, Massachusetts, 1939

PROFESSOR DAVID BROSSLER crossed Harvard Yard at a pace and did not stop to admire the new flowers. Spongy carpets of spring pansies had just been planted but failed to draw his attention, despite his recent interest in gardening. He simply felt that his aging body could not carry him fast enough to his destination, and yet his destination was one he was not sure he wanted to reach. A pit rumbled in his stomach.

Brossler was the head of Harvard's art history department and well known for his gesticulating lectures and devastating exams. His passion was van Gogh, but he was truly moved by everyone from Rembrandt to Goya. He made no secret about his distaste for Caravaggio and there was a long running debate within the department over whether or not Brossler had allowed himself to be influenced by the seedy and allegedly murderous personality of the painter. Professors Quark and Williams thought he had. Professors Niven and Jameson thought not and accused the others of failing to accept the fact that not everyone admired Caravaggio. This debate vaulted back and forth for years and the students were amused by it. Despite his concrete opinions, Brossler was well loved and respected for his gentleness and his generosity. No question was too ignorant, no student too naive...

that sort of thing. He spent hours with his students in the libraries and galleries to help them understand how to properly research and present an art history paper. He conducted one-on-one meetings with art history majors to discuss their thesis ideas, and art in general (and he did this each term, not just twice a year like most of the other professors). He adored teaching. But sometimes he committed himself to his students so completely in order to prevent himself from thinking too much about his past life. Or, that's what his wife said anyway. Though he didn't know it as he half-ran away from campus, his past life would rejoin him tonight.

He approached Richard Paulson's stately colonial house, which was attractively set back from the road and semiobscured behind a high black, rod-iron fence and very well maintained boxwood bushes. Once on the front steps, Brossler could see through the front windows a group of men sitting around the dining room table, a gray blanket of cigarette smoke hovering above them. Brossler straightened his glasses and rolled his tongue over his teeth just before he knocked on the front door. The lady of the house, Joanna Paulson, wore a tight and worried smile when she welcomed him in and took his brown sports coat.

"So glad you are here," she said nervously. "We were not sure you were going to come."

"I had a meeting…forgive my lateness."

"They have not started yet. I'll bring you some coffee."

She disappeared down the hall leaving Brossler to make his own entrance. As he walked into the dining room, the men stood and offered their hands. One man remained seated at the table and a glazed and weary strain was evident on his face. His small body seemed dwarfed by the long cherry dining table, which was a grand antique carved in Paris in the eighteenth century. Brossler made his way toward the man, who seemed lost in thought.

"My God, Friedrich!" Brossler cried as they embraced. The others in the room turned away in respect. Fassbinder buried his face for a moment on Brossler's shoulder.

"David…it's been so horrible. I don't know how to explain."

"You are here and you are safe. Jutta is with you?"

"Yes, she's with me. She's safe. How is Lotte?"

Brossler shook his head slowly. "It's been too hard for her. Leaving Germany was not something she wanted. Even now, she's very nostalgic and doesn't find it easy to live here."

"And Erik?" Fassbinder asked, regaining composure.

"He's still in London working on his PhD at the Courtauld Institute of Art. Lotte is desperate for him to come home."

"I can imagine."

Brossler smelled the aroma from the coffee that had been silently slipped in front of him. He turned to thank Mrs. Paulson, but she had gone. He then realized that the others were waiting for the meeting to begin, so he took his seat, as did Fassbinder.

"Let's bring this meeting to order," announced Richard Paulson. This seemed overly formal to Brossler since this was not a meeting of a regular group or club, but a gathering of professors, art dealers and collectors in the area who were interested in hearing firsthand about the situation in Germany. Richard Paulson had made a fortune in rubber and was the greatest art collector in the Boston area. He had many connections to artists and dealers in New York and in Europe, and one of those men was sitting in front of them now, wiping the sweat from his forehead with one of Mrs. Paulson's embroidered white linen napkins.

"As many of you know, this is Friedrich Fassbinder," Paulson continued. "Fassbinder has been an art dealer in the Munich area for over twenty years. He and David were good friends."

"*Are* good friends," Brossler interjected, smiling at Fassbinder.

"Excuse me, *are* good friends," Paulson continued. "He has obtained ten works for me and at least double that for my associates in New York. He has an interesting story to tell. Some things we already know, some we do not."

Paulson sat abruptly and turned toward Fassbinder, who seemed to shrink even further under the expectation.

Brossler was grateful that Paulson recognized this meeting was the wrong venue for one of his speeches on art and conservation, two topics that Paulson alone esteemed himself qualified to speak about. "Just because one *owns* art, does not mean one *understands* it," Brossler was fond of saying. Paulson liked to retort with, "you never *own* art, art *owns* you." They sparred from time to time, but in general were good friends and the respect was mutual. Of course, Paulson had given quite a bit of money to Harvard, his alma mater, and a number of paintings, including a Monet, to the university's Fogg Museum.

Brossler now turned his attention to Fassbinder, who had struggled to his feet. Suddenly something became deadly apparent. Fassbinder was thinner than he had ever been. He'd always been a small man, but now he looked almost childlike. Brossler didn't understand why he hadn't noticed it right away. A lump appeared in his throat.

"First of all," Fassbinder began, "I want to thank Mr. and Mrs. Paulson for funding my voyage from Rotterdam and for hosting me here in their beautiful home."

Paulson nodded graciously, accepting the thanks on behalf of his wife who was not in the room. He gestured for Fassbinder to continue.

"I feel I have a story to tell you that will, I dearly hope, incite you to act."

Fassbinder's Bavarian accent brought tears to Brossler's eyes. He had forgotten, or tried to forget, how much he missed Munich. The Brosslers had immigrated to America in 1933, the year the Nazis came to power and enacted the "Law for the Restoration of the Professional Civil Service." Many deemed politically opposed to the regime, or Jews, were fired from their jobs and this included a great number of academics. Not only did Brossler lose his lectureship at Ludwig Maximillian University, but he was personally attacked for his support of expressionist art in the Nazi newspaper *Völkische Beobachter.* After this, he was unemployable in Germany or Austria and they made the difficult decision to sell the house and the Klein silver collection (Lotte was devastated) and emigrate. When they sailed for New York, they left behind not only friends, but many relatives including his wife's mother who said she couldn't possibly leave her beloved Munich. Looking at Fassbinder, Brossler now realized how wrong she was to stay.

"Several years ago, in the summer of 1937," Fassbinder began, "I attended the opening of the Haus der Deutschen Kunst (House of German Art) in Munich with my great friend and client, Dietrich Junger."

There was a quiet murmuring at the table. Junger was one of the brightest stars in German modernist painting. Some said he was Chagall meets Kandinsky, though Brossler never thought so. He saw him more as an ultra-modern van Gogh (though Brossler thought all modern painters were more or less a version of van Gogh). Regard-less, Junger was recognized, even in America, as an explosive talent. His abstract landscapes were captivating and his heavy use of layered paint gave some of them an almost three-dimensional feel. An art critic from *The New York Times* called Junger "unafraid and dismissive of both tradition and convention." He meant that as a compliment. Three of Junger's massive canvases now hung in the Museum of Modern Art in New York. A show of his work was a major success at the Art Institute of Chicago in 1935. A number of other museums, including the Museum of Fine Arts in Boston, owned a Junger.

Brossler smiled, thinking of his old friend. He hadn't heard from him in years. Brossler wondered often about Anke, and he knew Erik still thought of her. He knew their parting in Munich had been the hardest moment of his son's life. There had been several attempts to tempt Junger and Anke to emigrate, but Junger had politely refused. Erik and Anke had maintained contact for a few years, but she stopped writing in 1936. The last they heard she was planning to leave Germany and continue her studies in Belgium, at the University of Ghent.

Brossler shrugged off his thoughts and returned to Fassbinder who was now standing and pacing back and forth. He looked right at Brossler.

"David, you should have seen the affair! Thousands of people parading through the streets, young women in formation, dressed as maidens from a Greek temple, escorting huge pieces of sculpture on floats…medieval knights on horseback with the swastika emblazoned on their shields….banners hanging everywhere and pine branches…it was unbelievable. A thousand years of Germanic cultural history paraded through the streets…it took hours! Junger and I started the day want-ing to laugh, wanting to find it all so hilarious…and why wouldn't we? But then Hitler came to the podium to give a speech. I had only ever seen him in person once before. I jotted down some notes while he was speaking…here are some of the best bits:"

"Works of art" that are not capable of being understood in themselves but need some pretentious instruction book to justify their existence—until at long last they find someone sufficiently browbeaten to endure such stupid

or impudent twaddle with patience—will never again find their way to the German people…we will, from now on, lead an unrelenting war of purification, an unrelenting war of extermination, against the last elements which have displaced our art.

Fassbinder knew he had everyone's attention. Coffee cups were left on their white porcelain saucers and cigarettes smoldered in the ashtrays. Nobody had even touched the vanilla Bundt cake.

"After that, I'll admit, I wanted to go home. But Junger wouldn't hear of it. He said it was our duty as humans to observe this. So we went inside the new House of German Art with the hundreds of others and let me tell you, it was one of the most ridiculous displays of art either of us had ever seen. With the exception of a few Cranachs, Holbeins, and the occasional Dutch or Flemish Old Master, most of the art was mediocre at best, downright amateur at worst. The propaganda paintings of the Nazi party were the dominant works, including many portraits of Hitler and even more of German soldiers. Hitler's birthplace in Austria…lots of landscapes of that. Some decent paintings, some good technique, but mostly…romantic, folk art. Nothing by modernist painters, no cubists, no expressionists. No communists. No Jews."

Another murmuring, but Fassbinder hardly paused, his heart was beating too fast.

"Junger and I left after about an hour, disgusted. But nothing would prepare us for what happened a few days later. I got a call from Junger early one morning and he was upset. He told me that men who called themselves "Nazi art representatives" appeared at his apartment in the middle of the night and demanded that he turn over his entire portfolio to them. They had four trucks waiting outside. He refused, but then his daughter, Anke, who was visiting from Ghent, appeared and the men threatened to arrest her. It worked because Junger opened his studio and let the men have the paintings. He told me that Anke slapped him across the face for allowing his canvases to go out the door. But she was all he had. Her mother died when she was a baby. He and Anke were very close."

Fassbinder suddenly needed to sit down. Brossler was disturbed by Fassbinder's use of the past tense but decided to bite his tongue.

Instead, he got up and poured a glass of water from the elegant Italianate pitcher at the center of the table and handed it to the grateful man. Slightly revived, Fassbinder continued his story from his seat.

"Junger and I had known for several years that the Nazis were taking modernist paintings and sculpture out of German museums, but we hadn't heard of an artist's entire portfolio being confiscated from his studio. As it turns out, Junger was not the first, not by far, and would not be the last. I mean, the Gestapo confiscated one of Oskar Kokoschka's canvases and cut it into four pieces! I was losing faith fast. But typical of Junger, he soon after insisted that we attend the opening of *Entartete Kunst*, the exhibit of so-called 'degenerate art' at the old archaeological building. Anke delayed her return to Ghent and came with us. None of you will believe me when I tell you what I saw on that day. For a start, the exhibition curators described expressionist art as," Fassbinder again consulted his notes, "'an inferno of Negro grimaces, crippled figures, and infantile demonic spookery.'"

Those around the table glanced at each other uneasily. Brossler's skin was crawling.

Fassbinder continued, gesturing with his glass of water and spilling it slightly.

"When we entered the exhibit, we came first to a section entitled *Works which insult women, workers and the farmers of Germany*.

"Here was Marc Chagall, Paul Klee, Max Ernst, Emil Nolde.... Here was Max Beckmann and Pablo Picasso! The lighting was abysmal and the paintings were slapped up on the wall, crooked and crowded together. Everything was intentional and there was graffiti written on the walls...insults and propaganda. There was an entire room dedicated to *A representative selection from the endless supply of Jewish trash that no words can adequately describe*.

"Can you imagine? Junger, Anke, and I just wandered around...we couldn't believe our eyes. Lots of people were shaking their heads, and I knew they were upset. We saw several people, friends of ours, but we said little to them. Nobody wanted to talk or say how they really felt. Junger's own paintings were hung in a corner, four of them. Under one of his country scenes was written *Nature as seen by sick minds*.

"Sick minds! I couldn't believe it. Junger was stoic but Anke was devastated. We left immediately because she said she felt ill."

Fassbinder leaned over and wiped his eyes. Brossler placed a reassuring hand on his shoulder, despite feeling quite ill himself. He noticed, for the first time, that Fassbinder hadn't lost his hair naturally, it had been shaved off. Small amounts of coarse, gray hair were now growing back.

"I'm sorry, David," Fassbinder said, his voice trailing to almost a whisper. "I have wanted to tell this story for so long, but I still can't believe what I am saying."

"Don't apologize, Friedrich. Just continue when you are ready."

"Yes. I must continue, because the worst is yet to come." He looked up at Brossler's worried face.

"Within days of the opening of the degenerate art exhibit, most of the German modernist art professors were fired. Paul Klee was ejected from the Bauhaus School in Düsseldorf, Beckmann in Berlin…Walter Hofer too. Oskar Schlemmer was called a Jew by a former student, even though he is not. He is now painting camouflage on military buildings. Willi Baumeister has been forced to work in a varnish factory in Stuttgart."

Fassbinder paused briefly for the gasps. He took a cigarette out of a silver case (a gift from Junger), and held it between his fingers without lighting it.

"Junger was arrested early in '38. They said he had been ordered to stop painting, but had refused. New canvases were found in his studio. He was taken to the Dachau concentration camp north of Munich. Anke returned from Ghent to lobby for his release but nobody would even talk to her. She was threatened with imprisonment. I told her to return to Ghent and that I would write as soon as I had news. Two days later I was arrested myself and sent to the Mathausen camp in Austria. I was there for six months. I was beaten with a whip and forced to dig stone in a gigantic quarry. I…I…will not say anymore. I *will* say that had they thought I was a Jew or a homosexual, I would most likely be dead. But, I was just a lowly art dealer who had sold too many modern and expressionist works. I was released five months ago.

When I returned home, my wife told me that Junger had been sent home a month prior and was in very bad health. I went immediately to see him and did not recognize the man who stood in the doorway. He had lost nearly seventy pounds…he was a skeleton. I was malnourished and sick as well, but not as bad as Junger. Anke informed me that her father had gone on a hunger strike in protest of the arrests of artists and intellectuals. This, of course, had no effect on the Nazis who no doubt intended for him to die. This man was a decorated soldier…he fought at Verdun…it's just incredible to me."

Fassbinder blew his nose into a white handkerchief and returned it to his breast pocket.

"But he didn't die. He survived. Anke nursed him night and day. By now, Austria had been annexed to Germany and everyone was talking about war. Junger felt it was too dangerous for Anke to stay in Germany and wanted her to return to Ghent, where she had friends. Not only did she refuse, but she insisted that her father begin painting again. She said it would make him well and I agreed. Junger could hardly hold a paintbrush when he returned from the camp, but he was getting stronger now. He sat up in his studio for hours, staring at a blank canvas. He could not paint. Anke tried sitting with him and she tried leaving him alone. This April, on the eighth of the month, she found her father hanging from the cord he used to bind his giant canvases together for transport. He was brought to the hospital, but could not be revived."

The cracking in Fassbinder's voice now melted into a soft sob. Brossler buried his face in his hands and wept, his shoulders shaking.

Moist eyes regarded them, though no one spoke out of respect. After a few moments, Brossler looked up at Fassbinder who was shaking his head at him.

"We knew there was nothing left to do but leave, David. I sold several paintings from my collection, the rest of which is now in the hands of the Nazis no doubt. My wife and I bought visas, with the help of Mr. Paulson, and booked passage on a ship from Rotterdam to New York. She is staying with friends in Manhattan, where I will return after our meeting here."

"And Anke…where did she go?" Brossler asked, wiping his eyes with a handkerchief shifted across the table by Paulson.

"She went back to Ghent. I never really got to say goodbye, everything happened so fast after Junger died. There was no funeral. He was buried in the churchyard at the Peterskirche and I think Anke was the only one to attend the burial. She said that's what she wanted. Before we left, I wrote her a letter with our New York address and sent it to the University of Ghent. I pray she received it."

Fassbinder slumped backward in his chair, exhausted by the emotion. Then, as if he forgot something, he straightened up again.

"All 'degenerate' works were removed from German museums. Meanwhile, the degenerate art exhibit has been traveling around Germany. Millions have seen it, but it only represents a small percentage of the art that Germany has produced. The Nazis burned the confiscated art that they didn't think they could sell. Over a thousand paintings and sculptures and nearly 4,000 drawings, watercolors, and other graphic prints were reduced to ashes at the Berlin Fire Department headquarters in March. And…there is talk of an auction."

"Auction?" Paulson suddenly found his voice.

"Yes, an auction…to raise money for The Reich."

Paulson's mind raced. To buy art from the Nazis, even if it meant giving them money for their war effort, was surely worth it, especially if the art would be destroyed.

"We can't possibly buy art from the Nazis," Brossler said, almost in a whisper. Paulson's face turned pink.

"One of the items up for bidding is van Gogh's *Self Portrait*," Fassbinder added, nonchalantly.

Brossler turned to him, astounded. "How can that be?"

"It was in Munich's Neue Staatsgalerie. They removed it around the time Junger was arrested. No one has seen it since. They are going to sell it."

"Where's the auction going to be?" Paulson asked.

"Lucerne."

"When?"

"In two weeks."

"Lord! Two weeks? It takes two weeks to *get* to Switzerland!"

"Then you must leave right away," Brossler commanded, shocking everyone.

Paulson ran his fingers through his thick, white hair. "You just said that we can't buy art from the Nazis. Now you want me to go to the auction? Why, because of the van Gogh?"

"Yes. We must save it."

"Someone will buy it. A Dutch dealer, surely."

"You should go and see what is going on, we need someone to give a firsthand report."

"Why don't you go?"

The glaringly obvious answer to this question, that Brossler was Jewish, embarrassed Paulson and he immediately apologized. Brossler nodded, absolving him.

"Is this what we want to do?" Paulson asked, addressing the group at large. Williams and Niven said yes at the same time. Quark was more reluctant, but agreed. Jameson nodded but looked thunderstruck. The feelings of Brossler and Fassbinder were obvious.

The meeting broke up when Mrs. Paulson entered the room and insisted that Fassbinder be taken off to bed, since he was clearly exhausted. Even though it wasn't expressed in so many words, everyone understood that Richard Paulson would get on the first ship heading east and attempt to make it to Lucerne to buy, at the very least, the van Gogh.

Brossler and Fassbinder embraced again and Brossler promised to see him tomorrow for breakfast. A sad silence passed between them as they parted, knowing each would shed more tears for Junger that night.

As Brossler walked slowly home though the darkened streets, he wondered if Erik knew about Junger. Perhaps it was reported in the British papers? Maybe this news would finally push Erik to come home to Cambridge like his mother wanted. London was too close to the action, too close to this evil that seemed to be spreading now. Brossler made a promise to himself that he would insist that Erik abandon his studies, for now, and return to America.

Brossler paused at his front door and sat down instead on the front porch swing. He took his hat off and ran his fingers across his balding head. His eyes filled again.

Junger wanted to die. It was all falling apart.

≈

IN LATE JULY, Brossler received a letter from Paulson.

David,

This has been quite the eye-opening experience, to say the least. You will be pleased, I am sure, to know that I bought the van Gogh for a fantastic price. I also bought Matisse's Bathers with a Turtle! I thought Maurice Sauval would be here, but he is apparently arranging a giant Picasso exhibit in Paris. I am going to take it in before I return, though I have shipped the pieces home already. There were a couple of Picassos, several Noldes and Chagalls up for bidding at the auction, many of them bought by a Belgian group. The German auctioneers were sarcastic and generally demeaned the art. Not surprising, I suppose. I spoke to one German dealer who was present, a Herr Groeben, and he seemed very conflicted about Rembrandt. He clearly thought of him as a Nordic painter, but he found fault with the fact that he chose to depict so many Jews. Can you believe these people? He also told me that there were more works up for sale in Berlin: Kandinsky, Klee, Beckmann. I might inquire....

Apparently Hermann Göring, the head of the Luftwaffe, is quite the collector. He isn't afraid of degenerate art, it would seem, by the choices his buyers were making. I propose we organize an exhibit of exiled works, perhaps at the Institute of Contemporary Art? Sauval's agents have bought a number of paintings here, I am sure he would agree to loan them.

I did manage to meet with your son, he came to see me at the Dorchester. He's a thoughtful and highly intelligent young man and he does you great credit!

Take care and best to Lotte,

Richard

July 30, 1939

$\boxed{2}$

The Fugitives

Bury them in caves and cellars, but not one picture shall leave this island.
—Winston Churchill

Eᴿɪᴋ Bʀᴏssʟᴇʀ emerged from Marble Arch Underground Station and headed northeast toward 20 Portman Square, the home of the Courtauld Institute of Art. It was a muggy August day and London was desperate in the heat. Everything seemed to warp and swell, the wooden doors in his flat, the benches in the underground station, even the polished wooden banisters at the institute. This kind of weather was awful for paintings and despite the Herculean efforts of many of the Courtauld staff, Erik himself included, too little or too much moisture was a constant problem. A regulated temperature and humidity inside the institute was attainable, but not without numerous glitches, delays, and failures. But this wasn't what made Erik speed down the sidewalk despite the heat. He considered himself a levelheaded young man, and most would agree, but the summer of 1939 had infused him with an apprehension that he had never felt before in his life. He wanted to reveal what he now knew.

His decision to choose the Courtauld for his graduate work was a difficult one for his parents, who preferred that he stay as far away from Germany as possible. But London, Erik knew, was becoming very popular with art historians, especially Germans. In 1933, not long after he and his family left for America, an entire group of scholars from the Warburg Library in Hamburg sought exile in England to escape the cultural pressures of the Third Reich. The founders of the

Courtauld helped secure them a place in London, later known as The Warburg Institute, and from their knowledge and their extensive collection of classical texts, a new appreciation of the study of art history was forming in London. Erik wanted to be a part of it and his father couldn't refuse him that.

But in recent months, the information coming out of Germany had gone from upsetting to downright alarming. His father had managed to organize a group of Harvard academics and art dealers into an informal protest association bent on helping German artists (and their portfolios) emigrate from Germany to the United States. Erik recently received this letter from his father.

Dearest Erik (or should I write Dr. Brossler?),

I hope this letter finds you well and that your work at the Courtauld is stimulating. To think that you are already embarking on a post-doctorate! Your mother and I couldn't be more proud and I mean that.

I had an experience of some consequence the other evening. You remember Richard Paulson, the art collector who donated that Monet to the university's museum? Well, he recently helped a contact of his from Munich immigrate to America with his wife. It was Friedrich Fassbinder! He told me, and I am so sorry to tell you this, that Dietrich Junger committed suicide in Munich. It wasn't reported in the American papers and I assume if it had been reported in the British press you would have told me. His portfolio was confiscated by the Nazis a couple of years ago and he was later imprisoned in a work camp because apparently he tried to create more canvases despite being ordered not to do so.

I have found out that Anke is at the University of Ghent, working on the Ghent Altarpiece I believe. I don't know how far along she is with her degree, but she's been there a few years at least. Fassbinder and I met again privately and we were just in tears over Anke. I've sent letters to her, as has Fassbinder, but there hasn't been a reply.

If we were wondering just how far the Nazis would go to push their "cultural agenda"—well I think we have our answer. Fassbinder said Junger was too broken by his time in prison and too afraid for Anke to paint ever again, and that was what caused him to take his own life.

Anyway, you know I feel that it would be best if you returned to America and I also know that you are your own man and will do as you please.

Your mother is extremely worried and this story about Junger has set her on edge even more. It's simply incredible! The Nazis are destroying Germany's preeminence in modernist and expressionist art! Junger is just the latest victim and I know there will be many more.

With all our love, Papa

The news about Junger brought Erik back to a place he thought he had left behind. His separation from Anke had been the most painful part of leaving Germany and it took about three years before Erik stopped thinking of her as his girlfriend. He had fantasized often that she and her father would also come to America, as so many were doing, and that he would marry her.

Erik scoffed at his own thoughts as he waited in the August heat for his supervisor to put the phone down and open his office door. Lord Brigsworth-Jones, eminent art historian and Professor of Medieval Art at the Courtauld Institute, had just returned from a last-minute trip to Geneva to see a hastily organized exhibit of art treasures from the Prado Museum in Madrid. The civil war in Spain had forced the curators to evacuate most of the collection, which was now homeless and consigned to traverse the country in trucks. Finally, a joint effort by the Committee for the Salvaging of Spanish Art Treasures and the League of Nations allowed the collection to be moved into France, and finally to Geneva. Several British art agencies were involved in the deal, one of which was overseen by Brigsworth-Jones, just one of his many official duties in the art world.

Erik jumped off the sticky wooden bench as Brigsworth-Jones's large frame filled the doorway. He motioned for Erik to enter with the lit cigarette in his hand. His mentor's appearance was that of someone who had not slept recently and had not changed his clothes in a day or two. To be fair, Brigsworth-Jones was hardly a dapper English gentleman; he was Welsh for a start. His seat in the House of Lords was permanently empty and he cared little for appearances. He loved rich food (pheasant and other fowl were his favorites) and wine (must be Bordeaux or Rhone Valley) and art (Hieronymus Bosch was his specialty). He did, however, usually wear clean shirts and comb his thinning hair. Erik felt out of sorts seeing him…out of sorts.

"Erik, sit down." Brigsworth-Jones leaned up against his desk, which slid backward along the floor ever so slowly under the pressure.

"Professor," Erik began, but stopped when Brigsworth-Jones shook his head.

"I have a lot to tell you and I need you to listen and then do exactly as I say. Is that clear?"

Erik wasn't used to this kind of talk from the professor. Their relationship had always been more like colleagues than professor/student. This seriousness unnerved him.

"Completely clear, sir."

"Good chap. As you know, James McMasters and I went to Geneva to see the Prado exhibit. It was astounding. There will never be another one like it."

He glanced at a piece of paper he held in his hand. Erik leaned forward expectantly.

"There were 174 paintings in all. Thirty-eight of them were Goyas, twenty-six El Greco's, not to mention all the good Velasquezs and Dürer's *Self-Portrait*. Oh, and Pieter Bruegel's *Triumph of Death*. Of course, the main reason I went was to see the Hieronymus Bosch triptych, *The Garden of Earthly Delights*, which was only given to the Prado this year. But this isn't why I asked you here."

The professor lit another cigarette and offered one to Erik, who declined. As the smoke encircled his head, Brigsworth-Jones returned to his desk chair and sat.

"McMasters was an art dealer before he was tapped for the Cultural Council and he still has lots of contacts in that world. We met with one of them in Geneva...Christophe Melker, a sweet old chap from Leipzig. He told us some rather upsetting things."

"Hitler is planning to attack Britain," Erik offered.

"Well, yes...I think that's a given at this point, but that's not what he told us. He was talking about art. He said Hitler has grand plans for a new museum in Linz, Austria...apparently it's his hometown. He also said that a man named Hans Steiglitz has been chosen curator of this new museum and is actively buying up art, mainly Old Masters and Germanic art, at a rapid pace and seems to have no budget ceiling."

"I wonder," Erik said, "if this was why the Germans refused to lend their paintings to the Rembrandt show at the Rijksmuseum last year. Plus, the Belgians had to beg the Germans for their Memlings for the show in Bruges."

"You went to that show, didn't you?"

"The *Polyptych of the Calvary* was there, from Lübeck Cathedral. I couldn't resist."

"Of course not, you're a Memling specialist."

Erik smiled, but thought of just how close he had been to Anke and hadn't even known it. Bruges and Ghent are only an hour apart by train.

Brigsworth-Jones took a long drag. "Melker said that Jewish art dealers have been cleaned out, their collections stolen outright."

"Hitler was rejected from the Vienna Academy of Art, wasn't he?" Erik asked, knowing the answer.

"Was he?"

"Yes. I've read about him, his early years. He wanted to be a painter, but he was rejected from the academy. Many on the admission committee were Jewish. My father had some of them as professors when he was in art school there. Those who hadn't retired lost their jobs last year and several of them left Austria. Alois Breckenbauer and his family stayed with my parents in Cambridge for a month after they left Vienna. Now he's at the Met in New York."

Brigsworth-Jones knew he had the right man sitting before him. Erik Brossler was connected, either by blood or friendship, to a huge web of art historians, dealers, and artists through his father. David Brossler was offered a position at the Courtauld when he made it clear he was leaving Germany, but he chose to go to America. His position at Harvard gave Brigsworth-Jones a solid ally on the American side, though the distance would make it difficult to make concrete plans. That's why he needed Erik. Though still honing his skills, Erik was a talented writer and his analysis on Memling was more than insightful. More importantly, he was young and strong. There was lots of heavy lifting to do.

"Chap, I am going to be blunt. I need you to keep all of this information private at all costs. Please do not tell your father or any of his colleagues anything until I give you permission."

"Of course. Not a problem."

"We are closing the National Gallery tomorrow. The works will be moved to several castles in Wales. The Royal Train has been donated to help transport them. I need you to get over there immediately and help organize the packing. You know how to do it…you've packed paintings here. You are my representative and I have told the curator that you are coming to help. Don't expect much of a welcome though. That little runt Irving is still in charge until Giles Merchant gets back from India. Regardless, I want you to keep me apprised of the progress. We need to get the bulk of the collection into hiding as soon as possible."

Erik tried to digest the certainty. The bombs were coming. He envisioned the galleries on fire, the canvases scorched, the paint melting. A sour pit rumbled in his stomach.

"What about the Courtauld? Where will this collection go?"

"Most of it will go to the country. The remaining students will be taught in Gilford. This building will be boarded up and sandbagged, most likely. But I don't need you here, I need you at the National Gallery."

"I'll go right now," Erik said, standing. He'd never had a job like this and was surprised by the exhilaration. He turned to leave when his mentor added, "Be sure to pack a few things. You'll be sleeping there for the next week."

WHEN ERIK ARRIVED in the main hall of the National Gallery, he saw Leonardo da Vinci's *Madonna of the Rocks* float by him like driftwood on a wave, the man carrying her obscured behind the panel. This was one of two almost identical altarpieces painted by da Vinci for the Confraternity of the Immaculate Conception in Milan. The other, more finished version is in the Louvre. The Virgin, with the infants Christ and St. John the Baptist, sit amongst rocks in a grotto type landscape. The man eased the Madonna gently down against the east wall, next to Rubens's *Samson and Delilah*. Erik's former Renaissance painting professor called this the most erotic painting in the world. Samson lies in Delilah's lap, his muscled body exhausted from the passion they have shared. She gazes down at him, her breasts still exposed, while another man cuts Samson's hair, robbing him of the source of his strength. Philistine soldiers wait at the door, ready to take Samson away.

Erik stood admiring the masterpiece when five new people appeared, all carrying paintings that represented the cream of the crop of the gallery's collection.

"Dr. Brossler?" a nasal voice came from a tiny man carrying a folded altarpiece. "I am Rupert Irving, the assistant curator. I informed Lord Brigsworth-Jones that we had everything under control, but I see he insisted on sending you to observe."

"Observe? I am here to help. I can pack paintings."

Erik's German accent had been purposely diluted by his years in America and Britain, but it was still noticeable to some people. Irving was one of those people.

"I had not planned on anyone outside of gallery staff actually handling the works of art," Irving said awkwardly.

"Do you think Brigsworth-Jones sent me to report on you? He wants to help. He got the Royal Train to take the paintings to Wales."

The look on Irving's face told Erik that the destination of the paintings was not common knowledge. Erik could have kicked himself. Irving probably thought he was a spy.

"The Royal Train…well, that is helpful." Irving handed Erik the folded altarpiece. "You can start by packing this. I need not remind you it was painted in the late fourteenth century."

Erik nodded and cradled the piece like a newborn. He followed Irving into the next room where wooden packing crates covered the floor and were piled up in every corner. Hundreds more sat outside the door in a long gallery lined with empty ornate frames. The bizarre and desolate image was burned in Erik's memory.

Before placing the altarpiece in the closest box, he stole a peek. As he suspected, it was the *Wilton Diptych*. The artist was unknown, but it was painted principally as a portable altarpiece for King Richard II of England, whose own likeness was depicted in the left section. The young king kneels in front of the Virgin and eleven angels. This was one of several works Erik studied in detail as a graduate student and was undoubtedly one of the most precious art treasures of Great Britain. Now he was packing it for an uncertain journey. He wrapped the edges with thick paper and buried the diptych in crunchy straw. This work had its own box, but others would be packed together no doubt. As he got up to get his next painting, he heard one of the other workers driving the nails into the top of the box, sealing Richard and the Virgin inside.

Erik was disappointed to discover that the museum's admirable collection of Memlings had been packed before he arrived. Amongst them was *The Donne Triptych*, which had formed a part of Erik's PhD thesis. The triptych had been commissioned by Sir John Donne of Kidwelly, Wales. He was a well-connected and wealthy courtier/soldier of the fifteenth century and a very distant relative of Brigsworth-Jones, who had turned Erik onto the idea of studying the triptych. Brigsworth-Jones had sent a note to Irving specifically requesting that Erik be allowed to pack *The Donne Triptych*. Since Brigsworth-Jones was on the board of directors of museum, Erik assumed his wishes would be granted. Irving, as it turned out, was not a fan of Brigsworth-Jones or his meddling in gallery affairs. This was no major surprise; more people disliked Erik's mentor than liked him. Perhaps that is why, at forty-six, he was still a bachelor. But what did surprise Erik was Irving's use of the Memlings to prove a point. They had been hastily packed, several to one crate, in the hours after receiving the note from Brigsworth-Jones, but before Erik arrived. When Erik insisted that his only care was for the art and suggested repacking the Memlings in a calmer, safer manner, Irving refused. Had Erik known what the following years had in store, he might have allowed Irving his power trip. But he didn't know, and so he cursed Irving under his breath time after time until even he grew bored and gave it up.

The packing staff slept at the gallery on mattresses donated by St. Bartholomew's Hospital. On his fourth night, Erik managed a spot of privacy by dragging his mattress into the "pre-1700 Dutch and Flemish painting" room, where he felt most at home. He found himself staring at the spot where van Eyck's *The Arnolfini Portrait* had been. This painting was famous for, among other things, the convex mirror that hung on the wall, just behind the richly dressed figures of Giovanni Arnolfini and his wife, Giovanna. In the small mirror, two other figures were visible though their identities remain a mystery. Erik always supposed that van Eyck was one of them, since above the mirror there is a Latin inscription: *Johannes van Eyck fuit hic.* Johannes van Eyck was here.

Nearby, the massive frame that held van Dyke's *Equestrian Portrait of Charles I* leaned lifelessly against the wall. Fitting, Eric supposed, since van Dyke's position as official painter to the English court of Charles I leant itself to the grand, idealized styling of the king astride a magnificent horse. Just two years after the painting was finished, King Charles was beheaded by his subjects after England's civil war.

In an adjoining room, *The Ambassadors*, by Hans Holbein the Younger, was still hanging and would be the first for Erik to pack tomorrow. Erik could vividly remember the first time he had seen this painting on a trip to London as a boy. Two wealthy English gentlemen stand in front of a table laden with musical instruments, globes, a Protestant prayer book, and a number of other items loaded with sixteenth-century religious and political symbolism. Erik recalled how his father slowly walked his son to the right, and then stood him in a position to gaze back on the painting from an extreme angle. From there, Erik saw that the design in the foreground, which he hadn't been able to identify and had therefore ignored, was in fact a large human skull. *The Ambassadors*, his father explained, was the most famous example of the use of anamorphic perspective, which became popular during the Renaissance. This technique rendered an image viewable only from a certain angle, and not straight on. Erik had felt that day like he had been let in on a tantalizing secret. He then watched as other people approached the painting, admired it, then moved on never knowing what they had missed. Erik knew he wanted to be an art historian at that moment, when he was eleven. Now, having achieved his goal, he backed away from the painting and sank wearily on his mattress. A disturbing thought flashed. Despite Holbein's distinguished career in England, painting English subjects, he was German by birth and training. Surely Hitler would want any and all Holbeins for his new museum in Linz. Then, another thought put Holbein in the shadow. Memling was born in Germany....

"Can't sleep?" The voice was female and after Erik's initial shudder, he sat up and smiled at Shirley Brown. Shirley was a monitor at the gallery and had been packing since day one. She was younger than many of the other women, though still a few years ahead of Erik.

"I haven't had much of a chance to try," Erik said, resting on his elbows and regarding her. "Where is your dress?"

Shirley looked down at her slip and shrugged. "I don't know...maybe I packed it. They'll find it in Wales, wrapped around a Rembrandt!"

Erik liked this. He gestured for her to join him on his mattress. There hadn't been a woman in his life since he left his college girlfriend, Lucy, behind after graduating from Yale. Lucy wasn't the right woman, he had told his parents. They knew that was only because she wasn't Anke. His mother, in a fit of nerves and desperation at Erik's decision to go to London, reminded him he had to stop measuring every woman he met against a fifteen-year-old girl he last saw on a Munich train platform. Despite her later apologies, Erik remembered that comment like no other.

Shirley snuggled up against him, her skin damp with the August heat. He leaned over her, smelling the powder she used and the Chesterfields she smoked. It wouldn't be wonderful, or life changing, he thought. He did what he could and she seemed happy enough, though not so happy as to stay with him all night. When he fell asleep, she watched him for a while in the darkness. He was not her type in the least. She liked blondes and Erik had dark, wavy hair and big brown eyes, like hers. But still, she found him beautiful though she couldn't pinpoint why. Eventually she slipped her arm out from under him and snuck away, putting her slip back on as she went. She knew she'd be back the next night, but she couldn't bring herself to sleep next to him. When she found her own pallet a few rooms west, she reached under the mattress and twisted her wedding ring back on.

KING GEORGE VI appeared at the Tate Gallery to watch the packing of its treasures, but made no such trip to the National Gallery. Just as well, Irving told his staff, since it would have undoubtedly caused distraction and delay. Thanks to several packing drills he ran the year before, Irving was proud to witness his staff empty one of the larger galleries in just seven minutes. The special cutting of some of the giant frames, to allow easy removal of the paintings, had helped with efficiency.

The art was loaded onto the Royal Train and shipped west at ten miles an hour so as not to jostle the contents. Some staffers, including Irving, accompanied the art to Wales. Others were directed to bring any remaining artworks to the Aldwych Underground station, where they would be stored on the platforms and in the tunnels.

After the last piece had left the museum, Erik returned to the Courtauld and walked through the empty galleries to the small office he shared with another post-doctoral fellow, Dean Carlisle. Erik could see that Dean had cleared out most of his papers and books, but had left a letter for Erik on his desk. It was from Brigsworth-Jones, who had quit London for Wales to oversee the installation of the collections at Penrhyn Castle (which was owned by his cousin).

Dear Erik,

Thank you for your updates, they were most helpful. That rat Irving spoke highly of you; I think you have won him over. As you know by now, I will be in Wales for the foreseeable future. I have recently spoken with your father and we came to an agreement. With war an almost certainty at this point, I will be attempting to organize an Anglo-American art conservation committee made up of British and American art historians and curators, which will aim to protect and account for Europe's art during this inevitable conflict. Your father has already taken steps and organized a group at Harvard. I will do the same on this end.

I made a promise to him that when you were finished at the National Gallery, I would emphatically insist that you go home. I understand that you have secured a junior curator position at the Memling Museum in Bruges for next year and let me be clear: I could not be happier for you, it's the perfect place for a man of your talents. However, Britain is now at war and it is my feeling that most of Europe will be as well in short order. You need to go west, chap. This is not because I do not need you. However, your father needs you too and you will be a distinguished addition to their group. I ask you to please respect our wishes in this matter, especially since I gave your father my word as a gentleman that you would return to Boston as soon as possible.

It has been my great pleasure to work with you and I feel certain that we will do so again when this nastiness is behind us. God be with you.

Owen Brigsworth-Jones

August 30, 1939

Post-script: The next time you decide to have a thoughtless fling, please do not pick the wife of a London policeman!

Erik put the letter down in a combination of shock and disappointment. Not about Shirley, she'd admitted as much to him and their dalliance was ended quickly. But his aspirations of going to Bruges, to his friend Pieter van Maes, and helping with the evacuations of the Memling Museum seemed naive now. His parents would be devastated and Brigsworth-Jones would be embarrassed. Still, what could be done in America? He didn't want to sit on a committee. He could have been the last person on earth to see the *Wilton Diptych*. How could a committee at Harvard compete with that?

THREE DAYS LATER, Erik opened the *The Times* at the small kitchen table in his miniscule Camden flat and read about the German invasion of Poland and Britain's official declaration of war. One headline read, "Five Kent Towns Evacuating Children This Weekend."

He packed his bags and shipped his books and files to his parents' house in Cambridge. Then, he took a train to Dover, the ferry to Oostende, and got the direct train to Bruges. Bruges was the home to Hans Memling for most of his painting career, in the late fifteenth century. Though unproved, the story goes that Memling was in the military service of Charles the Bold, the powerful Duke of Burgundy, and was wounded in a battle. The Hospitaller Knights of St. John offered him shelter in Bruges, healed his wounds, and in return he painted a number of works for them. These paintings are still kept in St. John's Hospital, Bruges (also known as the Memling Museum), and among them is the Shrine of St. Ursula. This shrine is one of Memling's most famous works and was the subject of Erik's master's dissertation at Yale. The wooden shrine is believed to hold the relics of the saint herself, who legend says was murdered by the Huns in Cologne after undertaking a pilgrimage to Rome with 11,000 virgins.

Erik told himself that once he had helped evacuate the Memlings, he'd take the first ship west. He would *not* attempt to find Anke in Ghent. She'd stopped writing. She had moved on. He willed himself to stop thinking about her and thought about his parents instead. They had only one child. He tried to convince himself that his father would understand. His mother, he knew, would not. If she knew where he was headed she would yell: "Erik, you are going in the wrong direction!"

He could not help but sense, as he ran from the Bruges train station toward the museum with little more than the clothes on his back, that she might be right.

3

Just Judges

The period immediately preceding the completion of the Ghent Altarpiece in
1432 had brought with it a totally new kind of painting...this was Ars Nova,
a new art, as contemporaries were quick to realize—even abroad, even in Italy.
—Otto Pächt, Viennese art historian

AT THE SAME TIME that Erik Brossler was sliding across the wet pav-
ing stones of Bruges, Anke Junger was bicycling madly through
Ghent on her way to Saint Bavo's Cathedral. As she entered St. Baafsplein, she leaned her bike against a wall on the south side of the
square and hurried into the church. St. Bavo's was as good an example
of Romanesque and Gothic architecture as one would get in Belgium,
and parts of the building dated back to the tenth century. She tiptoed across the nave, not wanting to disrupt the Mass, and slipped into
the Vidjt Chapel. In this small, holy space was one of the undisputed
masterpieces of Northern Renaissance painting, *The Adoration of the*
Mystic Lamb, commonly known as The Ghent Altarpiece. At more than
eleven feet tall and eighteen feet wide, it was one of the largest altarpieces of its kind in existence, with twelve panels in two rows, eight of
which are painted on both sides. Hubert van Eyck began the painting
in the early 1420s as a commission for the merchant Joost Vidjt, but
died before he could complete it. His brother, the master painter Jan
van Eyck, finished the painting in 1432 and it is considered by many
to be his greatest work. While Jan van Eyck did not invent oil painting,
he was the first to fully use oil to create the realism he became famous
for. The egg-based tempera, which had been the main staple of artists

for many years, was unable to render the exquisite detail of oil-based paint, which dried slower. The strikingly realistic Ghent Altarpiece caused such ripples in the medieval art world that an entire era of art, the Northern Renaissance period, could be said to have burst forth from its panels. After the Mystic Lamb, oil paint became the norm.

The central panels represent the seated Christ, with the Virgin and John the Baptist flanking him on either side, while the outside panels show singing angels and Adam and Eve. The lower central panel shows the adoration of the Lamb of God by pilgrims, hermits, angels, and priests. The left lower panels are depictions of the commissioner of the piece, Joost Vidjt, John the Baptist, and the *Just Judges* (men on horseback who have come to honor the lamb). As Anke looked up at the altarpiece, the *Just Judges* panel was missing.

Everyone in the art world, and many outside of it, knew that in 1934 both the *Just Judges* and the John the Baptist panels had been stolen from the cathedral. Economic depression and the recent collapse of two major Belgian banks had perhaps inspired the crime, which was widely reported in Europe and America. Scotland Yard was involved immediately, along with many of the other major police services of Western Europe. It was quite simply the biggest art theft since pirates stole Memling's *The Last Judgment* triptych in the late fifteenth century. Commissioned by agents of the Medici in Bruges and bound for Italy, the Memling masterpiece ended up in Danzig, Poland, where it remained.

Soon after the theft of the *Just Judges*, the Bishop of Ghent received a ransom note demanding one million Belgian francs for the return of the panels. The Bishop would receive thirteen such letters over the next few months and was always instructed to reply to them via the *Avis Individuals* section of the Brussels paper *La Derniere Heure*. He did so, indicating his various responsibilities and pleading for the return of the panels. After receiving the third letter, the John the Baptist panel was returned, unharmed, to a railway station in north Brussels.

Anke and her father had followed the story very closely. She was working on a degree in art history at the University of Ghent and her thesis paper was on the history of the Ghent Altarpiece. She was two months from completion when the panels were stolen. At first she was questioned by the police, along with all those who had access to the Vidjt Chapel and the cathedral in general. She was immediately ruled out as a suspect but asked to remain in Ghent in case she might provide answers or expertise to the investigators. This attention buoyed her and she wrote to her father, *I think they see me as an expert on the altarpiece, a real art historian!*

Dietrich Junger had no trouble thinking of his daughter as an authority on the Ghent Altarpiece, he had hardly been able to drag her away from it for two years. She came home to Munich for Christmas and Easter, and for her father's birthday in July. But Munich, he knew, wasn't the same without Erik Brossler. So, he traveled to Ghent on her September birthday, and spent a month there during her first summer in Belgium. He enjoyed his brief breaks from painting and found, when he returned to Munich, that he even missed hearing Anke bang away on her typewriter at all hours of the night.

He was fascinated with how she looked at a work of art...what she saw in it. When he stared up at the altarpiece, which he did countless times on his visits to Ghent, he saw rich color, texture, unbelievable realism, and truly awe-inspiring technique. Despite being a lapsed Catholic himself, he found the work uplifting and majestic. But it wasn't until Anke told him of the altar's tempestuous history did he understand why she loved it so much.

The panels, she explained to him on her birthday in 1936 (as they dined on *moules* at an outdoor café in Ghent) had already been to hell and back before this latest disaster. In 1566, during a Protestant revolt known as the *Beeldenstorm*, the altarpiece was hidden in the tower of the cathedral for three years to protect it from anti-Catholic rioting. When the Calvinists were in power, the painting was moved to the city hall of Ghent, again to preserve it from the iconoclasts who sought the destruction of religious imagery.

In 1792, Napoleon's soldiers stole the central panels (the Adam and Eve side panels having been hidden in the chapter house) and took them to Paris. They remained there until Napoleon was exiled to St. Helena in 1815, when they were returned to Ghent. The following year, the altar was dismantled and sold to the King of Prussia, except for the for the Adam and Eve panels, which remained in Ghent and were nearly destroyed in a fire in 1822.

At the end of the Great War in 1918, the Versailles Treaty stipulated that Germany return the altarpiece to Ghent. At last, all the panels were reunited. All was well until the two panels were stolen in 1934. The *Just Judges* has never been found and the thief himself, who was eventually identified and who claimed to be the only person on earth who knew the location of the missing panel, mumbled clues to its whereabouts on his deathbed but those clues led only to more questions.

Junger had marveled at his daughter that night. She spoke of the altarpiece, and its rough passage through time, as one speaks of a family member, or a cherished pet. For her, the panels were like lovers and she fell in and out of love with each one of them at different times. The disappearance of the *Just Judges* was something he knew would occupy her thoughts for many years, especially if neither the panel, nor proof of its destruction, were ever found. An artist had been recently hired to produce a copy of the *Just Judges* and last they heard, he was painting on an eighteenth-century cupboard shelf.

JAN PEETERS, the cathedral's elderly janitor and night watchman, observed Anke from behind a pillar, as he often did. He had told his wife about the young woman, who he said looked like an angel, and how she came almost every day to sit at the foot of the altarpiece. Hundreds of years prior, the German artist Albrecht Dürer was reported to have spent hours staring at the panels in much the same way, once kissing the frame as he left the chapel. But this woman wasn't an artist studying technique, the janitor knew, but someone who felt connected to the work much in the same way he did himself. He watched her stare up at the void of the missing panel and imagined the ache its loss must have provoked in her. He did not know that this ache was eclipsed only by the death of her beloved father, a true artist.

IN MAY 1940, the day after the invasion of Holland, Jan watched his angel sitting in the chapel as usual, but noticed that she wasn't alone. Six men had joined her and they were deep in conversation. Jan crept closer, curious.

"We need to be extremely careful here," a tall, elegant man was saying, his hands rumbling the coin pieces in the pockets of his dark trousers.

"I agree," the angel said, "but we must do it now. There is no doubt that the Nazis will be interested."

Another man peeked around to the back of the altarpiece, as if he was contemplating taking it down. Jan shuddered at the thought of the Lamb of God leaving the chapel yet again.

"Who else knows?" the angel asked, pushing back one of her blond curls that had escaped its pin.

"Nobody," said one of the men, whose back was to Jan. "After all the press about the *Just Judges*, I'd rather do this quietly."

All nodded in agreement and two of the men removed their suit jackets and rolled up their white sleeves. The other two, Jan now noticed, were wearing the robes of priests. The angel caught his eye and came toward him. Her soft face radiated warmth, which calmed him, though her eyes were glassy. Jan realized she was as upset as he was.

"Mr. Peeters? Did you overhear us?" Anke asked, gently.

"Only a few words, *Fräulein*."

Despite having known her for years now, he always called her that. He was a very quiet man but he kept the Vidjt Chapel spotless and polished the candlesticks each week. Anke knew that he watched over the van Eyck and she felt better knowing he slept just paces from the chapel, in the rear of the cathedral. He couldn't be left out of this process.

"Mr. Peeters, we have arranged for the altarpiece to be evacuated to the Vatican, for safekeeping."

"Who are those men?" Jan asked, pointing.

"Two are art historians, from the University. Professor Pierre Dubois runs the art history department. The other is Dr. Niels Maarten, a religious art specialist. The priests, Father Biestman and Father van der Saar, work for the bishop."

"Bishop Coppieters ordered this?"

"Yes, of course. He wants to protect the altar as much as we do."

Jan seemed placated and offered to help. His stooped frame suggested otherwise. He and Anke stood out of the way as Niels and Pierre carefully separated the panels and handed them down, one by one, to Father van der Saar, who leaned them against the walls. Anke wrapped the edges with strips of cloth and then enclosed each panel in a wool blanket. Father Biestman then slid the panels lengthwise into large wooden crates. The temptation to repair small cracks and wipe away the caked dirt on the panels was intense, but Anke knew there wasn't time. Three hours later, there were ten crates in all, nailed shut and loaded onto three small trucks. Anke threw a small bag of her own into the passenger seat of the front truck.

"Anke, you're not going," Pierre said, wiping his sweaty forehead with his sleeve.

"What? I thought we decided…," she began.

"No. It's too dangerous. When the Germans invade…I don't want you found with the altarpiece. The Germans will want it back in Berlin."

Anke began again, her voice breaking slightly. "But, you said I was the best person to travel with it, I aroused less suspicion because I am a woman."

"No, I'll go. You should go stay with my wife, help her with the baby, keep a low profile. You've published on the altarpiece, but not in German, so hopefully they won't notice you."

"Professor…please, I…."

"Anke!" His voice chilled Jan, who was still hovering near his angel. Pierre tried to calm himself, running his fingers across his balding head. "This is the least I can do for your father."

Niels cringed, not quite sure if that was a good point or a low blow. Anke's devastation over the suicide of her only remaining family member was well known throughout the university and there were rumors flying that the rising star had drifted into melancholy and had lost her spark.

"Let her go," Niels chimed in. "I thought the whole point was to get the altarpiece out of the country before the Germans get here. If it is too dangerous to return, you can stay in Rome!"

"If I am going to drive nearly a thousand miles, then it is my decision," Pierre warned.

"Then I'll go," Niels said, heading toward the truck. "Anke and I will go. We will join the convoy from Bruges. Everything is going to the same place and we'll be safer if we stay together. You stay here, with Gisela and the baby."

Pierre could not pretend that this wasn't the exact scenario he had hoped for. His devotion to Belgian art notwithstanding, he dreaded leaving his wife and their new son, Piers, who was only a month old. He had suspected for some time that Niels was having an affair with Anke; now he was sure of it. Niels was fifteen years older than Anke, though neither was married and since he was not her supervisor, it was more of a tidbit than a scandal.

"I still think you should stay here, Anke. If they find you…you still have German papers," Pierre warned.

"Not anymore," Niels announced. "Meet Leida Maarten, my niece from Antwerp."

Anke pulled out a passport and identity papers from her leather backpack. The forgeries were impressive, someone from the university's art department no doubt. Pierre handed the papers back to her, a look of resignation on his face. He suddenly noticed that the elderly janitor was still standing quite near to them, listening.

"It's alright, professor, that is Jan. He knows me." Anke winked at Jan, who grinned and receded into the background. He watched as his angel was helped up into the cab of the truck by Niels, whose hand lingered for a moment on her thigh. Pierre double-checked the precious cargo, then waved off the two priests who were driving the other trucks. He then went to the window of Anke's truck.

"Be careful, Anke. You made yourself known to the Germans when your father was at Dachau. You were questioned by the Gestapo. I am sure they have a file on you. Someone might remember your face."

"The chances of that are so remote," Niels said, fumbling with the sticky gearshift.

"I'll be careful," Anke promised. "I think my father would want me to do this, don't you?"

Pierre shrugged nervously.

Niels revved the engine of the old truck and they lurched forward. Pierre watched, heart pounding, as they drove west toward Bruges. He looked back at Jan, who stood somberly at the door of the cathedral. Chilled and suddenly lonely, he waved to Jan and walked off across St. Baafsplein.

∾

IN BRUGES, Anke and Niels met a colleague, Pieter van Maes, who was a junior curator at the Memling museum. He informed them that the chancellors of St. John's Hospital would not release the Memlings for transport to the Vatican and had decided to hide them in Bruges.

"Hide them? Hide them where? It will only take one direct hit to blow the Shrine of St. Ursula to bits," Niels hissed, frustrated.

"I know, but they won't let them go. I should have shipped them to America with Erik while I had the chance," Pieter said.

"Who is Erik?" Anke asked.

"Dr. Erik Brossler, Courtauld Institute. He is a wonderful fellow. He was to be my replacement here when I move to the Rijksmuseum next year. He helped evacuate the National Gallery in London, then he came right here to help me, at great personal risk I might add. He's Jewish."

"I hope he's gone now!" Niels said.

"Yes, he's taken a ship from Rotterdam, for New York."

Anke's face had been drained of blood and she sat abruptly on a stone bench. Erik had been here, just days before. She hadn't known he was in London all this time. She tried to imagine what he looked like now, but found it hard. For a moment, she imagined boarding a ship and following him to America. She shook it off. He didn't think of her anymore. He never returned any of her letters. Niels sat beside her and assumed her sudden paleness was in reaction to the possible fate of the Memling treasures.

"We can't send the Madonna with you either," Pieter finally said. "The bishop won't let her go."

One of Belgium's most famous works, second only to the Ghent Altarpiece, was the marble *Bruges Madonna* by Michelangelo. Anke loved this Madonna more than any other because the Virgin looked like a girl, not a woman. She clutches her son's small palm with her left hand and in her right she holds a book. Was it a holy book? Or, was she reading to Jesus? Both figures gaze down slightly, perhaps resigned to their fates.

This was the only Michelangelo to leave Italy during his lifetime. A prominent Bruges cloth merchant family bought it for 4,000 gold florins in 1506. After it left the country, it was unknown in Italy to the point where Georgio Vasari, an artist and contemporary biographer of many Italian Renaissance artists, reported that the statue was made of bronze, not marble. Just like the Ghent Altarpiece, the *Bruges Madonna* was stolen by the French in the late eighteenth century and then returned after the final defeat of Napoleon. Anke never left Bruges without a visit to Notre Dame cathedral, to see her Madonna. She wondered now if she would ever be able to visit her again.

"The Germans will take the Madonna," Niels said, to nobody in particular. "The bishop is a fool."

The Bishop of Bruges, fool or not, arranged for Anke to stay with the Beguines, the lay sisters of Bruges. The Beguines lived in a monastic arrangement, very much like nuns, but did not take formal religious vows. Niels disliked the situation since men were not allowed to sleep at the Beguinage. He stayed with Pieter on the outskirts of the city and like nearly everyone else in Belgium, slept little on the night of May 28th. King Leopold III had surrendered to the German Army to the horror of the entire population. The official capitulation took place at eleven o'clock at night, and the fighting was to be ended by four o'clock in the morning. As Anke lay on her small cot in the cool, Spartan room on the second floor of the Beguinage, she listened closely to the noises outside as if she could hear the end of the battle, even though she never heard the battles in the first place. She also shed tears over Erik Brossler for the first time in years.

Holland had been subdued in five days and Rotterdam was bombed into dust. The very docks Erik had sailed from months before were reduced to splinters so no more ships could depart. Only the church, Sint-Laurenskerk, still stood in the city center. Belgium held out for another fourteen days, though the army was ill-equipped to repel the German *blitzkrieg*. Two of the three guard towers protecting the bridges over the Albert Canal at Maastricht were overpowered by special Wehrmacht units who arrived on gliders. Although the bridges were all rigged with explosives, the attacks were so quick and efficient that the Belgian guards didn't have time to set the fuses. Brussels surrendered on May 18, but the Belgians fought on long enough for the evacuation of nearly 400,000 British and French soldiers from the beaches at Dunkirk in northern France. It also allowed for the Belgian art convoy to begin its journey to Rome.

Once they finally got on the road, they made it only to Péronne, just across the French border. There, the road was blocked by a legion of tanks. At first, Anke assumed they had run into the French army, though she then realized that the tanks were going in the wrong direction.

"My God, they are retreating," Anke said, still unsure what she was looking at.

Niels leaned his head out the window and listened. One of the tanks turned and began to drive toward the convoy. A swastika flag stuck out of the turret and flapped in the wind.

"Jesus Christ. Anke, these are the Germans."

"What? France has fallen too?" Anke asked, astonished.

"They must be heading for the channel coast," he said. "Shit, look at them, have you ever seen anything like this?"

Inexplicably, Anke knew what to do. She got out of the truck and began to walk toward the tank that had stopped fifty feet away. Niels screamed at her, but she ignored him. Her dark blue dress blew up in the dusty wind.

A uniformed officer emerged from the tank turret and climbed down to meet her. Niels leaned his head out of the window again, listening. His German was good, but she was too far away. He saw Anke pull out her papers.

"Fräulein Junger. Can I be of assistance?" the officer asked, handing them back to her.

"No, thank you. I am sure you are very busy. I am escorting these trucks, which have some paintings in them, to a safe location. They are very old and we just don't want them destroyed, you understand."

"Yes. Of course. I understand completely."

"Would you like to see them?"

"No, no. That will not be necessary. We are…very much pressed for time. We're driving the British right into the sea!"

"Yes, I can see that," Anke said, smiling at him.

He smiled back and bowed to her. He then turned and climbed up to the turret again.

"It will be at least an hour before you can continue on this road," he called down to her, "you might want to turn off your trucks to save on fuel."

"Excellent suggestion, thank you!"

When she climbed back into the cab of the truck, Niels stared at her, dumbfounded.

"My instinct was right, Niels. This is the Wehrmacht. These are ordinary soldiers. They aren't interested in art or where we are taking it."

"Did he believe your new papers?"

"I showed him my German papers."

"I thought you destroyed them!"

"No, I kept them. I thought I might need them, and I was right."

"If you are searched and they find both sets…Jesus, if the partisans find you…they'll think you are a German spy."

Anke had not thought of this. They sat in silence as the column of tanks rumbled past, making one of the loudest noises either of them had ever heard. She knew that owning to her German identity would most likely get her shipped back to the fatherland immediately. Maybe that wasn't such a bad thing. The van Eyck altar would be at the Vatican. She could go home to Munich and do what she could to protect the art there. She wanted to get her father's canvases back, if they had survived the degenerate bonfires.

When they finally began again, they drove slowly so as to preserve their cargo the best they could on the bumpy roads. South of Paris, the streets became cluttered with cars and trucks full of people and their possessions desperately fleeing to the countryside. They rode a while next to two young girls who sat atop several old mattresses in the back of an open truck. Anke watched them slowly strip off layer after layer of clothing and pile it next to them as the June sun bore down on them. When their trucks turned southeast, away from the girls, Anke had a hard time getting their sunburned faces out her mind. Little girls, wearing everything they owned. She dreamt of them for several nights as they slept at an inn near Orleans and then several barns near Clermont-Ferrand and Nimes.

As they neared the Italian border, more than a week later, one of the drivers from Bruges honked his horn until Niels stopped his truck, thereby bringing the convoy to a halt.

"What is it? Are you out of fuel?" Niels asked, craning his neck out the window impatiently. They were so close now.

"No, no. We can't go to the Vatican," the man yelled. "There is no way now. I just heard it on the radio!"

"Why? What are you talking about?" Anke asked, leaning over.

"The Italians are with the Germans! Mussolini has just declared war on France and England!"

Niels slammed his head into the steering wheel as Anke burst into tears.

4

The Polish Count

Poland's existence is intolerable, incompatible with the essential conditions of Germany's life.

—*Adolf Hitler*

T HE FIRST THAW OF SPRING 1940 came as a surprise to many, including David Brossler, who stepped outside his house with a wool overcoat on. He rushed down the sidewalk, the sweat already beginning to accumulate under his shirt, fearing he would be late for a meeting at the Paulson's, yet again. He did not want to miss anything tonight's distinguished guest would have to say.

The trickle of European artists and intelligentsia to America had begun as early as the 1920s, but it had become a downright deluge in recent months. The United States had even set up an agency in Marseille, the American Rescue Center, the sole purpose of which was to organize the secret emigrations of artists and intellectuals to America. The German invasions of Czechoslovakia and Poland had sent many with means into exile in Switzerland, Great Britain, Canada, and America and no doubt there were many waiting for entry visas. One of these exiles was at Paulson's tonight and Brossler had much the same feeling in his gut that he had on the night he went to hear the story of Friedrich Fassbinder.

Fassbinder's testimony had started a frenzy of sorts, a rush of activity, which occupied nearly all of Brossler's non-teaching time. There was the American Defense Harvard Group itself, which had welcomed several new members who were now making lists of European works of art that might be in peril. There was also his continued dialogue with the curators of the yet-to-open National Gallery of Art in Washington, DC, who sought the advice of the ADHG with regard to the well-being of their own collection, donated mainly by Andrew W. Mellon. Brossler was acting as the main spokesperson for the ADHG and his son, Erik, was in charge of compiling the lists.

Erik's return to Cambridge was "the greatest thing that has ever happened to me" Brossler told his colleagues (admitting afterward that it was actually a close second to Erik's actual birth). Lotte Brossler wrote to a friend in Baltimore:

> *When Erik emerged from the ship, David and I felt as if we might faint right there on the dock. It was so overwhelming to see him again. He is the handsomest man I have ever laid eyes on.*

His parents' doting aside, Erik was finding ways to keep busy with the ADHG and felt, despite his obvious connection through his father, that he was being treated as an art historian in his own right. His time spent in London, closer to the threat, as well as his involvement in the evacuation of Britain's art treasures, helped to bolster his credibility with the much older and more experienced members of the group. (He never mentioned his last-minute trip to Bruges). Once the works were safely in their Welsh castles, Brigsworth-Jones had written a rather elaborate letter, co-addressed to Henry Paulson and David Brossler, praising Erik's assistance with the evacuation and recommending that Erik serve as a liaison between the ADHG and the British art defense committee that Brigsworth-Jones was heading up. Though he was not as well known in America as in Europe, a solid endorsement from Brigsworth-Jones was nonetheless a résumé enhancer.

Erik tried hard to see his new life in America as important and worthwhile. He tried *not* to think about just how close he had been to Anke Junger when he was in Bruges and *not* to question constantly his decision to take the ship from Rotterdam without first going to Ghent to find her. He wasn't sure she wanted to be found.

Brossler arrived at the Paulson's five minutes past the start time, which was eight o'clock. Paulson was speaking to the men around the dining table, as usual, and Mrs. Paulson took Brossler's jacket and handed him a cup of coffee. It suddenly occurred to him that these meetings were the only occasions when the Paulsons did not use maids or butlers to serve their guests. Brossler glanced at Erik, who was seated at the end of the table and already taking notes. Tonight's speaker sat next to him, calmly sipping his coffee and returning the cup to the saucer he held in his other hand, just to pick it up again seconds later.

"Good, David is here, let's begin," Paulson said, standing up. Erik glanced up at his father as if to say, *what could possibly be more important than this?* Brossler took the seat next to his son, which he noted with pleasure, had been saved for him.

Paulson cleared his throat. "Tonight we are very pleased to have Count Stanislaus Borowski, from Krakow. The count and his family have been through an unimaginable ordeal. Their townhouse in Krakow was raided by the Nazis and nearly every piece of his art collection was either stolen or taken off to be destroyed. He did, however, arrange for the sixteenth-century Jagellonian tapestries, from the royal castle at Krakow, to be shipped by barge down the Vistula, then driven into Romania. From there they went to the Vatican, but the pope refused to hide them for political reasons, so they were taken to France and finally to England. I believe they are now bound for Canada, is that right, your grace?"

"Yes…indeed," the count replied, as if he was surprised to have been asked a question.

Paulson sat down and the count now understood that it was his turn. He stood slowly, revealing an immaculate black double-breasted suit, red tie, and a wilted purple crocus hanging from his breast pocket. His salt-and-pepper hair was thinning on top, but was still bushy and in need of a trim on the sides. His face was lined with recent worries but his high cheekbones and big, blue eyes promised a handsomeness that could possibly return. Erik put him at forty-five years old.

"I am very glad to be here speaking with you today. I understand I am not the first exiled European you have spoken with and I am quite sure I will not be the last. My nation has been overrun, plundered, and the people have been either murdered or cast out to die. Though there is little we here in this room can do about this crime, we must do whatever we can."

Erik glanced at his father, reminding him of their family's ongoing conversation. His mother has been living in a state of heightened anxiety over the fate of her family back in Germany. She felt, quite naturally, that her husband and son were spending entirely too much time worrying about pieces of art that may or may not have been stolen, or would be stolen or destroyed in the future, when they should be thinking of ways of saving *people*. This was not an argument that David or Erik felt they could win, nor did they want to. They granted her the point; there was no claim they could make against her. But, with each new day, they were more and more obsessed with the idea that saving art and saving lives were more closely linked than Lotte realized. "Saving art is saving humanity," David espoused at one of the ADHG meetings, to the impromptu applause of those gathered. That applause was not forthcoming when he said the same thing to his wife later that night at the dinner table. Her tears sent her rushing from the room and Erik chasing after her. David ate alone, again.

"I firmly believe that to destroy a work of art is like destroying life itself," the count continued, as if he heard their thoughts. "We must view this pillaging of our cultural heritage as a threat equal to military occupation!"

Paulson sensed an ongoing lecture and attempted to get down to specifics. "Count Borowski," he said, "can you tell us about the paintings which you hid in your country house?"

"Yes, of course." The count lit a cigarette and began smoking in a decidedly aristocratic manner.

"Not two days before the Nazis arrived in Krakow, which they have made their eastern headquarters mind you, I drove my three masterpieces to my country house, about two hours away. My groundskeepers walled the paintings up in a special room…bricked them in. They are da Vinci's *Lady with an Ermine*, Rembrandt's *Landscape with a Good Samaritan*, and Raphael's *Portrait of a Gentleman*. The Germans found them not a week later and hauled them off, along with our Dürer engravings and our Limoges enamels. My wife and I nearly died of devastation. Of course, they have no idea what they are doing…not on the lower levels anyway. After they took our collection, they targeted a cousin of mine, examined his wife's exquisite jewelry collection, and decided it was fake. They left it behind."

"But," Brossler interrupted, "*someone* knows what they are doing."

"You could not be more correct," the count replied. "There are clearly art experts and dealers within the German entourage, who are handpicking items to take back to Germany. They knew I had a Rembrandt, so I was targeted. But they think of him as Aryan, you know. They stole the Veit Stoss altarpiece from the Church of Our Lady in Krakow because Stoss was born in Nuremburg, Germany. I grew up with that altarpiece. It is quite simply the soul of Krakow."

"Was the altarpiece hidden?" asked Brossler.

"Yes, it was taken apart and hidden in pieces, some at the University Museum, but mostly at the Cathedral of Sandomierz. I was consulted on the decision in my capacity as committee chairman of the Fine Arts Museum of Krakow."

"The city has been left intact, is that correct?" asked Professor Quark, who had visited Krakow in 1935 and thought himself an authority on Wawel Castle, the seat of the Polish kings since the twelfth century.

"Yes, the city has not been touched, other than the removal of art. Of course, the Germans think of Krakow as Germanic, God knows why. It will not suffer the same fate as Warsaw, which has been destroyed beyond all imagination. Warsaw castle, which has been a Polish beacon of hope for hundreds of years, has been badly damaged. I heard that the Germans placed dynamite within the walls and have threatened to level it completely if the Poles don't stay in line."

"There has been a line drawn across the country," Erik added, "and southern Poland, with Krakow, will be 'Germanified' and Polish culture will be called German. Hundreds of university professors, art curators, and other intellectuals have been sent off to concentration camps in Germany. But Warsaw and the north...the Germans see that as Slavic land and therefore beneath them. They are going to destroy it completely and start again. They see no worthy culture there at all and they are simply pillaging and murdering their way to the Soviet Union."

"Where are you getting this information, Erik?" his father asked.

"Right here. The latest from Brigsworth-Jones." Erik pulled a letter out of his notebook and handed it to his father.

Brossler read for a moment, then turned to Count Borowski. "Lord Brigsworth-Jones is a British art historian, your grace, with whom we are well acquainted. My son worked with him in London to help evacuate the National Gallery."

The count, seeming to truly notice Erik for the first time, nodded his approval.

"Brigsworth-Jones," Brossler continued while still reading, "seems to have quite a bit of information at his fingertips. He has…friends, I believe, in Poland. He…."

"He has partisan connections, you mean," the count said, raising an eyebrow. "Well, good. I am sure he and I know some of the same people. It was the partisans that got my wife and I, and our three children, out of Poland. It was to them that my cousin gave most of his wife's jewelry. I dearly hope more lives can be saved with it."

Brossler nodded his agreement while continuing to read the letter. He shook his head in disgust several times.

"Brigsworth-Jones reports here, well…he says he's been in contact with a Polish art historian, a woman, and she said that the Germans toppled the statue of Adam Mickiewicz in Krakow."

"That must be Sabina Walczak, the first woman to attain a professorship in art history in Poland," the count remarked nonchalantly. "I've met her several times. She is, in fact, a distant relative of mine."

"The Germans also dismantled Frederic Chopin's monument in Warsaw and sent it off to a smelter," Erik added somberly.

"Do you see what is happening?" the count asked, becoming agitated. "They have taken Poland's most honored poet and composer and removed them from view. They cease to exist. They are unimportant now. Their effigies melted down, to be reused for the Nazi war effort no doubt. The Poles are nothing but dirt under their boots."

Brossler looked at his son. "They'll be after Memling's *Last Judgment* in Danzig."

"I know, and that shouldn't even be there. It was stolen from the Medici. Please, no offense, your grace."

"No offence taken at all," the count replied. "You are quite right. Art theft, in any form and by any nation or individual, is simply unacceptable and must be stopped!"

The count paused, wondering if his sudden flair for the dramatic had soured his image. He then turned to Brossler and asked, "Why do they think in this way? Why do they destroy Warsaw and say there is no culture worth saving? I ask you, because you are German. Your son is German."

Brossler and Erik exchanged looks. This was the association they had always feared. The answer must be emphatic.

Erik spoke first. "Your grace, please do not confuse being German with being a National Socialist. There are National Socialist parties in many countries; they just don't hold a majority. Poland itself has its National Socialists, but you are not one of them. My father and I are not either. When they began to expand in Germany, we came here. We don't understand or agree with their ideology any more than you do. I, for one, would give my life to stop them. We are exiles just like you, except…we are also Jews."

The count look surprised, as if the idea had never occurred to him. Then he extended his hand to Erik, who shook it.

"YOU SHOULD HAVE seen him, Lotte," Brossler said, as they prepared for bed that night. "He was magnificent. He told the count the truth, and he was so strong…yet gentle and respectful."

"I wish I had seen it," Lotte said, not looking at her husband but down at her legs as she removed her stockings.

"You could come with us to a meeting, would you like that? Mrs. Paulson is always there."

"I have nothing in common with her."

"Of course you do. You…."

"David! I have nothing in common with a woman like that. She is rich. She and her husband travel the world buying art. I left that life behind when we left Munich."

"You make it sound illegal, or dirty, or something."

"Well, I am sick of hearing about it. Erik could talk of nothing else when he got home except some altarpiece from Poland which the Nazis took to Germany."

"Lotte, for goodness sake! Erik is an art historian, like me. How can you ask him not to care about these things? The Veit Stoss altar is one of the most important gothic altars in the world. He was a master carver. I am not as well versed in medieval art, but this is Erik's specialty."

"I know, I know!" she cried.

"Keep your voice down!"

Lotte slumped on her side of the bed, defeated. Brossler saw then that she had something in her hand. He climbed across the bed and knelt down in front of her. He pulled the letter from her grasp.

"What is this?"

"A letter…from Shimon."

"Your brother finally wrote? What did he say?"

"Read it."

Brossler read the letter and looked up at his teary wife.

"I don't think this can be true."

"No? You've told me yourself that Jewish art, possessions, homes…all these things have been taken by the Nazis. You don't think they are capable of making people disappear?"

"I don't think we should presume that your mother is dead. She poses absolutely no threat to the Nazis whatsoever. She may have been forced to leave her home, but she will follow others in the same position, to a safe place, and from there we will bring her here. Your brother is in Palestine, and God knows what kind of information he is getting there."

"He said there are Jews from Germany who are arriving in Palestine all the time, and they have told him what is going on. That seems like better information than we have! We've got Polish counts who have lost their Raphaels."

"Lotte…that is not fair. What would you have us do? We know about art…maybe we can help…maybe we can…."

Brossler found himself in the usual place and hated himself. His wife didn't understand, but she was right not to. They turned out the lights in silence.

DOWNSTAIRS, Erik sat at the dining room table, piled high with art books from Harvard's art library. He had begun a list of Polish works that were likely targets of the Nazi art looters, as well as pieces that may have already been destroyed, like those by Jewish artists or with Slavic or Jewish subjects:

Rembrandt (or studio of?), "Portrait of Martin Soolmans" (1634)—little is known.

Rembrandt, "Landscape With the Good Samaritan" (1638) one of only eight landscapes ever painted by the artist. (Borowski collection)

Raphael, "Portrait of a Young Man" (c. 1504)—some consider it a self-portrait. (Borowski collection)

Da Vinci, "Lady with an Ermine" (c. 1489-90)—one of only four portraits of women painted by the artist. (Borowski collection)

Veit Stoss, "Altar of Our Lady Mary of Krakow" (c. 1484)—considered one of the most important carved medieval altars

Hans Memling, "The Last Judgment" (c. 1470)—commissioned for the Medici in Bruges, now in Danzig, Church of Our Lady

He worked all night. When his head finally sank down on the table, Erik had identified more than 350 works within Poland that were going to be on the Nazi loot lists. There were undoubtedly thousands more, but this was never going to be a comprehensive list. His books were too old and his instructions were to keep this top level as it would be given to the US government. What they would do with it, Erik had no idea. He planned to send a separate copy to Brigsworth-Jones, who might actually be able to use it. His next list would be of vulnerable works in Holland, then Belgium. After that, France and Italy. These lists, he knew, would be colossal.

5

The Arma Christi

The Führer loves art because he himself is an artist. Under his blessed hand a Renaissance has begun. —Joseph Goebbels, Reichsminister for Propaganda and National Enlightenment

AFTER A FRANTIC CALL to the Bishop of Ghent, a haven for the van Eyck altarpiece and the other Belgian works was found at the Chateau of Pau, near the Spanish border. It was a fitting shelter Anke decided as they drove up the hill toward the dominating structure, which overlooked the city and swiftly flowing *Gave de Pau*. It was the birthplace of King Henry IV of France and the holiday home of Napoleon. Once everything was unpacked and installed in the chateau's uppermost rooms, the drivers returned to Bruges, while Niels and Anke spent most of the summer in Toulouse. Niels felt they were safer in the unoccupied zone, though they were friendless there.

The heat of their affair dampened now, Niels soon decided to return to Ghent. He hoped that despite the occupation, he would be able to continue lecturing in the art history department at the university, a job that usually required serious planning and preparation starting in August. As for Anke, he guessed that without the altar, Ghent seemed like an empty shell to her. She spoke little and seemed to hardly notice him anymore.

"I am going back," he declared one morning as they ate bread and cheese at their small hotel. "Our money is just about gone and I need to get back...for school. You do too, actually. Dubois will want your last chapters...this is your last year."

"Don't be silly," Anke said. "Do you think it will be that easy? They've had time to organize. We can't just drive into occupied France."

"We should go separately. Use your Belgian papers. Tell them you were visiting friends in Toulouse for the summer. Lots of people spend their summers down here. Burn your German passport. Unless…you want to go back to Munich."

Anke visualized their apartment, ransacked and empty.

"No. I can't go back now."

"So, go to Ghent. Dubois was right, if you stay with him and Gisela and lay low, you will probably arouse no suspicion. Even if they look for the van Eyck, they won't know to come to you unless they have someone reading the Flemish art journals."

"I am sure they've read everything," she said, sounding defeated.

"Fine. Stay here. Stay in Toulouse for the rest of the war."

Little was said after that. Niels left two days later, in the truck. Their goodbye was awkward, as it is for former lovers. They both felt they were abandoning the other, and being abandoned themselves. Anke stayed another week in the sweltering hotel room, watching the *fleur de lis* wallpaper slowly peel down from top to bottom. She cried much of the time, not for Niels, but for her father and the world he had inhabited.

When she finally decided that her father might be watching, she abandoned her brief thoughts of suicide, scrubbed her clothes in the sink, and packed her small suitcase. The train to Paris took her only as far as Orleans. The French army had blown the bridges over the Loire as they retreated south and there was no train service from points south of the river. She began asking around for a ride, but no one was going north, everyone was fleeing in the other direction. She finally found an Alsatian family headed for Chartres, and rode in the back of their truck with the children and several goats.

Less than an hour from Chartres, Anke drifted to sleep despite the jolting motions of the truck. She had a vivid dream. Her father sat across from her, on a bale of hay. He was wearing his best dark suit, the one he wore on their infrequent trips to the Peterskirche, their church in Munich. He looked content and relaxed. His graying hair was worn longer than the fashion and blew wildly in the wind. This was her father before Dachau, before the hollow skeleton with a shaved head. But, hanging around his neck was a cord like the one he had used to hang himself. He seemed not to notice it.

"Anke," he said softly. "Where are you going?"

"I don't know. I don't know what to do," she stammered, staring at him in horror.

"Yes you do. You must stay with the art."

"You mean…I should have stayed in Pau? There is a curator there to guard the panels. I was told I couldn't stay…the bishop himself…."

"Shhh."

Anke felt bolted to her seat, which was nothing more than her suitcase. She thought she would want to run to him, wrap her arms around him. Instead she was terrified. He smiled and leaned forward, resting his arms on his knees. The cord dangled. He spoke in a whisper.

"Anke, liebling. You have always had wonderful instincts. Use your skills. They will save you. Stay with the art. Follow it. Stay close, listen, find others to help you."

He leaned back, satisfied. His gaze seemed distant, as if he wasn't really seeing her. She began to tremble.

"Are you…in a safe place?"

"Yes," he answered. "Safer than you."

"If I hadn't told you to start painting again…."

"No, liebling. It was my fault. It was my failure."

He always called her that. She used to bristle because it made her feel like a little girl. Now, she wanted to hear it again. Say it again!

She woke suddenly, as the truck came to a halt at a German checkpoint. She looked around, confused. There were several cars in front of them, so she had a few minutes. She took her suitcase from underneath her and rifled through it until she had her German papers in her hand. She took out her cigarette lighter, which Niels had given her, and lit it under the passport and identity card. When the flames were crawling toward her fingers, she flung the burning papers onto the road and watched them crumble to char. The children regarded her, amused. There were no cars behind them, so the burning went unnoticed. At the checkpoint, her Belgian papers were accepted and the truck was waved on by the young German guard.

⁓

AT CHARTRES, Anke left the Alsatian family and their goats behind and walked to the cathedral. The first thing she noticed as she approached one of the pinnacles of gothic architecture was that all of the stained glass windows had been removed. The cathedral was dark and there were German soldiers carrying tables and chairs inside. An old man who was passing by explained that the Germans intended to make the cathedral into an officers' club.

Anke more or less walked to Paris. From time to time, she was offered a ride in a truck and once on a horse, but for the majority of the fifty-five miles, she was on foot. So were many others, but they were headed in the opposite direction. Few people spoke to her, though she managed water and a slice of bread or cheese from the cafés along the way. Her feet were blistered and bleeding and she was down to the clothes on her back, since she jettisoned the suitcase six miles outside Chartres, keeping only her Belgian papers, keys, and money in a small purse. In the outskirts of Paris, the German presence increased. She was so exhausted and thirsty that she actually accepted a ride in a car driven by a German soldier. In the back of the car was a Bavarian woman and her small dachshund. Anke sat in the front, next to the driver.

"You are German?" the woman asked.

"No, Belgian," Anke answered, getting out her papers.

"That is not necessary," the woman replied, "I am not the police. Where are you going?"

"Ghent. I have been in Toulouse for the summer."

"We are going to Brussels! That is close to Ghent, yes?"

Anke couldn't believe it. The woman prattled on in German about how beautiful Paris was, but Anke only half listened. She closed her eyes and saw her father again.

At Brussels, they dropped her at the central train station. Here the trains were running and she took the local to Ghent with her last francs. She arrived late at night and found her way through the blackened streets to her apartment near the university. Everything was as she left it, which surprised her. She pushed the books off her bed and tried to sleep, but the image of her father haunted her. She wasn't sure what the dream had meant, or if it had meant anything at all. She was almost afraid to close her eyes.

SHE WOKE WITH A START nearly ten hours later. She bathed, for the first time since Toulouse, and put on a clean dress. Her feet were still cracked, but the bleeding had stopped. She decided to take her bicycle to St. Bavo's to check on Jan. She couldn't face walking. When she went out into the hall, she found that her bicycle had been stolen. The door on the landing below creaked open.

"Anke?" a shrill voice called out. Mrs. Roop, the landlady, had three small children and never seemed to go out.

"Yes, Mrs. Roop, it's me. I am back."

"Where have you been?"

"I paid my rent in advance."

"Yes, yes. It isn't about that. I was worried about you. I thought maybe you went back to Germany."

"No, I was visiting some friends in Toulouse."

"Oh, I didn't realize you had friends there."

Anke knew something was wrong.

Mrs. Roop never asks questions, liebling.

Suddenly, Mrs. Roop stepped forward onto the landing and a tall man, in full SS uniform, appeared in her doorway. He was holding her young daughter, Margriet, in his arms.

"Fräulein Junger. Good. I've been looking for you."

Anke's knees buckled and she sat on the stairs.

"I think we have much to discuss," the man said pleasantly. "Have you had breakfast?"

Anke shook her head. The man handed the child gently back to Mrs. Roop and thanked her politely for her hospitality. He gestured for Anke to follow him and, after a paralyzing moment when her aching legs just wouldn't move, she got up and followed him down the stairs. Mrs. Roop's eyes were moist as Anke passed by.

Once they were outside, the man turned to her and introduced himself.

"I am SS Oberleutnant Franz Bauer, Art Protection Division. I am here to interview you about the van Eyck altar. Shall we get some coffee?"

For the first time, Anke looked around and saw German occupied Ghent in the daylight. Swastika flags hung off every major building and the streets were crowded with trucks and open topped cars full of German soldiers. There were German traffic signs hanging below all the Flemish signs, and *Joden* was painted across the windows of the Jewish shops. Despite this, all the stores were open and the sidewalks were full of mothers pushing their children in prams and enjoying the September sun.

Bauer walked on ahead, not expecting her to argue. She hurried to keep up, but her feet were so sore she limped like a peddler. Bauer did not notice and turned down a side street and into a small *Koffiebranderij*. Two old men immediately got up from their table to allow him to sit down. He thanked them in Flemish and pulled one of the chairs out for Anke. She sat, but his manners unnerved her. All this civility must be building up to something.

The waiter anxiously took their order, which Bauer decided would be two milky coffees and two *mattentaarts*. He remained quiet, watching Anke until their breakfast arrived, which was only moments later.

"I must say, I love these mattentaarts," Bauer said, picking his up and taking a big bite. "They are like a kuchen, but maybe a little sweeter."

Anke nodded and began to eat hers with a fork. He looked surprised, then embarrassed.

"Was I supposed to use a fork?"

"Oh…some do, some don't. There are no rules."

"I see. That is a relief." He smiled at her as he took a sip of his coffee, blowing lightly on the frothy milk first.

Anke found herself smiling too, almost enjoying herself. Then she noticed that everyone had left the café, except for the waiter who stood behind the bar and out of earshot. She was on her own.

"Fräulein Junger, I know this last year must have been very hard for you."

Anke had no idea how to respond, so she just looked at him.

"I know what happened to your father, the suicide, and I must say I was very sorry to hear it. I know his works were considered degenerate, but I, for one, felt a great sympathy for him. I admired him."

"How can that be?"

"Art, as you know, is not an exact science. The Führer is right when he says we must guard against art that would demean and belittle the German people. But, I am not sure your father's paintings always did that. Some of them, especially his landscapes, had a quality of reality about them. His earlier works were, I feel, of a very high value. His later canvases…well…some were hard to understand."

"You sound like you know quite a lot about my father's career."

"Well, it has been my job to know and now it is my job to know about art in Belgium. That's why I have come to you."

"What is it that you want?"

"Well, first I would like to know why you remained here in Ghent when the order for all German nationals to return to the Fatherland was issued in June?"

"I wasn't in Ghent, I was in Toulouse, visiting a friend."

"May I have that friend's name?" He took out a small notebook and a pen.

"I…don't think she is there anymore. She has moved on."

"Her name?"

Anke felt stupid for allowing herself to be caught in a lie so quickly. She hadn't thought any of this out.

"It doesn't really matter," he said after a minute, deciding not to press her. "What I really want to know is the location of the van Eyck altarpiece."

"I have no idea."

"Not true! You drove the panels into France yourself with your friend…," he consulted his notebook, "Niels Maarten. You see, we have already spoken with Dr. Maarten. He is now at our holding facility at Fort Breendonk."

Anke felt a trickle. She was peeing on the seat.

Bauer took another sip of coffee and ate rest of his *mattentaart*. He regarded her thoughtfully. She was very attractive, even in her distressed state. She didn't look like an intellectual, at least, not like any of the intellectuals he knew. Although she was thin, she wasn't fragile; she looked strong and robust, like the farm girls from his home in Saxony. She wore her wavy blond hair just like his sister, Gretel, with the strands swept to the sides and held with pins. Her eyes were blue, but not icy. They were warm as they stared at him in horror.

"Don't worry, he didn't tell us where the altarpiece was. He held out admirably. He did offer you up, of course. He said you were using Belgian papers. May I see them?"

Anke reached into her backpack, pulled out her papers and placed them on the table.

"And your German passport?"

"I burned it."

"Why?"

"I didn't want to go back to Munich. Too many memories."

Bauer grimaced and shifted position, crossing his legs under the table. He lit a cigarette and held out his gilded silver cigarette case. She took one and leaned in when he held out the flame of his fancy SS lighter. She took a deep drag and started coughing. Smoking was something she did only on occasion. This seemed like a good time.

"It doesn't matter if you tell me where the altarpiece is or not. We will find it soon enough, I guarantee it."

"Why do you want to find it?"

"Two reasons. First, the Führer has declared it to be a top priority. Second, because it belongs to Germany."

"Are you referring to the panels bought by the King of Prussia in the last century?"

"I am."

"The Treaty of Versailles returned those to Belgium."

"That treaty is now invalid."

"Well, one is missing anyway... *The Just Judges.*"

"Yes, what do you know about that?"

Anke shrugged and took a more successful drag on her cigarette. "I know no more than you. Arsène Goedertier died before he could reveal anything helpful. I was questioned at the time, as you know, and I was cleared of any involvement."

Bauer smirked. "Yes, I've read your file. I have also read your articles on the altar... very impressive. You have been studying its history for several years now."

"Eight years."

Bauer drained his coffee cup and another was immediately placed before him by the waiter.

"What do you know about...the Arma Christi?" Bauer said, non-chalantly.

Anke wanted to laugh. This extremely serious SS officer could not possibly be a conspiracy theorist.

"Well," she began, "the Arma Christi were the tools used to complete Christ's crucifixion...the nails, the spear, the crown of thorns."

"I know that!" Bauer spat. "What do you know about van Eyck and the Arma Christi?"

"Van Eyck sometimes painted the Arma Christi, usually near to Christ's body. In the Ghent Altarpiece, the angels who surround the Mystic Lamb hold the Arma Christi. But this isn't unique to van Eyck. Lots of painters used the same symbols. There is no evidence to suggest that van Eyck had a special connection to the Arma Christi."

"That's it? You've never probed any further?" Bauer was incredulous.

"I am an art historian, Herr Oberleutnant, not a conspiracy theorist. I deal with facts that can be proved, that have been written down somewhere or are there, staring back at me from the paint."

Good, liebling.

"I see. Well, let me tell you a story. As I am sure you are aware, in the early fifteenth century Jan van Eyck had one main patron, Philip the Good, the Duke of Burgundy. The Duke paid him well, so well that van Eyck did not feel he needed to join the guild of painters in Bruges. He painted mostly portraits...in fact the altarpiece, that he finished after his brother died, was his first non-portrait painting. This work, as you know, took years. Would the Duke of Burgundy, who commissioned so many works from van Eyck, allow him to spend years on one painting just to help his dead brother? No. The altarpiece was special, it had a purpose... to reveal clues to the location of the Arma Christi."

Anke was speechless. She'd heard these rumors before, but ignored them. All art historians ignored them.

Bauer went on, excited now. "There was a secret society formed to protect the Arma Christi, after Christ's death. They have sometimes been called the 'Allahists,' sometimes the 'Ebionites.' Van Eyck was a member of this group and he made that clear in one of the panels."

"Really? Which one?"

"The Singing Angels. The Kabbalistic acronym AGLA is written on one of the floor tiles. It stands for 'Ateh Gibor Le-olam Adonai... The Lord is Mighty Forever.' There is a strong connection to alchemy. Did you know van Eyck was an alchemist?"

"I've heard the rumor."

"It is no rumor; he was. You should read *Spiegel der Kunst und Natur* by Stephan Michelspacher. He published it in 1615. Very interesting. It would have been on your reading list if you had studied for your degrees in Germany."

Bauer surprised her. He was clearly well-read and quite thoughtful. He was also completely insane. She had heard that the SS was involved with the occult and was traveling extensively doing archeological digs in hopes of finding clues to the history of the Aryan race. Alchemy played right into this. She needed to tread carefully here.

"I have read it. My father owned a copy."

"That doesn't surprise me. He was obviously very intelligent about art."

Anke couldn't decide if Bauer was patronizing her, or if he really admired her father. She decided to assume the former.

"You can see," Bauer continued, "how 'Allahists' could come from 'AGLAists.' Plus, the members of this society had a particular view of Jesus, one that the Vatican did not support, and this view was represented in van Eyck's altar."

Now this was something she knew about. Van Eyck portrayed Jesus, in the central panel, as Christ *Pantokrator* (Greek for "God rules all"), which is mainly a Byzantine format. In fact, some art historians doubt it is Christ at all, but rather an image of God the father. His right hand is raised, as if to bless the altar gazer, and he sits on a throne with his eyes staring straight out and not up or down as was common in Latin paintings of the Passion. He seems to be personifying God the father, as well as God the son. A phrase from Revelations 19:12-16 is written on the hem of his robe. This verse claims Christ to be the "King of Kings."

"I can see your mind working," Bauer said, smiling. "You know I am right."

"I concede that van Eyck's depiction of Christ is interesting and different for a painter in the western European tradition. I have published on it, as you know. Van Eyck was a very learned man and had very…unique views about the church. Some say he was ahead of his time. But, here is *my* question. Are you telling me that you are looking for the missing panel? Is there a clue about the Arma Christi within the *Just Judges*?"

"Perhaps."

"Do you think I know where the panel is?"

Bauer thought for a moment. He lit another cigarette. "No, I don't think you know where it is, but I am surprised you accepted the official line about the supposed thief, Arsène Goedertier."

"What do you mean?"

"Well, what was his motive? Money? He had over three million francs in his bank account when he died. Did you know that?"

"No, I didn't."

"He is an unreliable suspect. He may have been the one who found the real thief. His wife testified that he was obsessed with mystery novels."

The Nazi's "logic" made Anke's head throb. She asked for a glass of water. Bauer nodded to the waiter, and one was quickly provided.

"I still don't see how I can help you. I don't know where the missing panel is. I don't even know where the other panels are. You seem to know more than I do about the connection to the Arma Christi."

"You are right. I don't need you. I was interested in talking to you… mostly because of your analysis of van Eyck, but also because of your father. I used to work with a man named Otto Rahn, who knew much more than I on this subject. The Reichsführer-SS, Himmler, was very interested in Rahn's work and wants me to continue it, here."

Anke had heard of Rahn. He was a medievalist who was obsessed with the Holy Grail and the history of the Cathars. He was in the SS for a period of time, but was found dead last year, frozen on an Austrian mountainside.

"You want me to help you?" Anke asked, timidly.

"No, I don't think you would be much help. Frankly, you don't believe and I need believers. I could have you sent to a prison camp for hiding your German nationality. I could also say you are withholding information on the whereabouts of the Ghent Altarpiece. But I think it would be more profitable to the Reich to put you to work."

"Put me to work? On what?"

Bauer whistled and a young SS trooper entered the café from the street. Anke had never noticed him, not even when they were walking from her apartment. The soldier handed Bauer a black briefcase, saluted, and left the café. Anke looked for the waiter, but he was gone too.

"This is the Kümmel Report," Bauer said proudly. "Only six copies are in existence. We have been compiling it painstakingly for years. It lists all pieces of art, including literary and musical works, that have been stolen from the German people in the last 400 years. Many items on this list were taken by Napoleon's armies, of course. We are going to get every single surviving German work of art back, every single one."

"Including the *Just Judges*."

"Absolutely."

"You want me to find these works for you?"

"Lord, no. We are very good at finding things. I need you to add expertise and analysis of some of the Dutch and Flemish works. Special catalogues are being made for the Führer, with pictures and descriptions of each piece of art. But some of the descriptions are too vague, too shallow. As you know, the Führer is an artist himself and he has a great mind for art history. This catalogue must respect that and not be merely a list. You will compile this catalogue, starting with all artworks extant in Ghent, Brussels, Antwerp, Bruges, and then moving into Holland. You will do this…and your friend Niels Maarten will be released from his imprisonment. If you refuse, you will join him at a labor camp in Germany."

Anke felt a chill and tried to repress a shiver. Bauer's chuckle was evidence that she failed.

6

The Jeu de Paume

To destroy images has been something every revolution has been able to do.
—Alfred Rosenberg, Chief
Philosopher of the Nazi Party

THE STATE OF AFFAIRS in northern Europe as Anke began her Nazi art history commission was dire. The Belgian government had fled, first to France, then to London. King Leopold, thought by most to be a collaborator, was negotiating with the Germans for the release of Belgian prisoners of war. Soon he and his family would escape to exile in Switzerland. Marshal Petain and the French government was in Vichy, though General de Gaulle and the Free French had escaped to England. Anke and Niels had heard de Gaulle's patriotic BBC radio address in Toulouse, but she was depressed to find that most in Ghent had not since the Germans jammed the transmitters during the invasion. London was being bombed nightly by the Luftwaffe, but the Royal Air Force bombers had reached Berlin as well. Seventy-three British children were killed when the ship evacuating them to Canada was sunk by a German U-boat.

To avoid reading the news, Anke worked ten hours a day, seven days a week, on the catalogue. She needed to since the Kümmel Report included all works taken from Germany since 1500, all works by German or Austrian artists (or their descendants), all works commissioned or completed in Germany, and all works deemed to be in a Germanic style. She was allowed to conduct her research at the Ghent University library and Bauer even encouraged her to continue with her degree, though she would have little time to complete her dissertation. She was not to discuss her project with anyone and Bauer made it very clear that he was aware of the involvement of Pierre Dubois in the removal of the altarpiece and warned that it would be a shame if Dubois had to leave Gisela and little Piers for a work camp in the east. Anke understood that the pressure on Niels must have been very great for him to give up Dubois, who had been his mentor since he arrived in Ghent ten years ago.

Bauer kept his word and Niels was released from Fort Breedonk and was back at the university. He looked frail and there was evidence on his face that he had been beaten. He avoided Anke and when they finally met alone in a stairwell, he nodded but couldn't look her in the eye. She allowed him his shame and stayed away from him.

Several weeks into her research, she began to identify certain people in and around the university who seemed to have information on various works of art. Some of these people had firsthand knowledge and some were merely passing on rumors. One tasty morsel was that the Rijksmuseum had evacuated Rembrandt's world renowned *Night Watch* and a number of other Dutch masterpieces to a castle north of Amsterdam. The gigantic painting was taken off its dowels and rolled up for storage. Anke also learned that officials at the Louvre had removed its massive collection, including the *Mona Lisa*, and driven everything south of Paris to a number of chateaus. Anke met one woman, Danielle, who had been present at the evacuation of the Louvre. She described how the *Winged Victory of Samothrace*, a ten-foot statue of the goddess Nike sculpted from marble in the third-century BC, had descended the long staircase that lay in front of her on an improvised wooden ramp while the staff watched anxiously. In comparison, Anke realized that the Belgians had been rather low-key about their evacuations since the Memling show in Bruges had remained open even after the declarations of war.

At no point did she reveal to anyone that she had taken part in the evacuation of the Ghent Altarpiece, despite the constant queries about its whereabouts. Many, she discovered, thought the Germans had already stolen it and shipped it to Germany. One old man, whispering to her in the stacks of the art library, told her that the Nazis had been the ones who were planning to steal the *Just Judges* and St. John the Baptist panels back in 1934, but were beaten to it by Arsène Goedertier who had discovered their plan and taken the panels to "protect them." Anke wondered if Bauer had heard that one. This man did, however, have several solid pieces of information: The eleventh-century *Bayeux Tapestry* had been rolled, placed in a lead box, and hidden in a "safe" location. The priceless medieval stained glass from St. Chapelle in Paris and the cathedrals of Chartres, Bourges, Reims, Amiens, and Metz had been removed and were well-hidden. Anke told him about the officer's club at Chartres and he shook his head in disbelief.

Despite the rumors and the bits of misinformation, Anke sensed that people were heart-warmed and uplifted by the stories of the removal and hiding of Europe's great art. These objects became, even for those who had previously been oblivious to them, a source of national pride and the efforts to hide them from the Nazi art plunderers became a cause for which many ordinary citizens would fight. Anke made mental notes, hoping to write an article on the subject someday, when the war was over. It then occurred to her that for this to ever be possible, Germany, her own nation, *must lose the war.*

Ironically, the Germans had been quite helpful in a number of situations. This was the German art protection spirit Bauer had insisted was rife throughout both the SS and the Wehrmacht. When it was deemed that Rembrandt's *Night Watch* and other Dutch masterpieces needed even better protection from Allied bombing, the Germans constructed concrete shelters, with air conditioning, to house the treasures. In Brussels, they helped the locals take down the stained glass windows of St. Gudule Cathedral and store them safely. In Antwerp, they built an elaborate wall defense around *Descent from the Cross*, by Rubens. This would have pleased her father, Anke knew, since it was his favorite Rubens. She remembered him sitting in Antwerp Cathedral for more than an hour staring at the triptych, his eyes glazed with emotion. When he finally got up to leave he whispered to her, "Look at Christ's body, look at the color…drained of blood…the bruises." The skill to render that kind of detail always impressed her father, but it wasn't Christ's skin that Anke saw when she closed her eyes and recalled the painting, years later. It was the weight. As Christ is lowered from the cross, there are two women, with blond locks, waiting to receive him. But neither bears the weight of his muscled frame. Another person, a man in a red cloak, supports Christ's left thigh and lower back. He is holding all the weight, and yet he does not seem taxed. Rubens painted the weight, the gravity, into Christ himself and into the angle and drape of his body as it is lowered, not into those holding him. Anke couldn't think of another painting that did that with the same effect. Nor could her father.

A CATALOGUE OF 200 pages was produced by Christmas and Anke handed it over personally to Bauer at his office in Ghent's old market building. He had sent underlings to check on her several times since September, but had not been in contact with her himself. He flipped through it quickly, happily noting that Anke had included works in private collections, as instructed. He smiled and handed it to a secretary who was told to type five copies. Anke wondered how long that would take.

"You should be thankful that your job involved only books and a typewriter," Bauer said, noting her sullen expression.

"What happens now?"

"Now, we go to an exhibit."

"Excuse me?"

"Paris. The Jeu de Paume. There is someone I would like you to meet."

"May I ask who?"

"No, you may not. Pack a bag, you won't be returning to Ghent in the near future."

With this, Bauer walked out, leaving Anke standing in the large office alone. The pool of secretaries typed away in an adjoining room, never looking up from their work.

ANKE SAT NEXT TO BAUER in the back of the large Mercedes, dressed in her best black suit. She had spent a long time working on her hair using curlers borrowed from Mrs. Roop. She had makeup on too, which was rare for her. Bauer had demanded all this and Anke felt she could not refuse. He was silent most of the drive and read a copy of her catalogue cover to cover.

"This is outstanding work, Fräulein Junger," Bauer said when he was finished. "You have a superb mind for art and I think that will be much appreciated at the ERR."

"The ERR?"

"Yes, the Einsatzstab Reichsleiter Rosenberg. You have not heard of Alfred Rosenberg?"

"I have. He wrote some articles condemning my father's paintings as degenerate."

"Yes, he did. I might not agree with everything he says, but he has a brilliant mind. He has been one of the strongest voices within the party. Now he is leading the charge to protect the cultural heritage of Germany."

As they approached the Tuileries, Anke leaned forward to catch a glimpse of the Louvre. She imagined the empty frames lining the long galleries and the vacant spot at the top of the grand staircase where the *Winged Victory* used to stand. Bauer watched her.

"Are you thinking about the Louvre?"

"What do you mean?" she asked nervously.

"You know it is empty. It was silly of them to evacuate. We had no intention of bombing Paris. That would be madness."

"You are bombing London," Anke reminded him.

"The British refuse to capitulate. They are the destructors of their own cities. The French were much more practical."

Anke was about to speak when she realized that they were parked in front of the Jeu de Paume. A soldier opened the door and held out his hand. She took it and waited outside while Bauer straightened his uniform jacket and put on his hat. When they went inside, she was shocked to find at least fifty people milling around in the main gallery. A waiter in a white coat appeared and held out a serving tray packed with champagne flutes. Bauer took two and handed one to Anke, who accepted it anxiously. The peculiar nature of the situation dawned on her as she looked around and realized that she was at an exhibit of some of the most famous works of art in the world.

Bauer took her arm and steered her toward a distinguished gentle-man who was flanked by hangers-on and standing in front of a small Rembrandt, which Anke could not immediately identify. The man was dressed as a civilian, in a black suit, but seemed to have some official capacity since he was still deciding whether or not the Rembrandt was hung in the right place. Anke agreed that it was not.

"Your grace," Bauer said, addressing the man. "May I present Fräulein Anke Junger, the daughter of Dietrich Junger. Fräulein, this is his grace, Count von Essen."

To say this introduction raised a few eyebrows would be an understatement. One woman, standing next to the count, took in her breath so sharply that von Essen flinched, clearly embarrassed. He literally shooed the woman away and gestured for Anke to approach him.

"I was sorry to hear of your father's death, my dear."

"Thank you."

"How is it that you are in Paris?"

"Fräulein Junger is an art historian," Bauer answered for her. "She is an expert on Dutch and Flemish masters, especially van Eyck. She will be working here with the ERR."

Von Essen nodded, though he seemed displeased. He looked at Bauer with a combination of distaste and indifference. Finally, he turned his attention back to the Rembrandt.

"It is glorious, do you agree?" he said to Anke.

"Boy with a Red Beret," Anke said, now seeing the painting close up. "I've never seen this before, only in books."

"Yes," von Essen said uncomfortably. They stood for a moment in silence, then he led Anke away toward a number of neo-classical statues. Bauer was left behind and joined a group of officers looking at an imposing fifteenth-century tapestry.

As Anke wheeled around the rooms with von Essen, they came to stand in front of Vermeer's *The Astronomer*. One of only two known Vermeer paintings to have a male as the main subject, the astronomer sits at his desk gently caressing a spinning globe with his right hand, his left hand gripping the table. Light pours in from the window illuminating the globe, a notebook, and the astronomer's face. His long, wavy brown hair is tucked behind his ears and his dark, puffy robe melts into the soft folds so ubiquitous in Dutch and Flemish painting. Again, Anke had never seen this work in person. There was a reason for this.

"What do you think, Fräulein? Is this subject a self-portrait? Is that Vermeer we see as the astronomer?"

Anke took a moment to prepare. Von Essen was no amateur; he was curator of Rhineland-Westphalia and had been a professor at the University of Cologne. Von Essen was the consummate intellectual, down to his insistence on remaining a civilian despite the perks of joining the SS. Anke had read several of his books and Bauer had informed her that he was now the head of the *Kunstschutz*, the German organization dedicated to protecting art and monuments in times of war.

"Nobody knows for sure, your grace, but certainly it would be very difficult to create a plausible self-image by looking at oneself in the mirror, in profile, with both arms outstretched."

"Quite. I must say, I agree." The count regarded her with a satisfied smirk. "Any other thoughts?"

"Well," Anke continued, stepping closer to the painting, "the real question is this: is this an astronomer at all? There is no telescope. It is broad daylight. Perhaps this is an astrologer. Astrology and astronomy, as well as physics, were all lumped together in the sixteenth century. Even Johannes Kepler and Tycho Brahe were practicing astrologers."

The count took a step back and removed his glasses, as if he might now see the painting differently. "I must say, he said, "the same thing has occurred to me. It is completely true that paintings often received numerous names and usually after the artist himself was long dead. How fascinating!"

Anke couldn't hide her pleasure. It felt good to talk like this again. The obvious question nagged at her but she tried to ignore it. She failed.

"Your grace, may I ask you a question?"

"Of course, my dear." The count gave her his full attention, despite the members of his staff who were swarming just feet away, waiting impatiently for him to finish with the young lady.

"These works of art...I thought they were in the private collections of Paul Rosenberg, Andre Seligman and the Rothschilds. I mean...I am sure *The Astronomer* is owned by the Rothschild family."

"Better not to ask those questions, my dear," the count said, sternly.

"You approve of this?"

He leaned in, close to her. "I have safeguarded many of France's treasures…the Louvre repositories will be safe. I cannot prevent *them* from taking Jewish-owned art!"

He suddenly straightened and looked at her as if she was unfit to associate with him. She felt the sting of tears coming but a commotion at the entrance to the museum distracted her. A portly man had entered, wearing a large gray overcoat and a matching fedora. He looked thrilled and sauntered straight to a painting, the crowd peeling back to allow him a close inspection. Anke recognized him now; this was Reichsmarschall Hermann Göring. His reputation as an art collector was infamous. He stood in front of the painting, which Anke now saw was one of Pieter de Hooch's interiors with a woman and child. Göring took a few steps back, then went up close, as if he would smell the paint. Eventually, he moved on to a woodcut by Lucas Cranach, who, von Essen whispered to her, was the Reichsmarschall's favorite.

An hour passed in this way. Göring walked from piece to piece, examining them with diligence, and finally sat in a large chair and drank down a glass of champagne after sending up a toast to the crowd. There was a murmuring of "Heil Hitler," but it was tepid at best. Anke, who had been deserted by von Essen, stood alone near Gainsborough's *Portrait of Mrs. Thomas Hibbert*, which, despite its blurred dreaminess, she did not care for. She watched the young soldiers fawn over Göring. They even took some smaller paintings off the walls and brought them to him in his throne-like chair so he could view them without getting up. He was probably sitting on an eighteenth-century antique from Versailles, Anke mused.

She then noticed a small, dark-haired woman with round spectacles pop briefly into the room, then exit quickly though another door. She was dressed as a civilian and did not seem to fit in with this crowd. Anke thought about following her, but found herself face to face with quite another woman, whose strong, floral perfume brought the glassiness back to Anke's eyes.

"You don't remember me?" the woman said, waving her champagne flute at Anke. "I drove you to Brussels! Well, my driver did, actually." The woman was resplendent in a black cocktail dress, very high black heels, and an ornate diamond necklace that looked heavy and cumbersome on her dainty neck. She had had too much to drink.

"Of course I remember, thank you," Anke said, hoping she would go away.

"What are you doing here?" the woman asked, accusingly.

To Anke's surprise, and relief, Bauer appeared at her side. The woman smiled at him and retreated quickly, rejoining the circle of ladies who stood in the center of the room, laughing and drinking and thoroughly ignoring the art.

"Do you know her?" Bauer asked, looking surprised.

"She gave me a ride…it was months ago."

"Interesting. She's Sobel's mistress," he said, indicating a gray-haired man in a Wehrmacht uniform who sat on a yellow settee across the room and was in deep conversation with yet another woman, whose emphatic gestures with her champagne glass had soaked her skirt.

Bauer laughed and mumbled something about "these people" and escorted Anke back to the car. He took her suitcase out and started walking toward the Rue de Rivoli.

"You'll be happy, I'm sure, to see that we've found a room for you at Le Meurice."

"Isn't the German command headquarters in that hotel?"

"Yes, I thought you would be pleased," Bauer said, smirking.

ANKE'S FIRST DAY as an art historian on the "Special Staff for Pictorial Art," was January 6, 1941. She ran the short distance from the hotel to the museum to avoid the snow flurries that were whipping up from the Place de la Concorde. When she reached the front door it was opened by the small bespectacled woman who Anke had seen briefly at the art opening. She nodded to Anke and led her into the foyer. Apparently, Anke was the first to arrive.

"I am Anke Junger, pleased to meet you," she said in French.

"My name is Delphine Corot," the woman replied.

Delphine offered Anke a small cup of coffee, which was bitter and tasted nothing like the rich brew she had been served at the hotel, but which she nonetheless accepted with gratitude. Delphine seemed to study her as they stood silently in the foyer, awaiting someone more senior to arrive. Within minutes, an elaborately uniformed man stepped out of a large, shiny Mercedes-Benz and was welcomed inside by Delphine, to whom he made no acknowledgement.

"Ah, you must be Fräulein Junger. Bauer speaks highly of you, von Essen too," he said, taking off his overcoat and laying it across the arms of a uniformed underling who had appeared beside him. He started toward the stairs and Delphine rushed ahead of him to unlock the door at the bottom.

"Mademoiselle Corot was curator here…she is now in charge of the building. She does not speak German and she is not involved in our work."

He was looking at Anke, who nodded. He obviously thought she knew who he was, but she didn't. He passed through the door and Anke followed, leaving Delphine behind in the hallway.

The large room they now stood in was so full of paintings, drawings, sculptures, rugs, tapestries, furniture, decorative arts, and books that it was obvious new storage space would soon be needed. The walls were blanketed with paintings to the point where only a tiny bit of the wallpaper was visible. More were propped up on wooden tables that were lined up in rows. Despite the chaos, this was a room that would bring any art lover to her knees.

The man began leafing through what looked like a catalogue, and brought it to Anke.

"This was created for the Führer…not unlike the one you made in Ghent. We need one like this for the Reichsmarschall, whose tastes are…broader. Do you understand?"

"I think so. You want a catalogue of everything in this room?"

"More is added daily. Additional rooms at the Louvre may be needed. But things will leave too, for Germany. You are concerned with the Reichsmarschall's pieces only. A member of my staff will furnish you with a list."

He walked out, just as two men and a woman walked in and crossed through the room, to a smaller room that adjoined it. They ignored Anke at first and went immediately to their various desks, which each held a sizable stack of books. One of the men, a youthful blond, took a drawing from a folder and studied it, then opened one of his books. She walked over to him and he looked up as if he was expecting her.

"Dürer?" she asked, looking at the drawing.

"Yes. Isn't it amazing?"

"Of course."

"I am Leopold Wurtzer."

"Anke Junger," she said, taking his extended hand.

"You are working here?"

"Yes, I just arrived a couple of days ago."

"From where?"

"I was in Ghent, working on my doctorate."

"Working on it?" another man asked, coming over to them.

"Yes, I am almost finished. I hope to continue when…."

"The war's over? Don't worry, it won't be long!" the man said.

"This is Kurt Walder-Schmidt," Leopold said, "and that is Wanda Fuldenbach over there."

They had all gathered at Leopold's desk when a young man entered the room and handed Anke a stack of papers.

"Ah…your list." Wanda said, smiling.

Anke thumbed through it quickly. "Cezanne…Pisarro…Boucher…Ingres…Manet…Monet…Cranach…Memling…Pieter Bruegel the Elder…Rubens…."

It read like a curator's dream; a collection any major museum would be lucky to have.

"Göring is an even greater collector than the Führer," Bauer had told her before he returned to Belgium. "He has wider tastes…and he admired your father, though he would never admit to it."

Before Anke could digest her list, and what it all meant, a soldier appeared carrying a wooden desk. He set it down between Wanda and Leopold's and left, returning a moment later with a leather-bound chair. Anke sat at her new place awkwardly, feeling her poached eggs on toast rumbling in her stomach. She noticed a pile of books sitting on the floor, collecting dust.

"Are those for me?" she asked, to no one in particular.

"Depends," Wanda said. "Can you read French?"

"Yes."

"Then, they are all yours. Our German books were shipped in from Aachen."

"Do I get a typewriter?"

"Just write it all down, one of the secretaries will type it for you. They make several copies."

Anke soon spotted her colleagues' specialties. Wanda was an authority on Italian Renaissance art and was often dealing with sculptures that were too heavy to move, so she walked to and from the repository room constantly, her heels clicking as she went. Anke quickly learned to tune it out. Leopold focused on German and Austrian art and spent much of his time on Dürer drawings and Cranach paintings. Kurt worked on modern French paintings, as well as Italian painting. It was his job to recommend possible buyers for any degenerate works, which had not made it onto Anke's list for Göring. Kurt was older, with salt-and-pepper hair cut very short and small round spectacles, not unlike Delphine's. He kept several photos of his wife and daughters on his desk, which was much larger than Anke's. She decided he must be the senior art historian, though no official hierarchy had been explained to her. What *was* explained to her was that all this art was being sent to various places in Germany and Austria to preserve it for the German people. It was not being stolen, but repatriated, to save it from any possible destruction during the war. Anke was advised again not to ask questions.

"Who was the man who showed me in here?" she asked, ignoring the question rule immediately.

"You mean von Bahn? He's the head of the ERR in Paris. Nobody told you that?" Wanda was incredulous.

"No. I met Count von Essen last night at the party."

"Von Essen is the Kunstschutz, he has little to do with us. Von Bahn works directly for Alfred Rosenberg, the head of the entire ERR," Wanda said, cleaning a small bronze statue.

"So, is von Bahn an art historian?"

Her query was met with giggles and eye rolls. Leopold walked to her desk.

"He thinks he is," he whispered, "but he doesn't know a Cranach from a Kandinsky. He throws parties; that's what he does. I'm sure he was at the one here last night, but you just didn't meet him. He probably blended in with all the other uniforms, even though he is a civilian."

"He's a civilian, but wears a uniform?"

"Yep. That's von Bahn."

Anke didn't need to ask any more questions.

AS NEW PIECES CAME IN, Anke photographed them, noted their previous ownership (almost always Jewish art dealers), and entered them into her catalogue. Index cards were also kept alphabetized in large cabinets. The artist's name and title/provenance of the piece (if known) would be followed by an abbreviation of the name of the collection it came from (R for Rothschild, *Sm* for Seligman, etc.) There was a routine, a hum and pulse of the office. Everyone was pleasant, but no one talked too much. Anke wondered if any of them knew about her father.

After they left the office, Wanda and Leo (as he liked to be called) went directly to the Meurice for dinner. They seemed to like each other quite a bit and Anke felt she couldn't really invite herself along. Kurt went on long walks around Paris and boasted that one evening he walked until well after curfew. He said the empty streets, shuttered windows, and near-complete darkness gave him a sense of peace that he hadn't felt in years.

"It's like the war doesn't exist," he said.

Anke tried it one night and found herself escorted back to the Meurice by a German sentry whose lookout post she had mistakenly stumbled upon near the Bastille. Konrad the sentry, as chance would have it, was coming off duty and found Anke more receptive to his ideas than he thought she would be. There was none of the tenderness that had been there at the beginning with Niels, who had been her first. It was nothing like she had imagined it would be with Erik. Konrad was a tank who rolled over his lovers. Despite this, Anke accepted his invitation for dinner the following night. As she watched him devour a piece of veal, Anke wondered how she ended up here, in a Parisian restaurant, with this stranger who drank too much and knew nothing of art or history. Konrad casually remarked to her, in between bites, that Germany would soon invade the Soviet Union, which, as he put it, would be *kinderleicht*. Dead easy.

7

The Transporter

✝

In Prague, big red posters were put up on which one could read that seven Czechs had been shot today. I said to myself, "If I had to put up a poster for every seven Poles shot, the forests of Poland would not be sufficient to manufacture the paper."
—Hans Frank, the Nazi Governor General of Poland, 1940-1945

A T THE DAWN OF SUMMER, 1941, Paris was ablaze with the frenetic energy of German officers robustly enjoying themselves. The opera was playing to packed houses, as were the cinemas and dance halls. If you could find an outdoor seat in a café in St. Germain de Pres, or the Luxembourg Quarter, you were doing well. Anke and her frequent escort, Konrad, dined at the supper clubs in the Marais district on Saturday nights and drank wine at Café Simon in the Latin Quarter during the week. She compiled her catalogue, sifting through thousands of pieces of artwork and furniture downstairs at the Jeu de Paume, while upstairs there were frequent exhibitions of *Kunst der Front*, which were "frontline" paintings and drawings by amateur artists of the Wehrmacht. The lack of originality and mediocrity of these works made her cringe time and time again, though she complimented them with all the others. She had little choice. Her mind was dulled, as was her heart. She never dreamed of her father anymore. He had left her.

It dawned on Anke one morning, as she blew the dust off a Degas, that the truth about her situation was not widely known. Bauer had long since returned to his duties in Ghent and it appeared that the truth about her circumstances went with him. None of her colleagues, or Konrad, knew anything about the Ghent Altarpiece, Niels Maarten, or her relationship to the degenerate painter, Dietrich Junger. Junger was a common enough name for her knowledgeable coworkers to dismiss any possible connection. Konrad wouldn't have known who her father was anyway; he paid no attention to such things. Konrad had grown up on a farm near Dresden and had never once entered a museum. His first trip to the cinema was on a training excursion to Berlin just before he was posted to Paris. Since then, he had seen *Citizen Kane* six times, three of those with Anke.

Despite her misgivings, Anke felt freer in Paris than at any point since her father was arrested. She knew this sentiment was only loosely based on reality, but she used it to take risks nonetheless. As part of the giant catalogue she was now creating for Göring, she began inserting opinionated comments into it, right under the descriptions and dimensions of the piece. Nobody was checking her work, so the comments were sent along to the Reichsmarschall himself when the catalogue was finished in early June. Not a week after receiving it, Göring made another trip to the Jeu de Paume. It would be his sixteenth visit since the ERR began using the museum to house their confiscated works, about a year ago.

He arrived with his usual pomp, but this time he was wearing his light blue Luftwaffe uniform, complete with sword, scabbard, diamond-encrusted pistol, and Marshall's baton. He swung briefly around the upstairs galleries, then asked to be shown downstairs to where the art historians were working. His entrance into the main repository room nearly caused Kurt and Wanda to collapse in shock. Leo kept his calm and stood next to his desk, bowing slightly to the Reichsmarschall. Of course, Göring walked right past them with hardly a nod. He dwarfed Anke as he stood at her table, his face erupting into a goofy smile.

"Is this the little Fräulein who has been making her opinions known to me in my catalogue?"

Anke had the same weak-kneed feeling she had experienced when Bauer discovered her at her apartment in Ghent. Could she be this stupid twice?

"Well?" he demanded. His smile gave way to chuckles, which calmed her nerves, and those around her.

"I…knew you would appreciate the comments, Herr Reichsmarschall, or at least I thought you would."

"Oh, I do, I do! I especially like the fact that you admonish me for my love of Boucher and Fragonard. You dislike the Rococo style I presume?"

"It's not my favorite."

"And Gainsborough?"

Anke shrugged. "I can see the beauty in those portraits, just not the soul."

Göring creaked down onto Anke's chair and perused the books on her desk.

"You gave me an essay on Memling's Madonna. Did you get all that from these books?"

"No. Memling…I know a lot about him, about his paintings, I mean. I admire him almost as much as van Eyck."

Anke stopped suddenly and obviously. She shouldn't have mentioned van Eyck. If the Reichsmarschall noticed, he didn't let on. Instead he laughed, stood up, and put his arm around her. He steered her toward the door.

"I am taking the little Fräulein to lunch! I need to pick her brain a bit."

Leopold, Kurt, and Wanda stared at each other as Anke and Göring disappeared up the stairs. None of them knew if she was coming back.

AT THE MEURICE, Göring ordered the rabbit. They sat at a corner table and he saw to it that they were not disturbed. Several of his lieutenants sat nearby, but out of earshot. Göring removed the weapons from his belt and laid them on two of the ornately upholstered red chairs. His girth caused him to shift quite often in his seat, trying to find the most comfortable position. Apparently there wasn't one.

"I like you," he began. "I know your story. I've spoken with Bauer. He likes you too. I'd watch out for him, if I were you. His wife is ill and…well."

Anke just looked at him.

"Anyway, it doesn't matter. Bauer doesn't matter. I like you and that's what matters. I like your notes about the paintings. I think you are right, most of the time. You and I have similar tastes."

"Bauer told me you admired my father," Anke finally spat out.

"I did! I was sorry to hear what happened to him. That was unfortunate. But that does not need to be your fate. You have a wonderful future ahead of you. You could run a museum someday."

"I haven't been able to finish my doctorate."

"Don't worry about that. There will be time for that. When we've won the war, there will be many new museums to fill with artworks and we will need the best art historians and curators to run them. I can introduce you to some very influential people."

"Why me?"

"Why not you? I would think you would jump at the chance. There are not so many young women in your field. You could set a great example."

"But young women like me are supposed to have children for the Führer. I was detained by the Gestapo in Munich for not having joined the League of German Girls."

Their food arrived and Göring dove into his rabbit, while Anke looked at hers with disinterest. After a minute, he wiped his mouth, took a sip of Claret, and leaned forward.

"You should not focus on these things. There are many opportunities for people like you...people with skills. Forget about what happened, it was unfortunate. Don't you see? I like you *because* of your father, not despite him. Bauer feels the same way. He thinks he can turn you into a Nazi. Imagine that! I don't care if you are a Nazi or not. Think about your future. Think about the impact you could have on the art world. Your opinions...your way of wording them. You would be a very effective art critic. You should submit something to one of the art journals, *Die Kunst im Deutschen Reich*, or even *Kunst dem Volk*. I would lend you support."

Anke nodded appreciatively while slowly slicing her stringy rabbit. She got the sense, just as she had with Bauer, that all this was leading up to something.

"All I am saying is that there is more to you than making catalogues in the basement of the Jeu de Paume. You are more capable than that. I need capable people."

"What do you need me to do exactly?"

"For a start, I need you to transport something. Three things actually."

"What things?"

"You will find out when you get there. They are in Krakow. I need you to take them to Berlin."

"Paintings?"

"Yes. Don't ask me why you again. I trust you, that's why. I know you will take care of them. I know how much you cherish art…just like your father."

"I suppose I have no choice."

"No choice? You should be flattered I am asking you!"

"I am, Herr Reichsmarschall. I didn't mean to offend…."

"Let me ask you something, Fräulein Junger. Why did you include all your remarks and opinions in my catalogue, but not in the one you made for the Führer in Ghent?"

"I…I don't know. I guess I felt that you would appreciate it more."

"You were right. The Führer would not have appreciated it, not at all. He and I differ in this way. Do you understand?"

"Yes."

"You are very lucky to be dealing with me. Very lucky."

"Thank you, Herr Reichsmarschall."

Göring gave her a reassuring pat on the head as he left the table. One of his entourage sat in his place to give her instructions. Anke paid close attention because she was forbidden to write anything down.

TWO DAYS LATER Anke arrived in Krakow. She had been there with her father as a teenager to see the Veit Stoss altarpiece, but her memories were vague. She followed the crowds from the train station and found herself on the main medieval square, with the old cloth trading hall on one side and Our Lady of Krakow on the other. A tall pediment stood in the square, not far from the church. On it used to stand the statue of Adam Mickiewicz, author of a number of famous poems including the epic *Pan Tadeusz*, which was required reading in all Polish schools and many in Germany as well. Anke had read it several times and adored the love story between members of two feuding families in nineteenth-century Lithuania. One of her favorite pictures of her father was taken as he stood beneath the statue of Mickiewicz.

She swallowed hard and entered the church. It had been renovated since she was last there and looked cleaner than she remembered. Poland was a pious country and there were at least twenty people sitting or kneeling in the pews at noon on a Tuesday. As she proceeded up the main aisle, the incense assaulted her senses and the familiar pit returned to her stomach. The altarpiece that hung before her was *not* the masterpiece by Veit Stoss. The Stoss altar was gigantic, the largest Gothic altarpiece in the world. Its intricately carved wooden figures nearly jumped out at the gazer, or at least that's how Anke remembered it. The scenes were mostly from the life of the Virgin and nearly everything was coated in gold leaf, giving it an iridescent quality that reflected the flickering candles. The current altarpiece was much smaller, with two carved central figures and four painted side panels. Though it was a medieval altarpiece, and a lovely work in itself, it was not what people traveled miles to see and worship in front of. She glanced around at the resigned faces and saw that several were tearstained.

Anke felt a heaviness pulling her down and quickly sat in a pew near the front. She wept quietly, covering her eyes with the sleeve of her cotton blouse. A woman touched her shoulder from behind and said something in a soothing voice.

"I'm sorry, I don't speak Polish," Anke said, turning around. The woman was quite old, but well-dressed and wearing a warm smile. She reminded Anke a little of her maternal grandmother, Magda. Anke's mother had died when she was only two, of heart failure, and Magda had come to help out for a while. A while turned into six years, and Anke watched Magda die from complications from a stroke when she was eight. Besides her father, Magda was the only family member she had known well. Both her paternal grandparents had died young and Magda's husband, Andreas, was an alcoholic who rarely left their house in Mannheim. Anke realized, years later, that Magda had been looking for a reason to leave him for a long time.

The old Polish woman nodded gently at Anke and offered her a handkerchief.

"You are German?" the woman asked, in German.

Anke was tempted for a moment to use her Flemish, but she felt the pressure of keeping up a pretense too exhausting.

"Yes. My father was an artist and he took me here when I was very young to see the Stoss altarpiece. Where has it gone?"

"It was hidden, but the Germans found it and took it to Nuremburg, where Stoss was born. Or so I heard."

Anke nodded, her eyes filling with tears again. "I hope it will be returned here very soon."

"Yes, we all do," the woman said, slowing rising. "Krakow is not the same without it."

"And…the statue of Mickiewiez?"

"Pulled down last year."

The old woman turned her back on Anke and walked down the aisle, her warmth ebbing away.

AN HOUR LATER Anke was at the checkpoint at Wawel Castle, where the Nazi administrator of Poland, Hans Frank, had set up residence. Her instructions were to hand over a letter to him personally, which would confirm her identity and allow for the paintings to be released to her. Frank, she assumed, was expecting her.

She and her father had also visited Wawel Castle on their trip to Krakow and though it was now awash in swastika banners, it looked much the same. The kings of Poland were all buried here, in the main cathedral, along with Adam Mickiewicz, whose remains were transferred here from Paris sometime around the turn of the century. Anke wondered if the Nazis would dig him up again just for spite.

Thankfully, the breathtaking Italianate courtyard was still the castle's centerpiece and Anke was led through it by one of the guards who met her at the checkpoint. Up the stone stairs and along the galleried, alfresco corridor. She decided this would best be used as a set for a staging of Romeo and Juliet; the ivy-strewn balconies for the lovers' scenes and the great courtyard below for the duel between Tibalt and Mercutio. Add a little dust and on a hot day, this could be Verona, not Krakow.

Eventually the guard came to a halt outside a handsome black, iron door. After a moment, it creaked open from inside and a female secretary allowed Anke in. The guard retreated back down the corridor and disappeared.

"Please wait here," the woman said, gesturing for Anke to take a seat on a long black leather couch. Even though this was only the anteroom to Frank's office, it was sumptuously decorated. Fine artwork hung on the walls, covering equally extravagant striped wallpaper. Anke thought she saw a Caravaggio, but it may have been a copy. Heavy silk drapes and thick wool carpets added to the atmosphere. The air, however, was wet and despite the castle's perch atop a hill, there was little breeze.

Anke uncrossed her legs because the sweat was trickling down from behind her left knee, soaking her stockings. She was startled when the phone rang loudly. The secretary answered it and then nonchalantly got up and opened the mahogany door at the end of the room.

"The governor will see you now, Fräulein Junger."

Anke walked in with all the confidence she could muster but shuddered slightly as the secretary shut the door firmly behind her. This office put the anteroom to shame. Tasseled drapes, oriental carpets, and a number of ornate chessboards were immediately obvious. The dark-brown leather chairs gave it the feeling of a gentleman's club.

Hans Frank was standing near his enormous oak desk, looking out the window. He was dressed in a black, double-breasted suit and a red tie. His thin, brown hair was slicked back and he had a severe widow's peak. Three packages, wrapped in brown paper, sat on his desk. Frank turned his beady eyes on her.

"Well, Fräulein. You made good time from Paris."

"Yes, Herr Governor."

"Have you had the opportunity to walk around?"

"A little. I was here once before, years ago."

"Beautiful city, isn't it? Such a difference from Warsaw. There is nothing there worth seeing, I can assure you."

"I've never been."

"Give us a few years and it will be rebuilt, an example of what our Reich architects can do. It could rival Krakow yet!"

Anke didn't know what to say, so she handed over her letter.

He opened it and read it quickly, then crumpled it and threw it on his desk. He seemed exasperated.

"Here they are," he said, indicating the packages on his desk.

"I will ask you to keep them wrapped please. I don't really under-stand what all the fuss is about. I told the Reichsmarschall that I would take them to Berlin myself next month, but he insisted on sending you."

He paused and lit a cigarette, not bothering to offer one to Anke.

"It doesn't matter. They aren't mine, of course, they belong to the Reich, to the German people. They are as much yours as they are mine."

Anke nodded, understanding clearly that he wanted to keep them. It was amazing how a small thing like an appreciation for art could soften her toward someone who would otherwise seem vile to her. She noted this and wondered if she could stop allowing it to happen. This man was the chief occupier of Poland. Warsaw and Krakow had been plundered. They stole the Veit Stoss altarpiece. God only knows what was wrapped up in those packages.

"May I ask what are in the packages, Herr Governor?"

"I don't think it is necessary to go into that."

"If I have no knowledge of what I am transporting, then why, I wonder, did the Reichsmarschall insist that I come?"

"That is precisely my point, Fräulein, but it is not for you and me to question him."

"Of course."

Anke knew she would get no further. She opened the large can-vas bag that she had brought with her and began gingerly placing the packages inside. Thankfully, none were too large. Frank regarded her closely, but did not interfere. He sat at his desk and dialed the phone. A moment later the secretary returned to escort her out. Frank nodded at Anke as she left, but said nothing.

Outside the castle, Anke again mentally consulted her instructions. She was to take the packages immediately to Berlin, to one of Göring's associates at the Kaiser Friedrich Museum. She was told not to delay in Krakow and that she could sleep on the train. However, even after she and her bag were safely installed in a first-class compartment (courtesy of the Reichsmarschall) on the 8:15 to Berlin, she couldn't sleep despite having slept only a few hours the night before. She stared at her three companions, which were arranged on the seat next to her. The train was not full and she threw her empty bag and an umbrella on the seats opposite to discourage anyone from joining her in the cabin. As they passed Wroclaw, the sun had set and she ordered a cup of tea and biscuits. When they left Dresden, she opened the first package.

As she carefully removed the soft paper, she noted that this was a panel, not a canvas. A gentle, young face greeted her when she parted the folds, a brown-haired woman wearing a black, beaded necklace and a square-cut bodice. In her arms was an ermine. Anke felt a tingle. She was a holding a painting by Leonardo da Vinci. In the upper-left hand corner of the panel there was an inscription:

La Bele Feroniere Leonard Da Winci

The French was butchered and Leonardo's name had been spelled in the Polish manner. This inscription was made after the Polish owner had obtained it from Italy, whenever that was. Anke tried to recall something her father had said about the portrait, something about a Polish aristocrat who had bought it, but she couldn't come up with the name. She knew this was not "La Belle Ferronniere," which was a nickname for the mistress of Francis I of France. That portrait hung in the Louvre and was now, God willing, safe in some French chateau. However, this painting was similar in likeness but most art historians agreed that it was of Cecelia Gallerani, the very young mistress of Ludovico Sforza, the Duke of Milan in the late fifteenth century. The ermine was a symbol of the Sforza family and was included in Ludovico's coat of arms. An ermine was a Christian symbol for chastity, an ironic twist since Cecelia was only seventeen at the time this portrait was painted but had already given Ludovico a son. Anke could see, on closer inspection, that this painting had been grossly retouched. Cecelia's delicate and nearly transparent veil, which was commonly painted on women in this period, had been filled in to look like her dark, brown hair. The effect made it seem as though her hair was wrapped under her chin.

Anke's medieval and Renaissance Italian painting classes had prepared her well, she now admitted. She tried to imagine what her father would say if he could see her now, sitting on a train with a Leonardo on her lap. Would he laugh? Would he be horrified? Would he understand that despite the situation, she felt elated?

She carefully repacked the painting and opened the second package. This one was a landscape, also on a wood panel. Several figures are visible though they exist in a stormy, dangerous environment. The sky is swirled with ominous dark clouds and the figures, one of them on horseback, seem to be lost in the semidarkness. Anke was fairly sure that this was a Rembrandt and if she was right, she was holding one of only a few Rembrandt landscapes in existence. She turned the panel over and sure enough, there was a small inscription in Polish:

Rembrandt Van Rijn, Landscape with a Good Samaritan
Borowski Collection

Borowski. That was the name she had been looking for. Both these paintings had been taken from his collection and most likely the third as well. Who was he? The name didn't sound Jewish, but maybe it was. Anke opened the third package while the Rembrandt was still on her lap. This one was slightly larger, another panel, another portrait. A young man looked back at her this time, with a beret-like hat perched on the back of his head, his long curly brown hair cascading down his back. A fur shawl is draped over his left shoulder and he grasps it with his left hand. The delicate folds of his white shirt are exquisite; no doubt the work of a master. Behind him, a window shows a glimpse of the Italian countryside. Anke hoped for an inscription to confirm her hunch that this was a Raphael. She turned the panel over.

Raphael of Urbino, Portrait of a Young Man, 1514

The young man's dark eyes stare out with a serious softness, not at all unlike those of the Mona Lisa. Anke gently, so gently, touched his slightly curved lips with her index finger. This could be what Erik looks like now, she thought. Tears stung her eyes.

A jolting, the changing of tracks, told her she was nearing Berlin. She wasn't sure how long she had sat staring at the young man's portrait. She composed herself, replaced the Raphael, and rewrapped all the packages and stowed them in the canvas bag. She knew she had little choice but to deliver them to the Kaiser Friedrich Museum as she was instructed. There was nowhere to hide them and no place to escape to. At least in a museum they would be safe and taken care of, unlike with Governor Frank who, Anke had noted, had hung several oil paintings directly over a heater.

AT THE KAISER FRIEDRICH MUSEUM, a large, cherub-cheeked man (who reminded Anke slightly of Göring) accepted the paintings and even invited her to his office for a cup of tea. She declined, saying that her instructions were to return to Paris as soon as possible. The man, whose name was Kroger, nodded enthusiastically and made a comment that she must be "much in demand these days."

Anke walked through early-morning Berlin toward the train station. Official buildings were everywhere, all bedecked with the swastika. Nearly everyone seemed to be in uniform, even many of the women. This city, despite the bustle, could not have been more different from Paris. Berlin was all business.

Nevertheless, there were museums to visit and there was, in reality, no real rush to get back to Paris. However, something told her she did not want to stay here. Berlin was never a place where she had spent large amounts of time, other than a few trips to visit the museums with her father. She saw now that it was the capital of the insanity that had gripped her country, and most of Europe, and for which she couldn't find the right word. It was more than war. It was…something else.

8

The Consultant

✝

To accept, today, the work of German painters such as Holbein and Dürer and of Italians like Botticelli and Raphael, and of painters of the low countries like Van Dyck and Rembrandt, and of famous Frenchmen, famous Spaniards—to accept this work today on behalf of the people of this democratic nation is to assert the belief of the people of this nation in a human spirit which now is everywhere endangered and which, in many countries where it first found form and meaning, has been rooted out and broken and destroyed.
—President Franklin D. Roosevelt at the dedication
of the National Gallery of Art in Washington, DC,
March 17, 1941

ONCE THE BOMBS began to tear London to pieces, Erik Brossler became a very popular young man. Brigsworth-Jones had been on the phone to numerous curators in the US to coordinate efforts and solicit funds. Erik's name usually came up.

In March he was flown to Washington, at the expense of the newly formed Committee on the Conservation of Cultural Resources, to advise the National Gallery on packing and evacuation techniques. He'd never been to Washington and was impressed enough to call his parents and describe the finer details of the Lincoln Memorial.

Erik strongly suggested the removal of all cultural objects to safe, bombproof locations, just as was done in London. His recommendations were met with enthusiasm but absolutely no funding. Each museum or archive was left to its own devices, and more importantly, its own budgets. To help, Erik crafted an instructional pamphlet, based on one he'd seen at the British Museum, that gave step-by-step directions for the successful packing and storage of cultural items. He was assured it would be published and distributed immediately.

Meanwhile, the elite contents of the National Gallery would be evacuated to Biltmore, a French Renaissance mansion in Asheville, North Carolina, that was built as a mountain retreat by the millionaire George Vanderbilt in the late nineteenth century. It was fireproof, near the railway lines, and the nearest residence was miles away. According to Erik's guidelines, it was perfect.

The Metropolitan Museum of Art in New York decided to move its extensive collection to an empty mansion outside Philadelphia, once owned by an associate of JP Morgan. This was Erik's idea, since he soundly rejected the museum's first proposal to move its works of art into a tunnel that ran directly under their building (a result of a new water main installation in 1939). Much too damp, Erik told them, and they ultimately agreed. The Met had a number of Memlings.

Evacuation drills were running frequently at the Museum of Fine Arts in Boston and Richard Paulson was personally scoping out possible repositories for the museum's collection outside the city. The same could be said for almost all of the museums in major US cities, and many in smaller cities as well. The task was so daunting that Erik wrote frequently to Brigsworth-Jones, seeking information on what was happening with the English collections. His former mentor did not disappoint and sent not only information, but also photographs.

As Erik prepared a presentation for a meeting of the major museum directors in New York, his father sat at the dining room table next to him, editing the speech. Lotte was having lunch with Mrs. Paulson in Boston (after much cajoling, Lotte finally attended one of the Paulson's art meetings and found that she very much liked Joanna Paulson).

"Must we listen to the football game? I am trying to read here," David said.

"It helps me think. I like background noise," Erik said, smiling.

"He's up to the twenty-five, now he's hit and hit hard, at about the twenty-seven yard line...*we interrupt this broadcast to bring you this important bulletin from the United Press...flash...Washington...the White House announces Japanese attack on Pearl Harbor....*"

Erik rocketed up, knocking a pile of slides to the floor. By the time he reached the radio, the game was back on.

"What? What did he say?" David asked, breathless.

"The Japanese attacked Pearl Harbor! That's the Navy, Papa!"

"What are they doing?" David hissed, "Why is the game back on? Change the channel! Go to CBS…CBS!"

Erik swung the dial.

"The Japanese have attacked Pearl Harbor, Hawaii, by air, President Roosevelt has just announced. The attack also was made on all naval and military activities on the principle island of Oahu."

"My God! The Japanese. This will mean war." David sat back down at the table. Suddenly he felt his wife's all-consuming fear.

"Let's hope we declare war on Germany at the same time," Erik said, turning the channel again.

"Do you think…a war on two fronts?"

"Hitler is doing it. Someone needs to stop him."

"I know, of course, but will Congress agree to such a war?"

"There are many people who think we should have been in it a long time ago, me included."

"Erik, I understand your feelings, but please."

"I am joining up, as soon as possible."

Erik bent down and began to gather the slides from the floor. David had paled, but tried to remain calm. Yelling at Erik never got him anywhere.

"Your mother…she simply would not survive that, Erik."

"Stop it. Don't use her. I am joining up and you know I am right."

"That may be true, but I am giving you a simple fact. It will destroy her."

Erik walked out of the room just as his mother walked in, festive in a sparkly black hat.

"Have you two had a fight?" she asked, stopping Erik in his tracks. She hadn't heard. They didn't have a radio at the restaurant.

ERIK ARRIVED EARLY for the meeting in New York, the weekend before Christmas. A number of reporters were tipped off and had gathered outside the hotel.

"Are all US museums evacuating?"

"Where will the Met's paintings go?"

"Is it true you will use abandoned mines like the British have?"

Erik ignored them and strolled through the main entrance with his two briefcases. Once a quorum was reached inside the meeting room, he began his presentation. The curtains were drawn, coffee served, and the slides were projected onto the far wall of the room.

The first slide was of the *Grand Galerie* of the Louvre—empty. The elegant frames leaned against the walls; the floors were strewn with the detritus of desperate packing. Just visible were the chalk inscriptions on the wallpaper, indicating which painting had been in which spot.

The second slide showed the bombed Tate Gallery in London, the floors of which were blanketed with shattered glass from the hundreds of skylight panels.

The third, and perhaps most moving, was of Canterbury Cathedral—England's masterpiece of medieval architecture. The nave was now filled with hundreds of tons of dirt dug from the fields outside Canterbury, to help absorb the shocks of the explosions. The irreplaceable stained glass windows were removed.

After several more slides in the same vein, Erik shut off the projector and the lights came back on. He then produced the most recent letter from Brigsworth-Jones, which he read aloud.

To my American colleagues, I hope this letter finds you all well and hopeful this Christmas. To say the least, this is a difficult time and we need now, more than ever, to work together. Let me first relate some of the recent developments on this side of the Atlantic.

Now that the Germans are attacking our midland cities from their new airbases in France, the National Gallery collection has been moved to even more secure locations. For obvious reasons, I cannot disclose those locations. Suffice it to say, several lucky new landlords of British-owned art have benefited from the installation of electric heating at the government's expense. Dryness has been a problem and we've come up with a rather inelegant solution: wet blankets are hung amongst the paintings.

German bombing intensity, however, has forced us to go underground. This, in itself, provides us with a host of new problems, amongst them the lowering of a road to allow passage of our largest painting, van Dyke's

*equestrian portrait of King Charles I. Dr. Erik Brossler can attest to the
awkwardness of this gigantic canvas since he packed it himself.*

*I can provide you with news from outside England, but I must warn that
in many cases this information is not firsthand, though I will say that it
comes from sources who I trust implicitly. Many of the Jewish art dealers
who fled occupied Europe, some of whom are now in Britain, now know
that their collections have been vigorously looted by the Germans. Even the
objects which were sent to bank vaults have been, in some cases, stolen by
the Nazis. Miriam de Rothschild, who I have had the pleasure of meeting
on several occasions, has thankfully escaped but had her art collection hastily buried in a sand dune near Dieppe. Unfortunately, she was not able to
be more specific.*

*Henri Matisse, who had been staying with the art dealer Paul Rosenberg
in Bordeaux, was too horrified by the crush of people fighting to leave
France that he decided to stay and is now, God willing, somewhere safe in
the unoccupied zone. Rosenberg sailed for New York and may be sitting
with you all now. If so, please give him my warmest regards. As I understand it, he has lost the majority of his collection. The bulk of the Louvre's
collection has been moved to chateaus south of Paris. Our own RAF pilots
reported that there were gigantic letters spelling out "Musee de Louvre" on
a lawn outside a chateau in Le Mans, but that was nearly three years ago
now. However, I do not have any solid knowledge to indicate that any of
the Louvre's collection is in Nazi hands.*

*In the Low Countries, the Germans seem to be attempting to make nice.
They apparently view these nations as "Nordic" or "Aryan" and therefore are simply incorporating them into their greater "Reich." A reliable
source has told us of an SS-associated group called the "Ahnenerbe" which
has the mission to discover the historic ties between modern Germans and
the ancient Aryan people. They are heavily involved in archaeology and I
recently heard a report that one of their representatives was sent to The
Hague to make friends with the Dutch intelligentsia, who they hope will
assist them in fostering a German-Dutch alliance. First tasks: eliminate
the Catholic Church, communists, freemasons, and Jews. According to my
Dutch contacts, this program is not going well due to the virulent Dutch
hatred for the Germans.*

*An establishment known as the "ERR" (what exactly that stands for is
unclear) is operating throughout Europe, but especially in France where
they are actively looting private collections and storing their prizes at the Jeu*

de Paume museum in Paris. I have it on good authority that the Germans have art historians there sifting through the thousands of art objects, classifying them, and then shipping them off to Germany on trains. Books, manuscripts, original music, and scores…nothing is off limits.

The outrage I feel is, I am sure, felt by my honorable American colleagues as well. We must endeavor to join forces in a more palpable way if we are to recover, and save from looting or destruction, the cultural patrimony of Europe.

Your faithful and humble friend,

Owen Brigsworth-Jones

December 1, 1941

"As you can see by the date," Erik said, "Brigsworth-Jones wrote this before Pearl Harbor and the declarations of war on Germany and Japan. No doubt we will receive another letter soon, though this may become more difficult due to the impending war in the Atlantic."

He then turned to Friedrich Fassbinder, who had been asked to attend the meeting to report on the influx of artists, dealers, and art objects into the United States. Since his arrival in America, Fassbinder had amassed an impressive number of contacts and associates, both within the art world, and amongst the government officials whose job it was to monitor the European-owned assets now streaming into the country.

"Paul Rosenberg couldn't be here," Fassbinder said, lighting a cigarette, "but he told me he very much fears that the majority of his collection is gone. To give you an idea, his collection represented about six times that of the National Gallery in Washington."

Most around the table shook their heads in disbelief. Side conversations started up and the tension rose.

"I'm sure most of you know, of have heard of, Martin Fabiani," Fassbinder said, regaining attention. "He shipped a massive collection, nearly 700 pieces, on the *SS Excalibur* last year. There were over 400 Renoir paintings, drawings, and watercolors, not to mentions over sixty Cezanne's, and a number of Gauguins as well. By the time the ship arrived in Bermuda, the British had decided that all French assets were now 'enemy assets,' since France is occupied by the Germans. They are afraid any profits from these assets could ultimately assist the Nazis, and they clearly don't trust Fabiani. The collection is now in Canada and it will take a work of God to get it released."

"At least it is safe," commented Gerald Longhorn, the director of the Museum of Modern Art.

"For now," Fassbinder said, ominously.

"We are all here to make sure all the art, within our control, stays safe," Erik said, diffusing the tension. "Let's talk about our current measures. What are we doing right now...today."

"Our situation is untenable," said Longhorn, blowing out a plume of cigarette smoke. "We are taking down the cream of the crop, which most of you know are hung on the third floor, and putting them in a sand-bagged storeroom each night. We re-hang the paintings each morning before the public arrives."

"We have closed the Japanese galleries indefinitely," said Anthony Bracken, curator at the Museum of Fine Arts in Boston. "The board is afraid of vandalism disguised as anti-Japanese patriotism. Richard Paulson is still looking for a suitable repository for the collection outside of Boston."

"We are closing at dusk, to avoid anyone being caught there in a blackout. God knows what might happen," said Daniel Casey, curator at the Metropolitan Museum of Art. "Sam Goldman at the Frick could not make it to this meeting, but told me that they have blackened out their skylights."

Erik wondered what kind of exhibit they could offer without natural light, but held his tongue. Skylights, so essential to any museum, were also easy prey to overhead bombers, as seen at the Tate in London.

"I did receive a letter from Anders de Graff, curator of Dutch paintings at the Rijksmuseum in Amsterdam, that indicated that the Germans have been enthusiastic about protecting Dutch art because they believe they now own it all," Longhorn said, taking the letter out of his briefcase and putting on his glasses.

"De Graff himself was allowed to recently inspect a number of paintings, including Rembrandt's *Night Watch*, which are hidden in some purpose-built shelters in the sand dunes outside Amsterdam. He found that the paintings are being kept in absolute darkness. He warned about what happens to varnish in darkness…it yellows."

Nodding heads lit cigarettes and reached for their coffee cups. Erik had to admit he had not thought of the danger of yellowing varnish. Paintings could be cleaned and touched-up, he decided. They couldn't be pieced together from ashes.

The meeting finally adjourned with no blanket policy, save one. The museums must be kept open for the public as long as possible. Many of the major museums would soon send their most valuable works into hiding, with as little disruption to the public as can be managed. Erik's instructional packing pamphlet, which had still not been mass published, was nonetheless handed out to everyone at the meeting in multiples.

ERIK WAS ASKED to personally attend the packing of the National Gallery's collection, which took place on New Year's Eve since the museum was closed to the public on New Year's Day. Seventy-five paintings were pulled off the walls and removed from their frames. Erik wrapped Memling's *Madonna and Child with the Angels* and *Portrait of a Man with an Arrow* himself, feeling that familiar rush of excitement and dread that he had felt while packing the *Wilton Diptych* in London. He also presided over the packing of Botticelli's *Adoration of the Magi*, three Raphaels, three Vermeers, and two sculptures by Verrocchio. The remaining staff then filled the holes with other pieces from the collection and rearranged the galleries to make them look more full than they actually were. Erik and the curators rang in the New Year with champagne from the roof of the National Gallery, though the blackout severely marred the view.

Erik accompanied the art, and the curators, to Philadelphia and was there when everything was unloaded at *Biltmore* on January 6, 1942. While there, he made a call to Richard Paulson who informed him that Boston's Museum of Fine Arts was shipping their collection to Williams College in Western Massachusetts and lookouts had been posted on the roof of the museum in Boston around the clock.

The Frick and the Philadelphia Museum of Art had decided to use underground vaults on their own premises, while the magnificent

Philips Collection in Washington, DC, moved its works to Kansas City. The major museums of San Francisco and San Diego sent their collections to Colorado Springs. Erik was dismayed, but not surprised, to hear that the Detroit Institute of the Arts had decided not to move any of their artworks under severe pressure from Henry Ford, who dismissed any chance of attacks on the American mainland.

Erik's reputation as an up-and-coming art historian and preservation specialist had reached even beyond the usual art circles. After returning to Cambridge, he received a phone call from a clerk at the National Archives informing him that the Declaration of Independence had been sent to Fort Knox. Erik sat silently at the dining room table for nearly an hour after receiving this information. It wasn't so much the actual information, but the fact that he, a German immigrant, received it. Ribbons of anxiety pumped through him. He needed to get closer to the action.

He immediately made his intention to join the US Army public knowledge. Calls from many in the art community flooded into the Brossler home, unanimously calling for Erik to reconsider and remain committed to spearheading the efforts to preserve America's cultural assets. In truth, many knew that Erik had done his job too well and his ideas and suggestions had been taken up by a host of others, working in many cities, who were busy compiling lists and organizing art protection guidelines.

"Erik feels he has done all he can here on this side of the Atlantic," his father explained to Walter Dillinger, of the National Gallery. "He wants to go back to Europe and be of assistance on the ground. His mother and I are set against it, of course, but he is his own man, as you know."

"Forgive me, David," Dillinger said, "but is Erik an American citizen?"

"Oh yes, we all are…we became citizens in 1936."

"Forgive me, I didn't know."

"Yes, well…part of me regrets it now. If he wasn't a citizen, he couldn't join the army."

~

IN FEBRUARY, Erik reported for basic training to Fort Monroe in Virginia. Six weeks and a sprained ankle later, he arrived at Fort Benning, Georgia, for Officer Candidate School. His father wrote to him daily and devoured the infrequent letters he received in return. Lotte did not write, nor did she read Erik's letters. She confined herself more and more to the house, eschewing invitations from Joanna Paulson and others to attend parties and art events. By the time Erik graduated, in September of 1942, Lotte had all but stopped eating and was described by a doctor as "being in a state of confusion and frequent paranoia." Brossler hired a nurse to care for his wife, but kept her condition a closely guarded secret, especially from Erik.

Sitting by his wife's bedside one evening, David read in *The New York Times* the reviews of two new exhibitions: "The Surrealists" at the Guggenheim and "Artists in Exile" at the Pierre Matisse Gallery. Nearly every piece shown would have been confiscated or destroyed had they remained in Europe, not to mention the artists themselves. David briefly thought of Anke Junger and wished she could see her father's pieces exhibited in New York, to interest and acclaim, and not ridiculed. It was then that an overwhelming sense of detachment and helplessness overcame him. He realized, with a shock, that he severely envied his son who was, at that moment, on a ship bound for England and the war.

9

M-Aktion

It is quite true that I received a governmental order to confiscate archives, works of art, and later, household goods from Jewish citizens in France.... I was informed that the Jewish people in question no longer inhabited their institutions, castles and apartments...."
          —Alfred Rosenberg, Founder of the ERR

DUE IN PART to Anke's influence, Konrad obtained a promotion. He left his sentry duties behind to take an entry-level position within the ERR. When Anke returned from Berlin, Konrad surprised her with the news at the Meurice. His new orders were top secret and even Anke, who was now known as the personal art historian to the Reichsmarschall, was left in the dark. Konrad himself knew little about the new project, other than that he would be in charge of a group of French workers provided by The Union of Parisian Movers. He knew better than to ask questions since this new job was almost certainly the only thing between him and a ditch outside Stalingrad.

Anke thought little about Konrad's work since they rarely spoke outside the usual topics: films, music, and his favorite subject: the inevitable subjugation of Russia (which he longed for but had no desire to participate in). Anke anxiously wondered what had become of the colossal art collection at the Hermitage Museum in Leningrad. Her father had taken her there when she was sixteen and getting lost with him in the maze of the Winter Palace was one of her fondest memories. If she closed her eyes, she could almost hear him say, *"Anke, we are back where we started. We've seen this Titian already."*

The city had been under siege for a year now. She heard they had evacuated everything to Siberia. She hoped it was more than a rumor.

BY NOVEMBER 1942, Anke noticed an increased flow of artworks into the repository room. A surge of new pieces, from time to time, was normal. The ERR staffers would clean out an art dealer's hidden holdings from a Chateau outside Paris and bring everything in at once. Anke and the others would work all night to make a rudimentary catalogue of everything before pieces began to disappear into the cars of various high-ranking officers. She was now working on a second catalogue for Göring, which was shaping up to be twice the size of the first one. Göring's appetite for art was insatiable and this time he furnished her with a list in person, on yet another visit to the Jeu de Paume. He listed the types of works he was interested in by time period/style and country of origin, but let Anke make the specific selections for him. This was an unimaginable honor, Kurt informed her, despite his rather obvious jealousy. Wanda and Leo rarely spoke to Anke anymore, though von Essen told her it was merely out of self-preservation.

"They may fear you would betray their idle chatter to the Reichsmarschall," he told her over coffee at the Meurice.

"I don't even know what to say to that," she replied, sickened.

"I understand, my dear. But now, do *you* understand my situation? You see…it's not so easy. It's quite complicated actually."

Anke did see that and it was in von Essen that she eventually confided. Though he was a Nazi-party member, he had remained a civilian by choice and was concerned about the reports of Nazi art looting that had been published in the newspapers of Britain and America.

"Your grace," Anke asked during one of their frequent breakfasts at the Meurice, "are you aware of the influx of…second-class art into the repository?"

"What do you mean by second class?"

"Well…some of the pieces are lovely, and quite a few are by major artists. But, the frames are often cracked or the paintings are in frames that are wrong for them. Many of the pieces are dirty, especially the sculpture. My point is…these are not from art dealers. I've seen inscriptions that lead me to believe these are from the homes of regular people."

"I am not aware of this. Can you be more specific?"

"Canvases with personal inscriptions written on the back, your Grace. 'For Sophie, Happy Birthday, love, Father.'"

"Come now Anke, there are personal inscriptions on items within dealer inventories. Those things can enhance the value of an artistic item, you know that."

"They can also lessen its value. No, this is different. These don't have dealer markings. Rosenberg and Seligmann always marked their works. The Rothschilds did too. Jacques Goudstikker marked everything in Holland, as you know. These are not works from dealers. A whole new trove of items is coming in now. You don't know anything about it?"

"I can honestly say I do not." Von Essen waved to the waiter for their bill.

Anke dropped the subject. Von Essen was uncomfortable talking about the looting and he usually steered their conversations away from it as much as possible. Still, she believed him. She believed that he didn't know anything because he chose not to know anything. He walked around with his eyes closed.

CHRISTMAS AT THE MEURICE was an elaborate affair. A fifteen-foot tree dripping with silver and gold ornaments stood in the main lobby just to the right of the grand staircase. The main dining room, where Pablo Picasso and Olga Koklova held their wedding dinner in 1918, was now hosting Christmas parties for the German top brass nearly every night. The white, twinkling Christmas lights created a fairyland feel and gave Anke a little hope each day as she descended the stairs and began again her surreal new life. The attention and favor of the Reichsmarschall did have its perks. Her tiny, windowless room at the Meurice, which Bauer had sweetly reminded her was actually a converted broom closet, had been taken over as a storage room for extra luggage. Anke was given a new, larger room on the top floor of the hotel with a view of the Tuileries.

By Christmas Eve, the city had emptied out somewhat. Thousands of German soldiers, those lucky enough to have leave passes, packed the eastern bound trains and headed home to their families in Germany.

The officers, carpooling in big black cars, sped out of Paris leaving a skeleton hierarchy in charge until the New Year. Konrad, who was not allowed leave, was left to command his temporarily depleted ERR unit. Feeling powerful for the first time, he made a dinner reservation at St. Clair, a fashionable restaurant on the Champs-Elysees. Once the wine was poured, he brought out a small, red velvet box and placed it on the table. Anke looked at it as though it was a poisonous spider.

"Don't worry, it's not an engagement ring," Konrad said. "I know you're not going to marry me."

Anke decided that was the most self-aware thing Konrad had ever said to her. She slid the box toward her, interested now. Inside, there was a shiny silver "A" suspended by a thick, braided chain. It was well-crafted and clearly an antique. A minuscule French inscription ran along the underside of the A. She couldn't make it out in the dim light.

"Don't you like it?" Konrad asked, lighting a cigarette.

"It's beautiful. Where did you get it?"

"What does that matter? At a jewelry store."

"What jewelry store?"

"Come on, Anke. Stop trying to figure everything out all the time. Do you like it or not?"

"I want to know where you got it from."

"Why?"

"There is an inscription, and it's not from you."

"Where?"

"Here, on the underside," she said, passing the necklace to him. He squinted and handed it back to her.

"It's an antique. I thought you would like that."

"I do. It's just that, I don't want this to be…I mean, this wasn't stolen, was it?"

"Excuse me?"

"Tell me where you bought it."

Konrad slammed his fist on the table, causing the woman sitting behind him to shriek. He turned to her and apologized. Anke was mortified and put the necklace into her purse. She knew she was right. It wasn't from a jewelry store.

After dinner, which they ate in silence, Konrad walked her back to the Meurice. He had to report to his unit by midnight. He told her he had guard duty.

"What are you guarding? People? Prisoners?"

"No. Not people."

"What then?"

"Just things, Anke. I guard things. It's nothing to worry about."

"Was the necklace one of those things?"

Konrad stopped and looked at her. "Yes. It was. Now it is yours, okay?"

"No, it's not okay! I don't want stolen property!" Her voice cracked.

"Shh! Anke, keep your voice down! Calm down…it's not stolen. I was given permission to take anything I wanted as a Christmas bonus. Every man in the unit got to take something for his wife or girlfriend, except Bohnmann who doesn't have a girlfriend, if you know what I mean. He took something for his mother."

"Where are these "things" coming from? Is this what your unit does?"

"We gather materials for German families who have been bombed out of their homes. We also send supplies to the soldiers on the Eastern front. What, exactly, is wrong with that?"

"You just steal it from people's homes?"

"The homes are empty—the people are all gone. These are abandoned items, Anke."

"Why, do you think, people would abandon all of their possessions?"

"I have no idea. Some have left the country, I guess. Jews. Lots of Jews have left. I can't tell you how many menorahs we have. I hadn't even heard of a menorah before I came to Paris, now I am up to my eyeballs in them!"

Konrad laughed heartily and lit another cigarette. Anke stormed away from him, then thought better of it and sat on the low wall that runs around the Place de la Concorde. Konrad stood in front of her, confused by her anger. It was snowing lightly now. He wrapped her scarf around her head and tucked it into her wool coat (also a gift from him, but one she had not questioned).

Follow the art, liebling.

"Take me with you tonight," she said softly.

"Where? To my post?"

"Yes."

"Why would you want to go there?"

"There might be some things of artistic value there. I want to… see."

Konrad thought for a moment then shook his head.

"No, Anke. I've already told you too much. This project is top secret. I could be sent to Russia for telling you anything. Is that what you want?"

"Of course not."

"Then drop it. If you don't want the necklace, fine. I'm sure I can find another girl to give it to."

Anke stood and placed the necklace in his hand. She walked alone back to the Meurice.

AFTER A WEEK without contact, Konrad decided that Anke was well worth the risk. He appeared at her hotel room late on the first Friday night of 1943. He told her she could accompany him to his post, if she still wanted to. Anke initially declined, but then changed her mind. Her father's voice was in her head now and she wanted it to stay there.

They rode south, in one of the ERR's trucks, to the outskirts of Paris and turned into a train depot. Large warehouses lined the tracks, some of which had trains sitting on them waiting for the dawn. Konrad had given Anke a pass, which she pinned to her coat, and a set of papers that belonged to someone called Frieda Kaltenbrenner. These papers were accepted without interest at the guard station and they were waved through and into the main compound.

Konrad parked in a dark corner and led Anke toward one of the large warehouses. There were lights on inside and Anke could hear voices, women's voices. When they walked in, she initially had trouble understanding what she was looking at. The shapes and textures were blurred at first, but they smoothed out as she got closer. She was looking at the largest pile of furniture she had ever seen. Stacks of wood crates, piled four high and nearly thirty across, served as a base for a gigantic assortment of tables, chairs, beds, armoires, lamps, benches, coat racks, bookcases, and sofas.

"What's in the crates?" she asked Konrad, who was studying a clipboard next to her.

"Smaller things: plates, saucers, cups, glasses, things like that. The art and sculpture is in another warehouse, we can go in a minute and you can take a look. I just need to check a few things here…I am technically on duty tonight."

Anke looked around at the women who were packing items into open crates. They wore shabby dresses and looked sickly.

"Who are they?"

"Communist prisoners. They help with the packing. All this is being sent to German families who have lost everything. It's an amazing operation. We call it *Möbel Aktion*—or *M Aktion* for short. Operation Furniture. Over here, these large crates contain everything a family would need to set up a new house…even a kitchen sink!"

Anke realized that Konrad thought he was impressing her. She played along.

He led her to a smaller side room that was packed with pianos, harpsichords, harps, and accordions. Just what any homeless German family would need to survive, Anke thought.

As they passed through the vastness of the warehouse, something caught Anke's eye. She walked toward another small adjoining room, leaving Konrad and his all-consuming clipboard behind. The room was dark, but her eyes soon became accustomed and she spotted small faces staring out from piles shoved up against the back wall. Dolls. Dolls sitting in small cribs. A dollhouse. A rocking horse, not unlike the one she had when she was little. Several small carriages on wheels.

"Oh, this is…for the German children, who have lost everything," Konrad said, coming up behind her.

"Where are the children who owned these toys?"

"I told you, they left."

"The children…they left and didn't take their dolls?"

"Well, you can't take everything."

"No, you can't. Not if you are leaving in a rush…," she trailed off as she spotted a large pile of children's clothing and shoes sitting in an open box. A baby's tiny white linen dress lay on top. Anke vomited on the floor.

Run, leibling.

Konrad leapt back in shock, then put his arms around her and tried to pull her out of the room. She had gone limp, so he picked her up and took her out the back exit. The freezing wind brought her back and she kicked her way free of him, ripping her badge off and throwing it to the ground. Konrad stood, frozen in fear, as he watched her run into the blackness. He saw her scale a chain-link fence and he gasped as her coat caught on the barbed wire. She worked herself free and disappeared across a small field, leaving her coat flapping on the fence like an injured bird. Konrad, not knowing what else to do, went back into the warehouse with his clipboard.

A WEEK LATER, Hermann Göring received a telegram from von Bahn.

```
Fräulein Junger has collapsed. She is suffering
from pneumonia and a possible mental breakdown.
She is at a sanatorium in Châtenay-Malabry. Is
she to be rehabilitated or replaced? Please ad-
vise. Heil Hitler.
```

10

The Monuments Men

Today we are fighting in a country which has contributed a great deal to our cultural inheritance, a country rich in monuments which by their creation helped and now in their old age illustrate the growth of the civilization which is ours. We are bound to respect those monuments so far as the war allows.
—*Gen. Dwight D. Eisenhower*

Palermo, Sicily, July 1943

CAPTAIN **TIM BRUNSWICK** scanned the nave looking for his best lieutenant. The twelfth-century church of San Cataldo had been home to his men for the last twelve hours and most of them were taking well-deserved naps, their boots dangling off the ends of the pews. Finally he saw him, sitting in the last row, eyes closed with his rifle lying across his lap. Erik Brossler had surprised Brunswick, and he was not used to being surprised. The battle for Sicily was the first action ever seen by the majority of the US Seventh Army and casualties had been heavy on the initial seaborne assault. Brossler, who had a funny accent and was known as "the professor" turned out to be as fearless as a young child.

"Bross. Wake up. I've got news."

Brunswick was a tobacco-chewing hydrant of a man from rural Kentucky who called everyone in his company by some abbreviation of their last name. He killed his first deer at the age of six. He had almost nothing in common with Erik Brossler. Almost nothing.

"What news? Are we moving out?" Erik asked, trying to wake up.

"No. Not news for us, news for you. Your prayers have been answered."

"What? What do you mean? Have they set up an art protection division?"

"Jesus, you're a geek. I should have known they wouldn't let you get yourself killed. You're going to some new operation…hold on, I've got the cable here…a special art-protection unit has been created by the War Department and was finally signed off on by President Roosevelt last night. 'The American Commission for the Protection and Salvage of Artistic and Historic Monuments in War Areas.' Shit, that's a mouthful. Anyway, you're supposed to stay with us for the time being, but you'll be moved closer to the front lines soon. This is a joint British-American operation, so you might end up under British command."

"I can't believe this. I had pretty much given up hope."

"Well, apparently there are others who think like you, Bross."

A feeling then came over Erik, one he had not expected.

"Captain, you trained me to lead men into battle, not to protect art. I will understand if you don't want me to take this assignment."

"Yeah, well, I don't make the decisions. Someone obviously thinks you'd be more helpful saving Michelangelos than shooting Germans."

"Captain…."

"No, Bross, leave it alone. Am I happy about losing one of my best platoon commanders? No I'm not. But I knew who you were when you came under my command. I knew you weren't going to stay in my company for long."

"Who will take over my platoon?"

"Sergeant Saunders, probably. He's a good man. He can handle it."

Erik nodded in agreement, swallowing over a lump in his throat. The sting of shame mixed with the lightness of excitement was an odd sensation.

"Ok. So, where is the company of art protection officers? Where should I report?"

"Ha!" Brunswick snorted. "It says here that besides you, there are only two others. No company."

"Only two others in the entire battalion? How the fuck, excuse me sir, but how are we supposed to protect monuments from an advancing army with three men per battalion?"

"No, Bross. Not per battalion. There's three of you in the entire Seventh Army."

ERIK SOON LEARNED that the other two monuments officers were in Syracuse, on the other side of the island. He was on his own in Palermo, sharing a tiny office with a public relations officer. Members of the press shuffled in and out, asking uncomfortable questions about the sixty churches and the National Library, which had already been damaged by American artillery. With no typewriter and no transportation, Erik immediately cabled his father and asked for supplies. His father was now working directly for the Roberts Commission, the stateside administrative arm of the art protection unit spearheaded by Supreme Court Justice Owen Roberts. Erik hoped they were better equipped than he was.

After five weeks without any support whatsoever, and no word from his father, Erik had hardly been able to reach the outskirts of Palermo. He had, however, been helpful to the public relations officer, Lt. Branson, since the war reporters were not especially versed in history and occasionally attributed roofless temples to the Allied invasion. Erik was thrilled to inform them, often after their articles were already published, that those temples had been roofless since the second-century BC.

After a particularly frustrating day during which it rained hard enough to fill the naves of several recently damaged medieval churches with a foot or two of dirty water, Erik sloshed back to his office carrying pieces of a fourteenth-century statue of the Virgin. How he was going to repair this 700-year-old stone effigy, he had no idea. As he neared his office, crammed in the back of battalion headquarters (housed in a former school), he heard a familiar voice and the blood returned to his heart.

Brigsworth-Jones looked ridiculous sitting on Erik's tiny desk, but it was the sweetest sight Erik had seen in years. On his chair, looking less ridiculous, was a typewriter.

"Your father called and said you had no supplies of any kind," said Brigsworth-Jones, rising to greet his old friend.

"My knight in shining armor," Erik said, gently placing the statue pieces on the windowsill and allowing himself to be embraced by the Welsh giant.

"You should have called me."

"I thought you were still guarding pictures in Wales."

"Come on, get your things, chap. We are getting out of here."

"We?"

"I am now your commanding officer, Lt. Brossler. You may address me as Captain Brigsworth-Jones. Or Brigs. That's my new nickname. Do you like it? I like it."

Erik laughed out loud. "Did Captain Brunswick call you that, by any chance?"

"How did you know? Let's go."

"Wait, wait a second. How many strings did you have to pull to get over here?"

"Too many. But that's not your problem, chap. We've got a job to do and we can't worry about what the rest of the army thinks."

"They think we are a bunch of jerks," Erik said under his breath as he gathered his papers, notebooks, and the Virgin.

Brigsworth-Jones had begun walking down the hall, but stopped.

"Did you hear what I just said?"

"Yes, Captain," Erik said, smirking. "They call us the Monuments Men."

"Monuments Men…I like it," said Brigsworth-Jones as Erik followed him down the hall.

Out on the street, the rain had slowed to a drizzle. Brigsworth-Jones had managed to obtain a car, though it was not army issue.

"Captain, this thing looks a hundred years old. If we are going to be transporting cultural items…."

"Stop right there, Brossler. This is all I could get and we are lucky to have it. At least it moves. I had it going about forty miles an hour on the country roads."

"I'm surprise it goes above ten," Erik said, sitting in the passenger seat with his broken statue.

They drove away, the mud flipping off the wheels.

"You now have transportation and a typewriter," Brigsworth-Jones said, sounding pleased with himself. "Where do we start?"

"We need to secure the National Library. Part of the roof has been blown away. Rare books have been lying in the open for weeks now. We need to make some sort of tarp."

"Do you have a weapon on you?" Brigsworth-Jones asked, simultaneously lighting a cigarette, opening a map, and driving.

"Just my pistol. I had to surrender my rifle when I transferred."

"Do you know how to shoot it?"

Erik stared at him. "Of course I know how to shoot it. I was a platoon commander."

"Platoon commander, eh? Did they make fun of your accent?"

"That's part of the deal," Erik said, laughing.

"Nobody thinks you're a spy?"

"Not that I know of."

"Was it hard to leave your men?"

Erik was quiet for a moment. "Much harder than I expected."

"Yes. I thought it might have been, chap."

ERIK ENLISTED THE THREE US soldiers who had been ordered to guard the heavily damaged library to help him make a set of giant tarps out of used parachutes, which Brigsworth-Jones coaxed out of the Eighty-Second Airborne. Many of the rare books were completely ruined, but a larger number survived. For the most part, Palermo's valuable paintings, sculptures, and drawings had either been well-hidden and protected or removed from the city before the invasion. The Museo Nationale had taken down the *Holy Family* by Rubens and placed it, with many others, in a basement vault.

After a brief stop at the Botanical Gardens to demand that the soldiers camping there stop sleeping on top of the rare plants, Erik and Brigsworth-Jones drove east to Syracuse where they met up with Tom Dearborn and Marshall Crawford, the other two American Monuments Men attached to the US Seventh Army. Dearborn and Crawford had managed to swing a larger office and two typewriters at the central command post. Crawford was a petite man and a former administrator at the Los Angeles County Museum of Art. He sweated profusely and seemed constantly anxious.

Dearborn was exactly the opposite. He was a rugged young Texan who had played football at Texas A&M all four years. Since graduating, he had completed half his graduate degree in museum studies at the University of Pennsylvania, his specialty being ancient Greek and Roman architecture. This was his third trip to Syracuse, which he described as a "heaven of temples, amphitheatres, and necropolises." It was clear to Erik that Dearborn went out and examined, repaired, lifted, and cleaned, while Crawford wrote the reports. As usual, Brigsworth-Jones saw an opening.

"Crawford, we are going to need several reports on Palermo typed up, using Lt. Brossler's notes here…are you my man?"

"Yes, sir!" Crawford finally understood that Brigsworth-Jones was the British captain they were told to expect. The largeness of the man, combined with his unbuttoned uniform and unshaved appearance caused some initial confusion. Brigsworth-Jones broke the ice by providing a number of bottles of Italian red wine and treating his new monument team to a little party on the beach.

"Have you heard about Operation Mincemeat?" Brigsworth-Jones asked Crawford as they settled themselves on the sand.

"No sir," Crawford replied, sipping his wine from a small glass he had brought along.

"No, of course not," Brigsworth-Jones said, prying the cork out of a second bottle of wine with an army-issue knife. "It was a covert British operation. No one has heard of it."

They all stared at him.

"Well, it's over now. I can tell you without worrying too much."

"If it's covert, how do you know about it?" Erik asked.

"How do I know any of the things I know? People talk to me, always have."

"You should have become a spy instead of a cultural officer, sir," Dearborn said, drinking his wine from the bottle.

"How do you know I'm not? Maybe I am undercover here, in this unit. How else would I know about covert operations?"

There was a moment of silence and exchanged looks before Brigsworth-Jones erupted in hyena-type laughter.

"You chaps stick with me, I have some stories for you!"

Erik felt a rush of contented calmness seeing his mentor and friend so invigorated, so lively. This was the Brigsworth-Jones of old.

Operation Mincemeat, he told them, was aimed at fooling the Germans into thinking that the Allies were planning to invade Greece and

Sardinia, and not Sicily. A corpse was purposefully dumped so it would wash up on the shore near Huelva, Spain, where a German intelligence officer was known to be working. A briefcase was with the body and was full of falsified papers that would lead the Germans to believe they had found real British military documents detailing the invasion plans. It worked because Hitler transferred two Panzer divisions from Russia to Greece, and Sicily was not reinforced at all.

"This sounds a little far-fetched," Erik said. "It's a nice story though."

"Well, I thought you chaps might enjoy it…who knows if it's true," Brigsworth-Jones said, sharing a newly opened pack of Chesterfields.

"I've got another operation for you chaps, but this one I know is for real," he said, watching the young men's faces. "Operation Avalanche."

"Avalanche. What is that, sir?" Crawford asked while ducking from a flock of seagulls flying overhead. Erik made the mental note that Crawford would be a liability in any sort of battle.

"Operation Avalanche is the invasion of mainland Italy by Allied forces."

Crawford nearly spit out his wine. He had envisioned a longer stay in Sicily.

"When, sir?" Dearborn asked.

"Not sure yet. Soon."

"Will we be with them?" Erik asked.

"Well, that is something I need to discuss with you chaps. If we take the advice I am being given and wait until the main assault is over, we will most likely be less effective in our mission. Severe architectural damage will already have occurred…in other words, we will be too late."

"I don't see the alternative," Crawford said, uneasily.

"We go in with the main assault force," Erik answered. "We stay to the rear, behind the front lines, but we are there to immediately assess any damage, attempt to prevent looting by civilians or, dare I say it, by our own army."

No one spoke for several moments and the waves crashing on the rocks hissed in the background.

"That is my vote, sir," said Dearborn.

"I haven't fired a weapon since basic training," Crawford admitted.

"I haven't fired a weapon since 1918," Brigsworth-Jones said, answering a question that Erik had long wanted to ask. "We'll be joining the US Fifth Army. Like Bross said, we'll stay to the rear. He was a platoon commander and Dearborn here looks like he could fight the Germans by himself. I think we'll be alright."

"Yes sir," Crawford said, regaining some of his color. "If it gets really bad, I can always throw my typewriter at them."

Surprised initially by Crawford's self-depreciating comment, their laughter became so loud that the Sicilian family sitting fifty yards away turned to see what all the fuss was about.

Carinhall

It used to be called plundering. But today things have become more humane. In spite of that, I intend to plunder, and to do it thoroughly.
—*Hermann Göring*

ANKE WAS RELEASED from the sanatorium, into the custody of SS Oberleutnant Franz Bauer, on August 1, 1943. She had been incarcerated there for nearly eight months and subjected to a plethora of treatments, most of which involved a four-inch syringe. It was the opinion of the head psychiatrist, Dr. Emil Laroche, that she was not suffering from paranoid schizophrenia or from any other serious mental condition. He informed Bauer that, "Mademoiselle Junger is suffering from a consistently depressed mood and seems to have lost the will to go on. The death of her father clearly obsesses her and she speaks to him from time to time, as if he was still alive."

Since Anke was rarely in a state of complete consciousness, she was unaware that in the back garden of the hospital, in the Velleda Tower where Chateaubriand lived from 1807 to 1818, the well-known French artist Jean Fautriere was hiding from the Nazis and painting a series known as *The Hostages*. What he could hear, but Anke could not, were the sounds of gunshots coming from the nearby forest dubbed *la Vallee aux Loups* by Chateaubriand. For those "hostages" being shot by the Germans, it was indeed the valley of wolves.

Bauer's orders were to collect the Fräulein and escort her to Carinhall, Göring's hunting lodge north of Berlin. Bauer decided to view this particular errand as a personal favor to the Reichsmarschall and therefore as an indication that his efforts in Belgium had been well received. Besides, he was glad for an excuse to return to Germany, if only for a few days. His wife, Krista, was dying of tuberculosis and living with her parents near Würtzburg. The guilt he felt due to his long absences from her was grating on him. They had no children.

As they drove east, Bauer tried to chat about art, revisiting several of the subjects they had discussed vigorously in Ghent, but found the conversation painfully dull and was eventually sickened by the sound of his own voice. Anke spoke little, offering only "please" and "thank you" when he offered her sausage, cheese, and bread on their journey. She ate sparingly and sipped a cup of tea for hours, long past the point where it had turned cold. She sat, wrapped up in a blanket despite the heat, and stared out the window at the passing landscape like a city girl on her first trip to the country. She never asked where they were going and seemed not to recognize Bauer. He could not account for the transformation. The clever woman he remembered, and thought of too frequently, was missing.

They arrived at Carinhall at four in the morning and Bauer's orders were to wake the Reichsmarschall's private valet when they arrived. The valet, Lukas, showed them into the house, which was completely dark save a few candles flickering in sconces along the walls. Anke was placed in a large room and slipped immediately into the feather bed, still without a question as to where she was. Bauer spent the night in a room down the hall, not sleeping but trying to ascertain exactly what had thrown his little art historian off the rails.

ANKE WOKE THE NEXT MORNING with a terrible taste in her mouth. She quickly drank down the glass of water that sat on a table next to the bed. She was sweating uncontrollably and her clothes were stuck to her. She stripped off and dunked her head in the washbasin. The cool water soaked through her matted hair, dripped down her neck, and slid down her back. She stood, naked and sopping, in a room that's bizarreness she had just begun to notice.

The walls resembled that of a log cabin and in every available spot hung a set of stag antlers. Anke counted seven stags in this one bedroom alone. They stuck out like sharp barbs, caging her in. A large stone hearth took up one wall, while the others had wood benches with dark, embroidered cushions. This was obviously a hunting lodge and she guessed she was in Germany, or perhaps Austria. Anke found a towel and dried her hair as she peered out the window. She saw only a thick mass of evergreens. She turned around and noticed her suitcase sitting at the foot of the bed and opened it to find some, but not all, of her clothes. She quickly put on her lightweight yellow dress and black pumps. There were no stockings. Konrad had given her several pairs.

It all rushed over her in a huge, violent wave. Konrad...the warehouse...an infant's tiny dress. She began to shake.

"Fräulein?" Bauer asked gently, from outside the door. "Fräulein Junger? It is Oberleutant Bauer."

She had no idea what to do. She stood frozen in the middle of the room. The door opened slowly and a familiar face broke into a smile.

"How did you sleep? How are you feeling?"

Anke was horrified. "I...don't know what is going on. What is happening to me?"

"Shh. Fräulein. Sit down, let me explain."

She sank onto the floor, awkwardly. Bauer didn't want to upset her further, so he sat on the floor too. Close, but not too close.

"You were found on a road in south Paris in January. It is August now. Do you remember anything?"

She shook her head, crying now. He edged closer.

"Well, you were nearly frozen to death. You had a gash on your leg and no coat. You were taken to a hospital. I believe you were given some strong medications there. The Reichsmarschall always wanted to bring you here, to have you recuperate here, but the doctors made him wait until they came up with a diagnosis."

"Which was?" Anke asked.

"Sadness, depression, loss of interest in life. Grief for the loss of your father."

"Grief?"

"It's understandable, Anke. May I call you that?"

"The Reichsmarschall wants to rehabilitate me?"

"He thought you might like it here, because of his collection. He wants you to help catalogue it. I know…another catalogue."

"This is his home?" she asked, looking around again.

"This is Carinhall, his hunting lodge. He named it after his late wife, Carin. He keeps most of his art collection here."

"Where are we exactly?"

"Brandenburg. In the Schorfheide forest."

Anke was quiet for a few moments. She wiped her tears, realizing how ridiculous she must look. She smoothed her damp hair with her fingers and stuck her curls behind her ears. Bauer watched her.

"Do you know why I was found on that street in Paris?"

"It was assumed that you were left there, after some sort of accident. Your friend, Sgt. Konrad Ackerman, was questioned and he claimed he had no idea how you got so far out of Paris on your own, without a coat, and severely injured."

"Did you believe him?"

"I wasn't there. He was questioned by the Gestapo, I believe. In any event, he was transferred to the eastern front. He died at Stalingrad in March, I'm afraid."

Anke was shocked. "You transferred him because of me?"

"*I* didn't do anything."

Anke suddenly felt clearer than she had in a long time, though she didn't yet understand why. She could finally see straight.

"I didn't want him to die," she muttered softly. "I don't want anyone to die."

They were silent for a few moments, then Bauer got up and straightened his uniform.

"Are you feeling better?" he asked, looking down at her.

"Yes, much better, but I don't know why."

"It's the medication. You aren't on it anymore. I informed the Reichsmarschall of your unresponsive condition and he ordered me to contradict the doctors and take you off the medication."

"I've lost eight months?"

Bauer extended his hand to Anke, who accepted it.

"It hasn't been a particularly good eight months. The Russian campaign is going badly and the British and the Americans have invaded southern Italy. We will repel them, of course, but it is straining our resources. We need to start thinking, and seriously, of protecting art treasures the best we can—the Allies are notorious already for destroying everything, regardless of historical or artistic value."

This sounded wrong to Anke, but she held her tongue. Bauer had already shown himself to be drawn to conspiracy theories. A pulse of excitement sparked in her and goose bumps broke out on her damp skin. The Americans were finally in the picture. She thought of her father's friend, Friedrich Fassbinder, who had immigrated to America with his wife right after her father died. She received a kind letter from him soon after in which he offered her a place to live in New York should she want to go. That was right before the Germans invaded Belgium. She should have gone. She could have seen Erik. No, he's probably married by now, she decided. He probably has children.

"Anke? Is it okay if I call you that?"

"Yes," she said, returning.

"Shall we find some breakfast?"

They descended the main stairs, past six new antler mounts. They arrived at a long and wide breezeway, not one inch of which was not draped with fine tapestries, covered with the paintings of Old Masters or Impressionists, or adorned with classical and Renaissance sculpture.

"My God," Anke gawped.

"I've heard about his collection, but I've never actually seen it," Bauer said, peering at a modern bust of Hitler that was horrendously placed next to a neoclassical statue of Venus.

"These are Gobelin tapestries," Anke said, further down the hall.

"Forgive me, but I am missing the reference," he said, joining her.

"The Gobelins were a family of dyers in Paris. They provided tapestries and other types of textiles to the French royal families from the middle of the fifteenth century until the end of the seventeenth. These are extremely rare. I wonder how he got these?"

"He bought them, Anke, just like anyone else." He grasped her arm. "Please don't forget our arrangement. It is the same now as it always has been."

He released her quickly with a sheepish look. She now understood Göring's warning about Bauer. The all too familiar chill scaled her spine but she decided to play along, yet again. She'd seen her father last night and that was a great comfort.

The main salon made the breezeway look downright sparse. It was now obvious that Göring intended Carinhall to be a museum that doubled as a hunting lodge, and not the other way around. The dark wall panels, dozens of mounted antlers, heavily embroidered sofas and old-fashioned country cottage windows seemed nothing short of grotesque when juxtaposed with choice pieces from the studios of Degas, Titian, and Pieter Bruegel the Elder. Woodsy and masculine fought against the delicate and serene beauty of one particular work, which Anke was overwhelmed to be standing in front of.

"This is a Magdalene portrait by the Master of the Magdalene Mansi Legend," she said, her eyes glassy.

"Who?" Bauer asked.

"His name is not known, though there are several theories. He was southern Netherlandish, working in the early sixteenth century. He painted, most often, scenes from the life of Mary Magdalene. His images were sometimes based on drawings and sketches by Dürer, which explains why the Reichsmarschall would want to own one, assuming he knows that. This piece is as fine an example as I have ever seen. Look at her eyes and the roundness of her belly."

"She looks pregnant."

"That's just how women's dresses were painted in that period, like in the Arnolfini portrait by van Eyck. This reminds me of van Eyck, actually."

"Yes, me too. She's holding the lid to her ointment jar up, like she is blessing someone…almost Christlike."

Anke, despite everything, could not help feeling proud of Bauer for a fleeting moment before reality returned. She turned her attention to a painting that Göring had displayed in a high-profile position in the middle of the room, with a brass light mounted on the wall to illuminate it. It was a depiction of Christ blessing a woman, with two skeptical men looking on.

"He seems to really like this one," she said, standing only inches away from it, then stepping back, just as Göring always did at the Jeu de Paume.

"I don't recognize it," Bauer admitted.

"Neither do I. The technique seems rudimentary. Not the work of a master."

"There's almost no detail whatsoever."

"None," she agreed, shaking her head.

A flurry of activity in the next room put a halt to their leisurely musings. A tall, wiry woman came flying through an arched doorway, followed by the valet, Lukas, who moved slowly and deliberately to show that he held his post in high esteem.

"Herr Reichsmarschall has returned from Berlin," Lukas announced. "Please, may I show you both into the breakfast room?"

They followed him, and the wiry woman, through a series of rooms furnished to excess with priceless art. There was little time to stop and examine, but Anke was sure she passed several Bouchers, a Fragonard, and the Memling *Madonna with Child*. She recognized these paintings in particular because she had catalogued them at the Jeu de Paume. They were all from the collections of Andre Seligmann and Paul Rosenberg. The Magdalene portrait, she was quite sure, was from the collection of the Dutch art dealer Jacques Goudstikker, also Jewish.

When they finally arrived at the breakfast room, which seemed a mile away from the main salon, Göring was already seated and buttering toast. He stood as they walked in and was immediately saluted by Bauer.

"Yes, Heil Hitler. Good to see you Bauer! I see you have brought our little Fräulein back from Paris, well done. You look well enough, Fräulein Junger, I would say!"

"I am fine, Herr Reichsmarschall, thank you."

"No need for thanks, not at all. Sit down and eat something. I hate to eat alone and my wife is taking the waters at Baden-Baden with her mother. They do it twice a year and swear by it. Have you ever been, Fräulein?"

"Yes, my father took me, several times. He enjoyed it very much."

Göring smiled and stuffed a boiled egg into his mouth. Bauer was ravenous and built a mountainous sandwich from the thick bread, black forest ham, and Munster that sat on an enormous platter in the middle of the table.

"You did an excellent job on your Krakow errand, before you fell ill," Göring said pleasantly. "It's a pity they didn't stay in Berlin for long."

Anke felt the heat of blood rushing to her face. "You mean the paintings, the Raphael, the Rembrandt, and the da Vinci?"

"So you did open them! I knew you would," Göring said smiling and sawing at his sausage. "Frank, excuse me, Herr Governor of Poland, threw a fit and demanded they be returned to him so he could hang them in his office. He's got the Führer dazzled, it seems. I was going to send you to return them, but you were…indisposed."

Anke imagined the delicate *Lady with an Ermine* hanging in Frank's office, over the heating vent. The Reichsmarschall wasn't the only Nazi intent on enriching his own art collection, she knew. She just hadn't pegged Frank as one of them. He seemed too…brutal.

"So, what do you think of my collection?"

"It's…quite impressive," she said, trying not to sound too excited.

"Did you see the Vermeer?"

"Which Vermeer? I don't think we saw…."

"*Christ with the Woman Taken in Adultery.* It's hanging in the middle of the main salon. You couldn't have missed it."

Bauer and Anke exchanged looks. His told her to be silent.

"It's exquisite, Herr Reichsmarschall. Fräulein Junger commented on how interesting it was."

If that is a Vermeer, then I'm a Nazi, she thought while busying herself with her napkin and cutlery.

Careful, liebling.

The valet returned a moment later with a telegram for Göring.

"Open it for me, Lukas, my hands are greasy."

The valet laid the opened telegram in front of the Reichsmarschall, who peered down at it with squinty eyes. Anke shrieked when Göring brought both fists down on the table at once, upsetting most of the crockery.

"Forgive me, Fräulein…but I've just received some rather unfortunate news."

"Your Vermeer's a fake?" Anke *almost* said, but swallowed it down.

Göring turned to Bauer, who sat at attention and gulped down his bite quickly.

"Mussolini has been arrested. The Italians are changing sides."

"Because of Sicily, sir? Surely…." Bauer began.

"Who knows why? They are imbeciles. We never should have trusted them. The Führer will be furious. I need to go to Berlin immediately."

This declaration sent the valet and the wiry woman, who was lurking outside the breakfast room, scrambling away barking orders to other members of the household staff.

Göring rose, his girth seemingly larger than ever, and looked down at Anke.

"I'd like you to remain here, Fräulein. My wife will be home soon to keep you company. I will send you instructions shortly. Bauer, return to Ghent and wrap up. We are going to need you in Italy to protect cultural items from the capitalist bastards. I'll speak to Himmler in Berlin and I'm sure he'll approve."

Bauer stood and saluted while Göring took a last swig from his coffee cup. For a moment, the stag antlers mounted directly above him seemed to connect to his head, like Devil's horns. Anke, unsure of what to do, cut a piece of sausage from her plate and forced it down.

"I killed that myself," Göring said proudly.

Anke nodded and faked a smile. She could taste the blood.

12

The Venus Fixers

Here is this beautiful country [Italy] suffering the worst horrors of war, with the largest part still in the cruel and vengeful grip of the Nazis, and with a hideous prospect of the red-hot rake of the battle line being drawn from sea to sea right up the whole length of the peninsula.
—*Winston Churchill*

NOT ONLY HAD *il Duce* been arrested, but his replacement, Marshal Pietro Badoglio, had dissolved the Italian Fascist Party and negotiated a truce with the Allies. Before Mussolini could be handed over to the Americans, as the truce stipulated, he was liberated from his house arrest at the Campo Imperatore hotel in the Apennine Mountains by a unit of *Fallschirmjäger* (German paratroopers) and whisked to Hitler's bunker in East Prussia. When Mussolini returned to Italy, it was as the puppet head of the newly formed Italian Socialist Republic which set up its headquarters at Gargnano, on Lake Garda. Meanwhile, the irate Hitler demanded that all who had opposed *il Duce* be executed, the Vatican be seized along with the rest of Rome, and the royal family be arrested. The latter two were deemed too difficult from a public relations standpoint and never came to pass. The king and Marshal Badoglio fled to Rome, leaving the Italian army without certainty about which side they were fighting for.

In Naples, there was no electricity or water. The *Carabinieri*, the Italian police service, had been dissolved by the Germans, which left little security at the city's museums and archives. The main university library had been deliberately burned by the Germans in retaliation for partisan activity in the city. Fifty thousand volumes were incinerated in Naples, while an additional 80,000 were ignited by the Germans at an archive in Nola, to the east. This wanton destruction came as a frightening surprise to the Italians who had spent days negotiating with the Germans on behalf of their cultural assets. It also happened just hours before Erik Brossler, Owen Brigsworth-Jones, Tom Dearborn, and Marshall Crawford drove into Naples at the rear of the Seventh Armored Division of the US Fifth Army, on October 1.

AFTER ERIK'S FIRST FORTY-EIGHT HOURS in Naples, he sat down exhausted and yet unable to sleep, to write to his father.

Papa,

Saluti da Napoli! I would love to tell you that everything is going to plan, but I cannot begin to describe to you the scene here. I have been utterly useless thus far, I can assure you of that. The city encountered much damage before we arrived, including the destruction of the university library and nearly all its contents. Now I see rare birds from the zoological collection riding around in US Jeeps. The archaeological collections have been infiltrated as well and decades of work undone. The Italians are desperate and furious, as they should be. I didn't expect such disregard from my own side and I've been disgusted by it. Even at the highest level, the disrespect is eyebrow raising. I can't send details, but let's say that the finest of Neapolitan art is sharing its quarters with American officers, of the highest rank possible. Those of lower ranks have ripped brocades and tapestries right off the walls. Nobody is listening to us and most are downright hostile. Brigsworth-Jones told me to expect this and that it will get better as the organization increases. Naples, he said, will bear the brunt.

I have, however, heard some stories to ease my pain somewhat. At Sorbo Serpico, the townswomen (the men are in the army) carried seventeen crates of paintings from the church up into the hills and hid them from the Germans. Due to the German retreat, those paintings are now safe. I have not yet had a chance to examine them, but just hearing the story gave me strength. I hope to God that it is true.

I've heard rumors that you have been instrumental in sending more Monuments Men over here, though I imagine they are still in Sicily or North Africa at this moment. We desperately need them on the mainland, now.

Give my love to mother and I do hope she is feeling better. Please do not show her this letter, I am sending another addressed to her with less despair.

Your loving son,

Lt. Erik Brossler, Monuments, Fine Arts, and Archives Division, US Fifth Army

October 3, 1943

ON OCTOBER 13, 1943, Italy declared war on Nazi Germany and the army again had an enemy. In fact, they had an enemy who had been funneling troops and supplies into Italy for weeks and who, at this point, had reoccupied most of the country north of Naples. This was going to be a costly and difficult campaign and the Italians feared there might be little of their beautiful land left over when the fighting was done.

Erik and Brigsworth-Jones shared this fear and sent Dearborn and Crawford all over Allied territory putting up posters:

TO ALLIED FORCES

NATIONAL MONUMENT

OUT OF BOUNDS

OFF LIMITS

IT IS STRICTLY FORBIDDEN TO REMOVE STONE OR ANY OTHER MATERIAL
FROM THIS SITE

SOUVENIR HUNTING, WRITING ON WALLS OR DAMAGE IN ANY FORM
WILL BE DEALT WITH AS MILITARY OFFENCES

DWIGHT D. EISENHOWER

GENERAL,

SUPREME COMMANDER,

ALLIED EXPEDITIONARY FORCE

BY ORDER OF
O. BRIGSWORTH-JONES
SQDN. LDR., MFAA

Special guards were placed at sites like Paestum, southeast of Naples, which boasted a number of temples built in the sixth-century BC. But with the minute number of Monuments Men actually on the scene, guards and posters did very little to sway the masses of American soldiers and support personnel to their way of thinking. Reports of looted coin collections, books, and *objets d'art* came in constantly. The ruins at Pompeii were vandalized, though not extensively. There was even a persistent rumor that Eisenhower himself, in a hunting lodge at the Palace of Caserta, controlled the rodent population by shooting them with his pistol. Erik insisted that this was a falsehood, since Eisenhower would never shoot his weapon inside a treasured building like those at Caserta, but Brigsworth-Jones wasn't so sure. He made a few angry and somewhat frantic calls to London, and Erik sent off his first full report to the Roberts Commission in Washington, outlining each and every Allied misstep regarding art and architecture. Still reeling from the negative press about the botched Allied bombing of Rome, which destroyed the basilica of San Lorenzo Fuori le Mure, the Allies were looking for ways to assure the world that they would be a conquering, but not a pillaging force. Thus, slowly, a new protective spirit emerged, as did the following directive from Eisenhower:

> IF WE HAVE TO CHOOSE BETWEEN DESTROYING A FAMOUS BUILDING AND SACRIFICING MORE OF OUR OWN MEN, THEN OUR MEN'S LIVES COUNT INFINITELY MORE AND THE BUILDINGS MUST GO. BUT THE CHOICE IS NOT ALWAYS SO CLEAR CUT AS THAT. IN MANY CASES THE MONUMENTS CAN BE SPARED WITHOUT ANY DETRIMENT TO OPERATIONAL NEEDS. NOTHING CAN STAND AGAINST THE ARGUMENT OF MILITARY NECESSITY. THAT IS AN ACCEPTED PRINCIPLE. BUT THE PHRASE "MILITARY NECESSITY" IS SOMETIMES USED WHERE IT WOULD BE MORE TRUTHFUL TO SPEAK OF MILITARY CONVENIENCE OR EVEN OF PERSONAL CONVENIENCE. I DO NOT WANT IT TO CLOAK SLACKNESS OR INDIFFERENCE.

> IT IS A RESPONSIBILITY OF HIGHER COMMANDERS TO DETERMINE THROUGH A.M.G. OFFICERS THE LOCATIONS OF HISTORICAL MONUMENTS WHETHER THEY BE IMMEDIATELY AHEAD OF OUR FRONT LINES OR IN AREAS OCCUPIED BY US. THIS INFORMATION PASSED TO LOWER ECHELONS THROUGH NORMAL CHANNELS PLACES THE RESPONSIBILITY ON ALL COMMANDERS OF COMPLYING WITH THE SPIRIT OF THIS LETTER.

This directive worked better than Erik thought it would. The whole monuments division was re-energized and the units of monuments officers still waiting in Palermo were immediately sent to Naples. Overnight, Erik's operation went from four to twenty-four, though they were divided up and attached to several different battalions. Erik immediately had small, pocketsize booklets made up of important historical monuments, buildings, and works of art in each area that the front-line divisions would encounter as they drove north toward Rome. The lists that he had begun at his parents' dining room table more than three years ago were now in the pockets of all officers and NCOs.

Needless to say, David Brossler received another letter from his son in December.

Papa,

Saluti de Cassino! We are in pursuit of the Germans, all hopes are we will be in Rome by the New Year. The situation here, though still confusing and chaotic, is much improved since my last letter. General Eisenhower issued a strong directive that seems to have taken hold. The soldiers now call us "the Venus Fixers" rather than whatever insult they could come up with. I've noticed a real spirit of cooperation when it comes to clearing up a bombed church (and there are plenty of those) or gathering the fragments of a broken statue, etc. Interestingly, all paintings and pieces of art are referred to as "Michelangelos" by the rank and file. I'm sure you would prefer they were called "Van Goghs," but we are in Italy!

I still have my usual gripes about the Allied HQ (at the Palace of Naples) and the installation of not only a bar, but an officers' club and a cafeteria. This, however, I will never change and so I have decided not to speak of it again, except to you of course.

We now head straight into the Gustav Line, which the Germans have dug in around the monastery of Monte Cassino—perched on top of the mountain itself. I don't need to tell you what ancient and medieval treasures lie inside the abbey, but in addition, many of the pieces from the Neapolitan collections were moved to the abbey months ago. I have some concerns that the Germans will loot this stash, but I won't know if they did or did not until we get there, so there is little I can do but wait.

I will write again as soon as I can. Give all my love to mother.

Lt. Erik Brossler, MFAA Division

December 12, 1943

Years later, David Brossler would return to this letter and wonder how either of them could have seen it coming.

13

Monte Cassino

*Public discussion of this subject [the monastery] has started off on
the wrong foot, and people are getting badly confused about it...the issue is now viewed as one between dead matter and young living bodies.*
                                                            —*John Maynard Keynes*

BAUER HAD ARRIVED in Italy in October as a newly promoted *ObergruppenFührer* SS and with a new title, Special SS Cultural Liaison.
He was immediately attached to the Hermann Göring Panzer Division,
part of the German Tenth Army commanded by Field Marshall Albert
Kesselring. Bauer was very aware that his promotion was entirely due
to a misguided notion, harbored by the Reichsmarschall, that he was
Anke Junger's lover. What Bauer could not decide was whether or not
Göring himself had a romantic interest in Anke and had therefore
sent him to Italy expressly to have her to himself. This question preoccupied him and he found it hard to concentrate on his duties, which
were vaguely described to him in a cable from Göring that arrived a
day ahead of him at the division's headquarters in Spoleto.

He was informed that he was to see to the "evacuation" of all art
treasures housed at the Abbey of Monte Cassino, which numbered in
the thousands. He learned several hours later that not only were they to
take the monastery's own works of art, but also the crates from Naples,
which contained the elite of the city's art collections. After convincing the skeptical abbot that he only desired to protect the art from the
brutal Allied advance, Bauer hired Italian civilians to pack the items,

which took three weeks. He then rode in the lead truck as the convoy winded its way up and down the serpentine dirt roads that led from the monastery northward across a range of mountains to Spoleto.

As the abbot watched the trucks recede into the mountain mist, he uttered a curse, which he later regretted. His frustration was shared by most in the Italian art community, as well as many within the Catholic hierarchy. The Germans were their occupiers now and the lust for art shown by the Nazis had not gone unnoticed. A massive Italian effort had been underway for weeks to convince the Vatican to accept and house all displaced Italian art from a number of disparate repositories, but this agreement was not solidified until early November. Therefore, the monastery's impressive collection, including works by da Vinci, Titian, and Raphael as well as the remains of St. Benedict himself, were now in German hands and would not, the abbot feared, find their way to the Vatican without the interference of the Allies. Not at all surprising, after the stories he had heard, was the fact that the division that transported these items over hundreds of miles during an all-out Allied offensive was named for Hermann Göring.

"THIS IS RIDICULOUS," Erik said, pacing back and forth in the large tent where the monument officers were working. "Everyone is now fixated on the monastery. We don't even know if the Germans are in there!"

"Allied airborne recon have consistently reported German vehicles up at the monastery," Brigsworth-Jones replied testily, a Chesterfield dangling from his lips as he sat on a rickety chair inspecting a pile of mail from London. "What are we expected to think?"

"Well, they may be up there, using it as an observation post... but...."

"But what? Look at this press. *The New York Times* is reporting that the monastery is clearly occupied by the Germans, but that we don't want to bomb it because it is too precious. Do you think that all those American parents over there, reading that, think their sons are less precious than a building?"

"Of course not, but...."

"No, you be quiet. Listen to me. Listen to what was said in Parliament the other day," Brigsworth-Jones donned his glasses, becoming the professor again as he picked up a cable from London. "The Arch-bishop of Canterbury and the Bishop of Chichester stood in the House of Lords and asked the Allied armies not to bomb 'the lovely cities, towns, and villages of Italy.' They don't have any idea what is going on here. We are losing thousands of men."

"Destroying that building will not change that! Kesselring has said, several times, that his army is not seeking cover in the monastery."

"You believe him? I dismiss anything a German says, immediately. What makes you think he's genuine?"

Erik paused, unsure how to proceed. He was rarely reminded of his German background anymore, he felt as American as the next guy. His accent, with effort, was almost unnoticeable now. Those who did pick up on it could not identify it, they just thought he sounded a little different. How could he explain that he felt sure that a Field Marshall like Kesselring would, first, not use an ancient monastery as a shield and second, not lie about it?

"I don't know how to explain it," Erik said, finally. He sat on a cot, defeated.

"Look, chap. The uncanny fact that you spent your childhood in the same country where these bastards come from amazes me every day. You are like a son to me; you know that. What I am telling you is that in this instance, in this particular case, we need to put the needs of the boys first. We need to break this line in order to get to Rome. Beyond Rome, there is Florence. You know full well what we will find in Florence. Christ chap, Florence!"

Erik nodded, giving in. This wasn't the first time they had argued about this. Erik went to the tent opening and looked up, for the hun-dredth time, at the majestic monastery. The Benedictines had erected their abbey on the site of a temple of Apollo, around 529 AD. When they began to build, they first destroyed the altar of Apollo, not want-ing any pagan remnants on their new Christian site. They dedicated the monastery to John the Baptist and from here Benedict, the originator of the Benedictine Order of monks, wrote the "Benedictine Rule" that remains one of the most important foundations of monasticism. The abbey was sacked and rebuilt several times, but the current building was mainly of the thirteenth century, with several areas and much of the stone foundation dating back much further. Being Jewish, Erik felt little spiritual connection to the site. As a scholar of medieval art, he felt like it was his home.

OVER THE NEXT FEW DAYS, the battle lines were drawn within the Allied high command. The British and the New Zealanders, the latter preparing another attempt to take the mountain in concert with several Indian divisions, were in favor of bombing the abbey. The Americans and the French were against it. Finally, on Feb 13, General Sir Harold Alexander, Commander of Allied Forces in Italy, gave the order to destroy the monastery. Tons of leaflets were dropped by Allied planes onto the abbey to warn the monks and civilians who were sheltering inside to evacuate immediately. Not all did and many, the actual number is unknown, died when the bombs fell the next day. The majority of the structure was reduced to ruins, which the Germans then occupied and used as an effective defense against further attacks. It took only hours for the Allied commanders to realize that the German troops had not been in the monastery, but entrenched on the mountainside around it and therefore not particularly affected by the precision bombing raids.

The elderly abbot, along with several surviving monks, and a number of orphaned children and local villagers, crept out of the detritus after a day or two living in the deep, cavernous crypt. They wandered, dazed, down the mountain road where they were given medical attention by the Germans. On the other side of Monte Cassino, Erik Brossler wept at the edge of the Allied encampment, alone, in a cluster of cypress trees.

14

Neuschwanstein

Opera, next to Gothic architecture, is one of the strangest inventions of Western man. It could not have been foreseen by any logical process.
—*Lord Kenneth Clark*

BAUER WAS PLEASANTLY SURPRISED to receive orders to report to Göring in Berlin. In late April 1944, he found himself at a meeting at the Reichstag, which Hitler attended for about ten minutes, marking only the second time he had been in the same room with the Führer. The honor was brief and in truth, Bauer was underwhelmed by both Hitler's words and appearance. Their immortal leader seemed quite mortal, looking frail and appearing nervous at the meeting. The future of Italy's cities was the topic, but few concrete decisions were reached, other than that Florence should be spared from destruction. Hitler's pronouncements were vague at best, downright incomprehensible at worst. Göring was also present and sat to Hitler's immediate left, wearing a bored and sullen expression.

After the meeting, Göring cornered Bauer in the long hallway outside the main meeting room.

"That was pointless," Göring remarked, looking around to make sure he wasn't overheard.

Bauer nodded and smiled, but did not comment.

"Did you bring the newsreels, like I asked?"

"Of course, Herr Reichsmarschall."

"Well, let's go see our little Fräulein then. She's still at Carinhall, though I don't know how long I can keep her there. She's catalogued the whole place, twice."

"I'm sure she has," Bauer said, grinning. He followed Göring outside to an awaiting car.

"I was saddened to hear about your wife's death, Bauer," Göring said as they drove north, out of Berlin.

"Thank you, Herr Reichsmarschall. It was a blessing in the end. She was in a great deal of pain and discomfort."

"Yes…tuberculosis. Terrible disease. Well, my condolences."

"Your wife sent a lovely note and flowers."

"Ah, my Emmy. She has a big heart. She has become quite attached to Fräulein Junger, I should tell you. I think she would be upset if I sent her away."

"Where would you send her, if I may ask?"

"Not sure. Any suggestions?"

"I think they have their hands full at Neuschwanstein. She'd be a big help…," he trailed off when he saw the look on the Reichsmarschall's face.

"I find it interesting, Bauer, that you would send her there. Have you told her about the van Eyck?"

Bauer shifted uncomfortably. He should have known Göring would know everything.

"No, I haven't told her. I was ordered to keep it a secret."

"Good man," Göring said, staring out the window. "Send her where you like…she can't do any harm at this point."

Bauer nodded, relieved. The order to remove the Ghent Altarpiece from Pau in France and transfer it directly to the castle of Neuschwanstein came from Hitler himself and circumvented Göring and his art designs completely. Technically Bauer worked for Himmler, so Göring couldn't say much about it, although many SS art- and cultural-related units reported to Göring in a semiofficial manner, as a courtesy. The ERR did the same thing. Bauer couldn't tell Anke any of this, though he desperately wanted to. He could at least send her in the right direction. Then, it would be up to her.

When they arrived at Carinhall, Lukas the valet ran alongside the car as it pulled into the giant pebbled driveway, opening the door the instant the engine quit.

"Welcome, Herr Reichsmarschall!"

"Thank you, Lukas. Run and find Fräulein Junger for us, will you? And also my wife, Lukas. We will be in the projection room."

Göring led Bauer through a series of rooms on the backside of the lodge, far from the grand salon that he and Anke had wandered through back in August. Bauer noted with amusement the multitudes of stag mounts, remembering how Anke had scoffed at their close proximity to the priceless masterpieces Göring had amassed. He found himself sweating with anticipation and a nervous pit rolled around in his stomach.

They reached the projection room, which was sparsely furnished and had a large screen erected against one wall. Göring settled himself in a sturdy leather chair and began threading the film reel through the projector that sat on what looked like a Japanese lacquered table. A moment later, Mrs. Emmy Göring entered the room, breezy in a yellow floral dress, followed by Anke, who had gained a little weight and looked significantly healthier than when Bauer had last seen her.

"Hello my dear," Emmy said to her husband, patting him on the shoulder, a gesture he returned with a smile.

"I've brought back your friend, Fräulein. Bauer has much to tell you about his adventures in Italy. I think you will be much impressed."

Bauer registered this with pleasure. The Reichsmarschall was most certainly on his side. He sat on the leather divan next to Anke and suddenly felt as if he was on a first date. She looked at him with a combination of familiarity and skepticism. He then remembered his threats, the *mattentarts*, the discussion of her father. He wished he could take back the comments he had made about the Arma Christi. He had been following a script, a script that was unraveling rather fast now. The blood rushed to his face and he quickly turned it to the screen in front of them as Göring began the newsreel.

ALLIED ATTACK ON ABBEY OF MONTE CASSINO.

The ruins of the monastery still smoking, German soldiers were shown assisting civilians, carrying injured children, and helping monks into the back of a open-top truck.

HERMANN GÖRING PANZER DIVISION SAVED PRICELESS WORKS OF ITALIAN
ART FROM MONTE CASSINO AND SAW THEM SAFELY TO THE VATICAN IN
ROME.

Bauer himself was shown organizing the unloading of trucks in front
of a cheering crowd in Rome. Another shot of Bauer and various
other officers in front of the Colosseum, all in their best uniforms.
Several people were making speeches; the crowd roared its approval.

ALLIED DESTRUCTION IS TOTAL AND UNRELENTING. CULTURAL ITEMS ARE
SMASHED IN THEIR WAKE.

The ruins of several churches were shown, with German troops
helpfully repairing pews, sweeping broken glass, and carrying large
pieces of stone around. Anke noted Bauer's expression as he watched
and it was not what she had expected.

The reel ended and the room was dark for a moment, despite it
being midday. Emmy opened the heavy drapes and the spring light
poured in, illuminating Göring, who was rewinding the reel studiously.
He and Emmy then declared it was time for lunch and disappeared out
the door, without an official invitation to Bauer and Anke. They sat in
silence for a few moments; the clanking of trays in the distance.

"How have you been?" he asked.

"Better, thank you."

"No visits from the doctors, I trust?"

"No, none."

"I've thought about you, quite often."

"I was sorry to hear about your wife."

"Yes, thank you."

"The Reichsmarschall had mentioned something to me, about her
being ill, when were in Paris, before I was...."

"Yes, everyone knew. She was ill for years."

"I'm sorry."

"Thank you."

"Have you found the missing panel from the Ghent Altarpiece yet?"

Bauer laughed. "I can't believe I said all that to you. I was under
orders, you understand."

"I do."

"There are lots of theories in the SS."

"I realize that. I heard about some intensive archaeological digs in North Africa."

"Yes. Looking for clues, I suppose."

"Clues to what?"

"Ancient Aryans I think. I'm not sure anymore."

She smiled. He inched closer to her. She didn't move, but turned to look at him. His hand found her left knee, under the thick cotton of her dark skirt. She flinched, but did not protest. He pulled her toward him, kissing her gently on the neck, then on the mouth. The feeling she recalled, from the first time with Niels, returned with a greater force this time. Konrad had never elicited this sensation but she was too numb to notice at the time.

They lay back on the divan, his hands fumbling under her slip, releasing any and all clasps he encountered. Her breath was heavy, which made him feel powerful. He made love to her the way he had never once made love to his wife, who was fragile from the moment he married her. Anke's strong legs wrapped around him as she struggled to get his uniform jacket off, button after button. Bauer moaned loudly and Anke whispered to him that the door was still open. He collapsed on top of her, crushing her down into the soft leather. Anke relaxed under the weight, smelling the soap from his brown hair and wrapping her fingers in it. They lay like this for some time, their bodies entwined, his head resting on her breasts.

"IF YOU THINK I DID that because of a newsreel, you are wrong," Anke said, as she and Bauer sat by the pond that evening.

"I told the Reichsmarschall you wouldn't be so easily impressed," Bauer said, smiling at her.

"Why did he bring you back here?"

"I think he's a romantic."

"That's obvious."

They both laughed. He kissed her again and gently brushed his fingers across her collarbone, tracing a pattern up her throat to her chin.

"He's not just a romantic," she said, looking him in the eye. "He's also an art collector. Do you mean to tell me that he sent you to Italy, to liaise with the Panzer division named for him, in order to rescue art, deliver it to the Vatican, and take nothing for himself? Nothing for the Fatherland?"

Bauer grimaced, then shrugged. "I didn't say that."

"So, what did he take?"

"*He* didn't take anything."

"What did you take, then?"

"Nothing originally from Monte Cassino, if that's what you are suggesting. There were hundreds of crates being stored there from the museums of Naples. They never thought the Allies would bomb the abbey. Neither did I. Anyway, let's just say that when everything was evacuated, some of the crates never made it to the Vatican."

"Where are they?"

"I'll tell you if you admit you drove the Ghent Altarpiece to Pau."

"I don't need to admit it. You know I did. Niels Maarten told you."

"No. He never mentioned your name. I lied about that."

Anke blanched. "What do you mean? How did you know about me then?"

"We asked the janitor."

"The janitor? What janitor?" she stopped abruptly and put a hand across her mouth. *Oh God. Jan from St. Bavo's.*

"Did you...torture him?"

"Absolutely not! He told us everything immediately. All I had to do was ask."

Anke stood, away from him. She remembered how Jan had always called her *Fräulein*, which was odd for a Belgian man. Was he a Nazi sympathizer the entire time?

Bauer stood and took her hands in his. "Anke, this is all behind us now. You are with me, or not, of your own free will. I have no power over you. Face it, you are a favorite of the Reichsmarschall. You couldn't be more safe."

"What did you take from that shipment in Italy?"

"Fifteen crates. I don't know what was in them, other than they were from the Neapolitan museums. They were sent to Berlin."

"Those cheering crowds...staged?"

Bauer rolled his eyes. "Staged? Not exactly. But not completely authentic either. It's a propaganda film, Anke. It's for the German people."

"Yes, of course. To show that the Wehrmacht and the SS are protecting art from the Allies. All the while, Göring slips fifteen crates of priceless treasure out of the country, while the Romans cheer his Panzer division. Brilliant."

"It is, rather," Bauer admitted with a smirk, lighting a Roth-Handle cigarette and offering the pack to Anke.

"It's disgusting, and I am having a hard time understanding why you don't care," Anke spat back, waving him off.

"Anke, it is my job to do as I am ordered. I am a soldier. You are not; you are a civilian. You can do as you like, but I don't suggest you anger the Reichsmarschall. Your cushy life could disappear and you could find yourself in a much more…uncomfortable place."

"Dachau? Like my father?"

"I didn't say that. I wouldn't let them send you there."

"Maybe that's where I belong," she said, plopping down on the grass. "I feel like I've been living on borrowed time, for years now. I don't know what to do anymore."

"You don't belong there, Anke. Neither did your father. If the Reichsmarschall had been aware, I am sure he would have had him released immediately. It was an oversight, an overreaction by someone in the Gestapo. It never should have happened and it has poisoned you against us."

I was poisoned because you are all poisonous, she thought. Yet, she felt Franz Bauer was not the worst of the worst. She walked toward him and allowed him to wrap his arms around her legs.

"I know I was heavy-handed at the beginning and I know I misled you," he said, looking up at her. "I didn't know you then, I didn't love you. Now, I do. I would do anything for you. Tell me what to do."

Anke thought about this for a moment, both excited and apprehensive about the power she had over him. She thought of asking about *M-Aktion*, to see what he knew. She stopped short because she realized she wasn't ready to know what he knew. She wanted to keep him, a little longer.

"Get me out of here," she whispered, then bent down to kiss him.

∾

THREE DAYS LATER, Anke left Carinhall in one of Göring's cars. She was driven south first to Leipzig, then to Nuremburg, then to Ulm (she asked the driver to bypass Munich) and finally to Füssen, near the Austrian border.

Bauer had gone to Berlin the day before, to attend several meetings before returning to Italy. He had told Anke only that many of the looted works from the Jeu de Paume, those that didn't end up at Carinhall, had been sent to Mad King Ludwig's enormous fantasy castle in the Bavarian Alps. He knew she wanted to follow the art.

As she sat in the car, she wondered yet again...was she losing her mind? She wasn't sure. Fitting that she was now headed to the famous and thoroughly over-the-top castle of King Ludwig II, the ruler of Germany in the later nineteenth century. Ludwig was a known oddball who was obsessed with the composer Richard Wagner. He had gigantic murals painted all over the castle, depicting scenes from Wagner's operas. The composer's affair with the wife of one of Germany's premier orchestral conductors eventually forced him into exile in Switzerland and it was rumored that the king considered abdicating in order to follow his idol.

As they approached Neuschwanstein, she felt she was she driving into a world dominated by the fantastic. The castle was only accessible by a steep road, which she imagined was nearly impassable in snow. On this day, only the bottom half of the castle was visible, the upper regions, including the four pointy turrets, were cloaked in a heavy mist. A forest of fir trees encircled Neuschwanstein and separated it from the glassy lake that ran right into the foothills of the Bavarian Alps. To say the least, the setting was extraordinary.

The driver told Anke that they had gone as far as they could on four wheels and opened the door for her. She took her suitcase and walked up the uneven stone steps to the main entrance, the car receding back down the hill behind her. Several women emerged from a small side door and skipped lithely down the steps, paying Anke absolutely no notice.

"Fräulein Junger?" a matronly voice called out from the main door, which Anke now realized was ajar.

She walked through and into the main gatehouse, where a woman stood waiting for her. She had the look of a librarian, with the posture of a drill sergeant.

"This way, if you please, Fräulein."

Anke followed her through a number of rooms, which were opulently furnished with wall paintings and gilded mirrors, but most of the furniture was covered with white sheets, graying now from the dust. King Ludwig had spared no expense on his castle, invoking all the majesty and chivalry of the medieval German knights he idolized. This glorification of the Middle Ages was very common in the late nineteenth century and inspired an entire genre of painting and decoration known as "Neo-Gothic." If the Germanic Neo-Gothic movement had a spiritual and ancestral home, it was Neuschwanstein.

They went through no less than six rooms, two secret passageways, and up three steep, spiral staircases before arriving in a small room with an army-issue cot and a tiny window looking down on the gatehouse.

"This is all we can provide at the moment. Your arrival was...very last minute."

"I appreciate you accommodating me, Frau...."

"Kruger. Frau Kruger. I am facilities operator here. You will be cataloguing, am I correct?"

"Yes. Shall I start right away?"

"I believe they need you in room nine, which was the great upper hall in King Ludwig's time. Follow me."

Anke deposited her suitcase on the cot and they retraced their steps to a point, then went up another, much grander staircase. When they arrived in the upper hall, Anke saw that it was stacked, floor to ceiling, with crates of paintings. Special racks had been built to hold them, not unlike the luggage racks on the Munich trams. Five people were sitting at desks and two of them were typing with gusto.

"Jürgen, this is the new art historian, Fräulein Junger. Please see to it that she has what she needs," Frau Kruger said, before disappearing through a door opposite the one they had come through. Anke received a few nods, but little else. Jürgen showed her to a table covered with notebooks, which he brushed aside.

"Please, you can sit here, Fräulein. Gertrude, over there, will type your catalogue notes when you are finished. We have a small library here, which is in a room down the hall on the left. Everything you need should be in there. If you would like to start on this wall here, none of this has been catalogued yet. It all just arrived from Paris a week ago. We are quite far behind at this point."

"After the pieces are catalogued, do they stay here?" she asked.

"No, we have storage rooms, mostly on the lower floors and some in the basement. Everything goes up and down the main staircase. Local laborers come to do all the lifting so don't worry! Most items have already been included in the large catalogues, so what we need now is a supplemental index card for each piece, indicating any damage the piece has incurred and offering a recommendation for which Reich museum the piece is best suited for. Please keep in mind that Herr Steiglitz sends one of his deputies from time to time to choose items for the new Führermuseum in Linz."

"Which has not, as of yet, been built," Anke added.

"That is correct, Fräulein," Jürgen said, returning to his desk with a shrug of his shoulders.

Anke smiled; he seemed sweet enough. She wondered if he, or any of the others, had any idea who owned these works before they arrived here. Her question was answered in the next minute, when she went to peruse her stack of crates. Written in bold, block lettering on each crate (there were eighteen) was "D.W./Paris." D.W. was short for David David-Weill, an extremely prosperous Parisian art collector, Jewish of course. Anke picked up a crowbar, which sat on the floor, and began to pry open the first crate.

"Please, Fräulein! Allow me!" a chubby middle-aged man called as he rushed to her side. "My name is Hans. I deal with all the boxes, Fräulein. I wouldn't want you to hurt yourself."

Anke stood back and allowed him to do his job. He had the hands of a woodworker or maybe a blacksmith. There was a sturdy rugged-ness about him that reminded her of the village peasants in the paint-ings of Pieter Bruegel the Elder.

"Thank you, Hans," she said, as he lifted the paintings out, one by one, and leaned them against the wall. She knelt in front of the first one, a Cranach drawing that she had not come across at the Jeu de Paume. She consulted the large binder with the main catalogue, a copy of which Jürgen had left on the nearest table. She filled out a new index card.

Cranach, Lukas
Madonna with Child
Woodcut c. 1540
(D.W./Paris)
No observable damage
KFM Berlin

Anke had no idea where the piece should go, other than back to David David-Weill, who was now…God only knows where he was. She then decided the entire exercise was arbitrary and just wrote down the Kaiser Friedrich Museum in Berlin. It would be hard to argue with that for a German artist like Cranach.

She quickly realized this would be a tedious and depressing assignment. She looked at the enormous stack of crates and began to second-guess her decision not to accompany Bauer to Florence. At least there she could have helped, maybe even saved something from the war. Then again, if the Allies bombed Monte Cassino, they would have no trouble bombing Neuschwanstein. She could be needed in an emergency evacuation. She continued with her task, and made it through three crates before it became too dark to see the paintings properly. Her first night, alone in her sparse room, was a difficult one. Despite her instincts to come here, she couldn't help feeling she had followed the art to a dead end.

ON HER TENTH DAY, Anke decided to be bold. She found herself alone in room nine, the others having gone downstairs for lunch. She slipped down one of the back staircases and found, to her surprise, an unlocked door leading to a long, dimly lit hallway. If she was caught in a restricted area she could plead ignorance and say she got lost in the maze.

It wasn't long before her excuse became reality. After several turns, two more staircases, and a number of corridors, Anke was not at all sure she could find her way back. Her inner compass confused, she decided that snooping around was not only dangerous, but pointless. Anything they did not want her to find would be hidden, under lock and key. She wasn't even sure what she was looking for.

As she retraced her steps, she found herself in a storage room that was packed wall-to-wall with crates that had yet to be opened and catalogued. She had no idea how they would get through the inventory; it was simply immense. As she turned to leave and continue her reverse journey, a glint caught her eye. It was a shimmer really, from an exposed frame gilded with gold leaf but heavily worn from the years. The light in the room was dimmed by the heavy drapes on the windows, so it was miraculous that she even saw what she saw. Then again, she would have known that frame anywhere.

"This isn't happening," she said aloud.

She edged aside a stack of crates, not without difficulty, and revealed the piece, which leaned against the wall, unwrapped and in seemingly decent condition. *The Adoration of the Mystic Lamb.* Behind it, John the Baptist. Behind him, Adam. Behind him, Eve. All the panels, except the *Just Judges*, were here, dusty and cramped in a corner of a Bavarian castle. But Anke was there too, in this odd place. This was no mistake, she realized. Her father had known about this. He could see everything, from where he was. He was completely in control.

She pushed the crates aside with all of her reserve strength and was soaked in sweat by the time the panels had the room they needed to be arranged semi-properly. She couldn't hang them, of course, but she organized them in the usual order and placed them along the far wall. She stood back, shaking with excitement, relief, and rage.

She decided to say nothing and write to Bauer immediately. She would threaten to leave him. He would take the altarpiece back to Ghent and see it reinstalled. She would accompany him and inform Professor Dubois. She imagined old Jan's expression as she returned with the altar.

She sank on the floor, realizing that she could do none of that. Bauer didn't have the authority to remove such a valuable piece from Neuschwanstein and Jan would not be considered a collaborator until the Belgians had their country back. A few loud sobs erupted before she calmed herself down. She didn't want any of the others finding her in this situation. As it turned out, someone did find her nearly eight hours later, sleeping in the fetal position on the floor in front of the Ghent Altarpiece.

15

The Jewel of Europe

Florence as we knew it is no more...it will not be the Florence of the Medici, it will not be that perfection, that utterly harmonious atmosphere that made it unique in the world. —Herbert Matthews in The New York Times, June 1944

WHILE ANKE JUNGER cried herself to sleep in front of the van Eyck altar, Erik Brossler forced himself to stay awake while examining the new Air Force aerial maps of Rome. Finally, there was a coordinated military effort to avoid destroying the most beautiful cities in the Western world, and Erik was providing the words to go with the pictures. Once the maps were labeled properly, with museums, churches, and historic buildings, the cities of Italy were then put into categories: Category A cities were not to be bombed without official authority from Army headquarters (Rome, Florence, Venice, Torcello), category B were only to be bombed if it was considered essential (Ravenna, Assisi, San Gimignano, Urbino, Spoleto) and category C were considered important military objectives and could be bombed at will (Siena, Pisa, Padua, Orvieto, and many, many others). Erik and Brigsworth-Jones were sickened by this last category but had absolutely no authority to challenge the decision.

Every time an Allied bomb destroyed an Italian building of historical value, the German press wasted no time reporting it in gory, unsubstantiated detail. When an American bomb narrowly missed the Arena Chapel in Padua, sumptuously decorated by Giotto, even the Italian puppet government shouted about it in their fascist pamphlet: *The War Against Art.*

There was, however, an increased understanding amongst the generals of both the US and British armies that efforts toward art protection and historic preservation were extremely effective at creating positive press in the Allied home countries. This is why, on June 4, 1944, Erik Brossler entered Rome in the advance group, marking the first time in the war that a monuments officer had ridden ahead of combat troops. Erik's task was to drive around the city and record as much information as humanly possible regarding damage to works of art and/or historic buildings due to Allied bombing, before the hoards arrived and the city was brimming with soldiers looking for food, sex, and a semi-clean place to sleep. Being that Erik was in Rome merely an hour ahead of the combat battalion, he only scratched the surface and had to spend the next four days buzzing around on a motorcycle, identifying broken church glass, damage to libraries, and investigating charges of looting. The major museums were locked up and guarded twenty-four-hours a day.

After a few weeks of Allied occupation, these policies were relaxed and the Italian populace began to uncover the works that had been sealed in protective coating or bricked up for the last few years. Mosaics were revealed from behind cloth coverings and sculptures were liberated from their brick tombs, including Michelangelo's famous seated *Moses* from the sarcophagus of Pope Julius II in the church of San Pietro in Vincoli. Erik missed the unveiling due to his duties, but was assured by Dearborn, who oversaw the event, that the rebirth of *Moses* was greeted with shouts, applause, and quite a few tears by the assembled crowd. Moses's exquisite flowing beard, Dearborn added in his report, was not damaged and looked "as Moses-like as ever."

Pope Pius XII made a speech to thousands in St. Peter's Square praising God for sparing Rome. While Erik seethed at the Vatican's tepid attempt to protect Italy's art, Crawford was on his knees toward the front of the crowd, weeping and holding his rosary. Crawford had matured immensely since their first days together in Sicily and had often been Erik's companion on his rides around the city. Erik made a mental note to mention Crawford's devout Catholicism to Brigsworth-Jones, who had a habit of taking the Lord's name in vain, multiple times, in front of everyone.

The next evening a persistent hubbub rumbled through the city and shrieks of joy could be heard from soldiers and civilians alike. The news reached Erik as he teetered atop a giant wooden ladder, which gingerly leaned up against the Arch of Constantine. Italian workers were slowly dismantling the layers of brick protection that had encased the arch since the start of the war. Erik held a spotlight and searched for evidence of damage to the stonework itself. Brigsworth-Jones arrived by Jeep and shouted up to him.

"Come down old chap!"

"Now? Brigs, I am...."

"No, you're right," Brigsworth-Jones interrupted. "I am sure you don't want to hear this news. It's not strictly art-related. You'll hear sooner or later!"

Erik rolled his eyes and backed slowly down the ladder. The expression on the professor's face gave him butterflies.

"They've landed in France, chap. Normandy. Well over 100,000 men."

"Jesus!"

"I thought we weren't taking the Lord's name in vain."

"He's not my Lord."

Brigsworth-Jones erupted in laughter, which was contagious.

"Seriously, Brigs, is this it? Are the Germans finished?"

"I'd say yes, but I don't think they will lay down their arms just yet. Appallingly fierce, those chaps. Fighting to the death is their way, so it might be a few months yet. Over by Christmas I should think."

Erik looked back up at the arch, which was now almost completely clear of brick. The night was warm and suddenly strangely quiet. In the background, he could hear the meows of the many stray cats that lived in the ruins of the Colosseum, just yards from where they were standing.

WITH ROME SECURED and more monuments officers arriving every day, the team led by Brigsworth-Jones (on paper at least) rode north through the many villages of Umbria and Tuscany, toward Florence. The damage to the medieval hill towns was spotty; some monuments were blown to bits and completely unrecoverable while others were untouched. German artillery had left many parish churches partially roofless and some had no roofs at all. German looting in the village churches had been extensive: vestments, chalices, and other church ornaments made from gold or silver were often missing or scattered about. Graffiti-style inscriptions were found on the walls. Ironically, this vandalism often warned of the inevitable looting and destruction by the Allies. More than once, the monument team found the corpses of German soldiers littered around a bombed building or monument, left behind by the retreating Germans.

In a damaged and deserted church behind the Allied lines south of Florence, they waited anxiously for clearance to enter the city. Horrifying trickles of information reached them, some from the BBC, that the Germans had been removing artworks from various villas surrounding the city (where they were moved for protection from Allied bombing) and were now moving them north toward the territory controlled by the Reich. They also heard that the Wehrmacht had blown up all the bridges over the Arno except the Ponte Vecchio.

"They left the Ponte Vecchio because it was Hitler's favorite," Dearborn snarled. "I just heard that on the radio."

"Did they get the Vasari Corridor?" Erik asked tensely.

"Part of it I think. The part along the Arno was damaged."

"Jesus Christ!" said Brigsworth-Jones, who was now cursing more than ever. "How can Hitler save the Ponte Vecchio and bomb the goddamn Vasari Corridor?"

Though it was no longer open to the public, Erik and his father had walked that corridor once on a trip to the Uffizi Gallery in 1931. Erik was fourteen and just beginning his obsession with art and architecture. The corridor was designed by Giorgio Vasari, writer of the famous *Lives of the Artists*, which chronicled the lives and works of many Renaissance Italian painters. It was an indoor passageway that connected the Palazzo Vecchio to the Palazzo Pitti. The Grand Duke Cosimo I d'Medici ordered it built in 1565 to allow him to move around Florence without being seen in public. Part of the corridor runs through both the Uffizi Museum and the Ponte Vecchio.

"Wait a second...shh, listen to this!" Crawford hissed, holding the radio up so everyone could hear.

This is the BBC reporting from Montegufoni, Italy, this is Dickon Weatherhead…scores of priceless Renaissance paintings and sculpture have been hastily moved about by the retreating German army outside Florence… luxury villas had housed these treasures for months, though now some lie nearly empty…at the villa of Montegufoni, Italian refugees are hiding amongst the art, waiting for the battles to end. Troops of one of the allied New Zealand regiments now hold the villa….

"That's it," declared Erik. "We are going now."

"We have to wait for authorization," Dearborn said, wondering why on earth he even cared.

"We're not waiting. If we go now, we'll be almost there when they send the authorization," Erik said, heading for the Jeep.

"That's a bloody good point," said Brigsworth-Jones, who jumped in the passenger seat. Months of army rations had slimmed him down considerably and he loved his newly lithe figure, though he still occasionally dreamt of pheasant in butter sauce.

Crawford and Dearborn grabbed the rest of the gear and took the second Jeep, which they had driven across the sands of North Africa, through the villages of Sicily, up the Amalfi Coast of Italy, through Rome, Umbria, and Tuscany, and that was now going to carry them into the heart of Italian art…a city that even Hitler called "the jewel of Europe."

HITLER'S OPINIONS ASIDE, the soldiers who fought for him had decidedly less interest in Renaissance art. At Montegufoni, an exhausted art historian, Dr. Censari, greeted the Monuments Men with smiles and wide adrenaline eyes. He had only just arrived himself and led them to the main villa, grandly shaded by a bank of cypress trees and complete with its own bell tower, reminiscent of the famous one in Siena. Items from the *ricoveri*, the effort to protect Italy's great art, had been housed here and were now being guarded diligently by an Indian regiment from the British Army. What they found inside was nothing short of stomach-turning. Many works had been looted by the Germans, but a good number had been left behind as well. Most were stacked hastily in the corners of the rooms, though major damage was surprisingly rare. In the case of *Adoration of the Magi* by Ghirlandaio, the Germans had used it as a table on which to lay their weapons, food, and wine bottles. It was in horrendous shape. Erik and Dearborn lifted the painting and leaned it against the wall. Brigsworth-Jones got in close to inspect the damage, shaking his head and muttering.

"Did you know Ghirlandaio once tutored Michelangelo?" Dr. Censari asked, to no one in particular. He was a short, bald man who made even Crawford feel rather manly.

"Yes, I have heard that," Erik responded. "He also painted one of the wall frescoes in the Sistine Chapel, correct?"

"Indeed. I can see the Allies have sent the right men to me," Dr. Censari said, smiling.

Dearborn's voice could be heard from a few rooms away—the tone told Erik he'd found something important. Crawford reached him first.

"Oh! That...that's...."

"A Botticelli," Dearborn said, his arms waving in an aggravated fashion.

"Dio mio! *La Primavera*!" Dr. Censari cried, sweating now.

"Christ almighty...." Brigsworth-Jones added, helpfully.

Erik went close. This was tempera on panel, delicate, but seemed to be in decent condition.

"I don't understand," he said while gently running his fingers along the underside of the frame looking for damage. "They leave Botticelli's *La Primavera* just sitting here?"

"It's a gigantic painting, maybe it was too big to take," Crawford offered.

"The Italians managed to get it here—on a horse cart no doubt. Are you telling me that after all the looting they've done in Italy, and we all know they've stolen quite a bit, they just leave a masterpiece like this behind because they think it's too big?"

"I see what you are getting at, chap," Brigsworth-Jones said, stepping forward and getting his lit cigarette far too close to the painting for Dr. Censari, who grimaced. "The Germans are disorganized. They are in retreat and they aren't paying attention anymore. They're closing rank, taking only what they can handle. This is a good thing."

The others quietly digested this while gazing at Venus in the woods, surrounded by Mercury, Cupid, and the dancing three Graces:

Zephyrus, Flora, and Chloris. A late fifteenth-century allegory of the arrival of spring, that's what Vasari wrote anyway. A rebirth. European art could use one of those, Erik thought. A new Renaissance…without the Nazis.

"Sir, where should I put this?" an Indian soldier was standing in the doorway, addressing Brigsworth-Jones.

"What is it?"

"Not sure, sir. Looks religious."

Dearborn took the item from him and leaned it against the wall. A Madonna with Child…early fourteenth-century panel…Giotto.

"Mother of God!" Brigsworth-Jones lit another cigarette.

"Yes, that's what I thought sir," said the soldier, pleased with himself. He turned and left.

Erik and Brigsworth-Jones shot each other looks before erupting in laughter. Dr. Censari didn't get the joke.

OVER THE NEXT FEW DAYS, Dr. Censari accompanied the Monuments Men to other *ricoveri* sites to get a sense of what was where and what was damaged and, in some cases, missing. At Torre a Cona, they came across a garage that had only been very recently abandoned by the Germans. Inside, Erik saw two colossal crates obviously housing extremely large sculptures. He climbed on top of several smaller crates, like a young boy climbing a tower of rocks, and managed to peer down onto the head of Michelangelo's *Dawn*. This famous work had previously been a permanent part of the elaborate tomb of Lorenzo de Medici in the Medici Chapel, Church of San Lorenzo, Florence. Now it was sitting abandoned in a crate in a filthy garage southeast of the city. Erik leaned against the wall to catch his breath and find his composure. Brigsworth-Jones cursed the Germans so graphically that even Dr. Censari bristled slightly. Crawford, Erik noticed, had become accustomed and hardly registered the damnations as he quickly set up his typewriter on a crate and punched out a report on the major find. Crawford, it was turning out, was a tireless workhorse without whom they simply could not have managed.

The outrage, shared in earnest by Dr. Censari, was not always common amongst the townspeople and villagers who had been powerfully and brutally displaced by either the Germans, the Allied bombs, or both. In many cases Dr. Censari translated their impassioned approaches, which were too fast and full of spirit for Brigsworth-Jones, who thought he spoke Italian rather well.

"Why do you make a fuss over a statue when my family has nowhere to live? We are outside in the rain!" shouted one man.

"My children are young and have not eaten for two days," cried a young mother.

The monument team took the hint and helped the Indian and New Zealander soldiers erect temporary shelters and find food for the hundreds of roving civilians. Closer to the city, the once gorgeous Pitti and Bobili gardens were now teeming refugee centers. Unsanitary and dangerously overcrowded, the gardens held more than 6,000 Florentine citizens who had been evacuated by the Germans from the areas surrounding the blown bridges. The situation was slowly coming under control as more Allied troops moved into the area, so Dr. Censari accompanied the Monuments Men to the banks of the river where they witnessed the massive piles of rubble that were once the Renaissance bridges of Florence.

The Ponte Vecchio was still passable, though littered with debris. They crossed with care since German mines were everywhere. The smell was a combination of sewage from the damaged drainage pipes, and the acrid odor of char. Erik glanced back at Brigsworth-Jones and saw that he was in tears.

At the Uffizi, the windows and skylights were all blown out. Some frescoes were badly spoiled and were peeling from the walls. Dr. Censari was visibly moved and went to sit quietly on his own for a few minutes. Dearborn and Crawford wandered back toward the Arno with some mission that Erik was not privy to. A feeling of utter uselessness overwhelmed him as he watched Dr. Censari and Brigsworth-Jones attempt to gather themselves in the face of the partial destruction of Florence. Erik had never been a scholar of Italian art, nor had his father, nor had Brigsworth-Jones. Yet, Florence was the cradle of Renaissance art and from that cradle sprang so many artists, not just Italians but many in the northern schools as well. Erik calmed himself by noting that this was now the view of the Arno that Memling would have seen since the Santa Trinita Bridge was built well after his death.

Crawford and Dearborn returned, with six men in their wake. Erik knew they had an idea.

"These men are willing to dive into the river and try to retrieve the bridge stones," Dearborn said solemnly, as if he was reading their death warrants.

"Tom, the Arno is filled with sewage, the bombs hit all kinds of refuse pipes," Erik said, donning a fake grin for the men.

"I've made them aware of that, sir. They want to go in now."

Dr. Censari and Brigsworth-Jones, now composed, joined the group.

"This would be my honor," one man said to Dr. Censari, who nodded his approval.

Erik ceded authority to Dr. Censari, who was a curator at the Uffizi before the war. The Florentines turned around and marched back across the Ponte Vecchio to prepare for their dives. Before nightfall, citizens of all ages and genders had volunteered for both Arno diving and street patrols where statue or architectural fragments were picked up and dropped off at central sorting stations. Piece by piece, Florence would be put back together again.

Unfortunately, not everyone was this helpful. The US Army engineers got out their bulldozers and began eradicating both actual rubble and salvageable bits of stonework, sculpture, books, and other contents of the buildings bombed by the Germans. Despite several shouting matches and two frantic cables to Allied Command in Rome, neither Erik nor Brigsworth-Jones were able to stop this from occurring.

Erik, in a rage, wrote to his father:

Saluti da Firenze! You would not believe what the Germans have done to Florence, but I am sure you have read about it by now. What you probably have not read about is just how obtuse and pig-headed our Army can be. The engineers are "helping" us rebuild Florence with a sledgehammer. I am not being overly dramatic either. Watch, now this letter won't get past the sensors!

On a lighter note, and please convey this to mother, we did have an extraordinary day yesterday. Brigsworth-Jones convinced the engineers to drive one of their huge trucks out to a villa where the equestrian statue of Cosimo I de Medici had been sitting out the war. The Italians made the point to me, several times, that they had dragged him out on an ox-cart and could bring him back the same way if need be. But, we got the truck and managed to get him back fairly quickly. You should have seen the villagers along the way, Papa. They came out of their houses, or the ruins of their houses, and cheered us the entire way into Florence. A huge crowd gathered at the Piazza Signoria to see him placed back where Giambologna first erected the statue in 1598. A chant of "welcome home Cosimo" lasted for nearly twenty minutes!

Florence is in bad shape, but I know she will be rebuilt. The spirit here is intoxicating and the Italians have been accommodating and downright helpful so far. I would like to remain here longer, but I think we are needed in Pisa, which was hit even worse. I am sorry this is so short, but I need to pack my gear and get on the road. Love to you and mother.

Your devoted son,

Lt. Erik Brossler, Monuments Division

August 31, 1944

16

The Brenner Pass

One can have no smaller or greater mastery than mastery of oneself.
—Leonardo da Vinci

IT HAD BECOME quite apparent, to anyone who cared to notice such things, that the art-collection war between Hitler and Göring, which had been gathering steam for years, was now nearing its climax. Since much of Italy was now in the hands of the Allies, removing precious Italian art, especially Florentine art, became a top priority. As the Germans pulled out of Florence and headed north, there was a frenzy to evacuate much of the *ricoveri* to the Alpine areas of Italy, which had been annexed to the Reich and were therefore considered part of the fatherland.

In late July, Bauer found himself named the dedicated SS officer in charge of this mass evacuation, though he had a number of rivals swirling around him. One was from the *Kunstschutz* (von Essen's deputy), one was a representative from the yet-to-be-built *Führermuseum* in Linz, and there were several others motivated only by self-interest (these were the most dangerous). Technically, Bauer trumped them all since his orders came directly from Göring, who at least publicly still had Hitler's support.

His letter to Anke had gone unanswered and he didn't dare ask Göring about her since he was supposed to be focused on the task at hand. He wasn't supposed to be thinking of her night and day and he certainly wasn't supposed to be cherry-picking artworks that he thought she would like and would want to see protected. His system worked, he rationalized, because Anke favored many of the same pieces from the Northern schools that the Reichsmarschall and the Führer did, by coincidence only. He sent his men into the Villa Reale Poggio with strict instructions: Cranach, Rembrandt, van Eyck, Vermeer, van der Weyden, Dürer, Pieter Bruegel…he gave them a list. In some cases they took Italian art as well, quite a bit of it. But when time was short and their trucks were filling, they left behind unimaginable treasures… Botticelli's *Birth of Venus* and *La Primavera*, da Vinci's *Adoration of the Magi* and Michelangelo's *Doni Madonna*, just to name a few. Bauer's preoccupation with Anke and her whereabouts prevented him from worrying too much about these abandoned masterpieces, despite his knowledge that many displaced Italians were now squatting in these *ricoveri* villas, cooking, sleeping, and defecating amongst the art.

Let the Allies deal with it. Bauer repeated this to himself as they drove north to the SS headquarters in Verona. He knew for a fact there were several important pieces, a Raphael amongst them, missing from the shipments. He also knew if he ravaged the hotel rooms of several SS men, and the representative from the *Kunstschutz*, he would eventually find what he was looking for. However, if he did this he would open himself up for scrutiny, which would be unfortunate since he harbored a small van Eyck in his suitcase (*Madonna with Child*), encased between his soft, cotton undershirts. Anke would have her very own van Eyck. The image, of her beholding the panel for the first time, helped him sleep.

What Bauer was also aware of but chose to ignore was the official line being publicized by both the *Kunstschutz* and the German Army. Kesselring, the German commander in Italy, had promised publicly that all items from the *ricoveri* would be protected from artillery and bombing (to the best of his ability) and would then be either returned to Florence or handed over to the Vatican for safekeeping. Contrary to these statements, which the Allies had seemingly swallowed whole, were the orders from Berlin to stash the "cultural items" (more than 530 paintings and 150 sculptures) in the Italian Alps. Hitler stopped short of ordering them straight to Berlin, just in case the Italians might accuse them of looting. The idiocy of this statement amazed even

Göring, who had been emboldened by the success of the "repatria-tion" of the fifteen crates from Monte Cassino. Göring wanted all the Florentine art within Reich borders so he could eventually get some of it into Carinhall. After instructing Bauer to sit tight in the Tyrol un-til Hitler's directives could be guided to a more satisfactory outcome, the Reichsmarschall sent a Luftwaffe sergeant to retrieve Anke Junger from Neuschwanstein and return her to Carinhall so she could help prepare the hunting lodge for the arrival of the Florentine treasures.

When the sergeant arrived at Ludwig's castle, he found he had missed Fräulein Junger by less than twenty-four hours. She had given no reason for her departure and left no forwarding address. She was, as Frau Kruger put it, an "odd and unpredictable young woman." The sergeant departed with the distinct feeling that the Reichsmarschall would not be satisfied with this explanation.

AT THAT VERY MOMENT, Anke was passing through Innsbruck, Austria, in a car driven by Franz Bauer's orderly, Corporal Georg Wurtzer. They had driven straight, stopping only for food and the call of nature, since Füssen. Anke insisted she sit in the front next to Wurtzer, to avoid feeling like a passive participant in this new, dangerous adven-ture. Wurtzer, who looked no more than eighteen, initially appreciated the gesture and thought he could use Anke's banter to keep awake on the long drive. The Alps, even in summer weather, were a long haul and the steep passes and hairpin turns took the kind of concentration that few people were used to employing while driving. Unfortunately, Anke's light summer dress, clinging to her thighs in the damp heat, had the opposite effect. South of Innsbruck, Anke took the wheel and commanded Wurtzer to get some sleep in the back. He agreed, praying that this decision would not get him into trouble.

All Wurtzer knew was that his commanding officer had promised him three days of leave if he brought this woman safely across the Brenner Pass and into German-controlled Italy, where Bauer was waiting at a hotel in Bolzano. He assumed she was Bauer's lover and decided that he and his fellow corporals had not given their CO enough credit; Bauer had himself quite a mistress. Anke drove fast, but smoothly and Wurtzer slept peace-fully in the back as they snaked toward the Italian border.

Anke's plan had changed several times and she used the quietness of the drive to reformulate it once again. She knew Bauer would have no power to remove the Ghent Altarpiece and return it to Belgium; the war would have to end before that happened. She decided to use her sway with him to ensure the safety of the Italian works he had alluded to during their very brief phone conversation. He wasn't specific, but he indicated there was a cache of paintings that would concern her. His use of the word "concern" was the reason Anke decided to head to Italy. Had he said, "impress" or "interest," then she might have written the conversation off as an attempt by Bauer to entice her to his Italian hotel room, and his bed. But he didn't say either of those words, he said "concern." It was now Anke's opinion, though admittedly based on very thin information, that Franz Bauer was tiring of his role as looter lackey and was ready to do the right thing. The right thing, she knew, would most likely land him in a concentration camp if he was caught. Despite this, and despite their last meeting where he showed no signs of a faltering allegiance to the Nazi ideal, Anke felt Bauer was edging closer to her way of thinking. She had almost no explanation for this intuition, save one thing: when she last dreamt of her father, he spoke to her in Italian.

OBERGRUPPENFÜHRER BAUER sat on his small but fancy balcony at the Hotel Bolzano, facing north toward the mountains, toward the Reich. He had spent most of the day negotiating for the release of certain members of the Italian aristocracy, including a cousin of King Victor Emmanuel III. The Florentine SS and Gestapo were run almost entirely by Italian fascists and they had scores to settle that went far beyond what was necessary and beneficial to the German war effort. Bauer was disgusted by their tactics, which included arresting old ladies and torturing prominent Florentines for invented reasons. Bauer's official power was limited to the art and cultural evacuation, though his known association with the Reichsmarschall gave him an added aura of authority. Before he left Florence, he succeeded in shutting down most of the extracurricular activities of the Florentine Gestapo and especially those of its leader, Sandro Vini, a sadist in the extreme.

This extra work, which he had not expected and was outside his comfort zone, had left him exhausted and anxious. For the first time, he began to see just how uphill the battle was. The Russians were plowing west through Poland and were now well within Reich borders. Unstopped, they would be in Berlin in a matter of months. The Americans and the British were just south of him and the German retreat northward was unlikely to be reversed at this point. Western France had fallen to the Allies and the German defense line was creeping steadily east, despite their fierce resistance. Germany was being squeezed, excruciatingly, in the Allied vice. Of course, uttering this to another soul would have him shot in less time than it would take to actually utter it. Hitler had recently survived yet another assassination attempt and trusted almost no one. Defeatist talk was more taboo now than ever.

Bauer looked in the mirror and saw a man who had lost weight and looked older than his thirty-seven years. The fullness of his youth was gone, now he looked taught and hardened. His thick brown hair was still, thankfully, covering his head, though there was evidence of a slight retreat in his hairline. In a few years he'd have a widow's peak. He closed his eyes and imagined the sound of a car pulling up in front of the hotel, the door slamming shut, the click of heels on pavement, a knock on his door. She would be here shortly, he told himself. He knew what she would want from him and he was prepared to pay any price.

He was startled by a loud knock on his door. He hadn't actually heard the car, or had he? He rubbed his temples. *Am I losing my mind?* He got up and opened the door. She brushed past him and plopped on the bed, like a little girl in a hotel room for the very first time.

"Shall we talk later?" she asked, quickly removing her dress.

He nodded, understanding perfectly what she was doing. She had a mission, just like him. If they joined forces, he would have to choose between an Allied prison camp and suicide. Then again, those were most likely his only choices anyway, whether he joined her or not. Her naked form slipped under the satin covers and she looked at him expectantly. Her girlish prettiness, undimmed since he last saw her, seemed out of place in this new world he found himself in. She made him want to live. He shed his clothes and crawled in beside her. They lay together quietly for several minutes before and after they made love. Unwilling to let her go, Bauer clung to her long after she had fallen asleep, nestling his face in her neck as if her smell could sanitize the filth he'd seen. He couldn't sleep, despite his exhaustion.

"HOW FAR AWAY ARE THEY?" Anke asked, after the dinner trays had been brought up. Bauer sat at the desk while Anke lay on the bed, dipping her Tuscan bread in olive oil.

"Who?" Bauer glanced up at her while lighting a cigarette.

"The Americans."

"Crawling all over Florence by now. They'll be moving north and there isn't much to stop them at this point."

"Handing over the art will go a long way, I'm sure."

"I don't have the authority to do that, Anke."

"Of course not. That would be treason."

She sat up on the bed and looked at him. His shirt was unbuttoned and his hair was ruffled. He looked more like a boy now than he ever had. That's how she decided to see him, like a boy who got caught up in a naughty game. But now it was time to make nice.

"Anke, it has to be you. You can tell them where the stash is. They won't arrest you, at least I don't think they will. You can bring them here, then go north with them. There's Neuschwanstein, you can take them there. They'll love that." He smiled the smile of a resigned man.

"No, we need to do this together. If you tell them everything, maybe they won't put you in a POW camp."

"A POW camp would be fine."

"So, what is the problem?"

"The problem is that I will draw attention to us. If I leave Bolzano and head south to Rome, people will find out about it. They could move the art before we get the Americans up here."

"So, what do we do?"

"We wait."

"Wait? For how long? It will be winter soon, and everything will be harder to move in the snow."

"Anke, sweetheart. I know. I can't believe I am saying this, but I wish the Allies would move faster. I wish they were on our doorstep, right now. But they're not, they are hundreds of miles south of here and until they are closer, we can't risk Göring or Hitler moving the stash from the Brenner Pass."

"The Brenner Pass? That's…the hiding place?"

"Well, there are a number of buildings, houses and so forth. But yes, it's all along the Brenner Pass."

"I don't want to leave until I've seen everything," Anke said, beginning to dress. "I can't go back to Germany yet."

Bauer smiled. "I know, *leibling*. I've come up with a plan to explain why you left Neuschwanstein. Göring will love it…well, he'll appreciate it at least. He'll have no choice."

"What did you call me?" she asked, her voice quivering.

"What? I…I said, *liebling*. Why?"

"Don't call me that."

"Why not?"

Anke didn't answer and Bauer didn't ask again.

The Campo Santo

…We could never build again the Parthenon or the Pantheon or Siena Cathedral or the Campo Santo at Pisa or the Palazzo Vecchio or the Colonnade of St. Peter's.
—*Guglielmo Ferrero, 1914*

BRIGSWORTH-JONES had developed a chest infection, possibly from over-exposure to dust particles in Florence, and needed to recuperate for two weeks at an Allied hospital in Rome. Erik was left in command of their unit and had also been promoted to Captain. Despite the honor, Erik felt rudderless without the big man (and he wasn't even big anymore). Dearborn and Crawford were clearly exhausted after Florence and the news coming from Pisa was confused and contradictory. The German retreat had left not only damaged and abandoned artworks, but blown up roads, bridges, and heavily damaged churches and villages throughout Tuscany. A number of the glorious Renaissance villas, even some once owned by the Medici, were now ghostly shells filled with the detritus of excessive plunder.

Erik had also just received a letter from his father. His mother had died at home in Cambridge four weeks ago, though the cause of her death was not disclosed. Erik had known for some time that his mother was not well. He had not had a letter from her since he arrived in Sicily and he assumed, since his father rarely mentioned her, that she was still angry at him for joining the army. But he could not account for this sudden endgame. A rush of bitterness flooded over him as he realized he couldn't go to her funeral; he couldn't comfort his father.

He instead wrote several letters: condolences to his father, a bulletin to Brigsworth-Jones in Rome, and a few words of awkward sympathy to his grandmother in Munich. This last letter, sent to the house on the Leipziger Strasse where his mother had grown up and where he had played the piano so often as a young boy, was sent despite the fact that nothing had been heard from his grandmother in years. He had no faith that a letter from Allied Italy would even make it to the Reich, let alone find his grandmother.

Dearborn sensed Erik's looming depression and took on extra duties to compensate. When they rumbled into Pisa at midnight in mid-September, he found them a decent place to sleep and insisted that Erik rest for a few hours before they begin their cultural reconnaissance. The decent place he found was a roofless, abandoned house near the Leaning Tower. They set up their camp in the downstairs parlor, which still had a ceiling. Dearborn dragged a clammy mattress down from an upstairs bedroom and Erik collapsed onto it, wrapping himself in the clean sheets they had brought with them from Florence. Damp dust clung to everything and Erik was glad Brigsworth-Jones was not with them—he would have coughed himself to an early grave.

Erik slept for a time, a couple of hours it seemed to him, before he woke and realized he was completely alone. He hadn't been out of earshot of Dearborn and Crawford in months and their voices, and the hum dings of Crawford's typewriter, were the constant backdrop to his waking hours. The silence disturbed him and he sat up, looking around in the dim light. It was morning. He had been asleep all night, eight hours at least. He couldn't remember the last time he had slept that long, undisturbed. He fumbled with his uniform and staggered out into the morning sun, almost knocking over Crawford, who was on his way in carrying a small silver tray.

"I managed to find you some coffee sir," Crawford said grinning. He held a tin cup out as if it was a peace offering.

"Thanks, Crawford," Erik said, accepting the cup.

"Tom says...Lt. Dearborn I mean, sir...he says you should come see this cemetery. It's been badly damaged and he says it might not survive at all unless we do something."

"Cemetery? What…oh God." Erik nearly spit out the dark watery liquid he'd just sipped. "Are you…is it the Campo Santo? Is that what you are talking about?"

"Yes, sir. That's right. I forgot the name there for a minute. Campo Santo. It means, *holy ground*, is that right, sir?"

Erik handed the cup back to Crawford and was off running. He rushed past the Leaning Tower, which was leaning in the exact direction and to the same degree as before the war, though was now significantly pockmarked. Beyond the tower was one of the most sacred Christian sites in Italy and, arguably, in Europe. It also contained one of the most revered collections of medieval frescos in the world.

"Sir!" Crawford caught up to him, breathless. "You'll need this!"

A sandwich of some sort was thrust in his face. Erik thought he saw ham hanging out the sides.

"Not now, Crawford. I don't have time."

"Sir, you haven't eaten in over a day…Tom says, I mean, Lt. Dearborn…."

"Lieutenant…I can't eat that sandwich. I am Jewish and we don't eat ham." Erik had never kept kosher, but decided maybe it was time to start.

Crawford couldn't have been more taken aback if he was struck in the face. He looked at the sandwich as if it was a live grenade that might explode and kill them both any moment.

"Sir, I apologize. I didn't realize…I didn't mean to offend…."

"Forget it, Lieutenant. Get your typewriter. You'll need to send a report on this."

Erik sprung off toward the Campo Santo leaving Crawford, dumbfounded and embarrassed, standing in front of the Leaning Tower of Pisa with a ham sandwich.

"**CAPTAIN, HAVE YOU EVER SEEN** such a goddamn mess?" Dearborn said, taking photographs with the new camera the army had just assigned to them.

"No Lieutenant, I have not. I don't…I don't even know where to start." Erik was half amused, half annoyed that Dearborn was now speaking like Brigsworth-Jones.

"The roof, sir. We need to start with the roof."

Dearborn could not have been more right. The building was shaped like a cloister, with large glassless arched windows in the center to allow the light to illuminate the frescoes that adorned the outer walls. The roof of the Campo Santo was made entirely of lead and that lead had melted and rained down onto the frescoes and the ornate sarcophagi. Everything was exposed to the elements and had been for weeks.

"How did this happen, does anyone know?" Erik asked, lifting a rather small piece of lead from the ground and noting how heavy it was.

"What I've heard, sir, is that it was us. We were aiming for the Leaning Tower because the Krauts were using it as an observation post. But we missed the tower and hit the Campo Santo. It's a shame."

"It's more than a shame, Tom."

"Is it true, sir, that this place was built on earth that the crusaders brought back from the Holy Land?"

"Not just from the Holy Land, but from Golgotha itself."

"Golgotha…the place where Christ was crucified…." Dearborn trailed off. "Does Crawford know about this?"

"I don't think so. You should bring him up to speed," Erik said, running his hands along one of the stone window arches.

They tiptoed through the rubble, careful not to tread on fresco fragments that were lying all over the floor. Erik knew he needed a higher authority for this clean up. He turned to Dearborn, who looked overwhelmed but straightened up under his captain's scrutiny. Crawford appeared, sweaty, but with his typewriter tucked under his arm. He looked around for somewhere to set it down, but there was no place, so he just stood there.

"I'm sorry I've been so testy this past week," Erik said, looking down. "My mother died."

Dearborn and Crawford were stunned.

"It will be okay that I miss her burial if we can make something of this mess. But if we can't, I will feel…."

"We understand, sir," Crawford said, interrupting. "Should I send a cable to Rome?"

"Yes," Erik said, recovering. "Tell Brigs everything. Ask him to go up the chain of command. We are going to need to get the Italians involved in this. The mayor of Pisa would be helpful."

"I've heard he's a fascist," Dearborn offered.

"Well, then we just might have some leverage with him."

As Crawford ran off to the command unit, Dearborn began investigating the peeling frescoes.

"I hate to say, sir, but I don't know all that much about frescos."

"Neither do I."

"What I do know, sir, is that the majority of these tombs are Roman. This is second- and early third-century stuff."

"I think the medieval Pisans reused the sarcophagi. I read that somewhere."

"Yeah, that sounds right to me too. Sir, if we can get a roof on here, any kind of a roof, we can try to detach the rest of the frescoes from the walls. Isn't there a...a sort of an outline on the actual wall, underneath the fresco?"

Erik mentally traveled back to Florence and could hear Dr. Censari's voice.

"Yes, Dearborn, didn't Censari say something about this, in Florence? Didn't he say that a fresco could be detached and the sketch would still be there, on the wall?"

"Sir, I think he did. I wasn't listening as closely as I should have been, I think I was dealing with the river divers, but I remember him saying something about that. I think maybe we can save some of this. But not without a roof."

"No," Erik conceded. "Not without a roof."

THREE WEEKS LATER there was a roof over the Campo Santo. It wasn't much, wood slats with canvas stretched over it, but it kept the frescoes dry. A small army of Pisans had been wrangled by the mayor to help gather the lead wreckage from the floors of the cemetery and remove them via wheelbarrows. This took more than a week, but it made salvaging fresco and tomb fragments a much easier task.

Brigsworth-Jones arrived with great fanfare in early October, feeling much recovered and escorting Dr. Paulo Moretti, the most renowned medieval fresco specialist in Italy. Moretti was initially disconsolate at the sight of "his beloved Campo Santo," but he soon went to work instructing the group of art restorers and volunteers who had assembled to help despite the lack of edible food or drinking water in Pisa. They collected as many fresco fragments as possible, shored up the ones still on the walls with netting, and began to slowly peel them off, one by one, revealing the *sinopia* underneath. This *sinopia* was the original sketch that Erik and Dearborn had wondered about and it would allow, eventually, a fresco to be recreated even if the plaster had been damaged beyond repair. Dr. Moretti and his restorers uncovered the *sinopia* for the *Stories of the Anchorites*, the *Last Judgement*, and the *Triumph of Death* (all attributed by Brigsworth-Jones to the "Master of the Triumph of Death" and all quite appropriate for a cemetery). However, Dr. Moretti said that many of the main frescos were created by the Italian artist Bounamico Buffalmacco in the 1340s, just a few years before the Black Death extinguished at least one-third of the population of Europe.

Erik left Pisa more willingly than he did Florence. Perhaps it was the news of his mother's death, so closely associated with a charred cemetery that made him jump into the Jeep with more gusto than usual. But it may have also been because he was leaving the damaged site in good hands, a feeling he had rarely encountered before.

Crawford had scooped up a small mound of earth from the interior of the cloister and placed it in one of the tin boxes that had previously held a number of pencils. Dearborn must have explained things to him, Erik thought as he watched Crawford carefully label the box by scratching the words "Campo Santo" into the tin with his army knife.

"You alright, chap?" Brigsworth-Jones said as they rolled out of Pisa. "I'm going to need you tip-top for this Florentine business. We've had word that someone on the German side wants to negotiate and I think they are using the art to do it!"

"What are you talking about?" Erik's ears were pricked and he sat up in his seat. "Has someone contacted you?"

"Not me directly, chap. Not me directly, but OSS in Switzerland has heard from someone claiming to be moderately high in the SS chain of command. He says he can deliver the Florentine works to us and he wants to negotiate a peace treaty to officially end the war in Italy."

"You're kidding! This is amazing. Where....is there a meeting set up?"

"Not yet, chap. The Americans don't believe him. They are quite sure he is just trying to sow discord amongst the Allies."

"What does that mean, exactly?" Erik lit a cigarette. He had smoked more cigarettes since arriving in Pisa than he had in his entire life. Still, he was nowhere close to Brigsworth-Jones.

"It means, I think, that there are elements within the Nazi structure who are hoping to split us off from the Russians. They want us to believe that the Russians are more dangerous to us than they are, and if we join forces, we can crush Stalin together."

"Join forces...with the Nazis?"

"I know...bloody ridiculous idea. The British would never go for it. The Americans, I'm not so sure."

"What?" Erik's head pounded. "Brigs, are you serious?"

"Afraid so, chap. You Yanks hate the Fascists, but you hate the Communists just as much. The only people who hate the Communists as much as you are the Germans."

Erik was silent for at least two miles. The roof and side flaps of the Jeep were not well secured and gusts of cold November wind stung him repeatedly. He knew Brigsworth-Jones was a bit of a conspiracy theorist. He also knew he was a world-class cynic.

"Brigs," he said quietly, as they pulled into the small village of Rigoli, "I can't keep doing this if the Americans are going to join with the Nazis. I am a Jew. Do you understand this?"

"I understand, chap," Brigsworth-Jones said, even though Erik had never discussed his Jewish heritage before. He turned off the ignition outside the village church, which had lost part of its roof and was still smoldering from a recent hit. "I don't think it will come to that. But I wanted to be straight with you. I felt I owed you that."

Erik dragged himself out of the Jeep and forced himself to witness yet another instance of medieval architecture blown to bits. He watched the children, some without shoes, gather the fragments of a marble Madonna that had graced the entrance to the church. It was far too shattered to ever be repaired. He suddenly remembered the Madonna statue that he had lugged under his arm for more than a day in Sicily. That moment seemed like a hundred years ago now. He sat on a low stone wall and rubbed his face. The wetness he felt, he soon realized, was tears. The familiar dings began as Crawford sat next to him and began filing his report.

18

The Pawns

I am risking my life for my work, and half my reason has gone.
—Vincent van Gogh

IT APPEARED TO ANKE that Bauer's position was completely untenable. The location of the Florentine masterpieces was now one of the most sought-after secrets of the entire war. The Italians were demanding the return of the objects; even the Fascists were upset. The Americans and the British were driving northward toward the Reich and believed, at this point, that the SS was hiding the art with the intent to deliver it to Hitler's new museum at Linz (they were not aware that this museum was not yet built). Articles speculating on the whereabouts of the art treasures were front-page news in the presses of Germany, Switzerland, Italy, Austria, Britain, and America. Even the Vatican issued statements about the missing stash, insinuating that the Pope knew the hiding place but offering only a cryptic message regarding the location. Anke simply couldn't believe that a secret this big had been kept for so long.

Finally, in late November, Hitler capitulated to the growing international pressure and sent the Fascist Director General of Fine Arts in Italy, Giuseppe de Luca, to view the captive collection and report back on its safety to the various stakeholders. Bauer accompanied de Luca to the Brenner Pass and the director general did as he was told; he sent word to the newspapers that the art treasures were safe and cared for. He did not, however, reveal their location.

Meanwhile, Bauer's main plan began to take effect when Hitler's personal secretary, Martin Bormann, arrived at the Brenner Pass with an entourage of curators from the *Führermuseum* collection. Bormann informed Bauer that he and Himmler wanted the entire Florentine collection moved to Austria, for obvious reasons. This Bauer refused, citing lack of safe transportation for such delicate treasures. Since the Alps were snow-clogged by now, Himmler and Bormann settled for a photographic catalogue of each and every item, with accompanying description, which they would present to Hitler on his birthday, April 20. They accepted, without comment, Bauer's choice of Anke Junger as the art historian to compile the catalogue due to Bauer's insistence that she was Göring's favorite and that she had been instrumental at the Jeu de Paume, Carinhall, and Neuschwanstein. What Bauer left out was Göring's insistence that Anke return to Carinhall to assist with the packing of his own treasures, which he was now shipping south to Bavaria. Carinhall would be destroyed, Göring decided, lest it be occupied by the Russians. As it turned out, even if Göring's wishes had been made clear, Bormann would have insisted on ignoring them, such was the souring of their relationship.

Anke began her project under the scrutiny of Bormann and his minions, but they soon tired of the tedious nature of such a catalogue and returned to Berlin. Anke, armed with a new camera, photographed every piece of art, some of which were not well wrapped and were piled on top of each other without regard to their preservation. One of the main storage areas, she soon found out, was the decaying town jail at San Leonardo, near the Austrian border.

"They are prisoners!" she barked at Bauer after a long day cataloguing. "Leonardos, Titians, Raphaels…they sit, in the muck, unprotected, in a jail cell!"

"I'd call them pawns at this point, not prisoners, sweetheart," Bauer said calmly as he tried to eat his veal. He was careful with his terms of endearment now.

"Oh, is that what you would call them? Well, I did think that you, at least, would have taken measures to make sure your men prepared them for travel. I mean, some of the paintings aren't wrapped at all!"

"Are they badly damaged?"

"No," she admitted. "But that's just luck!"

"We were in a hurry, Anke. Look, I don't like this any more than you do. That's why I am trying to contact the fucking Americans! They won't talk to me. They don't think I am serious."

"Maybe I should try." She sat at the table, opposite him. The Hotel Bolzano was teeming with German officers, all eating, drinking, and laughing as if they were winning the war. It reminded her of the Meurice in Paris. She thought briefly of Konrad, frozen to death at Stalingrad. Bauer pushed some food across the table, but she had lost her appetite.

"You have no military authority, Anke. If they aren't taking me seriously...," he trailed off. He looked haggard and deflated. Anke felt it was only a matter of time before he stopped caring about anything, including her. She dropped the subject and poured the Chianti.

ANKE'S PATIENCE finally ran out on April 1, 1945. Bauer had continued his appeals to the American OSS branch in Switzerland and eventually traveled there for a meeting. Anke alone knew where he was going. The fact that he still trusted her was the only thing that kept her from abandoning him. Throughout March, Bauer felt he was making progress. Then, without warning, the Allies broke off all contact.

Anke's catalogue was finished and on its way to Berlin for the Führer's birthday. Everyone knew Hitler was ill (in mind and body) and the war was all but over. The Russians had crossed the Oder River and were driving into Berlin while the Americans and British were streaming into Germany from the west. Hamburg and Frankfurt had been bombed into rubble and the Wehrmacht and Luftwaffe were out of fuel. Still, life in Bolzano had changed little.

"The Americans think I am a double agent," Bauer informed her as he packed up his belongings in his hotel room. "I've done all I can, but now I have to move north. I can't prevent the collection from being taken into Austria, not anymore. Himmler is ready to throw me in a camp. I am losing what little authority I used to have."

"If Himmler wants to throw you in a camp, I suggest you go south!" she spat. "You can't go back to them now, Franz. You've left them. It's over."

"No, Anke. It doesn't work that way. It's not over until someone surrenders. I have a duty. I have been ordered back to Berlin and that's where I have to go. You, on the other hand…."

He said no more and neither did she. She knew she had less than a week to make contact, or everything would be moved into Austria. They parted in almost the same way as she and Niels did in Toulouse, years ago. Although this time she understood that she was not being abandoned. She was being set free.

Two hours after Bauer departed for Berlin, leaving her with a set of written orders from him regarding the release of the Florentine works to the Allies, Anke drove south toward Verona in one of his entourage cars. It took her two days to get there over the ruinous roads, most of which were flooded due to the spring rains. At Verona, she slept in a hotel filled with Italians who had been bombed out of their homes. She shared her space with two little girls wearing dresses three sizes to big for them. Anke told them she was Belgian and gave them chocolate (she had taken every last bit of food and drink from Bauer's hotel room just for this purpose). They gnawed on the chocolate and kissed her with their smeared mouths. She remembered the little sunburned French girls in the back of the truck, fleeing Paris. These girls were about the same age.

Anke cried herself to sleep, for the first time in months, and her father appeared to her again. He seemed content and spoke of nothing but the weather.

The spring rains are a rebirth of nature, leibling.

There was no evidence of the cord and Anke felt calmed by his presence. She slept for five hours straight before getting back in her car and driving south again. The girls asked her where she was going and she replied, "I don't know exactly. I suppose I'll stop when I find the Americans."

19

The Recoveri

Where they burn books, they will, in the end, burn people.
—*Heinrich Heine, 1821*

T HE MONUMENTS MEN of the US Fifth Army had been stuck south of Kesselring's "Gothic Line," which stretched across the Apennine Mountains like a lethal clothesline, for so long that Erik was complaining that he had been attached to the wrong army.

"The rest of the fucking Americans are already in Germany!" he fumed, to nobody in particular.

Dearborn was laid up with a badly cut foot (he had stepped on shrapnel while undressing for an outdoor shower). His foot became infected and caused their unit to wait in Lucca for nearly a month while he recovered. The lack of available antibiotics had left him feverish for weeks and he sometimes sleepwalked in his delirium. Erik found him wandering near a bombed out school in the middle of the night, naked. After that, they took turns sitting at his bedside until he finally shook the fever, in late March.

"You should have left me behind," Dearborn scolded, once he was lucid again. "I never would have expected you guys to stay here all this time."

"Where should we go, chap?" Brigsworth-Jones asked, feeding him watery broth. "We've been all over Tuscany, and the boys just broke through the German line the other day. It's still a mess and we've been ordered to hole up here. You haven't delayed us anymore than we already were."

Dearborn was relieved at that, but still felt awkward about being so helpless for so long. His foot was sore, but no longer infected since he had finally received a dose of Penicillin. He tried to get up from his cot, but found that his legs didn't want to move.

"You've been in a bed for weeks, chap. You are going to be bloody well weak in the knees. Take it slow, rest on me."

Brigsworth-Jones helped Dearborn hobble around the room, which was on the first floor of the local library. The books had all been either damaged by water or removed to other libraries (a task that would have been left for later had they been able to leave Lucca, but since they were stuck there, it seemed worthwhile).

In early April they were back on the road, heading north. Most of the Fifth Army was doing the same and the muddy, shelled roads could barely contain the onslaught. Erik had never seen traffic like this in his life.

"It's like Napoleon's retreat from Moscow!" Brigsworth-Jones sang out as they sat, gridlocked, outside Verona. "Stuck in the bloody mud!"

There was nothing Erik could do but laugh. He passed the time by writing again to his father and attempting to include as much positive information as possible so as not to depress him. He imagined the professor sitting at the dining room table alone, reading, as he so often did. He was overwhelmed with a desire to see his father again, but also to never, ever, go back to that house.

When they reached Verona, they set up in what had, until recently, been a bakery. The crusty smell from the ovens still hung in the air despite the direct hit the bakery took, which ripped apart one if its walls. Crawford happily settled himself against one of the remaining walls, directly under a gold crucifix, which was mounted above a small arrangement of dried flowers, now shredded and splattered with dust. Erik sat next to him, somehow calmed by Crawford's dedication to his faith. Erik had no idea how his Judaism could help him now, or how it had ever helped him. Then again, he couldn't imagine *not* being Jewish. It belonged to him and he belonged to it. That was something, he conceded.

Dearborn burst into the bakery just as Erik was beginning to doze off.

"Sir, there is someone you should meet. She was picked up by the MPs. She's German. She says she knows where the Florentine treasures are."

"Are you serious?" Erik jumped to his feet. "Where's Brigs?"

"He's with her now. He told me to come get you."

They passed a number of makeshift shower tents where the troops were hosing down after weeks of mud-soaked walking. Central command was set up in the first floor of a small hotel. They went through a number of rooms until they reached a back room off the kitchen. Brigsworth-Jones came to the door.

"She speaks English," he said. "But she's German. We need to debrief her now, before the intelligence boys get to her."

Erik walked into the room and saw a woman seated on a wooden dining room chair. He lost all feeling in his legs. Dearborn noticed right away and took his arm.

"Sir? Captain, what's wrong sir?" he asked. Erik's mouth was too dry to speak.

She stared at him with a confused, alarmed look. The hair on Brigsworth-Jones's neck stood at attention as he watched them.

"My God," she said. "My God." Her hands covered her mouth as she spoke.

"What is going on here, Captain Brossler?" Brigsworth-Jones demanded.

"I don't know," he replied, his eyes filling. "This can't be really happening."

"You never returned my letters," she said quietly. Erik's eyes widened.

Dearborn and Brigsworth-Jones glanced at each other and retreated out of the room. Erik and Anke hardly noticed and could hear little but the pulsing of their own heartbeats and could feel nothing but the rushing of blood to their faces. This produced, for Erik, a ringing in his ears.

"You stopped writing. It was 1936, I remember," Erik said, sitting down.

"No, Erik. I didn't stop then. I wrote dozens of letters, but you never replied."

He stared at her, then they both realized what happened. She put her head in her hands.

"They were monitoring you and your father," he said. "Your mail never left Germany."

"Did you write to me too?"

"For a while, then I stopped."

"You're all grown up. I almost didn't recognize you."

"You look the same. Still beautiful."

She smiled, choking everything back. Everything that she had done in the past few years seemed like a betrayal. She felt as though she had disappointed him. She thought briefly of Niels, Konrad, and Franz and shuddered.

"Are you married?" she asked.

"No. You?"

"No."

Erik tried to breathe, to calm himself. He thought his head would explode. He took her hand and kissed it.

At that moment Brigsworth-Jones reentered. His look told Erik that they needed to get down to business.

Erik stood. "Sir, this is Anke Junger. She and I were friends in Munich when we were children."

"I see. A stroll down memory lane, is it?"

"Yes, sir."

"Do me a favor and stop speaking German."

Erik hadn't even registered that he and Anke had been speaking in German. He hadn't strung three German words together in years, his father insisted on English at home the minute they emigrated. It had all come back to him so smoothly and effortlessly.

"Yes, sir," they both said, in English.

"Right," said Brigsworth-Jones. "Well Fräulein, we've got a rather big mess on our hands. You claimed you knew the location of the Florentine art stash. We need to find that art and bring it back to Florence."

"I understand. I want to help," she said.

"Well, that's all jolly well. However you are a German citizen, correct? This isn't going to go over well with the intelligence boys. We need to debrief you now, before they do."

Brigsworth-Jones gestured to Crawford, who was waiting by the door. He dashed inside and set his typewriter up on a small table.

Anke then began speaking, in near-perfect English, and Crawford typed madly, occasionally asking her to repeat something or to clarify a point.

She told them about the Ghent Altarpiece, the Jeu de Paume, her transports from Krakow, Carinhall, Neuschwanstein, and, of course, the Brenner Pass. She was as specific as she could be on the exact location and condition of the masterpieces. Dearborn brought in cups of strong coffee and a tin of olive oil crackers. Brigsworth-Jones sat, riveted, as she described her association with the Ghent Altarpiece. Anke teared up slightly when she described the room at Neuschwanstein where she last saw the altar, before she left for Italy. Erik mentally pictured her arranging the panels, alone, and sitting in front of them for hours. He attempted to take notes, but his hands were too shaky.

"Anke, you said you went to Bruges briefly to help evacuate Belgian works?"

"Yes. Pieter van Maes told us you had been there."

They looked at each other for a long time before Anke broke away, flushed. Brigsworth-Jones threw Erik a look: *Get on with it, chap.*

"They wouldn't release any Belgian works to us," Anke said sensing the tension. "The bishop wanted to hide everything in the city."

Anke told them about the repository at Pau and her trip back to Paris. She detailed the catalogue she prepared for Bauer in Ghent and the ones for the Reichsmarschall in Paris. She sped lightly over the Konrad affair and her incarceration in a mental institution…time for that later, maybe.

When she mentioned her time at Carinhall, Brigsworth-Jones nearly spit out his coffee.

"You actually lived at Hermann Göring's house?"

"For a summer, yes."

"Do you like him?" Crawford blurted out, looking up from his typewriter.

"Shut up, Marshall!" Dearborn hissed.

"No, it's fine," Anke said, smiling. "I understand how bizarre all this sounds. I understand if you think I'm a Nazi too. But I'm not. I've hated them since the day they came to power…since they began a war on art and on everything else that was decent in Germany. I stayed at Hermann Göring's house because he told me to and I had nowhere else to go."

"I hate to ask this," Brigsworth-Jones began, "but…," he trailed off after an imploring look from Erik.

"My father you mean?" Anke said softly. "Yes, you heard correctly. He killed himself. Seems like yesterday but it was actually almost seven years ago. I can't believe how long I've lived without him."

Erik reached for her hand and caught it, not caring what the others saw or thought.

"This Bauer fellow," Brigsworth-Jones said, lighting a cigarette and offering one to Anke, who accepted. "He's SS?"

"Yes, but he's been also working under Göring for art-related projects."

"Art-related projects?"

"Franz helped Göring steal crates of Neapolitan works from Monte Cassino, for one thing."

The fact that Anke used Bauer's first name made a pit in Erik's stomach.

"Do you know where Bauer is now?" Erik asked, trying to sound casual.

"I believe he went to Berlin, but I can't tell you his exact location. You understand, I…I don't believe he is an evil man. On the other hand, I have no wish to be associated with him anymore. I…we…we were…you understand, I had to protect my friends in Ghent. I…."

"We understand, Fräulein," Brigsworth-Jones said. "He was blackmailing you, using the safety of your friends."

"Yes, at first. That's true. But later…well, things changed and all I want to impress on you gentlemen is that Franz did the right thing at the end. I wouldn't be surprised if the Nazis have already imprisoned him, or worse. But, like I said, he did the right thing…in the end."

"These paintings you transported from Krakow," Erik said, changing the subject. "What were they exactly?"

"Da Vinci's *Lady with an Ermine*, Rembrandt's *Landscape with a Good Samaritan*, and Raphael's *Portrait of a Young Man*. I actually held them on my lap."

Erik raised an eyebrow. "Any idea where they had come from?"

"Yes, they had inscriptions. The name was Borowski. I remember my father telling me something, years ago, about a Polish family who bought a da Vinci...but I can't really recall the story."

"I've met him, the owner, Count Borowski."

"Recently?"

"Four years ago, in Cambridge. He came and spoke to my father and our art protection group. His story was compelling...he told us about the theft of the Veit Stoss altar."

Before the conversation could continue, the MPs appeared in their round metal helmets. They took Anke by the arms and began to lead her out of the room.

"Wait! Where are you taking her? We are in the middle of an interview!"

"An interview?" the MP asked, mockingly. "She needs to be debriefed by the interrogators. We shouldn't have left her here with you this long. She could be a spy."

"A spy? Are you serious? She's an art historian, like me. She's going to help us find the Florentine works."

The bulkier MP walked up and stood less than two inches from Erik. "You just keep worrying about your paintings. The interrogators will find out if she's the real deal, don't worry...Captain."

As they took her out, Anke looked serenely down as if to say, *don't fuss, this is supposed to happen.* Erik had seen that look before: Jesus's calm pose as he was arrested in the Garden of Gethsemane in Erik's favorite Caravaggio, *The Taking of Christ.* His father never cared for the painting. "Too shiny," he would say. But the gleam emitted from the soldiers' armor was exactly what drew Erik, and others, to the piece. Even from far away, it had a power. Christ was passive, but the taking was active and the viewer could feel the confusion, angst, and heartbreak of Christ's disciples. Of course, Erik was sure it was nothing compared to the heartbreak he felt now, for a woman who he hadn't seen in twelve years.

"LOOK, YOU DON'T UNDERSTAND. She's not a Nazi. Her father was killed by the Nazis!" Erik was shushed by Brigsworth-Jones, who stood next to him as they attempted to talk sense to the local head of Allied interrogation, Major John Flanagan.

"Excuse me, Captain Brossler, but I was under the impression that…," he paused to refer to his notes, "…Herr Junger committed suicide."

"He did, after the Nazis forced him to stop painting. Then they put him in a concentration camp and almost killed him. They confiscated his paintings. I know she's told you all this."

"Yes, she has. But we need to make sure that she doesn't know anything that could be of use to the army. I mean, she spent a summer at Göring's country estate for Christ's sake. There's a million things she could know!"

"Well, does she know anything?" Brigsworth-Jones asked, lighting a cigarette.

"Whether she does or she doesn't, it's above your pay grade, Captain."

"How long is this going to take?" Erik asked. "We need to get to the Brenner Pass as soon as possible."

"What's stopping you?" Flanagan asked.

"What do you mean what's stopping us? We need to take her with us!"

Brigsworth-Jones nudged Erik again. It was the *you seem to have forgotten you are speaking to a superior officer* nudge.

"Why? Why do you need her?" Flanagan barked. "You have the location. Go get the pictures and take them back to Florence. That's what you want isn't it? To be the big hero? So, go be heroes. Meanwhile, we'll keep talking to her and maybe she'll say something that will help us win the fucking war."

Flanagan shooed them out of his makeshift office.

"With respect, sir, the Germans are finished. I can't understand how she can help."

"After the war is won, Captain Brossler, there will be reprisals. People will be held to account. Horrific crimes have been committed. Stolen art isn't the half of it; trust me. I will release her when I am satisfied that she is who she says she is, a German civilian, and when I am satisfied that she has given us all relevant information. End of conversation."

The door was slammed with enough vigor to ripple Erik's hair.

~

WHILE ANKE WAS IN protective custody, President Roosevelt died. Erik and Dearborn heard the news as they reached Bolzano, which was still teeming with German officers wining and dining themselves despite the fact that the German commanders had already surrendered to the Allies in Rome. Apparently this was not yet public knowledge.

"Do these guys know they've lost?" Dearborn asked uneasily as they drove past yet another hotel adorned with the swastika and bursting with drunken soldiers singing and girls playing pianos.

"Thank God, it's not up to us to tell them. We've got the letters from Bauer, that Anke gave us. All we need to do is locate the storage facilities and send a cable to Brigsworth-Jones. We don't have to talk to anybody."

"Yeah, but...I mean, do they realize the war is over, it Italy at least? What if they want to engage us?"

"Tom, they won't even know we are here. I don't think they are paying much attention."

Erik sank his foot on the gas pedal and they sped up into the hills toward the Brenner Pass. A few minutes later, Erik could tell he wasn't convincing anyone because Dearborn was stuffing extra ammunition into his pockets. Neither of them had fired a shot since Sicily and despite their efforts to take the occasional target practice to keep their skills fresh, they hadn't done so since well before Pisa. Still, Erik knew Dearborn would be vicious in a fight.

They arrived at the first location Anke had marked on their map, the town jail at San Leonardo, just after dusk. A quietness hung over the village and Erik had the feeling that there were dozens of sets of eyes watching them through darkened windows and cracked doors, unsure of just who these uniforms were and what they wanted.

"Reinforced steel," Dearborn muttered, out of breath after his many jabs at the door with a shovel.

"At least the Germans *attempted* to protect the art," Erik said, peering in the barred window.

"We should have brought tools."

"I agree, if there were tools to be brought."

"Did Fräulein Junger mention how to get into this place?"

"No."

"But she got in, didn't she?"

"She had the keys."

They were about to get back in the Jeep when two men emerged from a small house across the square. One looked at least eighty years old, the other younger than thirty. The old man took a ring of keys from his pocket and shook them at Erik.

"Signori, are you...are those the keys to the jail?" Erik asked, knowing his Italian had too much Latin in it.

"I am the jail keeper!" the man yelled.

Erik proceeded with caution. "We are Americans...Americano.... we want to return the artworks to Florence...Firenze."

"Firenze?" the man asked, then went to open the door.

As it turned out, there were no fewer than six doors to open before they came to the main room where the paintings sat, some stacked, some leaning against the walls. It didn't take long for Erik and Dearborn to notice that Anke had organized many of the paintings by artist and had grouped them according to school (Italian, Flemish, etc.).

"How did she move these?" Erik wondered aloud. Some of the canvases were giant and awkward, even for them.

"Maybe she had a bunch of German soldiers in here helping her."

"She said she was here alone."

The Italian men stood in the doorway, watching the Americans and muttering to each other. Eventually they left and returned a few minutes later with yet another key, which opened the circuit box. The lights came on and illuminated just how grubby the place really was.

"Here's Bellini's *Pieta*," Dearborn said, dragging a panel into the light. "Or one of them at least."

The Italians crossed themselves at the sight of the Virgin Mary gently cradling the lifeless body of Jesus. Dearborn gingerly wiped the accumulated dust off with the sleeve of his uniform.

"Here's *Bacchus*!" Erik said, relieved it wasn't damaged despite the crowding together of many of the paintings without wrappings between them. He lifted the Caravaggio and stood it against the wall. The God of Wine looked back at him, resplendent in white toga and floral headdress.

"I love this one," Dearborn said, walking up close. "He's got the face of a little girl, but look at those biceps!"

"That's true. I've never really noticed that before," Erik said, smiling. "Now, where is the Cranach that Anke said Hermann Göring wanted her to bring back to him?"

"*Adam and Eve*, was it?"

"Yeah. Wait, there's some more stuff over here, under a sheet. For fuck's sake, it's right here."

Erik removed the filthy sheet and revealed the masterpiece. The Italians groaned when they saw it.

"Adamo!" the younger man exclaimed. "Eva!"

Erik and Dearborn just looked at each other. After that the Italians, whose names were Fabiano and his grandson Ezio, helped them gather all the paintings in the hallway according to size. By the time they were finished it was three o'clock in the morning. Ezio locked the building and brought Erik and Dearborn back to his house, which he shared with his grandfather. They insisted the Americans take their beds for the night. Erik slept fitfully on the tiny bed (Fabiano was no taller than five-foot-three) but the size of the bed wasn't the main problem. Erik was in constant rumination about Anke, her whereabouts, her condition and her…involvement with Franz Bauer. When Dearborn woke him at seven-thirty, Erik was sure he'd slept only an hour, two at most.

Dearborn looked at Erik's weariness and handed him a strong cup of coffee that tasted like burnt leaves.

"So, she was your girlfriend?" he asked timidly.

Erik shrugged. "No, we were just kids. I left for America before anything like that could happen."

They stepped out of the house into the still morning. It was strangely cold and then Erik remembered that they were up in the mountains.

"But, you love her," Dearborn said, sipping his coffee.

"Completely. Is that weird?"

"Nope. Just checking."

"Thanks Tom. Did you reach Brigs?"

"Yes sir. The troops have been mustered."

Dearborn had cabled Brigsworth-Jones, who was on his way with Crawford and an Army engineer unit. Local Italian workers had arrived in San Leonardo to help with the packing. Erik didn't dare ask, but he was fairly sure he had just spent the night in the home of the leader of the North Italian Resistance. Ezio seemed to know everyone and began directing people with authority and even put up a barrier around the jail to keep out dozens of villagers who had gathered to watch the show. Word spread quickly that the Allies had taken more than a thousand German prisoners of war down in Bolzano, no doubt including the reveling soldiers Erik and Dearborn had sped past the day before.

Four hours later, Brigsworth-Jones arrived with Crawford, two new units of Monuments Men sent from Rome, and Anke Junger.

"The interrogators are satisfied she is who she says she is," said Brigsworth-Jones as he crawled out of the Jeep. "They say she's all ours. They want a big deal made of this find. We are supposed to take everything back to Florence in high style. It will all be filmed, of course. The Americans are milking it a bit, chap...if you ask me."

Erik watched as the Italians wrapped and loaded each piece onto the trucks. Ezio directed traffic. A large crane arrived on the back of an army flatbed and proceeded to a building about a mile away that was housing many of Florence's most treasured sculptures, including Michelangelo's *Bacchus* and Donatello's *St. George*.

"Did you find the Cranach?" Anke asked, slipping next to him and handing him a cup of coffee, only toasted leaves this time.

"Yes, we did. We also found something else." He gestured to Dearborn who came trotting over with a small panel, wrapped in a blanket.

"This was in a corner by itself," Erik said.

Anke unwrapped the panel and gasped. "Van Eyck. *Madonna with Child.*" She shook her head. "I didn't see this when I was doing my catalogue here."

"Maybe it was added later? There's a note attached to the back," Erik said, then stepped a few feet away.

Anke turned the panel over.

Anke,

I hid this for you in my hotel room for weeks. I wanted you to have your own van Eyck. But I realize now how silly I was to think you would ever accept it. You have had every opportunity to take pieces of art for yourself

*and you have taken nothing. I hope you will understand that my decision
not to give this to you shows how I truly feel.*

Yours,

Franz

Anke folded the note and tucked it into her dress. She walked over
to where Erik and Dearborn were standing, trying to look like they
weren't watching her.

"This should go with the Dutch and Flemish paintings, Lieutenant,"
she said, handing the panel to Dearborn, who thanked her and ran off
to the trucks.

"That note was from Franz Bauer," she said. "Like I said, he is not
a bad man."

Erik nodded but said nothing.

She sipped her coffee, unsure if she had upset him. He seemed
tense.

"Do you want to come with us?" he asked suddenly, looking at the
ground.

"To Florence?"

"Yes. As an observer."

"Of course I want to come. Am I allowed?"

"You've been cleared as a spy, so I guess it's up to you now."

"I want to help, in any way I can. But…."

"You're worried about the van Eyck altarpiece."

"Yes."

"I will personally help you find it and see it returned to Ghent
when we're done in Florence."

Anke smiled and nodded and it seemed decided.

"Maybe we'll find some of your father's paintings," Erik said, walking with her toward the Jeep.

"No," she said with authority. "I'm sure they've been burned by
now."

Erik wanted to object, but then remembered one of the things
Anke had said in her debriefing statement. The SS had cut modernist paintings out of their frames with knives and then burned them

outside the Jeu de Paume, along with Jewish family portraits and anything painted by a Jewish artist.

Erik watched Anke walk slowly toward the trucks, her loss evident
in her slow, exhausted steps.

THE TRUCKLOADS OF FLORENTINE art were driven to the railroad depot
where everything was loaded into thirteen freight cars and heavily guarded
for the trip. As the train pushed slowly south, it passed the majority of
the Allied Fifth Army, which was now exiting Italy and moving toward
Germany. In its wake was destruction unlike Italy had seen since the Roman legions fought the Goths and the Vandals in the fifth century.

Brigsworth-Jones broke his own rule, that Anke and Erik should
be left alone to talk, because his news was just too big. He entered their
train compartment where Erik was recounting his experience at the
Campo Santo in Pisa. Anke was fascinated and hardly acknowledged
Brigsworth-Jones until he plopped down next to her.

"Sorry to interrupt, but Mussolini is dead. Shot. Strung up by a
mob in Milan. His mistress too."

Anke and Erik were stunned. "What does this mean?" she asked.
"Is the war over?"

"In Italy it is."

Brigsworth-Jones also had other news. The Russians had found
something in southern Poland, near Krakow. He called it an "extermination camp." Gas chambers were discovered, despite the attempts by
the Nazis to blow them up. There were crematoriums for burning the
bodies. There was evidence of torture, forced labor, starvation, medical experiments…even children were not spared. The prisoners were
mostly Jews, but also Poles, communists, and members of various gypsy
communities.

Then he said the Americans and the British had found similar
camps in Germany. He said there were likely dozens of them.

Anke stared out at the passing springtime landscape. Erik didn't
know what to say. He thought about his grandmother and all the friends
they had left in Munich. He was glad his mother wasn't alive to hear this.

An hour passed. Anke seemed frozen until she finally muttered
something.

"What? I missed that, Anke," Erik said, desperate to connect with her again.

"I was just remembering something that Heine wrote."

Erik thought for a moment, then said, "Where they burn books, they will, in the end, burn people."

Anke looked at him, tears pooling in the corners of her eyes. Erik looked down and concentrated on keeping his composure.

"Of course," Anke sniffed, "Heine was referring to the Koran being burnt during the Spanish Inquisition. Still...."

"Yes," Erik agreed. "Still...."

20

Hidden Treasures

PRICELESS WORKS OF ART, FROM FLORENCE'S BEST MUSEUMS AND PRIVATE COL-
LECTIONS, ARE RESTORED TO THE CITY BY ALLIED SOLDIERS.

A GERMAN ART HISTORIAN, ANKE JUNGER, WHOSE OWN FATHER, ACCLAIMED
PAINTER DIETRICH JUNGER, WAS A VICTIM OF THE NAZIS, WAS INSTRUMENTAL IN
THE RECOVERY OF THOUSANDS OF FLORENTINE MASTERPIECES.

THE MAYOR AND A MULTITUDE OF FLORENTINE CITIZENRY TURNED OUT TO WEL-
COME THE ART HOME.

TEARS OF JOY AND BOISTEROUS REJOICING MET THE MONUMENTS AND FINE ARTS
OFFICERS OF THE US FIFTH ARMY AS THEY RETURNED WORKS BY TITIAN, MICHEL-
ANGELO, RAPHAEL, DA VINCI, AND MANY MORE!

THE AMERICAN NEWSREEL captured the merriment of the occasion. The banners draped across the trucks read *le Opere d'Arte
Fiorentine tornano dall'Alto Adige alla loro sede* (The works of art of Florence
return from the Alto Adige to their home). The crowds were considerable and the city had gone to great lengths, even heralding the arrival of
the convoy with costumed trumpeters. Dr. Censari's face was awash in
tears as he stood in front of the Uffizi, shaking slightly at the thought
of the final triumph of the *ricoveri*.

The sight of Brigsworth-Jones and Censari in an emotional embrace had even Dearborn wiping his eyes. Anke's role in the recovery
of the collections was not hidden from the crowd and she was given a

bouquet of flowers by the Director of Italian Antiquities, Paulo Sorelli. Everyone had their picture taken in front of the trucks, then again with Censari, the mayor, and Sorelli. Choice paintings were taken out, unwrapped, and photographed. Erik was much in demand and gave several interviews to the American journalists. Brigsworth-Jones did the same for the British reporters and photographers. Anke wondered what the German papers were saying at this moment.

Once the formalities were over, a number of Florentines approached Anke and wanted to shake her hand, or embrace her. Her Italian was too rusty to make much conversation, but she found that a hearty smile worked even better. Erik, in a similar situation himself, understood all too well what the fake smile felt like. Today was jubilation, but he wasn't alone in his dread over what they might find, or not find, when they drove north toward Germany the next day.

Brigsworth-Jones passed out cigars that he said he had been keeping for a "celebratory moment." At the official banquet in the city hall, the wine flowed and Marshall Crawford became inebriated for the first time in his life. He told Anke she was the prettiest girl he had ever seen, before Dearborn dragged him off and stuck his head under a public water spout.

Anke stayed close to Erik, the whole event becoming more and more absurd as she began to obsess about what Brigsworth-Jones had told her the day before. What would her father think, seeing a party like this? But surely the safe return of priceless, irreplaceable art is worth a commemoration?

The wine had gone straight to her head and cheeks. She fled, flushed, out into the darkness of the Piazza Signora. Except for Cosimo I, the statues hadn't been replaced yet; that would be tomorrow's task. Most of the revelers had gone home and there was a dusty peacefulness to the square. She sat on a low wall and breathed deeply. The air was warm but did not yet have the stifling thickness of summer. She nearly wept with joy when she felt him sit beside her, his arm slipped around her waist. They spoke softly to each other for a few minutes before Erik kissed her. Anke would remember every detail of that moment for the rest of her life; his smell, of wine and garlic, and his rough, calloused hands cupping her face.

Anke spent the night at the home of Director Sorelli, as his guest. Erik and Dearborn left Brigswoth-Jones playing cards with a group of Italian soldiers and dragged Crawford back to a small hotel near the train station and let him sleep it off on the floor, while they collapsed on the flimsy twin beds. Brigsworth-Jones never made it to the hotel, but arrived bleary- eyed at the station the next morning. Where he spent the night was never discussed.

WHEN THEY GOT THERE, three days later, Neuschwanstein had been emptied of many of the most important works. The Ghent Altarpiece was gone, as was the cream of the crop of the ERR's French collection. What remained were numerous collections from Bavarian museums, sent to the castle to avoid Allied bombing. Frau Kruger was still there, though most of the art historians had left months prior. The old woman claimed she knew nothing about where the art was taken and even denied it being housed at the castle in the first place. She also pretended not to recognize Anke.

This was quickly sorted out when a giant room crammed with fastidious ERR records and catalogue cards was found by Crawford. Anke located hundreds of cards written by her own hand at the Jeu de Paume. Frau Kruger attempted to leave the castle after this embarrassing revelation, but she was "detained" by the MPs at the bottom of the hill. They returned her to the castle where Erik demanded she open her rather large suitcase. When she refused, Dearborn grabbed it from her.

"A bit heavy, don't you think Frau Kruger?"

"You have no right," she began, but Erik's look shut her mouth.

Dearborn ripped into the bag with a fury few had witnessed in him before. The clanking from the silver spilling out onto the floor brought Brigsworth-Jones in from the next room.

"Those are mine!" the woman stammered. "I...bought those."

Anke picked up one of the larger pieces and held it up.

"A candelabra, for my daughter...," Frau Kruger said, nearly weeping.

"It's not a candelabra," Erik said. "It's a menorah."

"A what?" she asked, incredulous.

Anke turned it over and looked at the bottom. The initials D.W. were carved into the metal.

"You should be looking for a big stash of silver and gold," she announced. "This belonged to David David-Weill, an art dealer from Paris. I'm sure there is more."

Erik and Brigsworth-Jones sent men in every direction, armed with pick axes, to find a hidden door, or safe, or room. Less than an hour later, two privates sent word that they had found something in the basement. Behind a steel door, draped with a dusty wall hanging, was hidden the Rothschild jewels and David-Weill's 1,200-piece silver and gold collection.

"Christ, there must be five million pounds worth of gold and silver in here," Brigsworth-Jones said.

"What are you going to do with it?" Anke asked.

"Leave it, under guard. We don't have anywhere to take it yet."

Upstairs, Crawford had been busy running from room to room, instructing newer members of the Monuments and Fine Arts division on how, exactly, he liked his reports to be typed up.

On the uppermost floor, Dearborn found enough antique furniture, rugs, and oriental carpets to outfit ten castles...and a hundred evacuated German children. Anke spoke to them and told them they were safe with the Americans. A cry of joy rippled around the room as, one by one, they comprehended that they were not going to be left to the Russians. The joy more than doubled when Dearborn brought out the chocolate bars.

The news of Hitler's suicide, which wafted around the castle like a whispering wind, had little effect on the children. They ate their chocolate and looked up at Anke with wide eyes. Clearly, they were wondering what was going to happen next. Leaving them, on their grubby cots, was as hard as leaving the van Eyck altar sitting in a stuffy room a few floors below. But leave them she did and drove east to Berchtesgaden with Erik, Brigsworth-Jones, and Dearborn. A number of Monuments Men stayed behind at the castle, including Crawford who was slowly recording the immense information contained in the ERR records room. A hefty military guard was posted outside.

Berchtesgaden, she told them, was the spiritual home of the Nazi party and most of the high-ranking members of the SS had second homes there, as did Hitler and Göring. She remembered Franz talking about it, about the unbelievable excess at a party he attended, but she had never been herself. One needed to be a Nazi party member to live there. She and her father would have been denied at the gates, God willing.

News had reached them that units of the US Third Army had found Carinhall, but it was in ruins. Göring had blown it up, but first shipped his art collection south. The final destination wasn't known, but Anke assumed it was Berchtesgaden. They arrived around noon and the town was almost completely deserted. Hitler's orders had been for the SS to make a last stand here, but even the most fanatic members had either scattered, surrendered, or been killed by the Allied onslaught. Swastika banners hung from balconies and flapped in the mountain breeze, but there was little noise aside from the drone of the Allied trucks. As they proceeded further into town they could see that the French had looted the Berghof, Hitler's vacation home, and had raised the French flag over the house.

"I don't begrudge them some payback, after what Hitler did to France," Brigsworth-Jones said, surveying the scene. "But it does seem that they've made a rather big mess of it. What do you say, chap?"

Erik looked around at the detritus. Statue fragments lay on the ground, forgotten in the rush. All the other houses were shuttered up tight.

"I think this place is creepy," Erik admitted. "Let's find what we can and get the hell out."

"I couldn't agree more," Dearborn said, wiping a piece of Italian marble clean on his pant leg.

The 101st Airborne was in command of Berchtesgaden and had taken up residence in many of the grander villas, including Göring's. When no apparent repository was found, Anke began to wonder if Göring had thought Berchtesgaden was too obvious and had shipped his collection somewhere else entirely.

A cable arrived in the early evening from the French interrogator who had spent the past twenty-four hours conversing with Hermann Göring at a prison in Augsburg. Göring, who spoke of the war without remorse or even consideration of the horrific damage done by the

Nazis, seemed very concerned about his collection, which he insisted was indeed at Berchtesgaden. Brigsworth-Jones wanted to send Anke to talk to him and get the exact locations, but relented when he saw the expression on her face. As it turned out, they didn't need Göring after all.

After breakfast on the second day, a well-dressed German man approached them in the main hotel and introduced himself as Andreas Pfizer, art dealer to Hermann Göring.

"I met him at Carinhall," Anke whispered to Erik. "He's a snake, but he probably knows exactly where everything is."

Brigsworth-Jones asked him to sit down and offered him a cigarette. Pfizer spilled the beans without much cajoling, and seemed not to see what the big deal was. There was a train, still packed with elements of Göring's collection, sitting on the tracks outside the town. There had been some initial looting by the local population, but that stopped when the 101st Airborne arrived. There were also a number of pictures in the tunnels that linked many of the main villas together.

"Tunnels?" Erik asked.

"Yes, much of the collection is stored in the tunnels."

"Not quite the place for works of art, Herr Pfizer."

Pfizer bared his teeth in what he must have thought was a smile. "You are German?"

"I was, but now I'm American," Erik shot back.

"I thought I heard a Bavarian accent. Welcome home."

Erik took his pistol out of the holster and cocked it. Pfizer was taken aback and immediately looked to Brigsworth-Jones, who said nothing and puffed away on his cigarette.

"Why don't you show us exactly where the collection is, Herr Pfizer," Anke said, trying to break the tension.

"I recognize you," he said, not taking the hint. "Franz Bauer's girlfriend."

"Certainly not," Anke said, calmly. "But I do remember meeting you at Carinhall."

"Yes, last summer. The Reichsmarschall was quite taken with you."

Erik leveled the pistol at Pfizer's head.

"Captain," Pfizer squealed, "I am a civilian! Surely you don't shoot civilians!"

"Why not? You Nazis do."

"I can assure you, Captain, that I have never touched a weapon in my entire life."

Brigsworth-Jones ended the stalemate by lifting the shaking Pfizer out of his chair by his arm. "Where's the bloody train? Which way?"

Pfizer pointed, still trembling despite Erik's re-holstering of his weapon. A few minutes later they were down at the train station looking at a string of abandoned cars sitting on the tracks. The doors to some of the cars were closed but not locked, indicating they had indeed been tampered with.

With the help of the 101st Airborne, the train was emptied in a little short of three hours. Hundreds of paintings, sculptures, rugs, furniture pieces, and tapestries were carried into the largest villas and grouped according to Anke's organizational system. She recognized many of them from the Jeu de Paume and those were placed in a special area, as were the several Memlings, which she wrapped in a tablecloth and placed aside so Erik could have a good look at them.

"Göring had more Memlings," Anke said. "There were several small ones. They're not here."

"Maybe he took them with him," Erik said.

"He's in custody. We'd have them if they were on his person," Brigsworth-Jones said.

"His wife," Anke said. "Has anyone checked his wife's belongings?"

They all looked at each other, then Brigsworth-Jones marched off to make a call.

WHEN CRAWFORD ARRIVED at Berchtesgaden the next day, he walked into the ballroom of the hotel, where Erik and Anke were bent over a small Memling Madonna. He teetered when he saw the walls lined with paintings, the colors blurring in front of him. His exhaustion was palpable. Brigsworth-Jones packed him off to one of the upstairs bedrooms with a ration kit.

The 101st Airborne's commander in Berchtesgaden, Major Randall "Randy" Summers, talked Brigsworth-Jones into allowing an exhibit of some of the art, a selection of pieces, so the men could see something that they might not ever have the chance to see again. Since they didn't have the transportation to move the collection anywhere, Erik and Anke agreed, but insisted on accompanying all personnel through the exhibit and setting a limit on how many men could be in the room at one time.

"Did you see the fifteen crates from Naples?" Anke asked Erik as they made lists of all the works found in Göring's train.

"Yeah. The ones Bauer *rescued* from Monte Cassino."

"I guess he did rescue them, in reality. He didn't know it at the time, of course."

Erik grimaced and rubbed his eyes. Sore subject. Anke felt guilty for bringing it up and excused herself to go get some rest.

"You two make quite the team, chap," Brigsworth-Jones said when Anke was gone.

"I guess so," Erik said awkwardly. "I mean, I don't know her that well. I haven't seen her since...."

"I understand, chap. Believe me, it's pretty obvious."

"What is?"

"Don't play the idiot with me. I'm still smarter than you."

Erik watched his mentor step out into the late spring evening and could still see the glow of his cigarette even after his form had disappeared into the darkness. The ballroom was still, though Erik could almost hear the roar of a Nazi dinner, the clanking of dishes, the pouring of champagne. He picked up a bread plate and turned it over to see the swastika. This was one of the last plates left. Nearly everything had been looted by Allied soldiers desperate for their little token of the Nazi establishment. Some took silver tea services; some took wall hangings and flags. Hitler's photo album from the Eagle's Nest was missing, so someone took that too. Erik stood up, exhausted by his thoughts, and ran up the stairs to Anke's room.

"What kept you?" she asked, letting him in.

"I have no idea. I think...I don't know what to think anymore."

She nodded, unsure how he really felt. He sat on the bed and looked at her. She was wearing her slip, the one Bauer had bought her. She immediately took it off and threw it across the room. There was no way Erik could understand the meaning behind the gesture, but he understood what to do next. Their fatigue was briefly forgotten and the bed was made of feathers so they sank into it like paint soaking a canvas. Anke wondered briefly who had been the last Nazi to occupy this hotel room, but Erik's mouth on hers stopped everything. She threaded her fingers in his hair and closed her eyes.

A loud banging on the door sent Erik flying off the bed and Anke scrambling under the covers.

"Captain! Sir!" It was Dearborn's voice. Erik, somewhat sheepishly, cracked open the door.

"Lieutenant…."

"Sir! They've surrendered! Germany has surrendered!"

Dearborn was flushed and a little drunk. He saluted, winked, and ran down the hall.

After registering that Dearborn had known exactly where to look for him (in Anke's room), Erik locked the door. He turned to Anke, who had heard and was weeping into her hands. He raced to the bed and nearly crushed her in his embrace.

"We might be the only two Germans crying out of happiness at this moment," he said softly, his eyes filling.

"No," she sputtered. "There are more, there have to be more."

They kissed each other and crawled under the covers.

21

The Underground

Fear has many eyes and can see things underground.
—Miguel de Cervantes

DESPITE THE WONDERFUL PR generated from the securing of Hermann Göring's art collection in Berchtesgaden, complete with his Vermeers, Cranachs, Rembrandts, Memlings, not to mention a sumptuous grouping of French Impressionists, the overwhelming majority of Nazi confiscated art was yet to be found. The Ghent Altarpiece was actively sought by the Belgian government and Anke was able to receive a phone call from Professor Dubois, who wept with joy when he heard her voice.

"We've been so worried. We had no idea...we thought maybe you'd been killed."

"No, I'm fine. I'm with the Americans. We are leaving Berchtesgaden today, to go north. How is...how is Niels?"

There was silence on the line.

"Professor?"

"Yes, I'm here. I'm sorry, it's just...Niels is dead. He killed himself, two years ago now."

Anke felt the blood drain from her face and the pale chill take over.

"Anke... he just felt so guilty about you. He felt he had abandoned you and led to your arrest."

"I was never arrested. I was...I was commandeered, yes, but not arrested. I never spent a day in prison."

"He didn't know that, none of us did. Your landlady told us an SS officer had come for you and you never returned."

"They needed my services, as an art historian. I was in Paris for over a year. Then I went to Germany. I found the *Mystic Lamb* in a Bavarian castle! It's gone now, we don't know where."

Her voice broke. Niels had killed himself because of her. But Bauer had admitted that Niels never actually gave her up, it was Jan the janitor at St. Bavo's. She couldn't talk anymore and let the phone drop. Erik picked it up and spoke to Dubois for a few minutes before passing the phone to Brigsworth-Jones, who spoke to Dubois for quite some time, taking notes down in his small black book.

"They found the stained glass from Strasbourg Cathedral," Brigsworth-Jones said after putting the phone down.

Anke looked up, not bothering to hide her tears. "Where?"

"A mine in Heilbronn."

"A mine?" Anke asked, looking at Erik, who sat beside her.

"Makes sense," he said. "Bomb proof."

"Let's get a list of major mines within thirty miles of here," Brigsworth-Jones said. Dearborn was off running before being officially given the order.

"Apparently the windows were packed well, in straw and wooden crates built especially for them," Brigsworth-Jones said, consulting his notes.

"Dubois told you that?" Anke asked. She thought of Chartres Cathedral and wondered if its stained glass had been found and replaced, assuming the German officer's club was now defunct.

"Yes. He had lots of information. Our Monuments Men have been in Belgium a while now and it looks like they've had their share of bombed churches to deal with. But the Bayeux Tapestry has survived and is going on display in Paris. The Louvre collection is safe as well."

"The entire collection?" Erik asked, incredulous.

"Looks like it. Everything was split up amongst a variety of chateaus south of Paris."

Anke remembered the man she met in the Ghent University library, who told her the Bayeux Tapestry had been placed in a lead box and buried somewhere, and the woman who spoke of the evacuation of the Louvre. It all seemed a lifetime ago.

"What happened, Anke?" Erik asked, unable to keep quiet about her obvious distress.

"It was another life," she said, still lost in her thoughts.

"What was?"

"I told you that I drove the Ghent Altarpiece to Pau, after trying to first take it to the Vatican."

"Yes."

"Well, there was someone with me. His name was Niels Maarten. He was a professor at the university. Not one of my professors…but I met him there and we had a…relationship. Anyway, when he returned to Ghent he was arrested. Bauer led me to believe that Niels had given up my name to save himself. He later told me that he had lied and that Niels never said anything about me, despite being badly beaten and God knows what else. It was someone else who dropped my name, someone from St. Bavo's."

Erik nodded and realized they were now sitting alone; Brigsworth-Jones had disappeared.

"After I left Ghent with Bauer, Niels and Dubois never heard what happened to me. He said they thought I was arrested and maybe killed. I guess Niels felt responsible. Maybe he couldn't remember whether he had named me or not…maybe he thought he had cracked. He killed himself two years ago."

"That is not your fault, Anke."

"I know that. I just don't know how much more I can take. The war is over, but I feel like the bad news is going to keep coming and coming."

"I know."

Anke stood, shaking slightly. "I've had nightmares. I see the van Eyck burning, the oil paint bubbling, only the panels merge…into my father's canvases. I feel like…maybe I am losing my mind."

"Of course you are not. You've slept ten hours in the last three days. I have nightmares too."

"I lost my mind once before, Erik. I've never told you about that either."

"When was this?"

"After Paris. I told you about the warehouses, the piles of furniture, the children's toys."

"How could I forget?"

Anke lit a cigarette. "I was in a hospital for months after that, in Châtenay-Malabry. I don't remember much…I was drugged. Bauer came for me eventually and took me off the drugs. That's when I was taken to Carinhall."

"Châtenay-Malabry?" Erik said. "I just read something about that place. Jean Fautrier was there too, before the liberation. His paintings, *The Hostages*, just went on exhibition in Paris."

Anke had a memory, but it slipped away. She closed her eyes but couldn't make it return.

"I don't remember. I wish I did. I lost so much time."

"Did you love him?"

"Who?"

"Bauer."

"No. But I didn't hate him. Not once he broke free from them. To think…what would have happened if more people had been able to break free…," she trailed off.

Erik could see Anke had said all she could at the moment. She needed to keep working, keep focused on finding, above all, the Ghent Altarpiece. He was sure her soul was somehow attached to the van Eyck in the same way his was attached to her.

DEARBORN DID MORE than find mines; he found miners. For some soup and a loaf of bread, several men who had worked in mines all over Germany highlighted on a map the mines they knew to be deep and cavernous enough to actually house large stores of art.

Armed with the map, a stockpile of food to bribe miners and whomever else they might come across, the Monuments Men abandoned their Jeeps (not without sorrow) and settled into two trucks provided by the US Third Army, Ninetieth Division.

"Riding with us, sir?" Crawford asked, sliding over to allow the Welshman in and remembering how much larger he was when they first met in Sicily.

"Yes, Lieutenant, I think I'll give the lovebirds some more time to shake out their demons."

"The lovebirds?" Crawford looked from Brigsworth-Jones to Dearborn and back again.

"Forget it, Marshall," Dearborn said, trying to suppress a laugh.

Several hours later, they arrived in Merkers, where there had been a report of a large mine used for hiding "Nazi gold." Erik had never considered himself much of a treasure hunter, but he had to admit it felt invigorating.

A small group of soldiers and one officer awaited them at the entrance to the mine, along with several local miners.

"We've heard a lot about your team, Captain Brossler," said Lt. James Gibbs. "You really tracked down that Florentine stash?"

"Actually, she told us where it was," Erik replied, nodding to Anke.

"You're the German art historian? Miss Junger?"

Anke nodded.

"You're well informed," Erik said, slightly unsettled.

"It was in the papers," Gibbs said. "We all felt…well, it was a great victory for the Allies."

"Let's not get ahead of ourselves, chap," Brigsworth-Jones said, stamping out a cigarette in the dirt.

"Sorry, sir. Please, this way."

They followed him inside and squeezed into the small elevator. Anke's hand found Erik's as they plunged downward into a complete void, bereft of any light whatsoever. After what seemed an hour, they arrived at the floor of the mine. It was damp and extremely cold. None of them, save the miner, had thought to bring jackets.

A number of hanging light bulbs now illuminated a huge cavern filled with row after row of cinched sacks. There was no artwork, furniture, or sculpture visible to the naked eye.

Dearborn picked up one of the sacks and found it heavier than he thought. He cut through the burlap with his army knife.

"Christ!"

Anke leaned forward and saw that Dearborn was holding gold bars in his hands.

"This is the Reich's reserves," Brigsworth-Jones said. "Look, here's some paper currency."

Brigsworth-Jones held up a pile of Reichsmarks then stuffed them back into the sack. They were worthless now. Anke and Erik followed him along the small track for the mining cars. There were hundreds of sacks arranged in perfect formation, like a military parade.

Toward the back of the mine there were some large crates, which Dearborn took a crowbar to. When Anke saw the crunchy straw her heart leapt. Erik helped Dearborn lift out a large oil painting, which they leaned against the crate.

"Manet," Brigsworth-Jones said. "*In the Conservatory.*"

A young woman in a bonnet sits on a bench with her closed parasol, a bearded gentlemen leans over the back of the bench, talking to her. She stares off into space as if his comments are either too boring or too shocking to pay attention to. Anke wondered if he was proposing.

"This was in the Kaiser-Friedrich Museum, in Berlin," she said. "The paintings I transferred from Krakow could be here, if they hadn't been taken back to Krakow by that horrible man."

Erik nodded, knowing the story. He and Dearborn took a few more paintings out, several more Impressionists and a pre-Raphaelite. Anke wandered to another crate, a few feet away, and saw that the top was not nailed shut. She opened it and saw a large folder labeled "DÜRER." Inside was an impressive number of woodcut prints by Albrecht Dürer.

"Dürer was a great admirer of van Eyck's altar, wasn't he?" Erik asked, joining her and flipping through a few of the prints.

"He was."

They were distracted by the voice of Brigsworth-Jones who had found an entire section of the mine filled with framed canvases, leaned against each other like volumes on a bookshelf. He gently browsed through them, calling out artists as he recognized them.

"These are German-owned works, put here for safekeeping," Erik said, somewhat disappointed.

"I don't even know what *these* are," Crawford said, standing over several gigantic crates in a dark corner.

Anke walked over to him and saw something glinting inside the crate. More gold?

"Wait a second," Crawford said, stepping back. "Oh my...oh my God!"

Anke was confused only for a second, then she saw what he saw. Gold teeth. Piles and piles of gold teeth. Surrounding the teeth were menorahs, gold necklaces, some with the Star of David, some with crosses, some lockets. Rings...hundreds of rings. Thousands maybe.

Erik stood beside her now, the rage evident on his face. He reached in and picked up one of the lockets. His fingers shook as he tried to pry it open. He finally managed it and the small lid creaked open. A little boy's face stared back at him, his dark eyes mirroring Erik's own. Anke walked slowly and deliberately back toward the elevator, without looking back.

ERIK FOUND HER SITTING in the truck outside the mine. She was morose. Her face brightened somewhat when she saw that he carried a gold bust of Nefertiti.

"Look what Dearborn found," he said, placing the bust in the backseat.

"I am surprised Crawford let you take it before he's written his report."

"Oh, he's down there writing it now."

"In that light?"

"I think he needs something to do."

Anke nodded and went silent again. She felt furious that the triumph of surviving art had to be so polluted with inhuman cruelty. How could these people care so much about art, enough to see it properly wrapped, packed and hidden in a mine, and also wrench gold teeth from...perhaps the very same people whose homes were ransacked and whose children's dolls were shipped to Germany? For the first time, she understood her father's state of mind as he stood on the paint-splattered table and wrapped the cord around his neck. How can one go on in the face of such unbelievable and vicious brutality?

Erik kissed her palm. A simple gesture, but one that convinced her, beyond all doubt, that she loved him. That, she decided, would save her. It hadn't saved her father, but maybe a daughter's love wasn't enough.

When the others returned to the light of day, they drove to the nearest Allied headquarters so Brigsworth-Jones could send and receive cables. As a rule, they avoided major cities to spare Anke having to witness the destruction. Everyone knew this rule would not last long, but so far they had kept to the country roads, which were more practical anyway since the main roads were shredded by the Allied bombs.

They descended into two more mines in the following days. They found the original manuscript for Beethoven's Sixth Symphony, vestments, gold and silver candlesticks and chalices from several German cathedrals, and the relics of Charlemagne in moldy boxes.

22

The German Count

A thousand years will pass and the guilt of Germany will not be erased.
                                                                —*Hans Frank*

THE MONUMENTS MEN had discovered that a young, attractive German woman could be quite a successful interrogator. While the frightened and half-starved inhabitants of the destroyed German cities shied away from Brigsworth-Jones and were reluctant with Erik, Dearborn, and Crawford, they were downright spouts of information when Anke sat down with them.

A woman in Bernterode told Anke that something suspicious had been going on at a mine outside town, just before the surrender. When they arrived at the location it looked initially like a huge munitions dump. They hoped that no art would be found in this extremely dirty and dangerous place. After several hours of searching, finding nothing of interest, a freshly made brick wall was discovered at the back of the mine. Soldiers from the US Third Army chipped at the wall with pick-axes until it tumbled down, then they came rushing up the mineshaft screaming that they had found Hitler's tomb. Anke was skeptical, but she, Erik and Dearborn went down nonetheless, leaving Brigsworth-Jones on the surface to spare his lungs.

A number of grinning privates stood at the entrance to the cavern, clearly thrilled with the story they would have to tell their children and grandchildren. Anke took one look at the caskets, wreaths, ribbons, and Nazi banners and realized this was some sort of shrine. Erik went to the first casket and there was a handwritten note attached to the top.

The coffin belonged to Field Marshal von Hindenburg, Germany's most decorated Field Marshal of World War I. The next one was that of Frederick the Great, the King of Prussia in the late eighteenth century. The third was Frederick William I, the King of Prussia in the early eighteenth century and the father of Frederick the Great. Banners from every Prussian war going back hundreds of years hung above the coffins, over two hundred of them. A box of photographs, mostly of Nazi field marshals posing with Hitler, sat next to one of the caskets.

"I can't believe Brigs is missing this," Erik said, squatting next to one of the caskets.

"There are some paintings over here," Dearborn called from a dark corner of the large space, "wait a second, there are tons of paintings over here!"

They found nearly 300 works of art, many from German royal palaces like Potsdam and Charlottenburg, including a series of Cranachs, along with a Boucher and a Watteau. They also found that the steel door, which sat directly behind the brick wall, was the only way in or out and had been locked from the *inside*. They looked around for the corpse of a dedicated Prussian history fanatic, but found no one.

TRUCKS WERE IN SHORT SUPPLY, so removing these items from their underground lair was slow going. Brigsworth-Jones ran out of favors to call in and was turned down by every army group within fifty miles. In the end, they had to move on and leave the art and the tombs under heavy guard until more transportation could be commandeered.

Once back on the road, Anke saw why the trucks were so in demand. Piles and piles of rubble were being hauled away each day to help make the search for survivors and war criminals an easier task. Unlike in Florence, ordinary people weren't sifting through the detritus looking for statue fragments. The German civilians were looking for only two things: food and shelter. Massive refugee camps were springing up along the main roads and the hollow eyes of children watched Anke's truck pass them as they stood in line for a bowl of soup. Brigsworth-Jones had reported that the concentration camp at Buchenwald had been re-appropriated by the Russians to be a POW camp "in less time than it takes to down a bottle of vodka." When the Allied trucks weren't hauling the remains of homes, churches, and buildings, they were transporting German POWS to their new camps, shuttling desperate civilians from temporary camps to makeshift shelters, and bringing home the first concentration camp survivors. Those faces were unmistakable, sitting in trucks on the road south from Weimar. Anke had seen that look before.

She wanted to close her eyes, but Erik's warmth beside her reminded her what was at stake. She knew if the rest of the van Eyck panels were lost to history, or destroyed, she quite simply wouldn't get over it. She hadn't heard from her father in a long time and she wondered if he was angry about her liaison with Erik. How could he be? He had always liked Erik and she was sure that when the Brosslers left for America her father had been as disappointed as she was.

She was blasted out of her reveries, which Erik always respected and allowed her without interruption, when she saw the flash of a familiar face as they passed a black car.

"Stop! Wait, that was Count von Essen!"

"Who?" Erik slammed on the breaks.

"The head of the Kunstschutz."

He turned the truck around, which was no easy feat on the muddy country road, and started after the black car. Brigsworth-Jones leaned out of the window of his truck, wondering what was happening. Without waiting for an explanation, Dearborn turned their truck around and followed Erik. The sudden movement woke Crawford, who had been dosing in the back of the truck on a pile of thin blankets they kept to wrap up any discovered paintings.

After about a mile, the black car pulled over to the side of the road and a well-dressed man emerged, a little grayer and more worn than the last time Anke had seen him, in the dining room of the Meurice.

"Fräulein Junger?" von Essen asked, surprised.

"Your grace," she said, jumping down from the truck.

"I must say, I am glad to see you. I was worried. I never heard about you again after that episode in Paris."

"Thank you. I...well, I survived."

"I see you are with the Americans."

"We are a joint American/British task force, sir," Erik said, joining them.

Von Essen took in his uniform and nodded respectfully. When Brigsworth-Jones walked up, a moment later, the count's eyes widened.

"Good God, Owen Brigsworth-Jones," von Essen said, in English.

"Von Essen. What the hell are you doing out here by yourself?"

"You know each other?" Anke asked, confused.

"Yes, we've met several times, before the war," Brigsworth-Jones said, lighting a cigarette and offering one to von Essen, who accepted.

"The last time must have been that conference in Strasbourg in '37. Seems like a million years ago," the count said, leaning in to the outstretched lighter.

"It was."

An uncomfortable chill was exchanged and von Essen looked shaken. It passed quickly and he turned to Anke.

"So, you blow with the wind don't you?"

"What do you know about the whereabouts of the ERR repository?" she asked, ignoring his comment.

"Absolutely nothing. I was never part of the ERR. You would know more than I do about that."

"I wouldn't be so determined to blacken Anke's name. She's already helped us beyond measure and her loyalty is without question," Brigsworth-Jones said. "I knew you to be a respectable man and a brilliant art historian. Don't disappoint me now."

"We just want to make sure the art is safe and returned to where it belongs, that's all," Anke said.

"I was not involved in any art looting, if that is what you are suggesting," the Count said, taking a long drag.

"We are suggesting that you were the head of the Kuntzshutz, a now defunct organization, and you are now in Allied custody. It usually helps when you tell us something," Erik said, using his best menacing tone.

It worked. Von Essen went back to his car and reached into the glove box. Dearborn leveled his pistol at him in case he was reaching for a gun, but re-holstered it when the count produced a map. He spread it out on the hood of his Mercedes.

"Here," he pointed. "I believe there is a large repository in this area. I am not sure where, exactly, but I've heard some talk."

"Austria?" Erik asked, looking at the map.

"Yes, the Salzkammergut, a mountainous region south of Salzburg."

"Wait a second," Brigsworth-Jones said. "That is where the SS were said to be mounting their last stand. You are sending us into the lion's den."

"To my knowledge, the German Army has surrendered."

"Yes, your grace, but I wouldn't put it past the SS zealots to put up some crazed defense in the Alps."

"Nor would I, my lord."

The use of his official title unsettled Brigsworth-Jones and he lit another cigarette before he'd finished the first one.

"May I speak to the count alone?" Anke asked.

The others nodded and backed away toward the trucks. Von Essen turned his attention to her, much as he had done that night at the Jeu de Paume as they discussed Vermeer's *The Astronomer*.

"Your grace, I know that you were not happy about what the ERR was doing. You made that clear on the night I met you. You may feel that I am betraying Germany by working with the Americans, but Germany betrayed me, and my father, years ago. I had no love for the Nazis and I know you didn't either."

"The Americans will never believe that."

"Why not? They believe me."

"Yes, well that young man, with the dark hair, he's clearly in love with you."

"He's the son of David Brossler."

"David Brossler, from Ludwig Maximillian University?"

"The same."

"Well, that's a strange coincidence. I knew him rather well. He wrote that wonderful book on van Gogh when he was only just out of school. He went to America, didn't he?"

"Yes, because he is Jewish."

Von Essen looked down for a few moments. "Yes, well I'm glad he went. I'm glad he survived. I'm glad his son survived. I'm glad you survived." His eyes were wet.

"Will you come with us?"

"No. I am too old for treasure hunting. You will find what you are looking for in the Salzkammergut. I believe there is a mine, perhaps at Alt Aussee. I don't know for sure, but I heard something about Alt Aussee."

"Thank you."

Von Essen turned to Brigsworth-Jones, who returned with a resigned look on his face.

"You must be interrogated, your grace. I can't be the one to do it."

"Certainly not! Our previous relationship might cloud your judgment."

"I would, however, like to extend the courtesy of allowing you to report to the local command center of your own accord."

"I appreciate that. I shall report by tomorrow."

Brigsworth-Jones extended his hand and von Essen took it, though made little eye contact. A moment later he was in his car, rolling up the windows. Anke thought that was strange since it was so hot, but she didn't put it together until it was too late. The shot made her jump and Erik yelled out her name, unsure of what was happening. Seconds later, Brigsworth-Jones opened the bloodstained door and the corpse of Count von Essen tumbled out, the gun still gripped in his hand.

Von Essen was the second dead body Anke had seen up close, the first being her father's. The effect was significant. How one moment he could be speaking to her and the next his lifeless body was rolling out of the car...

Anke felt queasy as she watched Erik and Dearborn lift the count's body onto a stretcher, which was then placed in the back of an army ambulance.

"I guess he knew his involvement in the looting would become public once we interrogated him," Erik said when he returned to the truck. "I figured he might be egotistic enough to think none of it would stick, like Göring."

"Maybe he just couldn't live with it," Anke said, feeling oddly defensive. "He was a true art lover. I think he regretted ever getting in-volved with the Nazis. I think there are many people in that position."

"It's best to figure that out when you can still do something about it, like you did."

Anke turned away from him as her nausea increased. Her face was greasy with sweat.

"I need a doctor," she said suddenly.

Erik paled. "Anke?"

She fainted, her body falling limply against the door of the truck. She woke almost immediately, the moment her head hit the window.

"Anke! Are you all right? Sweetheart?" Erik cried, cradling her head.

"I'm fine," she mumbled. He threw her into the seat and put the truck into gear. They sped into the nearest town, Shoppendorf, where Erik found a US field hospital set up in a church in the town center.

The pews had been removed to make room for row after row of beds for the wounded Americans, some so hideously injured Anke felt she might faint again.

"I can't take the doctor's time here! Please, I'm fine," she said, back-pedalling toward the door. Brigsworth-Jones appeared in the doorway and the look on his face turned her back around. She insisted that they wait until a doctor was free; she refused to take care away from a wounded man.

Several hours later, Captain Clay Bishop, a doctor from Greenville, South Carolina, came over and took Anke behind a partition made from bed sheets. Erik tried to follow, but was shooed away by a female nurse who was also a nun. Brigsworth-Jones took Erik outside and they smoked five cigarettes between them before the nun came out to get them.

"She's perfectly all right, it's normal in her condition," she said, then disappeared back inside before Erik could ask any questions.

"I thought that might be it," Brigsworth-Jones said, stifling a laugh.

"Excuse me?"

"You're going to be a father, chap."

ERIK FELL INTO a sort of trance over the next few hours, staring at Anke as if she were the most beautiful and yet most horrifying creature he'd ever seen. Anke, however, felt more focused than ever. Everything was falling into place. Though she had only fainted for a few seconds, she had seen her father in that time and he was radiantly smiling at her. There was no cord, no skeletal frame, just her father of old, the artist, at peace with himself and the world. She decided he must be very happy with her situation. Of course, he might prefer that she was married, but there was still time for that. Erik would need a little time.

"I feel fine, now let's get down there and see if von Essen knew what he was talking about," she insisted.

"Austria is a good three-day drive from here and we don't have that much fuel," Brigsworth-Jones reminded her. "That isn't even to mention the fact that you should really be resting, in your condition."

"In my condition?"

"Please Anke," Erik said softly, "he doesn't want to be responsible for...what if something happens to you or the baby?"

"No, of course! You are absolutely right. I will simply go...well, I'll go somewhere and I'll stay with...someone, and I'll just wait for the baby to come, seven months from now. Of course, this will completely negate the promise you made me that you would help me find the altarpiece and we would see it safely returned to St. Bavo's together."

"I fully intend to keep that promise, Anke."

"Then let's get going, please."

Erik looked at Brigsworth-Jones, who shrugged in a "you've got your hands full with her, chap" sort of way.

"We'll save on gas if we take only one truck," Crawford finally said. He was rewarded with a look of gratitude from Anke that he would not soon forget.

It was decided. They squeezed into one truck and convinced Anke to lie down in the back on a bed they fashioned out of empty sacks, straw, and the bedding they had carried with them since Italy. They lifted the canvas flaps enough to allow air to circulate, but not so much that it would be too windy to sleep. They each took turns driving and sitting in the back with Anke, who felt they were fussing too much but went along with it to keep her place in the expedition.

Along the way, they stopped at several American and British headquarters so Brigsworth-Jones could cable his superiors and alert them to a possible art stash at Alt Aussee in Austria. In return, he received the news that there had been some recent activity at the main mine in Alt Aussee and that it was now under military guard, awaiting their arrival. He also learned that fellow Monuments Men had found around 5,000 bells at a Hamburg dock, taken from churches all over Europe. The

Nazis hadn't had the time to melt them down, but had succeeded in damaging many of them in the transport process. Alfred Rosenberg's "Race Institute" had also been discovered in Berlin and an American chaplain was sorting through thousands of Torah scrolls that were dispassionately dumped in the basement.

"The chaps in Berchtesgaden are still running the Göring exhibition," he reported, trying to revitalize Erik who had become quiet and distant. "The 101st Airborne have turned out to be quite the art connoisseurs. They've had thousands of chaps through their exhibit...no problems yet."

Anke smiled, thinking of the treasures of Carinhall being shown to Allied soldiers by the "Screaming Eagles." Somehow, this was fitting and she wondered if Göring had heard about it, or if he was even still alive. She thought briefly about Bauer and it made her physically uncomfortable.

"Well, there was one little problem," Brigsworth-Jones said. "After much inspection, one of Göring's prized paintings turned out to be a fake. It's on display anyway."

"A Vermeer? *Christ with a Woman Taken in Adultery?*" Anke called from the back.

"Yes, how did you know that?"

Anke laughed, really laughed, for the first time in longer than she could remember.

"Neuschwanstein has been practically emptied," Brigsworth-Jones continued, realizing he wasn't going to get an answer from her. "Our chaps have moved nearly everything out, over 20,000 pieces. Bloody incredible! They built a wooden ramp down those stone stairs to slide the crates down. Goddamn brilliant."

"Where is everything going?" Erik asked, interested now.

"They've set up collecting points for anything found within the former Reich borders. The nearest one to here is Munich and that seems to be the largest one as well. The collection from the Siegen mine is going there, as well as pieces found in private homes. They just discovered some stolen paintings in Heinrich Himmler's castle, Wewelsburg. Joseph Goebbels also had a decent collection apparently."

"Does anyone find it strange that these men, butchers really, had such a love of art?" Dearborn asked, while navigating the truck along a partially flooded road.

"I think it was Hitler's influence," Crawford said. "The others were all just following the leader. Well, except for Göring maybe, he seemed to really love collecting. Of course, they didn't love *all* art. They destroyed some of it…like Anke's father's paintings."

"Marshall!" Dearborn hissed, but Erik put up his hand as he looked back at Anke; she had drifted off to sleep on her pile of sacks.

"It's okay Crawford, she's asleep," he said.

"Sorry, sir. I didn't mean anything by it."

"Don't apologize. You're right. Everything you said was right."

It was some time before any of them spoke again.

23

The Salzkammergut

The National Socialist Party in Austria never tried to hide its inclination for a greater Germany.
—*Arthur Seyss-Inquart, Reich Minister for Foreign Affairs*

WHEN THEY REACHED Alt Aussee on May 12, the US military presence outside the mine assured Anke this was the major cache of stolen art they were looking for. Here, surely, would be the Ghent Altarpiece, Michelangelo's exquisite Bruges Madonna, and the countless masterpieces that were still unaccounted for. She prayed she might also find the three paintings she escorted to Berlin from Krakow, but something told her Hans Frank would not have given them up without a fight.

An entire company of men was standing around the mine entrance, smoking and chatting in small groups and eating from their ration kits. Anke squinted into the bright sunlight as she emerged from the truck. Her back throbbed from sleeping on the hard sacks. A new awareness of her belly caused her to place her hand across it in a protective gesture. Suddenly a loud yell came from somewhere in the crowd. All the soldiers lined up in rows and stood at attention.

"At ease," boomed the officer. "These are the Monuments and Fine Arts officers we've been waiting for. Our mission is to provide them protection and physical support. Their commanding officer is Captain Brigsworth-Jones of the British Second Army. He is in charge."

The officer, Major Simard, consulted a piece of paper in his hand.

"The other officers are Captain Brossler, and Lieutenants Dearborn and Crawford of the US Fifth Army. You will do as they say. The lady is a German civilian and art expert who will be treated with the upmost respect. Is that clear?"

"Yes sir!" was sung out in unison.

"Now, we don't know what is down in this mine, but we think it might be a large stash of priceless artworks and other cultural items. We are not qualified to handle these objects unless under the direct supervision of these MFAA officers. You will wait for them before you touch anything. Am I clear?

"Yes sir!"

Major Simard turned and walked over to Brigsworth-Jones, who stood with his unit next to their truck.

"Captain, my men and I are here to assist you."

"Our most sincere thanks, major!"

"Not at all. I'm just glad we got here when we did. They almost blew the whole place up."

"What?" Erik and Brigsworth-Jones asked in unison.

"Yep. The entire mine. The Germans rigged it with explosives."

"Then, this can't be an art stash," Anke said, disappointed. "Hitler wouldn't have approved that."

"This was done after he was already dead," the major said. "It was the local Austrian district commander, actually. Might have been a power trip. Anyway, an SS officer overruled him and had the bombs removed less than a day before we arrived. We have him in custody. He told us all about it."

"You have the SS officer in custody?" Erik asked.

"No sir, the Austrian district commander. I don't know where the SS officer went."

"How do you know the district commander isn't lying to make it seem like he's a hero?" Erik asked, skeptically.

"Because they left behind some of the bombs. There's one in a box over there," he said, pointing to an area by a barbed wire fence. "It's been defused, of course."

They all walked over to the wooden crate, on which was written, *Marmor—Nicht Stürzen*. Marble, Don't Drop.

"Jesus Christ. These people never cease to amaze me," Brigsworth-Jones said.

"Well, there's got to be something important down there," Dearborn said. "You don't blow up nothing."

AFTER A BRIEF EXCHANGE over whether or not Anke should accompany them down into the mine, Anke stepped into the elevator with the two Austrian miners who had been paid wages by the Americans to be present during this investigation. Erik and Dearborn squeezed in behind her. Crawford set up his camp on the surface, content not to visit any more mines. The piles of teeth were still very much biting at him, especially at night. Brigsworth-Jones waited for the first load to go down, then planned to take three of the strongest-looking soldiers he could find down with him if word returned that there was indeed something worth removing.

As they descended, the air temperature plummeted by thirty degrees in the span of three minutes. Anke shivered with anticipation and wrapped her too-large army issue jacket tight around her. The miners switched on their helmet lights with their forever-stained hands as the elevator came to a stop. Erik and Dearborn turned their flashlights on, but despite this Anke could see almost nothing through the blackness. Her army helmet rattled around on her small head and she tried to tighten the strap but lost interest as soon as a tall figure came into view. She could see its outline, high and slender at the top, then wider toward the bottom. The quick passing of a flashlight beam illuminated, just for a second, the cherubic face of an infant. Everyone saw it at the same time and converged their lights on the same spot.

The Bruges Madonna.

"Oh, my God. Here she is," Anke said as the tears started to flow. Excitement mixed with the uncomfortable memory of a doll's face in a dark warehouse.

"Go get Brigsworth-Jones," Erik told Dearborn. "Tell him the Michelangelo Madonna is down here."

Anke gently rubbed her fingers along the smooth, cold marble. The statue was attached with twine to a grimy mattress but in otherwise good condition, aside from a thick coating of soot, which now covered Anke's hands. She couldn't believe how much her life, and the lives of so many others, had changed since she last saw this statue in Bruges before the war.

"If she's here, then maybe…," Erik began.

"Not necessarily," Anke said, shaking her head. "We don't know how they organized these mines."

Erik nodded, worried that he was getting her hopes up. They walked a bit further into the darkness, the miners' lights leading the way. What they saw, when the further lamps were lit, were rows and rows of purpose-built wooden racks, bins and shelves, all crammed with paintings, sculptures, books, and carved religious pieces. It was ten times the number or works found at either the Siegen or Heilbronn mines. It made the collection at Neuschwanstein look relatively minor.

They wandered through the stacks as if in a daze. On initial inspection, there didn't seem to be any obvious system; German works were mixed with confiscated French and Polish items. A cacophony of expletives announced the arrival of Brigsworth-Jones, who blundered past the Madonna and began browsing through paintings on a middle shelf like a woman sifting through dresses on a clothes rack.

"Six paintings in and I've found a bloody Vermeer. A real one."

Anke and Erik joined him as he held *The Astronomer* in his slightly trembling hands.

"Hitler wanted this for Linz. Von Essen showed this to me the night I met him at the Jeu de Paume," Anke said.

"Stolen from the Rothschilds, right?" Erik asked, blowing the dust off it.

"Right," Anke said. "So, that's a good sign. If the Linz collection is here, we will find a great many masterpieces."

"So, what you are saying is that this is Hitler's loot," Dearborn said, his smirk illuminated by his flashlight.

Everyone donned a Cheshire grin before plunging in.

Within an hour, Erik had found another Vermeer, *The Artist's Studio*, and six Rembrandts, including a self-portrait that he himself remembered seeing on a visit to the Kunsthistorisches in Vienna with his father.

Anke ventured further into the mine, which became labyrinth-like toward the back, escorted by one of the miners. The ceiling was so low at certain points that a sense of claustrophobia almost sent her retreating to the cavern area. There were so many wrapped packages, stuffed in every crevice, that she hardly noticed any single work as she searched for a sign, any clue in the gloom.

"Dead end," the miner said.

"Are you sure?"

"There's a door here, we need to turn around."

"Wait," she said, a tingling coming over her. "Shine the light there, at the door."

On the door was written, ST. BAAFS.

With wildly shaking hands, Anke looked for a door handle, a lock, anything. There was nothing. She ran back toward the cavern but smacked straight into Brigsworth-Jones, which sent her reeling to the floor.

"Christ! Anke, love. Are you hurt?" He pulled her up hoping Erik hadn't seen.

"No," she said, out of breath. "We need to push through that door. It says St. Baaf's."

"St. Baaf's?"

"St. Bavo's Cathedral," she stammered. "In Flemish they say St. Baaf's."

His eyes widened and he pivoted on the spot and began yelling out into the darkness. Two privates emerged from the shadows a minute later and pried the door open with a crowbar. Anke was the first one inside the chamber, but even with her flashlight she could see very little. She took a few timid steps, then her foot ran up against something. She bent down and shone her light down onto the dirt floor. Lying un-wrapped, on flattened cardboard boxes, was the Ghent Altarpiece. She had imagined this moment ever since she left Neuschwanstein, but was now struck by an intense fury at the injustice of these panels, amongst the most important artistic works in the world, lying on the earth in an Austrian mine. There was no visible damage, but the dirt was caked on and the vivid colors were reduced to shades of gray and brown.

She knew Erik was beside her before he spoke.

"We need blankets, lots. Mattresses too, if you can find them," she said.

"The boys upstairs have just gone to the nearest German field hospital."

Anke nodded, but felt lightheaded. Erik wrapped her in his arms and noticed that despite the fact that the mine was only about 47 degrees Fahrenheit, Anke was sweating and shivering at the same time. Her skin was on fire.

Hundreds of blankets and mattresses left the German field hospital and went down into the mine. Anke left the mine and went into the field hospital. The patients had already been marched or driven to the POW encampment north of Alt Aussee, but a few nurses and a doctor were still there when Anke arrived. She was given IV fluids and diagnosed with an influenza-like virus, from which, Erik was told, she would recover. Despite her protests, Erik did not return to the mine until her fever broke, two days later. In the meantime, the Americans removed more than 6,500 paintings, 2,300 drawings and watercolors, nearly 1,000 prints, and hundreds of sculptures, tapestries, suits of armor, books, furniture, and boxes of archives from the mine. The Ghent Altarpiece was left where it was because Erik insisted he carry the panels up himself.

Brigsworth-Jones came to the hospital to report that everything was being taken to the main collection point in Munich, where every piece would be sorted, cleaned, repaired, investigated, catalogued, and eventually returned to the country or place of origin.

"Other MFAA units have found lots of other caches," he said. "In cellars, in people's homes, in mines. There is stuff stashed bloody everywhere!"

"Any sign of the Veit Stoss altarpiece?" Erik asked.

"Yes! They found that in Nuremburg. Seems to be in good shape."

"I should have told you it was in Nuremburg," Anke said, struggling to sit up in the bed. "I was told that when I was in Krakow picking up the paintings from Frank."

"Who told you?"

"An old woman who comforted me in The Church of Our Lady of Krakow. I was a bit overwhelmed when I got there and then I saw a different altarpiece in the church and nearly collapsed. My father was very fond of the Veit Stoss, despite the fact that he was a lapsed Catholic. My father I mean, not Stoss."

"From what I've heard, the Nazis were anti-Catholic, anti-Christian, and anti-Jewish. Who bloody knows, maybe all this religious art wasn't destined for Linz after all. Maybe they were going to destroy it," Brigsworth-Jones said.

"Then why take the time to hide it in a mine?" Erik asked. "Why not just burn it?"

"The Nazi purists were a sect within the larger group," Anke said. "Most of them were just criminals. Thieves. Profiteers. Murderers." She rolled over and pulled the covers up, despite the heat.

Erik stayed with her a while longer before returning to the mine with Brigsworth-Jones.

"Why do you think an old woman in Krakow knew where the Germans were taking the Veit Stoss?" Erik asked as they drove back to the mine. "Did she know that he was born in Nuremburg?"

"I don't think the Germans were hiding it, chap. They probably told everybody, 'we're taking this to Nuremburg, just try and stop us!' Remember, it was not until recently that they even considered they could lose this war. Now they've lost and lost badly. I think we'll find that most of the really important art was only hidden in the last few months."

Over the next three hours, Erik and Dearborn personally wrapped and carried the panels of the Ghent Altarpiece to the elevator, rode up with them, and saw them safely installed in a truck that was reserved especially for the van Eyck. Erik then sent a runner to the hospital to tell Anke that the panels were safe and headed for Munich. When the runner returned, he had someone on the back of his motorcycle.

Brigsworth-Jones nearly choked with laughter. "I bloody love this girl," he announced, watching her delicately slip off the motorcycle. "She's let it out of her sight twice, and twice it was moved somewhere else. She's no dummy, chap."

24

Munich

Do not let spacious plans for a new world divert your energies from saving what is left of the old.

—*Winston Churchill*

I T HAD BECOME all too obvious to Erik that the art protection mission was going to be more complicated and political in peacetime than it ever had been during the war. Memos were flying out of the War Department like flocks of pigeons in Piazza San Marco, all insisting that as much looted art be indentified and consolidated within the American Zone as possible. The American Zone included Bavaria and Hesse, as well as several northern ports (Bremerhaven and Bremen) and the northern part of Baden-Württemberg (the French had the southern portion). The British had most of north and midwestern Germany while the Russians had the entire eastern half of the country, as well as the areas of Poland and Czechoslovakia that had been annexed to the Reich. It was never said out loud, but both Erik and Brigsworth-Jones knew that much of the looted art found in the Russian zone was already heading east to Moscow and Leningrad. They had absolutely no control over that, but still it bothered them.

What bothered them even more was the fact that the trucks at Alt Aussee were loaded and ready to depart, but word came from Allied HQ in Munich that the collecting point was not ready to receive the masterpieces just yet. They hoped it would only be a day or two, a week at most. It was forty-five days. The trucks were guarded round-the-clock and the Monuments Men were billeted in a school gymnasium in Alt Aussee. Anke reluctantly returned to the hospital for a few days, then took up residence with a local doctor and his family. Dr. Fuerst had been very helpful to the Americans and had operated on two officers who had been wounded in accidents since their arrival in Austria. His wife had died before the war and he had three young daughters. Anke was happy there, thinking it was only for a week or so, until the youngest girl, Greta, asked why Anke kept touching her belly. Dr. Fuerst showed considerable understanding considering he had an unwed pregnant woman living in his house with three young girls.

"She's been through a hard time, in the war," he told the girls. "But she's with the Americans now, and so are we."

The simplicity of the statement made Anke shudder. "Was this the amount of thought given to supporting the Nazis?" she asked him that night, when the girls were in bed.

He shrugged. "The Americans have the guns in this region. For my brother-in-law in Saxony, it's the Russians. I'm not sure this war is really over. The enemies are just changing, that's all."

After that, Anke begged Erik to let her live with him at the gymnasium. This idea was shot down by Brigsworth-Jones, who claimed that he needed to start playing by the rules if he wanted to call in more favors, like the honor to escort the Ghent Altarpiece back to Belgium.

While Anke was packing her things at the doctor's house, determined not to stay there any longer than she had to, it suddenly occurred to her that she could go home. The Junger apartment in Munich was owned by her father, which meant it was now hers since she was his sole heir.

"You don't know what you will find there," Erik said when she told him her idea. "There are probably American soldiers living there. It's likely been ransacked. It might be horrible for you to see."

"I want to go home. I haven't been home since he died. Don't you want to go home?"

"Home is America for me."

"Really? Before the war you were going to settle in Bruges."

"That was before the war."

They looked at each other for a while without speaking, sitting in a café near Alt Aussee. Then they drove back to the school. Erik requested permission to take Anke to Munich and assist in the preparation of the collecting point. Brigsworth-Jones wasn't fooled, but agreed anyway. They weren't allowed to take any of the rescued works of art with them and all the Army could spare was a motorcycle with a sidecar. They left most of their belongings with Crawford, who promised to bring them when the convoy got under way. Dearborn tucked a pillow, the one he had been sleeping on since Rome, behind Anke in the sidecar.

"You'll watch over them, Tom?" she whispered to him.

"You bet."

There was no question to whom "them" referred. Erik sped off and Anke left the van Eyck panels behind for the third time.

WHEN THEY REACHED MUNICH, they drove immediately to the Königsplatz, where the collection point was being set up in the former Nazi party headquarters. The huge square, now eerily empty and forsaken, had been the scene of The Day of German Art, eight years before. Though neither Anke nor Erik had witnessed it in person, they had heard it described in vivid, emotional detail. Erik remembered the words of Friedrich Fassbinder and the quotes from Hitler's speech from one of his father's many letters. Anke recalled listening to it all on the radio. They sat, lost in thought for a few moments, before Anke realized that she could ease her discomfort by simply getting out and walking. Erik drove the bike around the square to the collecting point, all the time watching her cross the Königsplatz. As she got closer, she could see that the collecting point was surrounded by a barbed wire fence. A protective measure surely, but a disconcerting one as well.

A guard at the door waved them in after making a phone call to someone inside. Though the outside of the building was relatively unharmed, the inside was a riot of destruction. The first room they came to, off the main hall, was literally a construction site. The walls were being re-plastered and they could see why; there were holes three feet wide and much of the old plaster had fallen off revealing the brick underneath.

A US naval officer noticed them and walked over, his eyebrow raised and a smile erupting on his face.

"Are you kidding me?" he asked, addressing Erik.

"Jeff?"

"Erik Brossler? I heard you were over here. I thought you were in Italy."

"I was. We've just come from Alt Aussee."

They shook hands, shocked smiles on both.

"Jeff, this is Anke Junger. She's an art historian and she's been helping us. She led us to the Florentine stash in the Italian Alps."

"You're reputation precedes you, Fräulein. I'm Lt. Jeffrey Lynch. Erik and I worked together at the National Gallery."

"Oh, wonderful to meet you. You were a curator?"

"Yes. Erik and I were put in charge of evacuating the gallery. I imagine they are planning the return of everything now. I wish I was there."

Erik looked down at the floor, which was littered with papers, pieces of furniture, and other trash. "Are you in charge here?"

"Sorry to say I am."

"Why are you sorry?" Anke asked.

"Because this is fucking disaster, excuse my language Fräulein."

"I'll admit, it doesn't look ready to receive anything," Erik said, trying not to sound too critical.

"Luckily, this is one of the last rooms we have attended to, many others are in better shape," Lynch said, lighting a cigarette and offering them around.

"This place was first trashed by the Nazis as they were all leaving, then trashed again by our boys when they first came in. Nazi Party HQ was a pretty big target. Then, I'm told to get this place ready, with no supplies, half-starved German workers, and hardly enough time to clean up three rooms, let alone thirty. The whole place needs to be weatherproofed, heated, and humidified. Oh, and they want a complete art reference library."

Erik and Anke looked at each other. He did have a point.

"I might be able to help with the library," Anke said. "My father had a massive art library. I haven't been to the apartment yet, but it is possible the books are still there."

"Anke, I don't want you getting your hopes up," Erik warned.

"Is your father Junger…Junger the painter?" Lynch asked.

"He was. He died seven years ago."

"I'm sorry. I know his work. He was incredible."

"Thank you. I think so too." Anke's eyes were wet, but she kept her composure.

"Look, any help you folks can give me, I'll take. I'm supposed to be receiving the Ghent Altarpiece in three days!"

Anke beamed at the thought, but kept her attachment to the van Eyck to herself. Lynch was stressed as it was.

"And the Bruges Madonna," Erik added, "along with just about the most incredible collection of art anyone has ever seen."

"Thanks," Lynch said, rolling his eyes.

Lynch took them on a tour of the building and gave them a run-down of his last few weeks. He had to turn out several units of American soldiers who were billeted in the building previously, then bring in the bomb units to check for booby traps and explosives left by the departing Germans. Holes in the roof and hundreds of shattered windows had to be repaired and replaced by local workers provided by the mayor of Munich. Easels had to be found or built to show the art to the experts who would be cataloging and restoring it.

"Who are these experts?" Anke asked.

"Germans mostly. The MFAA just doesn't have enough manpower to handle the quantities of art we are talking about. Munich will be the largest collecting point, but there is also one in Wiesbaden and another up at the I.G. Farben building near Frankfurt. We are spread pretty thin."

"Who are these Germans?" Anke said, realizing how odd that would sound coming from her.

"You mean were they Nazis? I've got these lists, which are supposedly of people who have been vetted and are considered not to be Nazis, but I've got my suspicions. I'm sure there are plenty of people who are just blowing with the wind."

"No question," Anke said uncomfortably.

Lynch shrugged as they entered the kitchen rooms, where meals would be prepared for the workers, truck drivers, art experts, and everyone else involved in this mammoth operation. The scale of the project was so overwhelming that they all just stood in the doorway for a moment, speechless.

"Where is the Haus der Deutschen Kunst?" Erik said suddenly. "I want to see that."

"The House of German Art? That's been commandeered by Patton's men. They've turned it into a mess hall and an officers' club. I was over there last night, what a party!"

This piece of information made Anke laugh out loud. "Finally," she said, "some justice in this world."

As THEY DROVE through the city toward Anke's old apartment, they digested a few other tidbits that Jeff had tossed out. He had recently inspected a number of paintings that were found in the possession of Hans Frank, Nazi Governor of Poland. He saw not only da Vinci's *Lady with an Ermine*, but the Rembrandt landscape as well. There was no sign of the Raphael, however, and although Frank was now in US custody, he refused to say how he obtained the paintings.

Lynch also told them that a few days ago word came that hundreds of medieval manuscripts were found floating down the Rhine on a barge. With great effort, an American MFAA officer had gathered a group of locals to help him secure the barge and transfer the manuscripts to an abandoned farmhouse, where he buried them in straw and covered them with wool blankets. These too would be on their way to the Munich collecting point as soon as it was operational.

Perhaps most disturbing was the story of Quedlinburg, a medieval town high in the mountains of Saxony, which became a shrine-like place for the SS because of its connection to the old Saxon kings. Himmler fancied himself the reincarnation of Henry I, the Dark Age Duke of Saxony and King of the Germans. The cathedral at Quedlinburg was taken over by the SS and used as a headquarters for their cult activities. The local clergy worried about the extra attention and eventually hid their most precious relics, illuminated Gospels and gold and silver ornaments, in a mineshaft outside the town. The hidden treasures were accidentally discovered by an American officer, who then ordered a guard posted at the entrance to the mine. This guard evidently allowed other soldiers to see the church's collection, and one or more of them stole most of it and shipped it back to America in cardboard boxes. An investigation, Lynch promised, was underway by the US Army.

Erik couldn't stop thinking this would be the tip of the iceberg. If German soldiers looted, Russians looted, Italians looted, Americans would loot too. He felt sick at the thought. Anke suddenly pointed from the sidecar and he brought the bike to a stop near the Ludwig-Maximillian University.

"It's right there," she said, still pointing, "17 Georgenstrasse."

Despite all the time they spent together as children, Erik had never been to the Junger apartment. All the festivities were held at his parents' house, in north Munich. They pulled up to an elegant apartment building. Ornate rod-iron balconies mixed with fancy scrollwork and masterfully carved stonework flourishes; this was not quite what Erik had expected from Dietrich Junger. Too old-fashioned.

"Our apartment is on the top floor—with his studio in the attic," Anke said, pointing to the topmost windows, which were larger than the others.

"I am amazed, after all that you have been through, that you still have your house keys," Erik said with a smile as she opened the front door.

"I almost lost everything in Paris, but Bauer brought my things to Carinhall...," she trailed off as Erik's face darkened.

Inside, there was silence and gloom. Litter covered the floor and the odor was of garbage and human waste. The elevator was broken, so they walked up the stairs. They heard murmurs from behind closed doors, the occasional radio, but little else. Erik knew the Americans had forced people out of their apartments to make room for billeting troops, but it did not appear that this building had been yet used in that way. Though it was clearly in disrepair and needed a good cleaning, the windows weren't broken and it hadn't suffered any major damage from the bombings. Anke was seriously winded by the time they reached the top floor.

"This is it. Five-forty-four."

Erik knocked. No answer. He took the keys and told Anke to stay back, next to the wall. He opened the door. A stale, musty smell greeted him. The apartment had not had fresh air in years. He walked in slowly, his gun raised, and went from room to room in the darkness. When he was satisfied there was nobody there, he gestured for Anke to come in. The light switches didn't work, so he used his flashlight. As the light beam crawled over the various surfaces, along the walls, and over the floor, they could see that the apartment was in perfectly normal condition, aside from a thick layer of dust clinging to every surface.

"It looks the same!" Anke said, rushing into the room. "The divan looks the same, the rugs, even the radio." She hurried into her father's study. "The books are here! I can't believe it!"

Erik stood, puzzled, in the living room as Anke ran upstairs to her father's studio. When all he heard was silence, he rushed up too. Anke was standing, her back to him, in the middle of a room crammed with canvases. *Dietrich Junger's canvases.*

"I…I don't understand," Anke said, beginning to sob. "They are here. These are the ones that were in the degenerate art exhibit," she said, pointing to several stacked in the corner.

"There must be a hundred canvases in here," Erik said. "This is his entire portfolio."

"More than that," Anke said. "Look, these are unfinished. This is everything that was confiscated from his studio."

"How can this be?" Erik asked.

Anke wiped her tears and leaned against the wall while Erik opened one of the skylights and the air improved immediately. They stared at each other for few moments before a strange look came over Anke's face.

"There is only one person who could have done this," she said.

"Bauer," Erik said, disappointed.

"Yes. Franz had the power to rescue confiscated works. But, these were all taken years before I met him. I don't understand, I thought they were destroyed right away."

"They must have been put in storage somewhere. Bauer found out where they were, perhaps to impress you, and had them all moved back here."

"Then why didn't he tell me? Why would he keep it a secret?"

"Because it would expose him. They were officially declared degenerate. He needed to wait until the war was over," Erik said. He had to admit, Bauer had outdone himself.

"He didn't trust me to keep the secret," Anke said, lost in thought.

"Unless he did it after he last saw you in Italy."

"My father's paintings," she said, sobbing again. Suddenly, she stopped and looked at Erik.

"Do you think…," she began.

"Do I think what?"

"The SS officer…they said an SS officer came down to Alt Aussee and stopped the bombing of the mine."

"What, you think that was Bauer too?"

"It could have been."

Erik looked away. Anke dropped the subject.

THAT NIGHT ERIK phoned his father. The conversation was brief and one-sided, but it was the most wonderful four minutes David Brossler had experienced in years. When David but the phone down, he sat bewildered at the dining room table. His son, his Erik, had helped find or repair the Ghent Altarpiece, the Bruges Madonna, Vermeer's *The Astronomer*, the Vasari Corridor, the Campo Santo, and that named just a few. His son, his Erik, was going to be the father of Dietrich Junger's grandchild. His son, his Erik, was going dancing tonight at the Haus der Deutschen Kunst, with the love of his life, in the city that David had taken him from twelve years ago.

ANKE DANCED until she couldn't breathe anymore. She wasn't the only German girl there this night, but one of many. She was, however, the only one with something substantial to celebrate. She, Erik, and Lynch walked across the Königsplatz after the mess hall had been shut down, not content to let the night die there. They told Lynch about the baby and he erupted in congratulations.

"What will you name him or her?" he asked, swigging from a whisky bottle and passing it to Erik.

"We've haven't thought about it," Anke admitted. "There's been too much else to worry about."

"How about Dietrich if it's a boy, and Lotte if it's a girl?" Erik asked. "In Jewish tradition, you name the baby after a deceased relative."

"Your mother died?" Lynch asked. Anke reeled back in shock.

"Yes, almost a year ago."

"Erik," Anke began, tearing up. "How can it be I didn't know? You never said."

Erik smiled. "Like you just said, we've had so much to worry about. I found out not long before we met in Verona."

"What happened, was she ill for long?" she asked.

Erik closed his eyes for a minute, as if he was concentrating on his answer. "I don't know why she died," he said softly. "But I think it was because her heart was broken."

The three figures walked across the square in the blackness and parted ways outside the collecting point. Anke and Erik returned to her apartment and slept in her bed, in the room she grew up in. It was fairly cleaned out because of her move to Ghent, but there were girlish accents here and there: an Escher & Beirschenck doll, a basket of ribbons, a child's paint set.

They pulled the floral bedspread up over their heads, recreating the feel of the night in the Berchtesgaden hotel on VE Day. Erik slept with his hand on Anke's belly.

25

Burying the Dead

Heroes don't often tolerate the company of other heroes.
—*Lord Kenneth Clark*

ON THEIR THIRD NIGHT in the Junger apartment, they went to bed early to prepare for the next day when the trucks from Alt Aussee would arrive. They had spent every moment at the collecting point, Anke assembling the art library from her father's books and the collections at local libraries, and Erik helping Lynch with the organization of the main offices. They hauled in furniture, including Hitler's own desk from his office at the Nazi Party HQ. This enormous desk would now be a sorting station for smaller paintings and drawings.

At six in the morning on the day the trucks were due to arrive, Erik was blasted out of bed by a series of loud bangs on the front door of the apartment. After ascertaining that it was US military personnel, he opened the door.

"Sir, we need you to step aside," the MP said.

"Excuse me?"

"We are not here for you, Captain. There is a German woman living here."

"So? What is your business with her?"

"All German civilians from this quarter are required to go to the camp at Dachau today, to bury bodies."

Erik blanched. "Dachau? What...are you talking about the concentration camp?"

"Yes sir. You wouldn't believe it if we told you. We need everyone from this building sir, between the ages of twelve and eighty."

"She's pregnant," he stammered.

"Not our problem, sir."

"She's been working with the Monuments and Fine Arts Division for months! She's been invaluable…."

The door was pushed open so hard Erik staggered backward, his left knee reeling from the blow. He ran back into the bedroom and locked the door. Anke was up and dressed, wearing a horrified expression.

"Anke, they are rounding up German civilians to bury bodies at the Dachau camp."

She froze.

"Don't worry, you're not going…I will…."

The bedroom door burst open like an explosive. The two MPs stood in the doorway, nonchalantly, but with rifles leveled.

"Miss…Fräulein, we don't want to harm you in any way," the first MP said, stepping forward. "If you just come with us, you can fulfill your duty and be home by sunset. Everyone in this neighborhood of the city is going today. The camp cleanup has been going on for two weeks already. You're lucky, you've missed some of the worst of it."

"There is no way she is going anywhere…her father almost died in that camp!" Erik yelled.

Go Anke. It might take some of the mystery out of it.

"It's my duty to go, Erik. I should see where my father was kept."

"Don't be ridiculous!"

The MPs looked at each other, unsure about this story. But orders were orders.

"Erik, please don't make a scene," she said quietly, leaning into him. "Like he said, I'll be back by sunset. I'll meet you at the collecting point."

"Anke, do you understand what you are saying?" Erik took hold of her, but the MP had her by the other arm. This was happening again. Erik's mind flickered to the Caravaggio ever so briefly.

"I should go. My father would want this. He'd have wanted me to see what they did with my own eyes."

Anke was told to dress in her finest, to respect the dead. She changed into her pale blue dress and heels she had bought the day before, since most of her clothes were still with Crawford and the truck convoy. It would not have been right to wear any of those clothes anyway, she decided, since they were bought for her by members of the SS and the Wehrmacht. She would give them away, to someone who desperately needed them.

Erik threw on his uniform and followed her downstairs and outside to an awaiting truck. Several other trucks had already departed; the MPs had started on the ground floor of the building and worked their way up.

"I'm going with her," Erik announced and jumped into the back of the truck.

"No! You need to be at the collecting point...the van Eyck is coming today."

She looked honestly distressed. The other people in the truck, her neighbors, began to slowly recognize her.

"Anke Junger?" one woman asked.

"Yes."

"My God! We thought you were dead. After what happened to Dietrich."

"I understand," Anke said, kindly.

"I'm Milke Schuler, you knew my daughter, Leni."

"How is Leni?"

"Killed by the bombs in Dresden."

Anke nodded solemnly. "I'm so sorry."

"You married an American soldier?" Milke asked, smirking slightly.

"We aren't married, yet. He's from Munich actually. His family moved to America years ago."

Meanwhile, the MPs had been having a private conversation about whether or not to allow Erik to accompany her to the camp. They decided to follow their orders to the letter and forced him off the truck.

"I'll watch over her," Milke said.

"She's pregnant," Erik said, hoping the repetition might force the MPs to relent. Instead, it made the neighbors erupt in whispers and gasps. Anke's face went red and Erik suddenly realized the position she was in. Munich was a traditional town. She would have preferred her situation was kept quiet for a while longer. But he was desperate.

"She'll be alright," Milke said, putting her arm protectively around Anke.

That was it. The back of the truck was pushed into place and the MPs drove off down the street. Onlookers had stopped to witness the departure, either remembering their visit to the camp or dreading the one that was to come. One man approached Erik with a sympathetic look on his emaciated face.

"Excuse me, but are you Jewish, by any chance?" the man asked, approaching Erik timidly.

"I'm sorry?"

"Please, I mean no harm. I should not have phrased it like that. That was silly of me. Of course you would be afraid."

"If I am afraid, it is for my…my fiancée. She's been taken to Dachau to bury bodies."

"Yes, I can see how you would be. It is very dangerous there right now."

"What do you mean?"

"There is a typhus epidemic. The prisoners who were liberated a couple of months ago…many of them are still there because of the epidemic. Of course, there is better food and sanitation now. The Americans are doing their best, but still, the prisoners are still being kept in the camp."

"Were you there yourself?"

"I was. Two years. I have been cleared of typhus and I was released a little over a week ago. I lived here, in this building. Now another family is living in my apartment. They have been kind and taken me in while they look for alternate accommodation. Their house was bombed…."

"Did you know Dietrich Junger?" Erik interrupted.

"Junger? Of course! He was quite famous in these parts."

"His daughter is my fiancée."

The man's eyes widened. "I would like to congratulate you, but I feel I should warn you that she is now in very grave danger. A large number of the citizens of the town of Dachau caught typhus when they were forced to bury the bodies after the liberation."

"So, then the bodies are already buried?" Erik couldn't believe they were discussing corpses in this way.

"Yes. There were many thousands. They were buried on Leitenberg Hill, sometime in mid-May. They were first paraded through the town on carts, so all the townspeople could see what had happened."

"So, if the bodies are already buried...." Erik started to feel slightly less nauseous.

"No, now there are new bodies, from the typhus epidemic. Right before the liberation, 400 people were dying every day. Now it is less, but still significant. The Americans don't want to handle the bodies, you understand."

"Oh my God." Erik wanted to run somewhere, but found himself rooted to the spot.

"Dietrich Junger was a good man and a gifted artist," the man continued. "I heard what happened to him when he returned from Dachau and I remember his daughter, though I have forgotten her name."

"Anke." Erik almost whispered.

"You must find a way to keep her out of that camp. I would hate to see Dietrich's daughter die of typhus. He was a good man. He hated the Nazis. He stood up to them, in his own way."

Erik's mind was reeling. Could he get to the collection point, commandeer a vehicle and get to Dachau before Anke did? His fear was causing paralysis. He was soaked through with sweat despite the sun being still quite low in the sky. Finally, after a few seconds that felt like hours, he turned and sprinted off toward the Königsplatz. Once across the street, he stopped and turned around. He looked at the man, who was still watching him from the other sidewalk. He noticed, for the first time, that the man's clothes were far too big for him and made him look like a little boy in a man's suit.

"Yes, I am Jewish," he called out.

"*Be'hatzlacha!*" the man replied, smiling.

"Thank you!" Erik said, not even pausing to reflect on the fact that he had instinctively understood that the man had wished him luck. Erik had never studied Hebrew.

The man waved and turned to another neighbor. "It's a good feeling, I can tell you, to be able to speak Hebrew in public again."

~

BRIGSWORTH-JONES had made excellent time. His truck, the first in the convoy, rolled up to the collection point at exactly nine in the morning. They had spent the last night not far from Neuschwanstein, south of Munich, so the last leg had been the shortest of all. He expected to see Erik and Anke standing on the front steps with triumphant grins on their faces. Instead, he saw only Erik, panic-stricken and white as a piece of raw marble.

"This isn't quite the welcome we've been hoping for, chap," he said, dismounting from the truck.

"Anke's been taken to Dachau. They have a typhus epidemic!"

"I've heard about Dachau. Why was she taken there?"

"German civilians are being used for labor… burial of bodies."

"Mother of God. How did they even find her?"

"We were staying at her apartment, her father's place. The MPs were going through the whole building."

Then Erik remembered something. "Wait a second," he said. "They knew she was there. I mean…they knew that we, specifically, were there."

"I wouldn't put it past someone to try to put her in her place. She got some good press about the Florentine affair. Maybe there is someone here in Munich who doesn't think a German should be getting any of the credit."

"So they'll kill her by sending her to a place where typhus is raging?"

"Lots of Germans are being exposed to this, chap. We'd look bad if we gave her a pass."

"*We'd look bad?*" Erik was incredulous.

Brigsworth-Jones lit a cigarette but kept his head down for a moment. Erik knew he was thinking.

"What do you need?" he finally asked, looking up.

"A vehicle of some sort."

"What happened to the bike and sidecar?"

"Requisitioned for army use, right after we got here."

"Right. I'll see what I can do."

Brigsworth-Jones disappeared inside the collecting point. Erik felt a rage brewing inside him, but he knew he wouldn't get a vehicle by exploding on anyone. A line of trucks twenty long was snaking around the Königsplatz, bringing all other traffic to a halt. She should be here to see this.

Crawford appeared with Anke's small suitcase and Erik's army pack. He had evidently overheard, because he looked like he might cry at any moment. Dearborn emerged from one of the other trucks and joined them.

"Where's Anke? I mean, Miss Junger?"

Erik couldn't explain it again. "Is the van Eyck okay?"

"Fine, sir. It's in that truck right there. I rode with it."

"Thanks, Tom."

Brigsworth-Jones reappeared, followed by Lynch, who looked concerned.

"There's not a bloody thing we can do, chap," Brigsworth-Jones said.

"I called the Fortieth Engineer Regiment," Lynch said. "They are pretty much running the show over at Dachau. They said there was no way they could wade into a crowd of German civilians, pick out one woman, and take her out of the camp. It would create chaos and too many questions."

Erik knew he was going to say that. "Ok, then I am going myself. I'll walk if I have to. Someone will pick me up along the road."

"Hold on, chap. Hold on," Brigsworth-Jones said softly. "She'll be back tonight. They've got the DDT spray now, which should contain the typhus."

"She should boil her clothes and take a hot bath or shower when she gets back," Lynch said. "Without prolonged exposure, she should be fine."

"If she's handling bodies, with lice on them…," Erik began.

"She won't be. The officer I spoke with told me that the men do the burying. The women clean, organize, and maybe help in the infirmary."

Isn't the infirmary full of people with typhus? Erik thought.

"The best thing you can do for her is stay here and help get us started with the off-loading. Don't you think that's what she would want?" Brigsworth-Jones asked.

Erik knew that this was exactly what Anke wanted, but that didn't seem to matter at the moment. He couldn't believe nobody understood. He looked at his watch: nine thirty. She was already there by now.

Lynch and Brigsworth-Jones went back inside to begin the process of filling the collecting point with some of the world's foremost art treasures. Crawford followed them glumly, not sure what else to do.

Erik and Dearborn stood staring out at the sea of trucks. At almost exactly the same time, they ran down to the truck carrying the Ghent Altarpiece and began unloading the crates. Together they carefully carried the panels inside, with Lynch pointing them to the correct room, unaware of any ulterior motives. It made perfect sense to unload the van Eyck first.

Forty-minutes later, the collecting point was buzzing with activity. Boxes and crates were coming in at a constant rate. Lynch stood near the entrance, directing traffic. Crawford was typing at a desk in the main office. Brigsworth-Jones was on the phone. MFAA officers, from a variety of Army and Navy groups, Americans, British, and French, were inspecting and cataloging an immense cache of art unlike any of them had seen in their lifetimes or would ever see again.

Nobody was going to miss one truck.

"You'll get hell from Brigsworth-Jones," Dearborn said as they cruised out of Munich.

"Yup. So will you."

"Yes, sir. I will."

THEY ARRIVED AROUND NOON after snarled traffic on the bombed roads. The town of Dachau was quaint and distinctly Bavarian. The townspeople looked down or away as Erik drove past. No one met his eye.

"The weird thing is, I've been here before," Erik said. "My mother had a friend who lived here. We went to her house a number of times. I wonder if she still lives here."

"If she's alive," Dearborn said.

"She wasn't Jewish."

"From what I've heard, Jews weren't the only ones taken to Dachau. I heard that pretty much all the intellectuals, professors, musicians, and even a bunch of doctors were thrown in the camp, along with anyone who disagreed with the Nazis in public. Lots of political prisoners. Lots of Germans. Oh, and lots of priests."

Erik shot him a look knowing that if they hadn't immigrated to America, his whole family might have been thrown in this camp.

"Crawford and I have been listening to the BBC," Dearborn muttered.

They drove through a small forest on the far side of town and arrived at the outer fence of the camp. The main entrance was a few hundred feet to their left and very crowded with American military personnel. Erik could see the same trucks that had left Anke's apartment building lined up near the entrance.

"They're not just going to let us in, are they?" Dearborn asked, secretly hoping the answer was no.

"Doubt it. But I am going to try everything."

"What will you do if they let you in, but don't allow her to leave with you?"

"I'll hold her hand."

Dearborn nodded, and swallowed down a mixture of pride in his captain, and jealousy. Someday, when this was all over, he would find a woman he loved that much.

They left the truck where it was, partly shielded in the trees, and walked to the entrance. They could see lots of activity inside the camp. People were walking between the wooden buildings, which they assumed were the barracks. There was barbed wire everywhere, with guard towers lining the periphery. Mounds of dirt and detritus were visible along the inside of the barbed-wire fence. The main gatehouse was a large stucco building with a rod-iron gate in the middle.

Erik walked up to a major who looked like he knew what he was doing. The major was barking orders to a number of privates, who then jumped in Jeeps and drove off toward the town.

"Major, may I have a word?"

"And you are?"

"Captain Brossler sir, MFAA division."

"What division?"

"The Monuments and Fine Arts Division, sir."

"Oh, Christ. Is the camp considered an architecturally sensitive site?" he asked mockingly.

Erik kept his cool. "Not at all, sir. I would like to help."

"We have all the help we need, thank you Captain."

"My wife, sir, is in there. She's a German civilian. I would like permission to join her."

"Are you serious?"

"Completely, sir."

"What's her name?"

"Anke Junger."

The major consulted a number of lists. "Jagger?"

"Junger, sir. J-U-N-G-E-R. It's pronounced *Younger*."

"You speak German, Captain?"

"Fluent, sir."

The major's face lit up and he smiled, revealing a set of teeth worthy of a medieval peasant.

"Follow me," he said, and Erik did.

They went up to the main gate. On the other side, a number of inmates were sitting on the ground looking dazed. Some of them wore pajama-like striped pants, clearly part of a uniform, and others had civilian clothes on. Just like the man who Erik met outside Anke's apartment, their clothes hung off them like laundry on a clothesline.

"We need German speakers to deal with these civilians. The prisoners, or ex-prisoners actually, are so used to doing what they are told that they aren't really a problem. Plus, they are so sick and weak that they have no energy to be difficult."

Erik wasn't listening. He was looking at some pictures that had been attached to the side of the gatehouse. He wasn't sure what he was looking at. The major followed his gaze.

"Oh, yes. You should see these. This is what the camp looked like up until about two weeks ago."

Erik looked at the first picture. A pile of bodies, reaching the height of a grown man, sat in what looked like the very place they were now standing, but on the other side of the fence.

Erik tried to breathe.

"You okay?" the major asked. "At least you can't smell it. I'll never get that smell out of my nostrils. Never."

"I can't believe what I am seeing. Is that a bulldozer?"

"Yeah, we used a bulldozer to remove the bodies. The townspeople buried them. You're wife is lucky she wasn't here for that. People were fainting and puking all over the fucking place."

"Where is my wife?" Erik asked, more determined than ever to get Anke out of there.

"Probably over there, with the other women. They are burning all the uniforms, clothes, sheets, anything that might have been infected with typhus."

"What are the chances she could contract typhus from doing that?"

He shrugged. "We spray them with DDT, that's about all we can do."

"Can I go in?"

"Nope. No unauthorized US personnel are allowed in the camp."

"Do you know who she is?"

"Don't care. Nobody is being spared. I've heard stories from tons of people who say they hated the Nazis, say they hid Jewish children in their basements…believe me, I've heard it all. There is no way we can know anything for sure until everyone has gone through the denazification process. Right now, they would say anything to avoid coming in here."

"Denazification process?"

"Yeah, forget I mentioned it. You'll know about it soon enough. It's a work in progress."

A young private came up to them and sprayed their hands with DDT. It smelled awful and Erik's eyes began watering. Then, through the smoke, he saw Anke. She was walking toward one of the bonfires carrying a load of clothes, mostly striped uniforms. Right behind her was her neighbor, Milke. He watched her dump her bundle on the fire. He called out to her but she didn't hear him and turned back toward the other women and the tower of clothes.

Erik was allowed to wait at the gate if he did some translating for the major. He spoke to several prominent people from the town of Dachau, who were supposed to be providing food to the camp's remaining ex-prisoner population, though they insisted they did not have enough ingredients for their own bread, let alone extra bread for the inmates. Erik calmly explained to them that unless they find a way to bring bread, they would be arrested by the Americans and thrown into a camp not unlike Dachau.

"You sound just like the Nazis," one baker said. "If you don't do this…we will send you to a camp."

Erik nodded solemnly at the man but had no further comment. He was doing exactly as the major instructed. He wanted to take Anke back to Munich himself and this was the deal.

At five o'clock, the German civilians were marched out of the camp, through the main gate, and loaded back onto the trucks bound for Munich. Most of them looked stunned and exhausted. There weren't any children in this particular group, but the major had told Erik that German children as young as twelve had been to the camp on many occasions, but were usually given the lightest of tasks.

"Sounds harsh to bring children here, doesn't it?" the major asked. "Well, it's not. It's downright Christian compared to what those camp children went through. The survivors, most of the them, won't make it a year."

Erik scanned the crowd for Anke, but refrained from calling out her name. He didn't want to draw attention to the fact that she would be taken home separately, by him.

When he saw her, he grabbed her hand and pulled her aside. She wrenched her hand away immediately as if it had touched something piping hot.

"Anke! Sweetheart, it's me. I'm going to take you home."

"No, you're not. I will go on the truck with the others."

"Please, Tom and I came to get you…I tried to get you out of the camp but they…."

"I told you I would meet you at the collecting point."

"I know, but…are you alright?"

Anke turned away from him and climbed into the truck. Milke had saved a space for her near the back. She avoided his stare until the truck started up and drove toward the woods. Erik was rooted to his spot until well after the trucks were out of sight.

"Sir?" Dearborn approached timidly. "Sir, if we go now, we can make it to the collecting point before she does."

Erik nodded feeling an uncomfortable, hollow feeling. They walked to their truck and Dearborn took the wheel. The major watched them drive off, still wondering why they had come at all.

"I should have broken my way in," Erik said, after a few miles of silence.

"Well, you could have done that sir, but then you would have been arrested."

"So what?"

"Well, it seems to me that if you were arrested they'd find someone else to take the Ghent Altarpiece back to St. Bavo's."

Erik just looked at him.

"It seems to me, with respect sir, that Miss Junger wants more than anything for that person to be you. I mean, for you to do it together."

"Did she tell you that?"

"No, sir."

"You think that's why she wouldn't come with us?"

"I don't know sir. Who knows what was going through her mind after cleaning up that mess. But I...," Dearborn trailed off.

"What?" Erik demanded.

"I just think that she did what she did because...I think she felt that her father would have wanted it that way. I think that's why she does lots of things."

Erik looked out the window. He wondered what Dietrich Junger wanted next.

26

Promises

War is not an adventure. It is a disease. It is like typhus.
—*Antoine de Saint-Exupery*

T HE MUNICH COLLECTING POINT had amassed such an assortment of priceless art that its staff joked that they worked for the greatest museum on earth. The art library was downright distinguished, as was the group of art historians who had been assembled to catalogue and repair the works of art. The German laborers grumbled about the heavy lifting, the constant building of new shelving, storage bins, and easels, but they knew they were lucky to have any work at all.

Germany was a shambles. There were shortages of food, water, coal, and fuel. Munich fared better than other cities because it was left with a good number of buildings still intact, but the train depots had been bombed, along with most of the tracks leading to and from the city. Since Munich was the springboard of the Nazi party movement, the Americans were extra suspicious of its inhabitants and assumed that Nazi sympathies lay behind all the broken and gaunt faces.

The art protection effort, however, was thriving. The new Art Looting Investigation Unit (ALIU) had formidable powers and had poached Captain Brigsworth-Jones to serve as an interrogator. In his first week on the job, he witnessed the interrogation of Alfred Rosenberg, creator of the ERR, though he did not question him personally. His first official interrogation was of some ERR staffers who had worked at Neuschwanstein. Amongst them was Frau Kruger who was distinctly more forthcoming than she had been when the Americans had first visited the "castle of art."

Not long after Brigsworth-Jones joined their ranks, Erik was also appropriated for interrogation duty in the ALIU. Erik approached his work with zeal. He and Brigsworth-Jones made an excellent team; Erik was the heavy, the screamer, the accuser, while Brigsworth-Jones was the calm one, the one who offered coffee and cigarettes and apologized for his partner's explosive behavior. Since Erik's rage seemed to work wonders, and people were singing like songbirds, Brigsworth-Jones let him vent his anger. He understood where it was coming from, everyone did.

Anke had never made it to the collecting point after Dachau. She and the others from her building were required to be isolation for one week after their exposure to typhus. By then, it was assumed, the symptoms would have presented themselves, or not. After bathing in hot water, which had to be heated over a wood fire since there was a major shortage of coal, Anke and Milke boiled their clothes and settled in to wait out their quarantine.

After a week, nearly thirty people in the apartment building were showing signs of typhus, including Anke and Milke. They had developed a rash all over their torsos, high fevers, and abdominal pain. Just as had been done at the camp, the residents threw the drapes, rugs, and linens from the infected apartments out of the windows and they were burned in a giant bonfire.

By the time Anke and Milke were transferred to an American hospital, they were delirious. When the doctors examined Anke, they found that she had recently suffered a miscarriage, though she didn't seem aware of it. After a week in the hospital, Anke improved enough to eat a thin soup by herself. After two weeks, she was transferred to the non-contagious ward and could stand on her own. She refused to see Erik, or anyone else, despite the fact that almost all American personnel had already received the typhus vaccine. She didn't want to take any chances.

Three weeks after entering the hospital, Milke died. Anke sat by her bedside for several hours before they removed the body.

She will be with Leni now, leibling.

A week later, Anke was given a typhus test and the result was negative. She had survived. She was issued a new set of clothes by the Red
Cross. The dress bagged over her shrunken form and her feet rattled
around in the heels, but she stuffed newspaper into the toes and wore
them proudly as she walked out of the hospital. Crawford was waiting
outside, alone.

"Where is Erik?" she asked, dumbfounded. She hadn't yet told him
about the baby.

"Miss Junger," Crawford said uneasily, shifting from right to left.
"Your apartment building burned down last night. Too many people
incinerating their clothes...."

Anke reeled and he steadied her with a hand on her shoulder. Her
father's canvases...they burned after all. Her stomach heaved.

"Please, don't worry miss! Erik, I mean Captain Brossler, and Lt.
Dearborn removed all your father's works, every last one. We moved
them to the collecting point this morning."

"How...how did they do that?"

"The fire started on the far side of the building, so they had a little
time...about an hour I'd say, before the fire reached your apartment.
They wanted to lower them out the windows, but the water from the
fire engines was too powerful...it would have ruined them, so they
carried everything down the stairs. I tell you, not a single piece was
damaged. Everything else in the apartment, I am sorry to say, was destroyed. They just didn't have time...."

"Where is he now?" Anke asked, her eyes dripping.

"They had to make a special place for your father's work at the
collecting point, because it is so over-crowded. When I left, they were
installing new bins in the basement. He'll be in good company, most
of the Austrian national collection is down there."

"Can we go there now?"

"That's why I'm here," he said grinning. He opened the door of a
black Volkswagen.

As they drove, Anke realized that her father's canvases were her
only remaining possessions. She recalled the moment she threw her
larger suitcase away on the road to Paris years ago. Now she had only
the clothes on her back, and they weren't even hers.

～

ANKE WAS FOLLOWING Lynch down the main hall of the collecting point when she saw Erik emerge from a nondescript door, which probably led to the basement. He was drenched in sweat and his face and uniform were covered in soot, like a chimney sweep. To say he looked exhausted would have been an understatement; he looked ravaged.

Anke was aware of her own appearance. She was thinner than she had been and even though the miscarriage had happened before she really started showing, she was sure Erik knew the minute he saw her.

He stood aside and opened the basement door for her. She understood and slipped silently down the stairs, passing Dearborn on the way. He looked worse than Erik and she almost didn't recognize him as she passed by. She calmly put a hand on his shoulder and he nodded with a weary smile.

Erik followed her down and they stood in front of a section of bays brimming with the Junger canvases.

"I wish I could explain to you what this means to me," she began. "I shouldn't have treated you like that, at Dachau."

"I understand."

"You could have been killed saving my father's portfolio."

"Well, it survived the Nazis and I couldn't watch it burn after all that. Not after Friedrichshain."

"Friedrichshain?"

"The flak tower. It burned down in May. Over four hundred paintings from the Kaiser Friedrich Museum were stored there. Everything was lost."

"My God!"

Erik sank onto an empty bay and rubbed the back of his neck. Anke sat at his feet.

"Allied bombing," he said, flashing a satirical smile. "Always there to back us up."

"There was nothing you or any of us could do. You can't climb up there and save 500 paintings."

"Nope. I didn't even hear about it until a few days ago."

"Erik...I lost the baby."

"I know," he said.

"Maybe it's better this way."

"Maybe."

They sat in silence for a few minutes, then they heard Brigsworth-Jones on the stairs. He'd taken to smoking a pipe and the tobacco he used could be smelled from yards away.

"You are a sorry sight, chap."

"He's exhausted," Anke said defensively.

Brigsworth-Jones stooped down and looked Erik in the eye.

"You need to get yourself washed up and rested. Members of the Roberts Commission are arriving imminently to inspect the collecting point. We need to be on our toes so we can get what we want. Are you with me, chap?"

Erik's big, dark eyes, still red and stinging from the smoke, looked up at him.

"Yes sir."

Brigsworth-Jones was visibly moved by Erik's cold tone. Unsure how to proceed, he frantically began repacking his pipe. Anke knew she was missing something; there was an unspoken issue between them.

"He's right, Erik. You need to take care of yourself. Where will we be staying?"

She addressed this last question to Brigsworth-Jones, who had no immediate reply.

Erik stood slowly and glared at his mentor.

"I need to speak to Anke alone."

"Right. See you upstairs," Brigsworth-Jones disappeared in a swirl of pipe smoke.

"The pipe is new," Anke said.

"He thinks it's more distinguished."

"My father smoked a pipe sometimes."

"Mine too."

Anke smiled. She put her arms around him and they kissed, slowly, for a long time. He rubbed the soot off her face afterwards.

"I'm in a bit of trouble, Anke," Erik finally said.

"What kind of trouble?"

"With the Army. The powers that be are cracking down on fraternization."

"You mean, with German women?"

"With all Germans. Brigsworth-Jones had to explain why a truck disappeared from outside here without letting on that Dearborn and I had taken it to Dachau. I wasn't supposed to stay with you at the apartment, but I did. I wasn't even supposed to be involved with saving your father's paintings. It was a civilian fire and we are not allowed to get involved...."

"I think you are all already involved!" she bristled.

"I know. It's ludicrous. None of this was really enforced before, but now I am in the ALIU and that is under British command. The Brits are taking this stuff very seriously."

"ALIU?"

"Art Looting Investigation Unit. That's where we work now. Dearborn is with us as well. Crawford is working here at the collecting point, pretty much running the research division."

"So, what are you saying? Are you calling it off?"

"God, no! Anke, I'm sorry...I haven't explained this well. It's just that I can't stay with you right now. I have to play by the rules so Brigsworth-Jones can get the promotion he is up for and then he can help us get the van Eyck back to Ghent. I haven't forgotten my promise."

"I know you haven't. I can stay at a shelter. Don't worry about it."

Erik shook his head. "You're not going to a shelter. You've just recovered from typhus and had a miscarriage. I've arranged for a family to house you. They live on the Leopoldstrasse."

"Thank you."

He took her hands in his. "Listen to me. I want to marry you, as soon as possible. Do you want that?"

She struggled not to break down. "Yes, of course."

"No American personnel are allowed to marry German civilians and until that changes, or I am discharged, we have to wait."

"I can wait."

"You shouldn't have to. It's fucking military politics and we're just caught up in it."

"Shh. It's okay. Let's go get you cleaned up," she said, leading him toward the stairs.

He walked with such heaviness that Anke tried to think of ways to lessen his burden. When they emerged, she could hear Brigsworth-Jones' booming laugh. What did he have to laugh about? She felt Erik stiffen next to her. A flash of fear washed over her as she followed his gaze down the hall, where she saw an older man standing with Brigsworth-Jones, looking back at them. Erik put his arm around her waist and walked her down the hall toward him. The man wiped his eyes with his sleeve and clasped his hands over his mouth. He was weeping. Before she knew it, the man was beside her embracing Erik. Erik closed his eyes and his arm left Anke's waist. She stood back and looked at Brigsworth-Jones.

"Professor David Brossler, Anke," he said, winking.

Anke gasped. She hadn't recognized him. He looked so much older, but then so did she. Brossler finally released Erik and turned to her.

"Good God, Anke Junger. Yes, look at you, I remember. When I last saw you, you had your hair in braids, with ribbons."

I remember those ribbons, leibling.

Anke nodded, overwhelmed with emotion. He kissed her on both cheeks and she beamed at him with everything she had. He glanced ever so quickly at her belly and she realized that Brigsworth-Jones had told him everything. It saved her and Erik having to do it, she thought.

"I am a consultant to the Roberts Commission," he explained, still looking at Anke. "They asked if I wanted to come inspect the collecting points and I couldn't get on the plane fast enough. We were scheduled to be here tomorrow but I just couldn't wait!"

Brigsworth-Jones laughed again, trying to lift the mood. "You three have a lot to discuss. Why don't you go back to my quarters?"

"No, no!" Brossler said. "I have a lovely place. Erik, you remember Friedrich Fassbinder. Anke, you knew him of course! He sends you his love. He set me up with some friends of his here. You might remember them, the Kellers? They knew your father, Anke. Anyway, their apartment is not far from here and they've got plenty of room. No soldiers billeted there yet…we can get you a nice bath and a soft bed, Anke. That's what you need…Professor Brigsworth-Jones brought me up to speed."

"Completely up to speed?" Erik asked.

"Yes." Brossler took Anke's hand. "Completely. Anke will stay with me and the Kellers."

"I couldn't impose, Professor," she said.

"Don't be silly, *liebling*. You've been through a horrible ordeal. You will stay with me until Erik is discharged. I still have a number of friends here. Of course, many of them are gone."

Anke marveled at her father's ways. He had guided Professor Brossler here, to them, at this moment. How was he doing it?

"I will never forget your kindness," Anke said, after a few quiet moments.

"Thank you Papa," Erik said, as they turned to leave.

"Don't give it another thought!" Brossler said, stepping out into the sun with Anke on his arm. "Erik, come with us and get cleaned up. You can rest for a while at the Kellers."

"I can't, Papa. It's against regulations to fraternize with Germans."

Brossler just looked at his son. "You are German, Erik."

"I am an American soldier, Papa."

"He has seventy-two hours of leave," Brigsworth-Jones said, interrupting. "I'll cover for him. Go. Wear civilian clothes and keep your bloody head down."

Erik looked back at him as he walked down the stairs. The big man had come through yet again.

AFTER HOT BATHS, still rationed to only twice a week, and an eight-hour sleep for Erik, he and Anke chose to spend his seventy-two hour leave with his father in Munich. They walked around the city, noting the heartbreaking destruction and seeking out old acquaintances. Although Anke did not really remember the Kellers, she did remember some of their friends, who were all part of her father's former art circle. A number of members were missing, of course. The Fassbinders were in New York. The Geshalts were Polish nationals and had disappeared in 1940. The Jewish members of Junger's crowd had left Germany before the war, except for Daniel Kahn, who was arrested by the Gestapo in 1942. Nobody had seen him since. Paul Klee had died in Switzerland in 1940, of natural causes. Anke remembered his paintings displayed near her father's in the degenerate art exhibit. Max Beckmann was in

Amsterdam, the last they heard. Oskar Kokoschka had immigrated to England. Some of the others had survived the war and continued to meet throughout at the Kellers, who had a large apartment due to Dr. Ernst Keller's status as a surgeon. Dr. Keller shipped his art collection to Switzerland in 1938 and was now in the process of having it shipped back to Munich. Amongst his paintings, he informed Anke, were two early Junger canvases.

Anke also learned that the whereabouts of her father's portfolio had become a mystery of legend in Munich art circles during the war. Some claimed to have seen it burned in one of the giant bonfires of 1939, others said that they heard, on good authority, that the Junger paintings had been sold to the Americans. Still others thought Anke herself had hidden them in Ghent. When Anke admitted that it was most likely a member of the SS who was initially responsible for saving the Junger collection there were gasps of shock and protests of impossibility. When she later revealed to the professor the reason that her father's paintings were currently safe in the basement of the collecting point, David Brossler turned a strange color.

"He still thinks I'm a little boy," Erik explained, hardly hiding his embarrassment as they walked back to the apartment.

"You could have been killed, Erik!" his father cried.

"Yes, Papa. I could have been killed each and every day since I left New York."

"No, you don't understand. I couldn't be more proud of you. Your mother...," he stopped, overcome with emotion.

This was the one and only time Anke observed Erik weep for his mother. She walked on and allowed him to share his father's grief, which was obviously still intense. Anke felt oddly comforted that she wasn't the only one struggling with death. She then realized that it would be odd to find anyone in Europe who hadn't lost someone to the war. The guilt of her self-pity was enveloping her when he heard the professor call out.

"Anke, *liebling*! Wait for us!"

"I don't think she likes to be called that, Papa," Erik said, wiping his eyes.

"No, it's okay. I don't mind," Anke countered. "My father used to call me that. He still does, actually."

The professor looked confused, but Erik just stared at her, understanding just a little bit more in that moment. He took her face in his hands and kissed her.

"To hell with their rules," he said. "Let them arrest me."

27

Denazification

It is lack of confidence, more than anything else, that kills a civilization. We can destroy ourselves by cynicism and disillusion, just as effectively as by bombs.
—*Lord Kenneth Clark*

September, 1945

ANKE SAT AT THE small kitchen table in Professor Brossler's new apartment and stared at the *Fragebogen*. It was a lengthy, in-depth questionnaire. All Germans had to fill one out. There were questions about everything from employment, to how often one went to church, to the birthplace of parents and grandparents, to views on the war. Anke had been working on it for days, but now it was due at the *Spruchkammer*, the civil court set up for the purpose of denazification. She had to report at noon.

She had been completely honest on her *Fragebogen*. She had listed Hermann Göring and Count von Essen as people she had previously associated with. She listed Carinhall as a place she resided for several months in 1943. She listed the ERR in Paris as a place of former employment. She reluctantly listed SS *ObergruppenFührer* Franz Bauer and Sgt. Konrad Ackerman as previous associates though she failed to mention the intimacy of the relationships. She also listed the issues relating to her father's demise and death, her involvement in the evacuation of Belgian works of art, her work with the Monuments, Fine Arts and Archives division of the US Fifth Army, and her current engagement to Captain Erik Brossler of the US Fifth Army.

Erik had been so preoccupied with the decision, by the Roberts Commission, to send 202 German-owned artworks to the National Gallery in Washington for a major exhibition that he had not paid much attention to her denazification hearing.

"It's nothing but a formality, sweetheart," he told her.

Anke was distressed by the sending of the German works as well since it seemed in poor taste after all that had happened, but she knew she had absolutely no clout with the Americans. In fact, as time passed and the denazification procedures were put in place, her position seemed less secure than ever. She hadn't lost her job at the collecting point, but she noticed that Brigsworth-Jones hadn't stopped by to see her in weeks. He was distancing himself from her and that's why she was fairly sure that her hearing at the *Spruchkammer* was going to be much more than a formality.

As Anke dressed, she tried for a conservative look, donning a shapeless black dress she had found at one of the Red Cross stations. She did her hair in the American way, curled and held back with pins. Makeup wasn't an option since she didn't have any. She looked at herself in the mirror for a long time, then walked slowly and calmly to the old school where the court for her district was recently set up. Though the occupying power was the driving force behind denazification, local Germans had been given the task of determining guilt in their districts. The Americans simply didn't have the time.

When she entered the hearing room, a bank of uniforms stood up to her far right. The hearing committee entered in front of her and the chairman told everyone to sit down.

"This is the hearing of Anke Karolina Junger," the chairman said. A woman sat in the corner and typed a transcript. She reminded Anke of one of the many secretaries who worked for Bauer and the ERR.

"Fräulein Junger, your character witnesses are as follows: Major Owen Brigsworth-Jones, British Third Army, Monuments, Fine Arts, and Archives Division; Captain Erik Brossler, US Fifth Army, Monuments, Fine Arts, and Archives Division; Lieutenant Thomas Dearborn, US Fifth Army, Monuments, Fine Arts, and Archives Division; Lieutenant Marshall Crawford, US Fifth Army, Monuments, Fine Arts, and Archives Division; Lieutenant Jeffrey Lynch, US Navy, Monuments,

Fine Arts, and Archives Division; Professor David Brossler, German-American civilian."

Anke nodded at them, touched and surprised that even Lynch had decided to show up. She registered with some pleasure that Brigsworth-Jones had indeed been promoted. The committee chairman, a small bespectacled man, cleared his throat.

"Fräulein. Your *Fragebogen* indicates a high level of interaction with Nazi officials, including the former Reichsmarschall Göring. You are aware, I am sure, that Herr Göring is currently on trial in Nuremberg?"

"Yes sir. I am aware of that," Anke answered.

"You maintain, however, that you were coerced into cooperating with said persons via threats made to you and your friends in Belgium, is that correct?"

"Yes, sir. I was threatened with imprisonment in a concentration camp, as were my friends."

There was a short break when several members of the *Spruchkammer* had a whispered conference.

"Fräulein Junger. We are aware of the situation with your late father, Dietrich Junger, and you have our condolences. We are also aware of your relationship with a number of British and American officers who have already testified generously on your behalf. Their comments are in the permanent record."

"Thank you."

"Fräulein. While we do not believe you are to be considered a major offender, we do feel that you were involved, specifically, in the systematic looting of art from France and Poland."

"Herr chairman, allow me to...."

"Please, Fräulein. You will be given an opportunity to address these accusations in due course. I must inform you that several Nazi personnel in Allied custody have mentioned your name during their interrogations. Former Reichsmarschall Göring is one. He testified that you transported several paintings from Krakow to Berlin in 1942. Is this correct?"

"Yes. Göring ordered me to. He wanted three pieces out of the hands of Hans Frank, the Governor of Poland."

"What were the pieces, please?"

Erik stood up. "Herr chairman, these are questions for the ALIU, not for a denazification hearing."

The chairman stared at Erik for moment, then decided to embarrass him.

"Captain, I am well aware of your connection to this woman. Since this is a denazification hearing, it is not the place to discuss your complete disregard for the non-fraternization policies of the American military government. However, that is for me to say that since I am chairing this hearing. You, however, will remain silent or I will have you removed from the room. Is that clear?"

"Yes, sir," Erik sat down as Brigsworth-Jones rolled his eyes.

"Fräulein," he continued, "could you please name the pieces you transported from Krakow?"

"The paintings were *Lady with an Ermine*, by Leonardo daVinci, *Landscape with a Good Samaritan* by Rembrandt van Rijn, and *Portrait of a Gentleman* by Raphael of Urbino."

"Thank you. Now, is it true that the daVinci and the Rembrandt have since been located by Allied forces and are now in safe locations?"

"Yes. The daVinci is here in Munich, at the collecting point."

"You work at the collecting point, is that correct?"

"Yes."

"You obtained that job before undergoing denazification, is that correct?"

"Yes. All the German art historians and restorers there were brought in almost immediately. There wasn't time for…."

"Thank you, that is enough. Is it true that, to your knowledge, no Allied personnel have taken into custody the painting by Raphael?"

"Not to my knowledge."

"Do you have any ideas where it might be?"

"Have you asked Hans Frank?"

"I will ask the questions, if you please Fräulein."

"I don't know where it is," Anke said, frustrated. "I think that many suspect it was found by the Russians."

"I see," he shuffled some papers. Anke glanced quickly at Erik. He shrugged and winked at her.

The chairman resumed the questioning.

"You are considered, by some, to be one of the foremost experts on the Ghent Altarpiece, is that correct?"

Anke wasn't sure how to answer. "I would aspire to that, sir."

"Now now, no false modesty please. Answer the question."

"I have studied the altarpiece for years and published a number of articles on it."

"And you were instrumental in removing it from Ghent and taking it to the château of Pau in 1940, is that correct?"

"Yes."

"The altarpiece was transferred to the castle of Neuschwanstein sometime in 1943, shortly before you arrived there, correct?"

"I believe so. I don't know exactly when the altarpiece arrived."

"Really? No idea? That strikes me as odd since it is the opinion of this committee that you were the driving force behind the removal of the altarpiece from Pau."

Anke was stunned. Her mouth went dry. "That's not true," she almost whispered.

"You were obsessed with the van Eyck, that is clear from your record. You took it to Pau, then appeared at Neuschwanstein, along with the altarpiece, and you expect us to see this as a coincidence?"

"I had nothing to do with the transfer of the altarpiece out of France."

"That is not the testimony of Herr Göring. He claims that you asked him to have the altarpiece sent to Neuschwanstein and then asked him to send you there to be closer to it. He said you had always wanted it back in Germany and that he had promised you a curatorship at the Führermuseum in Linz, where the altarpiece was destined to be displayed."

Anke glanced at Erik again and saw something in his face that made her want to throw up. His defiance was wavering. He was doubting her.

"I don't understand why you would believe Göring over me," she began, with a shaky voice. "He has every reason to lie, to divert blame from himself. If I wanted Germany to have all the art, why would I have told Captain Brossler and Major Brigsworth-Jones about the stash in the Brenner Pass?"

"Fräulein, I did not suggest that you wanted *all* the art. I am saying that you wanted the altarpiece."

"Well I did. I wanted it returned to St. Bavo's. I still do. It's what I want most in the world…other than to marry Captain Brossler and forget about all of this."

There was another discussion amongst the panel. She turned toward Erik and his expression had softened. Dearborn, Lynch, and Crawford looked confused, and Brigsworth-Jones just looked bored. Professor Brossler had the expression of an over-protective father watching his daughter being bullied in the schoolyard. Her father was staring out at her through Brossler's eyes. Anke shook her head and wondered, for the millionth time, if she was losing her mind.

The chairman told Anke that her case was still open, pending further investigation and more witness testimony. A second hearing would be scheduled within a few weeks. In the meantime, she was not to go within one hundred yards of the collecting point and was ordered to report to a convent-run shelter for women near the Marienplatz. A soldier was assigned to escort her there, but it was then decided that Professor Brossler would be allowed to take her himself.

Erik and the others had left without a word to her. She linked arms with her future father-in-law and walked with him toward the Marienplatz. The professor was quiet, but his firm arm and warm nature convinced her that he was sure of her innocence.

"Is Erik upset?" she asked.

"Of course. Not with you, *leibling*. He's in a difficult position. His spending time with us has not gone unnoticed, despite the heroic efforts of Brigsworth-Jones. Even going to your hearing further associates him with you."

"I know."

"Brigsworth-Jones told me in no uncertain terms that Erik will be court-martialed if he doesn't stop breaking the rules."

Anke wanted to scream, but she kept her eyes on the pavement.

"Anke?" The professor bent down to see her face.

"I just missed him. I…needed him. He needed me. We love each other. I never meant to get him in trouble."

"I know that. Everyone understands that."

She straightened up and looked at his kindly, graying face. How lucky Erik was to have him here. Perhaps he would agree to give her away, at the wedding. There would be a wedding, she told herself. Soon.

THERE WERE NO MEN allowed at the shelter. The food and care was provided by the nursing sisters of St. Bridget's priory hospital, which had survived the bombing, and the shelter was in the basement. It was so crowded with mothers, crying children, and pregnant women that Anke was only able to manage a small straw mattress on the floor. However, the nuns kept the place clean and the other women, several of whom were pregnant with the children of American soldiers, provided an envelope of empathy that Anke hadn't experienced since the initial days after her father died.

She couldn't tell her story, and so she remained just another German woman displaced by the war. Some of the women admitted that they had lived at the shelter since before the end of the war and the American soldiers had actually come to the shelter to pick them up and take them dancing. Many of them continued to see American men because they received extra food in exchange for their "companionship." The babies needed the evaporated milk and the scrawny children ate the tinned beans and chocolate bars.

Anke was consumed with both a fear and a desire to see Erik walk through the door and bundle her out of there. She knew he couldn't come. He'd gone too far and she regretted not sensing it until it was too late.

After two weeks, word came via Dearborn that Erik and Brigsworth-Jones were hatching a plan.

They stood just outside the shelter and around the corner of the building. "What exactly *is* the plan?" she asked him as he filled her pockets with US Army rations.

"Not sure. I am just supposed to tell you to sit tight. Oh, and get you to drink this."

He pulled a small glass bottle of cow's milk out from under his coat. Anke hadn't seen cow's milk since Carinhall. Dearborn put the glass in her hand and she drank it down so quickly that she coughed and sputtered like a child. He shoved an extra bar of chocolate, the last of his own ration (Erik had already sent the entirety of his ration) into Anke's hand. She stuffed it into her bra.

"Don't give it to the kids! Eat it. Please, Anke. He wants me to stand here and watch you eat it."

"I'll eat all of it, I promise," she said.

A nun appeared at the church door and told Dearborn that Anke needed to come back in. He left quickly. All the nun had to do was report him and Anke would be moved somewhere else...somewhere even worse.

Anke understood that and handed a canned tin of ham to the nun as she walked by.

"For the children, sister," she said.

An hour later, that tin of ham was empty and not one child tasted any of it.

28

A Reckoning

It is not love that is blind, but jealousy.
—*Lawrence Durrell*

ERIK KNEW BRIGSWORTH-JONES **was** up to something. The big man, as they still liked to call him, hadn't been seen in forty-eight hours and had sent word from Berlin that some sort of "prisoner-swap" had occurred with the Russians.

"My question is," Dearborn said as they sat awaiting their next interrogation at the ALIU unit HQ, "who would be important enough to get the big man up to Berlin? I mean, Hitler's dead, Himmler and Goebbels too. Göring's in jail awaiting trial, so is Rosenberg, Speer, Frank...."

"It's probably not someone of high importance to everyone," Erik said, "but someone important to *us*."

Dearborn turned and looked at him. "You know who it is?"

"I have an idea."

"Who?"

"Franz Bauer."

Dearborn's eyes went wide. "Bauer. Anke's old friend."

Erik shook his head. "Lover, Tom. They were lovers."

"Come on. She loves you now."

Erik went to the sink and threw water on his face.

"I don't know how she feels about him, Tom. I honestly don't know. But it's a chance I have to take. He might be the only one who can get her off the hook. He probably moved the fucking van Eyck out of France himself. If he didn't, he knows who did. Göring is lying to save his own ass and hopes he can hang this one around Anke's neck. No fucking way. Not my girl."

Dearborn smiled. This was the Erik of old. "Are they going to let you interrogate him, I mean, given the situation?"

"I don't know. I'm hoping the big man can work his magic...." Erik was cut off when the phone rang. Dearborn answered.

"Yes, sir. We'll be right there."

Dearborn stood and buttoned his uniform. "They're back."

"Is it Bauer?"

"He didn't say. Wants us down there straight away."

Erik combed his hair, straightened his uniform jacket, and stuffed a packet of Roth-Handle cigarettes in his pocket. The Germans preferred those.

Down one flight of stairs, Brigsworth-Jones stood in the hallway outside one of the larger interrogation rooms. Two armed guards stood with him.

"You'll never guess who I've got in this room, Capt. Brossler," Brigsworth-Jones said, flashing a grin.

"Please tell me it is Franz Bauer."

"Jesus Christ. Always one step ahead, chap?"

"Where did you find him?"

"In a Russian prison camp. They set one up in the Buchenwald concentration camp. Bloody brilliant those Bolsheviks! We traded a couple of POWs for him. I convinced central command that he could help us find a good number of works that are still eluding us. Maybe even the Raphael."

"Have you told *him* anything?"

"You mean have I told him that the chap who is currently engaged to the woman he still loves is about to interrogate him about the Ghent Altarpiece? No, I haven't told him."

"How do you know he still loves her?" Dearborn asked.

"Because I might have mentioned the Dachau incident. The look on his face told me everything I needed to know. He'll say anything to save her."

"Wait a second," Erik said. "What do you mean he'll say anything? Do you think Anke is lying?"

"Not for a minute, chap. I think Bauer was probably the one who removed the altarpiece, probably on Göring or Hitler's orders, but we won't know for sure until we go in there and interrogate him."

"Right," Erik said, trying to calm down. "Let's go."

They walked in slowly, deliberately nonchalant. Erik sat in one corner, Dearborn in the other, and Brigsworth-Jones sat at a table across from their prey. An interview recorder sat in an adjoining stall with his typewriter.

"For the record, I am Major Owen Brigsworth-Jones, MFAA, British Third Army. Assisting me in this interview are Capt. Erik Brossler and Lt. Thomas Dearborn, both MFAA, US Fifth Army. Please, state your full name."

Across the table sat a man who until recently had been living in the same clothes he'd been arrested in two months earlier. He'd eaten nothing but watery potato soup for weeks (not dissimilar from the soup fed to the former inmates of Buchenwald by the SS). He had lost all of his possessions. His parents and sister were either dead or starving near Wurzburg (he wasn't sure). The only person he'd ever truly loved had disappeared from his life in Italy in March and he wondered about her constantly. It hurt more than the sores and blisters on his swollen feet or the rumbling of his empty stomach.

"Franz Karl Bauer."

"Former rank?"

"ObergruppenFührer SS…Special Cultural Liaison."

"What does that mean, exactly?"

"I technically worked for Himmler, but I did what Göring wanted. I safeguarded Italian artworks, and later assisted Göring in removing his collection from his hunting lodge."

"Carinhall?"

"Yes."

"You also had duties in Belgium, in 1940, 1941, and 1942, is that correct?"

"Yes. I distributed the Kümmel Report to several art historians. It was my job to repatriate art from Belgium."

"You've used the words 'safeguarded' and 'repatriate.' Is this what you mean, or are you just used to speaking in this way?"

Bauer felt stung. He wanted to lash out, but realized he had absolutely no energy to do so. It was over.

"I accept responsibility for my actions, if that's what you are asking, major."

"You accept that what you were doing was looting?"

"Yes."

"Brilliant. That's a start. Now, I believe you have been informed that in exchange for verifiable answers to a number of questions we have, American High Command is willing to give you a light sentence. If you choose not to answer our questions, you will be transferred back to the Russian zone."

Bauer swallowed. "I am prepared to answer your questions."

"Jolly good. Let's begin."

Erik studied Bauer. He looked older than he had imagined him. His hair was thinning on top and the spotty and sagging skin on his face made him look like a banana that was starting to rot. Erik tried to picture him healthier, not so skinny, with shiny dark hair and rosy cheeks. A bile rose in his throat.

"May I, major?" Erik asked suddenly, standing up. Bauer squinted through the bright lamplight at the officer who he had hardly noticed, sitting in the dark corner.

"By all means, Captain Brossler," Brigsworth-Jones said, sitting down in Erik's seat.

Erik lit a cigarette and handed one to Bauer, who accepted and leaned forward into Erik's flame.

"We want to go through everything, piece by piece, Herr Bauer. But before we do that, we want to get a clear picture of what exactly happened to the Ghent Altarpiece. We have it in our possession now, thankfully, but we are still unclear on how it got from Ghent to Germany."

Bauer sat up straight and took a long drag. "The altarpiece, to my knowledge, was transported from Ghent to Pau, in France, not long before the Wehrmacht invaded Belgium."

"Who transported it?"

"A man named Niels Maarten. A professor at Ghent University."

"You remember his name? That's surprising."

Bauer shrugged.

"He did this alone?"

"To my knowledge, yes."

He's not going to mention her, Erik thought. He paced back and forth.

"How did the altarpiece get from Pau to Alt Aussee?"

"How exactly it got to Alt Aussee, I do not know. I took it from Pau to the castle of Neuschwanstein myself, in July of 1942."

"On whose orders?"

"Hitler's. He was obsessed with it. He wanted it more than anything else, except maybe Vermeer's *The Astronomer*. He knew that the Ghent Altarpiece was one of the undisputed wonders of European art and I believe he had special plans for it in the Führermuseum in Linz."

Erik looked to Dearborn, who stood up and walked to the table. Brigsworth-Jones nodded in agreement. Dearborn should do this part.

"Are you aware, Herr Bauer, that a German art historian, by the name of Anke Junger, has been accused of the crime that you just admitted to?"

Bauer looked stunned and his already white face paled even further.

"Anke Junger? You know her? She is…she is here?"

"I will ask the questions, Herr Bauer. What is your previous association with her?"

Bauer looked at Erik. Something in the eyes…his dark eyes staring at him from the corner. Yes. He had detected an accent when questioned by him. Was he German, or Austrian? It had sounded…Bavarian. Anke was from Munich. Was he someone who knew her?

"I met Anke in Ghent. She was one of the art historians to whom I gave the Kümmel Report. She's an authority on the Ghent Altarpiece."

"Did you threaten her?"

"Yes."

"With what?"

"I told her I would send her and her friends to a concentration camp if she didn't cooperate."

"Were you aware that she drove the altarpiece to Pau, along with Niels Maarten?"

"Yes."

"Why did you not mention this a few minutes ago?"

"I didn't want to bring her into it."

"You are trying to protect her?"

"Yes."

"Why?"

"Because she is innocent."

"And you protect the innocent, do you?"

Bauer should have seen that coming. The Americans would never understand. They'd seen Dachau and Buchenwald and they would never understand that he was capable of love. He didn't understand it himself.

"Herr Bauer." Dearborn leaned in close. "Remember our deal."

Bauer knew now how Anke must have felt when he first met her in Ghent. He could still recall the way she smiled over the *mattentarts* and blew on her hot, frothy coffee.

"I was in love with Anke Junger, Lieutenant. I still am and I would not want to see her harmed in any way. That is the truth."

"Were you the one who saved Dietrich Junger's portfolio?"

"Yes. They had been slated for sale. Anything that didn't sell was to be destroyed. I bought the entire portfolio in 1940."

"That must have been expensive."

"They were being sold cheaply, but yes, it was still expensive."

"How much?"

"In the range of 100,000 Reichsmarks."

"Your own money?"

"No. Göring's. He was a fan of Junger, before the war. He ordered me to find a safe place for them. Initially they were in a storage facility here in Munich. Once the Allies began the major bombing campaigns, they were moved to the basement of the Neue Staatsgalerie. In 1945, after I left Bolzano, I removed them and brought them to the Junger apartment. I thought they might be safer there—further away from the railway lines."

"You never told her?"

"No. I knew there was a chance they would be destroyed anyway, by bombing. I didn't want to raise her hopes of seeing them again."

"Did you know that her apartment building burned to the ground?"
He flinched. "No, I didn't."
"The paintings were saved, Herr Bauer. They are safe."
"Does she know?"
"Yes. She's seen them."
He nodded and smiled. He took a long drag on his cigarette and seemed to visibly relax.

Dearborn swallowed down his reluctant respect for this man.

"If you love her, you'll give us proof that you removed the Ghent Altarpiece from Pau. We need more than your word. Any court would consider you an unreliable witness. You have ulterior motives, Herr Bauer."

"Don't we all," Bauer said, looking directly at Erik.

EIGHT HOURS LATER, they had few answers and none of them had slept. Bauer, quite used to sleep deprivation in his POW camp, had fared better than the others. Erik had become enraged when Bauer insisted that his full cooperation was contingent on him being allowed to speak with Anke Junger alone. Brigsworth-Jones patiently explained that she was a German citizen and could not be compelled by any member of the ALIU to meet with anyone, but that excuse was obviously impotent before he finished uttering it. In the end, Dearborn had been dispatched to the shelter to see if Anke would be willing to speak to Bauer. Considering her future depended on it, Brigsworth-Jones was sure she would come. Erik was sure as well, but for different reasons.

He sat at the kitchen table in his father's apartment. He couldn't sleep. He'd eaten four saltine crackers in a twelve-hour period. His anger and resentment hung around him like a thick coat of grime, thicker even than the dust that rose up from the ruins of Monte Cassino.

He looked at his father, who sat across from him, immobilized by his son's anguish.

"She's talking to him right now," Erik said.
"Let's hope this ends the affair."
"The affair?"
"Oh Erik, you know what I mean! The affair of this ridiculous denazification process."

Erik nodded and rubbed his eyes. It was bizarre to him that with all of the Nazis who still existed in Germany, Anke Junger had been singled out as a threat. It was so preposterous that it almost made him laugh. He checked his watch. Dearborn had promised to come get him when Anke left the interrogation room. A knock on the door told him it was time to head back to the ALIU. It was one in the morning.

"Sir, she's back at the shelter," Dearborn reported. "I took her myself. Major Brigsworth-Jones wants us back at HQ."

Erik got his coat and followed him out, his father's sad eyes trailing him. Once they were outside, he looked at Dearborn expectantly.

"Don't ask me what they talked about because I don't know," Dearborn said. "I wasn't allowed in the room."

"How long was she in there?"

"Two hours. I heard laughing at one point."

Erik was speechless. He picked up his pace. He saw Brigsworth-Jones standing outside the HQ, smoking his pipe.

"Did we get *anything* out of this?" Erik hissed.

"Now settle down, chap. Of course we did. Bauer signed a confession. He admitted to lots of things, including taking the van Eyck from France to Germany. He admitted coercing Anke to work for the ERR. He mentioned paperwork in Berlin and Ghent to prove all this, but our chaps are still sifting through it. He even admitted taking fifteen crates of Neapolitan paintings from Monte Cassino for Göring."

Erik and Dearborn looked at each other. "That answer's that question," Dearborn said.

"That's not all, chaps. We know he tried to get our attention in Italy, Anke told us that. He wasn't authorized, but he wanted to negotiate surrender. What we didn't know for sure was that he also went to Alt Aussee, a day or two before we arrived, and ordered that the explosives that were packed into the mine be defused. He claimed to be doing so on Hitler's authority, even though Hitler was already dead."

Anke had suspected this. "So he's an art lover. Does that make him a great guy all of a sudden?"

"No," Brigsworth-Jones said, ignoring Erik's tone. "But it makes him a more decent individual than some of these other Nazi bastards. That's all I'm saying. Forgive her for her involvement with him. She might not have had much choice and even if she did, he's clearly not a monster."

Erik was silent. His mentor cut to the quick and as usual, he was dead on.

"Why didn't he surrender to us?" Dearborn asked. "He could have turned himself in after going to Alt Aussee, but he goes back north and gets caught by the Russians? It doesn't make sense."

"I think he felt he had something left to do," Brigsworth-Jones said.

"What?" Erik spat. He hated debating Bauer like this.

"I don't know. I just got the sense, from things Anke said, and she didn't say much, that he might have just given her some valuable information."

"The Raphael?" Dearborn wondered aloud.

"Perhaps. We won't know until we talk to her. His confession should put an end to her denazification hearing. She'll be off the hook."

"I need to talk to her now," Erik said, heading off toward the Marienplatz.

"Erik! You will do no such thing. We are going to get her name cleared tomorrow, but we still have the non-fraternization policy and until that changes you are not to be alone with her."

"What are you going to do, Brigs? Turn me in?"

Brigsworth-Jones had the look of a father whose son had taken the car without permission. "Yes, I will."

"No, you won't."

"Erik," Dearborn said, "Anke will be devastated if she get's the all-clear and then you end up in a military jail. Think of what she's been through."

Brigsworth-Jones went back inside the HQ, knowing that the matter had been settled.

ANKE STOOD in the long line for breakfast but had little appetite. Her nerves were in overdrive. One of the nuns, Sister Marta, had taken a liking to Anke and pushed two small slices of bread into her bowl.

"Eat it, Fräulein. I know it tastes like sawdust, but it will keep you going."

Anke felt her father's presence. He was watching. She smiled at Sister Marta and swallowed down both pieces of bread before she even got her porridge. She returned, with her steaming bowl, to her cot in the corner. At least she wasn't on the floor anymore. In the last week, ten new women had entered the shelter, but ten had died and made the beds available. Two babies died as well. After learning to sleep with the crying of infants, she found it hard to sleep in the cold silence. The older children had been transferred to a special hospital run by the American Red Cross. Even the pregnant women had been taken elsewhere. As the occupation became more organized, Anke realized that her Catholic shelter was one of the better places to be in Munich, and Munich was one of the better places to be in Germany. There were still plenty of people (displaced persons, survivors of the concentration camps, widows of German soldiers, orphaned children) who were living in bombed-out buildings with the rain coming right down on them. Winter was around the corner. Then again, they were all the lucky ones. They could be in Berlin.

She ran over her conversation with Bauer so many times that she began to wonder if she had imagined the whole thing. He had wept several times. She remembered that. He had asked for her forgiveness and she had given it to him. When he told her that he had ordered the bombs taken out of the mine at Alt Aussee, she had sincerely thanked him. When he confirmed that he had saved her father's portfolio from dispersal or destruction, she had squeezed his hand and said, "God bless you, Franz."

Their conversation was warm, as if it had been many years since their affair. But it had only been seven months. It was too raw for Bauer and he refused to reminisce.

"Anke," he said. "The child...was it mine?"

"No, Franz."

"Is the father of your child...the child that you were carrying...is he amongst the Americans who interrogated me?"

"Yes."

"The one with the slight Bavarian accent?"

"Yes."

"You knew him before the war?"

"Yes, when we were children. He emigrated to America with his family years ago. They are Jews."

Bauer took a deep breath. "Thank you for being honest."

"No more lies, Franz."

He nodded and took a drag on his cigarette. "I agree. No more lies. I intend to make a full confession. I won't leave anything out. You will be cleared of any involvement in the removal of the altarpiece."

"Thank you."

"Not at all. It wouldn't have come to this had I not been taken by the Russians."

"How did that happen? Why didn't you stay in Bavaria and surrender to the Americans?"

"It's complicated."

"You said you were a soldier...you had a duty."

"I lied about that. I was a soldier and I did have a duty, but I didn't care. That's not why I went back to Berlin."

Anke felt there was something close...a presence, in the room.

"Why? Franz, why did you go back?"

"I needed to check on something."

"What?"

"Something I had hidden for you. I left it too exposed. I needed to see if it was okay."

"Are you talking about a painting?"

"Yes."

"The Raphael?"

Bauer stared at her. "Yes."

"Where had you hidden it?"

"At Carinhall."

Anke furrowed her brow. "Carinhall? Why...."

"I thought if I placed it amongst his collection, right under his nose, it wouldn't be noticed. He was never there toward the end. I figured it would be packed up and evacuated to Berchtesgaden with everything else."

"We never found it. We were all over Berchtesgaden."

Bauer grimaced. "It must have been stolen then, or Göring's got it stashed away at Carinhall, buried somewhere."

Anke rubbed her eyes. "Why would he do that? The Raphael is an undisputed masterpiece, but he had a number of those and he sent them to Berchtesgaden. Why single the Raphael out?"

"You will discover the answers to these questions, not me. It's over for me."

"You'll go to jail, then you'll come out. It's not over."

Bauer smiled. "Perhaps," he said.

Sitting on her rusting cot, she replayed the conversation one more time. He left Bolzano to place her father's portfolio in her Munich apartment. He left Munich to go to Alt Aussee to prevent the mine from being incinerated. He then returned to Carinhall to find the Raphael, only to discover Göring had sent his collection south. Did he blow up Carinhall? He never directly answered that question, except to say that a unit of the Luftwaffe was involved in the demolition. That means he must have been there. He knows what was destroyed and what wasn't. He mentioned the possibility of buried items. The Russians might not have been that thorough when they looted the ruins. Her blood ran hot and she felt, for the first time since Alt Aussee, that her father was in a hopeful mood.

29

The Exile

I know how men in exile feed on dreams.
—Aeschylus

A S EXPECTED, Anke was cleared of any involvement in art loot-ing by the denazification panel. She received no apology, just a letter that declared her to be *Entlastet*, an exonerated or non-incriminated person. She was allowed to leave the shelter, which she did with rel-ish (though there were tears as she left behind some very depressed women who had nevertheless been kind to her). Professor Brossler welcomed her back into his apartment, though he informed her that the state of Germany was greatly weighing on him and he was consid-ering returning to America. She could hardly blame him. His impend-ing departure, however, seemed a painful reminder of how alone she was in Germany now. If it wasn't for Erik, she would have headed immediately back to Ghent. Her new classification allowed her travel internationally.

Erik sent her a message to meet him at the Königsplatz. Non-frat-ernization rules were slowly imploding under the weight of so many GIs flouting them. An officer or enlisted man was now allowed to speak to Germans and meet with them in public places. Private homes, clubs, and brothels were still off-limits.

As she approached the square and saw him leaning against a street-light, she realized that she hadn't been alone with him since the day she came home from the hospital.

He smiled as she approached. When she got closer, his smile looked fake. "Erik? What's wrong?"

He shook his head. "Nothing. You look beautiful."

"I'm skin and bones."

"We'll fatten you up," he said as he took a bar of chocolate and a tin of evaporated milk out of his pocket.

"Let's get this out of the way," she said, biting into the chocolate. "I talked to him and I think we have a major find ahead of us. He was pleasant and I am glad he won't be in a Russian camp for the rest of his life. That's it, okay? I don't have feelings for him. I never really did, not like the feelings I have for you."

Erik looked at her and his eyes got glassy. "I can't kiss you, Anke. Not here. But I can hold your hand. Will that be enough?"

"Yes. It will be enough."

They walked for a few minutes in silence while Erik composed himself. They sat on a bench, not far from an old German couple. Both Anke and Erik registered the couple since it was odd to see older people out in public in Munich. So many of them hadn't survived the war.

"So. Do you think Bauer was trying to lead you to the Raphael?"

"I think so, yes."

"Where did he say he had seen it?"

"Carinhall. He put it in Göring's collection himself. He thought it wouldn't be noticed and then it would be evacuated with everything else."

"He thought Göring wouldn't notice the addition of a Raphael to his collection?"

"He said that Göring was hardly at Carinhall toward the end. I don't know…Bauer must have been desperate."

"Where did he get it from in the first place?"

"He must have taken it from Hans Frank in Krakow, or maybe the painting had been brought back to Germany again before Bauer found it. I didn't get that far."

Erik nodded, then his face broke into a broad smile. Anke followed his gaze. Brigsworth-Jones was approaching, Dearborn and Crawford literally skipping behind him.

"Sorry to interrupt, lovebirds, but I've got some rather exciting news," Brigsworth-Jones said, sitting down next to Anke. "Nice to have the old gang back together, isn't it chaps? I, for one, rather miss the war!"

"Don't say that," Anke chided.

"Alright, I take it back. But you, Fräulein, have quite a bit to celebrate, it would seem."

"They don't think I'm a Nazi or a threat to American security. I'm touched, really."

Erik laughed out loud.

"Glad to see your wit has returned, Anke," Brigsworth-Jones said, lighting his pipe. "But if that touched you, hold on to your hat. You've been especially designated by the American government as a "cooperative German.""

"Does this mean I can help return the altarpiece?"

Brigsworth-Jones grimaced. "No, I am afraid not. The altarpiece has been designated as the first non-German work to be repatriated, but it must be a member of Allied personnel who returns it. The Belgians want to put it on display in Brussels for a few months before taking it back to Ghent."

"So who gets to return it?" Dearborn asked.

"I've been given the job of choosing the officer," Brigsworth-Jones said. He looked at Anke. "Who should I choose?"

"Erik," Anke said without hesitation.

"It's settled then. You leave tomorrow by plane, Brossler. You and the van Eyck."

"Yes, sir. It will be a honor."

Anke took one of Erik's cigarettes and he lit it for her. She blew out a plume of smoke and smiled at Dearborn and Crawford.

"So…I am a cooperative German. What does that get me, exactly?"

Brigsworth-Jones shrugged. "Not much. You are free to move about within the American zone without a pass. You can work at the collecting point if you want. That's about it for now."

"Can I go into the Russian zone?"

"Why would you want to go into the Russian zone?" Crawford asked uneasily.

Anke and Erik looked at each other. He spoke first. "Bauer told her he hidden something for her at Carinhall, Göring's hunting lodge. We think it might be the missing Raphael."

"We've been through Göring's stuff. The Raphael wasn't there. Carin-hall was blown up by the bloody Russians!" Brigsworth-Jones said.

"Bauer insinuated that Göring may have buried the painting and not evacuated it with the rest of the collection," Anke said. "Or, maybe it was Bauer himself who buried it. I'm not sure.…."

"This isn't much to go on," Dearborn said.

"I know. It could be nothing. But if we don't go…if there's a Ra-phael buried there…."

"Brossler, did you tell her about Frau Göring?" Brigsworth-Jones asked.

"Not yet. Göring's wife, Emmy, you knew her, Anke?"

"Yes."

"She was found with several small Memlings at her home, includ-ing the *Madonna with Child*. Göring was in custody, so the MFAA of-ficer forged a letter from Göring with instructions for Emmy to turn the painting over to him and she did. They took the painting into the office of General Jenness. Several hours later it was gone."

"Oh, Erik!" Anke clasped her hand to her mouth. "You wrote on the *Madonna and Child*, during your work at the Courtauld?"

"Yep."

"So, now we've got a Memling on the loose as well. Christ. I hate to say it, but it was probably one of our chaps," Brigsworth-Jones said.

"They won't be able to sell it," Anke said.

"Maybe they just want to have it, like Göring did," Crawford said, causing everyone to look at him with respect.

Brigsworth-Jones stood suddenly. "Right. Brossler will take the van Eyck home tomorrow. Then he'll join us at Carinhall. I'll get passes from the Russians to enter their zone. With your new status, Anke, it should be possible. They've been all over Carinhall and honestly I doubt they'll give a damn."

Anke couldn't remember the last time she had looked forward to tomorrow.

ERIK FLEW with the Ghent Altarpiece, well wrapped and sitting in the plane's seats like passengers, on a day of torrential rain across most of central Europe. When he landed at an airfield outside Brussels, there was no one to meet him. After an hour sitting in the plane on the soggy tarmac, a truck emerged through the downpour. Apologies were forthcoming; someone had dropped the ball. Pretty big ball, Erik thought, but tried to remain positive.

He and the altarpiece rode safely to Brussels, where the panels were put on display immediately at the Royal Palace. They had been thoroughly cleaned at the collecting point, so they looked pretty much as they had before the war. The press was allowed in, only several at a time, and there was no shortage of joyful tears. Brussels wasn't Ghent, but it was close. Hitler's greatest prize was almost home. Erik spoke briefly with Professor Dubois from Ghent University and was told to assure Anke that the panels were now in the best of hands.

"I think that will mean a lot to her, Professor."

"Captain, thank you. I don't know how to repay you for what you have done."

"No thanks needed. It was a honor."

As he watched Erik depart for the airfield, a thought crossed Dubois' mind. He made a note to speak to the Bishop of Ghent.

FOUR HUNDRED MILES east, Anke and the Monuments Men had reached Carinhall. Brigsworth-Jones had been right. The Russians were done with it and didn't seem to mind at all if a few Americans, a Brit, and a cooperative German wanted to poke around.

The ruins were a shock to say the least. Anke's memories of the lodge flooded back now, though it seemed like a lifetime ago that she had woken up in the antler room. The one and only time she was actually content with Bauer, albeit briefly, was here in this house. Now there was nothing but piles of bricks, plaster, and splintered wood. Even the lake was full of rubble, sticking out above the surface like dead reeds.

"Wow. There's really nothing left," Dearborn said, disappointed. "Where do we start?"

"We need to find a place where there could be an underground vault of some kind," Anke said, surveying the scene.

"How do we know it's not buried under the rubble of the house?" Crawford asked.

"We don't. This isn't going to be easy," Brigsworth-Jones said, puffing away on his pipe.

They wandered around the site, picking up fragments of neoclassical statues that the Russians had left behind.

"Christ, they made an awful bloody mess!"

"I wonder if this was the Luftwaffe or the Russians who smashed all these statues. These weren't even in the house, they were outside," Anke said, remembering her first foray into the grounds of Carinhall on a summer evening.

"I say the Russians," Dearborn said. "I hate to say it, but I think they've probably got the Raphael too."

"This is a fool's errand, is it?" Brigsworth-Jones asked, inspecting a small replica of the *Winged Victory of Samothrace*, which was still more or less intact.

Anke joined him. "The *Winged Victory*. I met a woman in Ghent who was present for the evacuation of the Louvre. She saw the statue taken down a ramp. I think they were all scared to death that she'd tip over and smash to pieces."

"I couldn't have watched, I'll tell you that," Brigsworth-Jones said, putting his arm around her.

"The altarpiece is in Brussels by now," she said.

"Erik's on his way here. Your knight in shining armor."

"You've orchestrated all of this. I don't know how to thank you."

"You'll convince him to stay in Europe, that's how you'll thank me. We need you both here, sorting things out. We can't lose everybody to America."

Anke digested this. She had never considered going to America. She realized now that Erik might want to. That was his home now, he'd already told her that.

"I'll try," she said.

"And if you can't?"

"You'll have to come visit us in Boston."

Brigsworth-Jones smiled. "Quite right, *Fräulein*."

WHEN ERIK ARRIVED, with a Russian escort, he found his fiancée up to her knees in mud and stabbing at the ground with a shovel that was far too heavy for her. The Russians took a look at the mess and returned to their posts on the outskirts of the estate as if to say, *Let them have it.*

"Dearborn, are you going to let her keep digging with that shovel?" Erik asked, irritated.

"I tried, sir. She insisted!"

Anke threw down her shovel and ran over to him as he ushered her to a small cluster of trees. They held each other quietly, trembling.

"Let's find this fucking Raphael and get out of here. This place is creepy," Erik said. He had said the same thing about Berchtesgaden and he was absolutely right. There was Nazism in the air here.

As night fell, they had found nothing of note. They were given accommodation at a nearby lodge, though they paid for their beds. The war hadn't touched this part of the Schorfheide forest and the autumn colors were just starting to appear. Brigsworth-Jones purchased a bottle of whiskey from the owner for far more than it was worth, and they drank it on the veranda. It was the best day any of them had had since the German surrender. They agreed that they would go back to Carinhall the following day but if nothing was found, they would have to assume that the Raphael was either looted from Göring's train outside Berchtesgaden, or found here by the Russians and shipped to Moscow or Leningrad. The Hermitage would have many new additions to its already immense collection; everyone understood that.

Anke and Erik made love that night for the second time, the first being on VE day. He promised her that the ban on marriage would lift soon and they would be husband and wife before the year was out. She told him not to make any more promises. She was living in the here and now and she was happier than she'd ever been since her father died.

AT EXACTLY THREE O'CLOCK the next afternoon, Dearborn struck gold. His shovel hit something hard in an area they guessed had been directly under the main salon. There was so much twisted wood and metal it was hard to know where to dig, but he had cleared a patch and was digging diligently, about three feet down, in every direction. His back ached, he was drenched in sweat, and he was hung-over.

"There's something here!" he yelled at the top of his voice.

The others rushed to his side and Erik and Crawford began digging around the spot. The shape of a large box became visible and Anke thought, at first, it was a coffin. Once they raised it slightly, she could see it was a rectangular trunk, the kind you might take on a long trip. Erik pried it open with a knife.

Inside was an object wrapped in blankets. Brigsworth-Jones smiled. They had it. The Russians never even knew it was there.

Erik and Dearborn carried it to a patch of grass and gently laid it down. Anke got a feeling in her stomach and she thought her heart would beat right out of her chest.

"It's much too big to be the Raphael," she said breathlessly.

Erik looked up at her, startled.

Dearborn unwrapped it and did not immediately know what he was looking at. Crawford had no earthly idea, though it looked familiar.

"Jesus fucking Christ," Brigsworth-Jones said. "Is that what I think it is?"

Erik's mouth went dry and he tried to swallow. "It's the *Just Judges*. The missing panel from the Ghent Altarpiece."

Anke fainted. Someone caught her. When she came to, she was sure it was her father.

Acknowledgements

I OFFER MY SINCERE THANKS to all those who have helped and supported me in the writing of this book. Especially Judith Harlan and Lucky Bat Books, my editor Jeff Posey, cover artist Guilherme Gustavo Condeixa, interior designer Louisa Swann, Dr. Heidi Gearhart, Jim Butterfield, my husband Andrew, and my parents, Jean and John Fogle.

Author's Note

THE ALTARPIECE IS, without question, a work of fiction. However, it does not stray too far from reality. The events relating to Nazi looting of European art, as well as the Allied effort to recover and protect that art, have not been invented but actually occurred. I made every effort to keep to the facts and only alter the truth when the story needed it. The research for this book focused mainly on Lynn Nichols's *The Rape of Europa*, Robert M. Edsel's *Rescuing da Vinci* and *The Monuments Men*, *The Faustian Bargain* by Jonathan Petropoulos, and *The Venus Fixers* by Ilena Dagnini. The artworks mentioned in this book really were stolen, damaged, and recovered with one exception. The missing panel from the Ghent Altarpiece, *The Just Judges*, has never been found.

Erik Brossler, Owen Brigsworth-Jones, Tom Dearborn, and Marshall Crawford are amalgamations of several real Monuments Men such as Deane Keller, James Romier, George Stout, Mason Hammond, Lincoln Kirstein, Lord Kenneth Clark, and Edgar Breitenbach. Dietrich Junger is loosely based on Ernest Ludwig Kirchner, a founder of the expressionist group "Die Brucke" in Dresden. He committed suicide in Switzerland in 1939 after 600 of his paintings were confiscated by the Nazis. Franz Bauer's character comes from a real SS *Oberleutnant* named Henry Koehn who was sent to Belgium to look into the whereabouts of the Ghent Altarpiece and its missing panel. Nazi art historians and dealers such as Kajetan Muhlmann and Andreas Hofer were additional influences on Bauer's character. Count von Essen is based on Count Metternich, who was the actual head of the *Kunstschutz* for much of the war.

Anke Junger is a character completely of my own imagination. I wanted to believe that there were people like her operating inside the Nazi machine and constantly pushing in the other direction (though sometimes subtly). If there was an inspiration for Anke, it was the cunning Jeu de Paume curator Rose Valland, who kept a log of exactly what the Germans were looting and became a national hero in France after the war. Rose made a brief appearance in this book as the bespectacled Delphine.

Hermann Göring is the only major character in this book who was an actual person. He was very much an avid art lover and looter, and his collection at Carinhall was in no way embellished.

About the Author

L AUREN FOGLE BOYD is a medievalist who teaches history at The University of Massachusetts at Lowell. *The Altarpiece* is her first novel.